I WILL NEVER LEAVE YOU

I WILL NEVER LEAVE YOU

KARA A. KENNEDY

DELACORTE PRESS

Text copyright © 2024 by Kara A. Kennedy
Jacket art copyright © 2024 by Carolina Rodriguez Fuenmayor

Visit us on the Web! GetUnderlined.com

Educators and librarians, for a variety of teaching tools, visit us at RHTeachersLibrarians.com

Library of Congress Cataloging-in-Publication Data
Names: Kennedy, Kara A., author.
Title: I will never leave you / Kara A. Kennedy.
Description: First edition. | New York : Delacorte Press, 2024. | Audience: Ages 12–18. | Audience: Grades 10–12. | Summary: "A teen girl is being haunted by the ghost of her toxic ex-girlfriend, who gives her a chilling ultimatum—help her possess another girl or go down for her murder"— Provided by publisher.
Identifiers: LCCN 2023052058 (print) | LCCN 2023052059 (ebook) | ISBN 978-0-593-70746-3 (hardcover) | ISBN 978-0-593-70747-0 (lib. bdg.) | ISBN 978-0-593-70748-7 (ebook)
Subjects: CYAC: Ghosts—Fiction. | Lesbians—Fiction. | Psychological abuse—Fiction. | LCGFT: Ghost stories. | Thrillers (Fiction) | Novels.
Classification: LCC PZ7.1.K5045 Iaw 2024 (print) | LCC PZ7.1.K5045 (ebook) | DDC [Fic]—dc23

The text of this book is set in 11-point Sabon Next.
Interior design by Ken Crossland

Printed in the United States of America
10 9 8 7 6 5 4 3 2 1
First Edition

Random House Children's Books supports the First Amendment and celebrates the right to read.

For Mom and Grandmom,
and all the other unbreakable girls

I am the hermit.
I search for bones as the hawk circles
    above my head.
My light is soft and low,
illuminating just as far ahead as is
    required for my eyes to see.
This walk is mine alone.
You are not invited
where I am going.

                —Anna Marie Tendler

PROLOGUE

NO ONE KNOWS Alana Murray like I do.

I was the one who held her hand on the first day of sixth grade, secret, so no one would know she was nervous. I was the one who edited her English papers for her. I was the one who kissed her behind a palm tree when we were fifteen, my heart cracking out of my rib cage.

I'll be the last person to touch her casket before it's lowered into the ground.

Funeral day dawns dark and cold and wrong, the Los Angeles sky clogged with watercolor gray. It won't rain, and I won't let myself cry. I practice in front of my bathroom mirror.

Alana died alone, I think, staring at my reflection until my eyes burn. *She thought of you every second. How she hated you. How she loved you.*

I sob until my throat goes dry, until I gag into the sink, fingernails scraping against the marble countertop. Then I wipe my makeup off with a warm washcloth, reapply my mascara, start all over. Alana always thought I cried too much, so today, I won't let the tears come. Even though I know what people will say about a girl who doesn't cry at her own girlfriend's funeral.

Monster. Heartless.

I am. But not for the reasons they think.

During the service, Alana's mom wears sunglasses with her black Chanel dress and ignores me. Lilies choke the inside of the funeral home. Everyone else watches me, whispers about me. *Maya,* the wind hisses my name, *Maya, what do you know?* I can feel it, a slow, creeping hate I might never outrun.

Outside it's a sea of dark clothes and soft sniffles under shady trees, a small pile of red roses laid across the top of the casket. We surround Alana's gravesite, and I can feel how the others loathe me because they think I know too much or too little. They track my movements and it feels like ice water dripping down my back.

Finally, everyone turns away, and the weight of their stares lifts. The cedar of Alana's casket is warm under my palm, and I try to remember the way it felt to loop a strand of her hair around my finger, to brush my knuckles across her lips.

A handful of orange California poppy petals slip through my fingertips and scatter across the coffin lid. When I turn my back, I allow myself the smallest of smiles.

Because I know better than anyone that death isn't the end. Not for Alana and me. Not even close.

CHAPTER ONE

ONE WEEK EARLIER

ON THE MORNING I decide to break up with Alana, the sky is crystal blue.

We're hiking the superbloom trail at Antelope Valley, our annual tradition. Liquid gold sunlight pours down on us, warming the pathway lined with electric-orange poppies bending in the wind. The gusts are almost strong enough to block out the obliterating desert heat. I was praying for rain last night, for a miracle that would cancel this outing, but the Southern California air is dry as ever.

"You're so tense and weird today," Alana says. She never breathes heavily on hikes. Everything she does, from schoolwork to hiking to insulting me, is effortless.

"Sorry." I take a swig from my water bottle while her back is turned. "I'm just stressed."

"Maya, what do you have to be stressed about?" Her brown ponytail swings. "It's a beautiful day. You're surrounded by wildflowers. Senior year's basically over. You have me. Relax."

I tilt my head back to face the sky. An eagle swoops overhead, low and silent. People come to see the famous superbloom from all over, cars lining the roads that feed to the Visitor Center. Ever since we got our licenses, we've made the trip up here each May. It's our thing.

If I break up with her, I leave all that behind. I start all over again.

It's what I need to do. I just don't know if I'm strong enough to stand up to her.

On the trail, it's quiet, but there are still plenty of hikers snapping photos and laughing. Everyone in the world is happier than me. At least there will be witnesses, I tell myself glumly, wiping the sweat off my forehead. Because I know what will happen when I initiate this conversation with Alana. Her anger, the way it accelerates so quickly it makes me dizzy. I can already feel the fear lodging in my throat, the kick-drum beat of my heart.

"Are you freaking out about graduation?" Alana asks, voice cutting through the quiet. "Because it won't be a big deal. We'll walk across the stage, we'll get our diplomas."

"Barely, in my case." I bite my lip and focus on the California poppies spilling out before us. Graduation is next Saturday, only a week away. "That whole thing is still a secret, right? You didn't tell anybody?"

Alana turns, walking backward, bouncing on the soles of her feet. Her sneakers are newer than mine, pristine despite the dirt path. Everything she touches stays perfect.

"Who would I tell?" she asks. "Besides, it's your personal business."

"And everyone else on the planet, when I stay here in LA this fall," I mumble, kicking a pebble. It ricochets off my sneaker, lands in a cluster of poppies and blue forget-me-nots.

"Do you know how shitty it feels, not getting into a single college?"

She pauses, waits for me to catch up. Beyond her is a sprawling wildflower field that goes on for miles, and in the distance, the white-capped San Gabriel Mountains. I swallow back that gnawing sensation I get at the sight of it. I've lived in Southern California my whole life and it never fails to knock me off my feet.

There was a time when I felt the same way whenever I looked at Alana. Now, the expectant set of her mouth floods my stomach with nausea. The copper taste of fear in my mouth, bitten back.

"You're being dramatic," Alana says. "Hardly anybody gets into Yale early decision. That was always a crapshoot."

This is a well-trodden conversation, one we've revisited a hundred times over the past few months.

"And then, what? Five rejection letters during regular decision?"

"Something like that," I say, like I don't know the names of the schools by heart. Like I don't recite them over and over in my head in a mantra of self-hatred before falling asleep.

"Well, it could've been worse." Alana squeezes my hand and the knot in my chest loosens. Alana is nice to me, she *is*—this is proof. "Nobody in our class knows besides me. So you show up at the graduation ceremony and act like you have every right to be there, because you do. Be brave."

I don't know if I remember how to do brave things, I think, wiping the back of my hand across my sweaty forehead and squinting into the Mojave Desert sun. It's almost impossible to believe that wildflowers can bloom in an environment like this.

Alana crouches down at the trail's edge as a couple of hikers holding hands with a giggling toddler pass behind us. I watch her brush her fingers gently against the soft petal of a poppy.

"Speaking of college." My throat constricts. Sunlight picks strands of gold out of Alana's deep brown hair. "I was thinking that it . . . that it doesn't . . ."

She mumbles something under her breath. It sounds like *Here we go.*

"What?" I ask, defensive.

"You're going to give me a big speech about how we shouldn't be together, right? Because long distance will be too hard?"

I'm silent.

She glances over her shoulder. "Am I wrong?"

"I just don't see how it can work," I whisper. "You being all the way on the East Coast for college . . . I mean, it's ridiculous, right?"

She's going to say I'm wrong, I tell myself, hope blooming in my chest. *She'll tell me that distance doesn't matter, or better yet, she won't go to Massachusetts at all.*

"Yeah," Alana says, thoughtful. She gets to her feet, brushing dust off her leggings. "Yeah, you're right."

A cold shock washes over me. "What?"

"We're going to be almost three thousand miles apart for four whole years."

I stare at her, feeling my hands start to shake. "You don't think it'll work either?"

"Maya, you literally *just* told me that you can't see how it can work between us. Were you messing with my head?"

"No! I—"

"That's really unfair." Alana sighs, folding her arms. "After everything I've done for you this year? Protecting you from all the drama, all the—"

"Sorry," I choke out. Ironclad panic squeezes my lungs. I can't cry in front of her. I *can't.*

The briefest of pauses, wind rustling through the wide-open fields.

"Are you crying?"

"No." My lower lip is shaking, and when I blink, a fat, hot tear spills over my lashes, trickling down my cheek, dripping off my chin before I can wipe it away. Alana watches it fall through narrowed eyes. More than anything, she hates when I cry.

This is why I need to end things, no matter what it does to me. I'm not happy, and I won't be any happier when she's across the country. I will always be at her mercy.

I'm dry grass and she's the wildfire. It takes nothing for me to burn.

"Sometimes I feel like . . . ," I start, but trail off. "Sometimes I feel like it makes me too sad, being with you."

"This again? Seriously?"

"I just don't think relationships are supposed to make you this sad."

"What's making you sad?" she asks. The words drip off Alana's tongue, slow and lazy like honey. "Is it your spooky ghosts again?"

I flinch like she took a swing at me. I should never have told her about the paranormal encounters I had growing up. She's always had a way of clinging to my childhood ghost anecdotes, like it was some kind of fun party trick and not a trauma I'd rather forget. "You know I haven't seen them since I was a kid."

She smirks. "Yeah, I know, Maya. You aren't being haunted by anything except your inner demons."

Goose bumps rise on my bare arms, thin hairs standing on edge even in the warm wind. Dimly, I'm aware of the other hikers ducking around us, trying to act like this never-ending wildflower field doesn't make it possible for them to hear every word. This is what Alana does: latches onto the ghosts of my past and resurrects them as soon as I'm vulnerable.

I could escape right now if I wanted. But the thing about Alana is that even when I feel so trapped that I can't breathe, she could give me a wide-open sky and I still wouldn't run. I love her too much.

"Seriously," Alana says again. "It's a favor from the universe that you didn't get into Yale. There's no way you could've lived an hour and a half away from me. I bet you would've lasted, like, a week, and then you would've just followed me to Smith."

"I would've been fine," I insist, but it comes out more whiny than forceful. It kills me to say these words, a jagged pain shooting through my lungs. "I'll be fine. We need to stop pretending that we . . . that we need each other."

She gives me a skeptical look, condescension dripping from her gaze. "Like you really mean that. Who's going to be there to protect you from your anxiety spirals? What would you have done if you'd seen one of those super-scary Instagram posts from Elise and the other girls from school having fun without you—proof that the world doesn't revolve around you?"

She laughs at her own joke, but I just glare. Another ghost that needs to stay in the past.

"Why would you bring that up? You know how bad it hurt when—"

"Maya, I realize you're perfect and we should all aspire to emulate your shining example, but honestly? You're not the best judge of character." Alana undoes her ponytail, brown hair ribboning in the wind. "Why else do you think you ended up losing every single one of your friends over the last few years?"

I stare at her, hating her so much it stings. Hands shaking, I step forward, sneakers scuffing in the dirt. I'm not actually going to hit her, but my heart is slamming against my rib cage, blood pooling in my cheeks, and I'm not so sure I can control what I do anymore.

"Hey," a voice says behind me, and I whip my head around. There's a hiker, blond and midtwenties, thumbs looped through her backpack straps. She looks embarrassed. "So sorry to interrupt. I just wanted to make sure—are you guys okay?"

I open my mouth, cheeks blazing hot, but before I can get a word out—

"Oh, I'm fine," Alana says, crystal blue eyes widening. Out of nowhere, there's a delicate tremble to her voice. "We're just, um, talking about school. It's no big deal."

The woman doesn't seem convinced. Her eyes flicker over to me, then back to Alana. "You're sure you don't need anything?"

She says this to Alana, not me.

"Yeah, I'm fine. Thank you so much. Have a great rest of your hike! Beautiful day."

I watch the woman as she heads off down the trail, wildflowers blooming in raging colors all around her.

"Good job, Maya," Alana says, a laugh in her voice, and I close my eyes to block out the rage simmering in my veins. "Now you're freaking out strangers."

"Listen to me. The stuff with our friends—none of that was my fault," I choke out through gritted teeth, squinting at her in the blinding sunlight. She will never believe me, but it's true. Livia, Elise . . . when they stopped speaking to me, stopped caring about me. "I keep asking you to quit mentioning it. You aren't giving me the space to heal."

"The space to heal," she repeats scornfully, waving her fingers in little quotation marks. "Your therapist is really getting to you. Maya, you're fine. Well, I guess you would be if you could stop crying every five seconds."

She steps closer to me. Doesn't stop until she's close enough to brush a strand of hair out of my eyes, fingertips soft against my forehead.

"As long as you're with me, you'll be fine."

Her touch stings like an electric current. I want to grab her by the shoulders and shake her, want to punch the smile off her face until I hear the crack of bone under my fingers.

I want to make her hurt the same way she hurts me.

"I don't need to be with you, Alana. We need to end this."

"You're breaking up with me?" Alana purses her lips. "Really?"

"You know we would both be happier that way." Rage pounds in my ears. "Didn't you just say it yourself? It's crazy to expect we could stay together when we're on different coasts. You don't *want* that. You want to go off and live your life, while I—"

Her blue eyes go cold, like the hottest edge of a flame. "Don't tell me how I feel."

"Why? I know you better than anyone."

"Oh, you'd love to think that's true," she says, but we both know it is. Over the years, we've twisted ourselves together into knots, carved our initials into the darkest parts of each other. You don't come back from that.

I bite my lip. "I-I'm sorry. But this shit about me following you around . . . it hurts my feelings, Alana. You don't think I can be my own person without you. I'm going to prove to you that I can."

"You're being crazy."

"You know what, Alana?" I step back, sneakers dragging in the dirt. *Crazy.* The word rings in my ears, pounding inside my skull. "I'm going home."

Alana laughs, the sound crackling like lightning.

"Maya," she says. "You won't leave without me."

"Watch me."

And I turn, pulling my car keys out of my pocket, swinging them around one finger. I drove us here, but she's resourceful; let her find her own way back home. Without a backward glance, I head down the trail the way we came, desert wind harsh on my face.

I leave her there.

CHAPTER TWO

WHEN I ARRIVE home in the afternoon, there's a deep blue Audi parked in the usually empty driveway. I rub the heels of my hands against my eyes, letting out a sigh, and kick my car door closed.

Wonderful. I get to close out my breakup with a heart-to-heart with Dad.

Heading up the brick walkway, I squint at the two-story house with a gable roof that's been home my entire life. When I think of my house, I think of empty rooms, of quiet. A leaky bathroom faucet drip, drip, dripping. A grandfather clock ticking in the hall. Me at my desk pushed up against the bedroom wall, trying to block it all out and finish my homework. Even when Dad's home from his job as head chef at a cushy Beverly Hills restaurant, the two of us aren't enough to fill up this echoey house.

I find him in the kitchen, humming along to a classic rock song playing from the speaker balanced on the windowsill above the sink. The counter is covered in ingredients: a giant sack of almond flour, a box of confectioners' sugar, the enormous stainless-steel mixer. Typically he's at the restaurant on Saturdays, prepping for a big weekend event. The sight of him bustling around the kitchen is so bizarre that all I can do is stand there and stare.

"Maya!" he calls over the crooning notes of Mick Jagger. Doesn't turn around. "I'm going to give you five options. Answer fast. Go with your instinct."

I hover in the kitchen doorway warily. "What?"

"Strawberry. Blackberry. Tiramisu. Mint. Salted Caramel."

"I'm sorry." I clear my throat. "What are you talking about?"

He finally turns, a smile fixed on his face. I know it well. Dad knows he's never around, knows he leaves me alone in this house with its echoes and shadows, and the smiles are a way to overcompensate. Saying the words out loud is, apparently, out of the question. But that's okay, really. I'm used to it.

"Macarons," he says. "Tough to make, but I'm giving it a shot. I thought this would be a great treat for your postgraduation reception, so this is a test run."

My hand presses against the wood of the doorframe. "You're . . . making cookies for my graduation reception?"

"Macarons," he says again, laying on a French accent a bit thick. Our ancestors are from the Provence region, but my grasp of the language is more solid than his after my years of French classes. "Come sit down, kid. How was study group?"

Study group. I don't move from my spot in the doorway, watching Dad meticulously sift flour and sugar into a large glass bowl. His words roll over me slow and sluggish as a storm cloud. All I can think about is Alana surrounded by wildflowers, blue eyes blazing. Her voice cutting through me: *Don't tell me how I feel.*

"Kiddo?"

I blink and Dad is looking at me nervously, pushing up the sleeves of his T-shirt. Trying to read me, failing like always.

I focus on him to ground myself amid the rising panic, finding traces of myself in his face. The same brown eyes rimmed with feather-long lashes, the same solemn set of our mouth. This is a ritual I began when I was eight, right after Mom died: anchoring myself to the parent I have left.

"Right." My voice comes out thin, faint. "Study group. It was, um, canceled today."

"Canceled, huh?"

"Yeah. It's okay, though. I have plenty of Chem notes that I can go over tonight."

Dad's eyebrows draw together. Thick, expressive—another feature we share. "Interesting," he says, "since your study group is for AP US History."

Goddammit. Another way Dad tries to compensate: my stupid class and activities schedule taped to the wall of his kitchen at the restaurant. Some kids might view that as strict, overbearing, but I know better. He's not really that invested, just desperate for conversation topics. If he doesn't ask me about school, there's nothing left. Only Mom, and neither of us will ever cross that invisible line.

"You were with Alana again." It isn't a question. There's something resigned in his voice. He adds whipped egg whites to the bowl, spatula in one hand, eyes focused on his work. "See, eventually I'll learn. Every time you're supposed to be somewhere for the betterment of your academic future, you're actually with Alana."

He's trying to keep his voice light, but there's something

14

biting beneath it. A reminder of the secret anger, the hidden grief, that neither of us will ever speak aloud.

"What academic future, Dad? I don't have one." Tears prick the back of my eyes. "I'm not going to college. Everything I did was a waste."

"*Maya.*" Dad thwacks the spatula against the counter, and I flinch. "What did we decide back in the fall? We take this day by day. You're graduating—"

"Barely."

"You're getting a high school diploma, and then we're getting you into community college for the fall. You'll keep up with therapy, with your meds, and when you're feeling better, we'll get you back on track."

But Alana, I bite back. The question tastes like bitter poison. *What am I supposed to do about Alana? Do we stay broken up? Do I beg for her forgiveness?*

I could ask Mom, an intrusive thought pipes up. *If she were alive, I could ask Mom.*

"We need to focus on the day-to-day." Dad's still talking. He picks up the spatula again, folding egg whites into the batter. "Tomorrow, go to your study group. You don't have to ace all your exams, Maya—you just need to *try.* You know how to do that, kid. You've been trying your whole life."

I squeeze my eyes shut tight. *Mom. Please. I need to see you.*

"And enough with Alana, okay? That girl's been nothing but trouble. If you can just keep your head down and focus on school for one more week . . ."

My eyes pop open. For a flickering second, I want it so badly that I almost convince myself that Mom's ghost is here: cross-legged on a stool at the kitchen counter, hair tied back in a long ponytail, laugh like a melody filling the house.

But she's not here. She never is.

I won't cry. I *won't*. I turn, backpack swinging over my shoulder, and run out the front door. Dad calls after me, but I can't make out the words, and when the door slams, it's heavy and certain and final.

● ● ●

I could chart the path to Alana's house with my eyes closed. East on Valleyheart, tracing the slant of the Los Angeles River, past the taco place on Ventura and the café with the world's best hangover food. Coasting down Colfax Avenue to Moorpark, cranking the steering wheel as I turn onto a tree-lined enclave just past Tujunga. Alana and I have roamed these streets for years, sometimes in the middle of the night, a flickering streetlamp lighting our way. A lot of girls in our class live up in the Hills or tucked away in Malibu, but the Valley is ours.

Alana's mom bought this house right after hitting it big as a screenwriter. It's objectively beautiful, all clean lines and crisp, utilitarian corners, but I always hated it a little bit. The gate is sleek metal, cold to the touch; after parking on the street, I punch in the security code and watch it swing open. Already, I'm dreading the conversation with Alana that awaits me, but it needs to happen. We can't just end things like that.

"Maya!"

I jump, scanning the manicured front yard for a glimpse of Alana, but it's just her mom. She's emerging from the garage, wrestling two leather suitcases. Shit—I didn't expect anyone to be here except maybe Alana, probably in a rage over her astronomical Uber charge.

"Sorry, Mrs. Murray," I say, digging my hands into my back pockets.

Melissa Murray is her daughter age-progressed thirty years, brown hair pulled back with a colorful scarf and eyeshadow highlighting her blue eyes. She smiles. "Nothing to be sorry for. I didn't know you were coming over today!"

"Oh. It's—I'm a surprise." I smile weakly.

For as long as I can remember, Melissa Murray has been a fixture in my life. She moved to LA to be a screenwriter and became successful when Alana was a kid, selling romantic comedy scripts that read like soap operas, eventually becoming head writer on a popular TV show. Sometimes my dad jokes that she lets her work bleed over into real life, hosting book clubs where the gossip flows like red wine, airing the latest sordid details of somebody's affair in the frozen foods aisle at Erewhon. She's always put together, always calm and in control.

"Sweetheart, any surprise where I get to see you is a great one." She releases a suitcase, stretching out her toned arms, and I walk into them eagerly. Mrs. Murray isn't Mom, but she's the next best thing. "But if you're here to see our girl, I think you might need to try somewhere else."

"What do you mean?" I ask, pulling out of the hug.

"My flight from Vancouver got in this morning, and do you think Alana bothered to answer any of my texts?" Mrs. Murray sighs. "It's like she's punishing me for traveling for work. You'd think a teenage girl would relish the opportunity to have a house all to herself, but no, she needs to be out on the town."

I force out a weak laugh, trying not to think about Mrs.

Murray's reaction if she knew that I'd ditched her daughter at Antelope Valley two hours ago.

"I actually just came over to borrow some shoes." The lie slips out easily. I can't risk worrying her. "For graduation. Do you mind if I . . . ?"

"Oh, honey, go ahead." Mrs. Murray waves me toward the house, distracted; her shrill ringtone is sounding from the pocket of her cardigan. My heartbeat skips—is it Alana calling for her mom to pick her up? Will she tell Mrs. Murray what I did? To avoid finding out, I dart past her, letting myself into the house.

The Murrays' husky, Balto, greets me in the foyer, hopping up on his hind legs to place his paws on my shoulders. As I head upstairs, he trots along at my heels, warbling a little husky proclamation until we get to Alana's room, then settles down in his plush dog bed. Her bedroom is on the second floor, windows looking out over the saltwater pool glinting in the afternoon light. I pick my way across her messy floor, discarded uniform skirts and crumpled shopping bags and tangled phone charger cables. She definitely hasn't been home yet.

A familiar whir of anxiety starts up in my brain and I close my eyes, trying to feel it and let it pass. It's only been a couple hours, and I had a head start before booking it down the freeway. *This isn't weird,* I tell myself, sucking in a deep breath. *There's no way Alana could've beaten me back to LA.* The thought occurs to me suddenly: Maybe if I can log on to her computer, I can access her texts and figure out if she's on her way.

Her desk is the messiest part of the room. I can picture her sitting in her pink velvet chair, long legs up on the desk, chatting to me over her shoulder as we work on history essays. I shove aside stacks of homework and piles of makeup, bottles of nail polish clinking together. Her iMac is covered in sticky notes. There's a sketch of a flower on one, a half-finished strand of poetry on another. I brush these aside, tapping the Enter key on the computer keyboard.

When it asks me for a password, I get in on my second try; she's used the same three since elementary school. The desktop wallpaper is a mood board culled from Pinterest photos and snapshots of the two of us together, pinks and oranges like a sunset.

There's a bang in the hallway and I jump, glancing over my shoulder. Mrs. Murray is struggling with her suitcases, dragging them along the hallway carpet.

"Honey," she calls, meeting my eyes. I freeze, wondering if an admonishment for being on her daughter's computer is coming. It shouldn't matter to her. Alana and I overlap, tangle together. *What's mine is yours,* I always jokingly tell her when she steals food out of my family's fridge or grabs pens out of my backpack.

"Do you need help?" I ask, rising from Alana's desk chair.

"Someone's calling me. Can you check? It might be Alana." She gestures toward an iPhone perched on the hallway table, plugged into a charger. For as long as I can remember, Mrs. Murray has been notorious for carrying multiple phones with her: one for work, one for managing Alana's activities, one for social engagements, one just because she got bored and wanted to try the newest model. I can never think too much about the expense, or it'll make me sick.

I reach the ringing phone right as it goes to voice mail.

"Nah," I call down the hallway, reading the numbers on the screen. "It's not her. Probably spam."

"Hate that crap," Mrs. Murray calls cheerfully from the master bedroom. From the sound of it, she's wrangled her suitcases into submission and is now digging through her dresser drawers. Balto has trotted off to help her. "Not to worry, I'll track down our girl."

But what if it was Alana? my anxiety pipes up unhelpfully. *What if she's stranded somewhere and had to call her mom from a store or somebody else's phone?*

No. Shut up. I shake my head hard. If it was Alana trying to contact her mom, she wouldn't call this number. The phone is unlocked, no passcode, a generic watercolor background; clearly, this isn't Mrs. Murray's main phone. Alana hasn't texted me in the two hours since I left Antelope Valley, and according to her mom, she hasn't been in touch with her either.

"Did you find the shoes you wanted?" Mrs. Murray asks.

"Umm . . ." The phone feels hot in my hand. I stare down at it.

"I think Alana has some cute red heels stashed in the back of her closet," her mother continues. "Can't remember the last time she thought to clean it out."

"Oh, I think I know the ones you mean." I'm stalling for time as I try to think. Alana has never enabled location sharing with me—*we have to have our own lives,* I can hear her lecturing me. But I'm sure all of Mrs. Murray's phones have access to Alana's location. She's strict about that, always getting on Alana for stopping at Starbucks before school.

I unplug the phone and slide it into my back pocket, ducking into Alana's room. It only takes a couple seconds for me to tap through the apps in search of one that's bright green. I'm in, and there's **Alana Murray, Los Angeles, CA.**

My heartbeat quickens. She's in LA. She made it home. I

focus on the whir of the central air coming through the vents, Balto's grumbling, the faint sound of chatter as Mrs. Murray turns on her bedroom television.

Is Alana close by? Maybe she's in an Uber right now heading toward me. Blue eyes blazing, already rehearsing for the fight we'll have the second she steps through the door. She'll be furious. With shaking hands, I press my thumb against her name. Mrs. Murray's contact photo for her daughter shows a kindergartener sticking out her tongue, brown hair tugged into two pigtails. She's younger there than I ever knew her; I only met Alana when she moved here in the fifth grade. The photo blinks back at me, framed in a small circle, as the phone works to pinpoint her location.

And then it loads: a street address on Mulholland Drive.

I freeze, staring at the tiny letters. Could she be in traffic? No—the circle isn't moving.

It's been over a year, but I still know Elise Carter-Holloway's address by heart. There's no way Alana would hang out with her—but the idea of her running to our former friend, furious with me, post-breakup, is enough to make my blood run cold.

Wordlessly, I grab a pair of heels from Alana's closet and duck back into the hallway, depositing Mrs. Murray's phone on the table where I found it.

CHAPTER THREE

A YEAR AGO, Elise Carter-Holloway was one of my best friends. Today, she's a ghost to me. And I know a thing or two about ghosts.

Her house in the Hollywood Hills looms up ahead of me, a Mediterranean monstrosity that overlooks the entire San Fernando Valley. The sun is brilliant and high in the sky, washing the sandstone in warm light, palm trees swaying gently in an afternoon breeze. Several cars are parked in the circular driveway, but there's no way to tell who they belong to; I can't brace myself for what kind of snake pit I might be walking into.

But I have to do it. I have to know why Alana is here.

I parallel park a couple houses down, scrubbing my hands over my face. Take in a deep breath, let it out slow.

Walking up the sidewalk, I try not to focus on the flood of memories of Elise, a girl I used to love like a sister. When I had my first-ever panic attack in seventh-grade math class, Elise was the one who talked me down in the bathroom, wiping tears from my cheeks. In loud, chatty groups, her eyes would always find mine, making sure I was okay. She was like my protector.

After Livia, I thought I'd never have a close friend again. But I did. Maybe Elise was Alana's friend first, but she welcomed me with an open heart.

Until everything fell apart.

I shake my head hard to clear it. Standing on Elise's front steps, I close my eyes and picture the foyer: sparkling white marble, giant bronze fish statues. Her parents—a director and a film composer, a full-blown Hollywood power couple—have the weirdest decor taste. Music is pounding deep inside the cavernous house, and that jars a memory too: her mother banging out a melody on the piano, blasting her latest composition over the sound system. *Girls, what do you think?* she'd shout at me, Elise, and Alana over the deafening roar.

Instead of knocking, I let myself in.

It's exactly as I remember, fish statues and all. There are no personal touches until I reach the living room, which is all polished white floors and an ornate fireplace filled with candles. As always, the air-conditioning is on full blast, making me shiver.

The group of girls staring at me might have something to do with that too.

Everyone is dressed deliberately sloppy, perched on the white couch or gathered by the enormous bay windows. Here and there, I hear whispers hissing like rain on hot coals. They aren't girls from my class, they're younger, but I still know them well—our school is so small.

"Maya," someone says. I glance over my shoulder; there's Elise's little sister, Isabelle, making a beeline for me, thick brown curls pulled into a bun, a White Claw in one hand. In my mind, Isabelle is a giggly preteen rather than a sophomore in high school; I do a double take at the drink she's clutching. "Are you—are you sure you want to be here?"

"I'm not really here," I answer as loudly as I dare. The bassline is pounding, rattling the framed family portrait that hangs over the fireplace. Outside the living room window, I catch a glimpse of a few girls hopping in and out of the infinity pool that overlooks the Valley. "Just stopped by to see Alana."

Isabelle steps back, eyes darting around the room. "Alana Murray?"

"Yeah." *Duh,* I think. I can't even count how many sleep-overs Elise, Alana, and I had at this house, occasionally allowing Isabelle to watch scary movies with us.

"Maya, this is my pool party," Isabelle says, biting her lip. "For my friends. I didn't invite Alana Murray."

"Oh." A warm flush creeps up my cheeks. What kind of moron crashes a fifteen-year-old's pool party? "Sorry—I must've made a mistake. I'll just . . ."

Before I can finish my sentence, there's a commotion in the foyer. Voices fight for attention, shrieking and squealing over one another. And then there's Elise, pushing through the knot of bodies congregating in the hall.

"I'm fine," she says loudly, placating her sister's friends, and even though I haven't spoken to her in a year, I can tell she's lying. Her face is covered in a thin sheen of sweat, and coiled tendrils of dark hair are slipping out of her ponytail. I can't remember the last time I saw her with her hair up.

"Where were you?" Isabelle asks her older sister. Elise's head snaps up. She sees me standing here with her sister, an unlikely pair, and her eyes widen. "Mom said you were supposed to be back by noon to study for AP Bio."

I miss Elise with a stabbing pain in my rib cage. I want to chime in, to tease her—she was *always* late to parties and school events, and always for dumb reasons, like that she needed Starbucks or had to pull over on the side of the road to take a picture of a cat. But I can't tease her about anything anymore because I'm no one to her.

"You don't have your license, Iz. You don't know what it's like to take the 405 this time of day, especially not in *my* crappy car." Elise's voice is forced into levity, but when the girls around her scatter back to the pool, she heads straight for me and her eyes are blazing fire.

"Wow." Elise grins, her teeth pearly white. It's a grim smile. If she feels emotional about the fact that we haven't spoken in a year, I can't tell. Her eyes sweep over me. "To what do I owe the honor?"

"I'm looking for Alana," I hear myself say. There's a weird ringing in my ears.

The last time I spoke to Elise was that day during junior year on my front lawn, shouting at her so loudly that the neighbors called my dad. I can't recall the exact words we exchanged, but I know what it was about. Earlier that day, she told the whole soccer team that I had to be on meds to get through the school day. About how there was a contingency plan among the teachers in case I had a panic attack in the middle of class. Elise, who used to help me breathe through anxiety, said all that to girls I've known for years, and she laughed.

"You and Alana aren't together? Well, hell must be freezing over." Her tone is dry, flat. "I figured you would crumble into dust if your girlfriend was ever out of your sight for two seconds."

It hits uncomfortably close to the things Alana said to me on the trail earlier. My voice comes out hard. "Have you seen her or not?"

Isabelle is looking between the two of us like she's watching a tennis match, eyes wide.

"If you're looking for Alana," Elise says slowly, scrutinizing every inch of my face. "Why would you come here? You haven't wanted anything to do with me in, like . . ."

"A year," I finish. Anger is making my hands shake. "Look, I didn't come here to have another screaming match with you. If Alana's not here, then I'm leaving."

"If she shows up, Maya, I'll ask her to text you," Isabelle interrupts. "I know you wouldn't come over here unless you were really worried."

"Oh," I say, too nervous to look at Elise. I force myself to sound casual. "Thanks, but I'm not worried. She'll turn up."

Before either of them can say another word, I'm walking briskly from the living room, through the foyer, sneakers scuffing up the marble. *I'm fine, I'm fine, I'm fine,* across the familiar front yard, ducking through the gate, hurrying down the sidewalk, unlocking my car.

As soon as I'm safe inside, I rest my arms on the steering wheel, breathing hard.

Alana isn't at home. Alana isn't at Elise's house. Alana isn't anywhere.

What if she's still up at Antelope Valley?

I know it's stupid—her phone literally pinged in Los Angeles. But I can see her there in my mind, pacing the parking lot, watching the warm afternoon sunlight wash the California poppies in gold. Furious. Hating me.

Waiting for me to go to her.

Maybe there was a glitch with her mom's phone—maybe it was an old ping. Did I see the date and time attached to it? I squeeze my eyes shut, trying to remember, but I can't. The shock over seeing Elise's address was too overpowering. If it was one of Mrs. Murray's old phones, it could easily not have been updated in over a year. It could've saved an old ping from one of the sleepovers or study sessions at Elise's house back when we were all still friends.

I swear under my breath and put the car in drive. I'm right back where I started. And there's only one place for me to go.

■ ■ ■

I've known the names of the superbloom flowers since I was a little girl and my parents brought me up here, carrying me along the trail on Dad's shoulders. Brittlebrush, sand verbena, evening primrose. Mom always pointed out the desert lilies, white and stretching up toward the sun-washed sky. But the California poppies were always my favorite. At Antelope Valley, the field fills with them, an ocean of golden orange.

Even today, heart in my throat as I scan the parking lot for a sign of Alana, the sight is stunning, washed in a warm glow. The petals ripple in the desert wind, and the dry heat warms my bare arms. I hug them across my chest, turning in every direction; Alana isn't anywhere, but then, I don't know what I expected. Her to be sitting cross-legged by the entrance like an obedient kid waiting to be picked up from school?

In the hour and a half it took for me to drive back up here, the cars lining the road have dwindled, the sun settling lower in the sky. Along the way, I must've dialed her number a hundred times. All unanswered. Worry cracks my heart, shaking along familiar fault lines. I have to know where Alana is. If I walked away from her, if I left her here alone, I'm the worst girlfriend ever. She'll hate me.

You're not even her girlfriend anymore, a voice in my head sneers—Alana's voice, probably. *You broke up with her.*

The wildflowers blur in front of me as I race along the line of cars full of people going home after a carefree day on the trail. Anxiety whirs louder in my head until all I hear is a hysterical buzzing; my palms are sweaty and time passes weirdly, lurching, so that before I know it, hours have gone by. I can't stay here much longer, since national park land is only open until sunset, but I can't *leave.* Not without Alana.

But there's no trace of her. I've scoured every inch of this place, even run halfway up the trail. My heartbeat kicks up when I glance down at myself and realize that my sneakers are covered in dirt, that there's a thin ribbon of blood trickling down my shin from where I must have tripped.

I sit down at the trailhead, pressing the heels of my hands against my eyes to ward off tears. *It's fine, it's fine,* I chant inside my head, trying to calm myself—but I know full well that nothing's ever been less fine in my life. Alana's gone, and now night is falling, and I'm here all by myself. If my anxiety tips over the edge into a full-blown panic attack, which seems inevitable, I'll be completely alone.

When I pull my phone out of my pocket with shaking hands, there are zero bars. Panic spikes through my chest, razor-sharp. I can't drive all the way back down to LA when

I'm this anxious, and now I can't call for help. There's a graduation rehearsal on campus tomorrow, but that doesn't matter right now. If I can just crash somewhere safe for the night, Alana will turn up in the morning. She'll be at school like normal, dramatic and flipping her hair and ready to dissect our entire fight. Everything will be chaos, but everything will be all right.

I suck in a long, slow breath, clutching my useless phone. I know where I can go.

INTERLUDE

———

SIX YEARS EARLIER

THERE IS A place, tucked away in the far reaches of Los Padres National Forest, miles north of the San Fernando Valley's urban sprawl, that is a secret all my own.

I took my first steps on the grassy lawn of our family's summer house, the lake winking playfully in the background. Every year, Dad takes me out on the water in the Sunfish, its brilliant orange-and-yellow sail billowing in the wind. I don't remember a single summer where I didn't spend time at Lake Ember. As soon as Alana enters my life, she's included on every trip.

Alana doesn't often say that she likes things. The shows on Disney Channel are lame. My new white Keds are stupid ("they're just going to get dirty"). The music at our middle school dances is boring. But she *loves* Lake Ember. I know she does. I can see it on her face when we wake up early to jump off the boat dock, when we walk down Mira Monte Road to buy ice cream in town, when we stay up late whispering secrets on my window seat looking out across the water.

We're two days into our Lake Ember summer, sixth grade finally behind us, when Alana asks the question.

My half sister, Jazmine, is twenty-one, a junior in college. She wears her Stanford baseball cap constantly, even at the dinner table while Dad passes around plates of burgers fresh from the grill. I stare at that hat, bright red with a green tree sewn across the front.

"What are you going to do when you graduate?" Alana asks, digging through the salad bowl with plastic tongs in search of the ripest tomato.

Jazmine gives her an indulgent smile across the table. "Well," she says, "I'm majoring in architecture, with a minor in Spanish."

I love listening to my sister talk about school. Architecture is the perfect thing for her to study; she's so detail-oriented, careful, thoughtful, and creative. She's the one who taught me to draw before I was even in kindergarten, explaining depth of field and shading.

"Yeah, but what are you going to do with that?" Alana continues. "Design buildings?"

"That's usually what you do with an architecture degree," Jazmine says patiently.

"But you live here." Alana gives a little snort into her salad. "What kinds of buildings would you design in Lake Ember? Boathouses? Seafood shacks?"

I glance sharply over at my best friend, ponytail swinging. I would never sit at the Murrays' dinner table and interrogate Alana's family about their jobs. Jazmine exchanges a quick look with my dad that they don't think I see. I'm embarrassed: *I'm* the one who brought this girl into our house. I'm responsible for her.

"I don't live here," Jazmine says politely, but I know my sister well enough to understand why her pink lips press into a tight smile. "This is Maya's dad's house. I'm here for part of the summer, just like you."

"Hey, Miss Alana," Dad interrupts deftly, passing the plate of hamburgers her way. "Grab that patty in the middle. I remember you like them well done."

He's teasing. Alana accepts the plate with a laugh.

"No! I like them medium, Mr. Rosier."

"Oh," he says, feigning confusion. "Nice and crunchy, right? Consistency of a potato chip?"

"No! Eww!"

We both giggle, and for a little while, I don't have to think about the way she spoke to Jazmine.

That night, I'm sitting on my bedroom's window seat, wearing pajamas, my hair still damp from the shower. Alana hasn't taken hers yet. She's carefully brushing the tangles out of her lake water hair. I watch her, admiring the color, deep brown like the coffee table in our living room back in LA.

"That was kind of mean," I tell her. "What you said to Jazmine at dinner."

Alana looks up, the sunset washing her summer-tan face in gold. She clutches the ends of her perfect hair between her fingers. "Your sister's an adult. Adults don't get their feelings hurt."

"Yeah, but ... college is a really big deal, and you were kind of ..."

"Maya. College is not that big of a deal for someone who went to Coldwater. We'll all go to college. Blah blah. It's not special." Alana glances out the window, lost in thought. "Do you ever think you cling to your sister a little too much?"

I flinch, stung. *But I don't have a mom,* I think. *Who else is there?*

"Do *you* think I cling to her too much?"

Alana considers this. She fixes me with her sapphire-blue eyes.

"I don't think you need her as much as you think you do."

She skips off into the hallway, but I can't stop thinking about what she said. At eleven years old, I don't know it yet, but she's planted the seeds that will take root and grow me into someone new.

A girl who doesn't need her big sister. A girl who doesn't even speak to her.

CHAPTER FOUR

I CREEP BACK into Lake Ember like a ghost.

By the time I hit Mira Monte Road, the main drag through town, night has fully fallen. Streetlamps flicker in the blue-dark, shops already closing because life moves so slowly in this godforsaken place. The sights are familiar: the 99 Cent Store where Alana and I bought flip-flops and Styrofoam pool noodles to splash with in the lake, the ice cream place where she'd get two scoops, one chocolate and one cotton candy. I always had to finish it for her.

I chew on my bottom lip until I taste copper.

Muscle memory guides me as I turn off the road, heading down a dirt path in between oak trees that creak ominously in the wind. I swallow hard against the memories that are trying to choke me, drag me down with spiny fingers. When I was a little girl, Lake Ember meant safety. It welcomed me summer after summer, lush and leafy with the predictable sloshing of water against the shoreline, rocking me to sleep.

I haven't been back since I was thirteen. I don't know what it means to me now.

Then I see it: moonlight winking off the water, just visible between gaps in the trees. And the house, a cottage with hyacinths out front, wind chimes singing a familiar refrain. I'm hit with a powerful wave of déjà vu. From the outside, the lake house doesn't look like much: a wooden cabin, front door painted in lemon yellow. Plants grow on either side of the front steps, tall and bending with the nighttime breeze.

With a heavy sigh, I jump out of the car, swinging my purse over my shoulder. Pine cones crunch under my sneakers. Behind the living room curtains, a golden light glows, so I punch the doorbell. Try not to think about what my sister will say when she realizes her little sister has turned up, dirty and bleeding, on her front steps.

I hear Jazmine's voice before I see her.

"Colin," she calls, laughing musically. "I didn't mean you guys should come over right *now*. Tomorrow would've been totally . . ."

The door swings open. I take in everything about her, the sister I haven't seen in years: dark wavy hair skimming her shoulders, a white tank top under faded overalls. Her brown skin is already summer tan, and if she smiled, I know the dimple in her left cheek would show.

But she doesn't smile. She just stares.

"Maya?" Like a word in a foreign language, one she's trying to recall how to pronounce. "You . . . What are you doing here? Are you okay?"

Her huge brown eyes, our most similar feature, flick up and down my body. We're half sisters and we barely share anything except Mom; she might have been the product of our mother's early mistakes, but Jazmine Reyes has been Miss Perfect for as long as I can remember.

We're so different, but when she brushes her fingertips against my shoulder, there's a crease in her eyebrows that I recognize from my own reflection. A creeping sadness.

"I was in the area," I say finally. "I needed a place to crash."

"And you chose me over a Motel Six? I'm honored."

There's no sharpness in her words, just a dry humor, but I wince anyway.

"Maya, I'm kidding." Jazmine kisses me twice: my temple, then my cheek. She holds me at arm's length, eyes still searching like I'm an indecipherable map. "Come inside. Does your dad know that you're here?"

I follow her into the living room, blinking in the golden light. It's surprisingly easy to brush past the memory of Dad making macarons back home just a couple hours ago, talking to me with an affection and worry I hardly deserve.

"He doesn't care. Half the time he's over at the restaurant for some private event or movie premiere. Doesn't come home until late."

"He seriously leaves you alone in that house at night?" Jazmine asks. I know she's thinking of how big it is, how cold.

"I don't need a babysitter. I'll be eighteen next month."

"Yeah, I know, but still."

We stand there in a once-familiar living room, staring at each other. The wood-paneled walls are the same as I remember, but everything else has been lovingly, carefully redone. A fuzzy white blanket thrown over the arm of a pastel blue couch, a record player perched on an end table. When I was a kid, our school photos lined the mantel. They're gone now, replaced by wax candles, a cactus in a red clay pot. There's one framed picture of me and Mom; I avert my eyes quickly, unwilling to acknowledge the tide of grief that's rising in my chest.

"I won't stay long." My voice is marble-hard, a tone I learned from Alana.

She blinks, surprised. "Of course you can *stay*, Maya. I'm just curious why you're even here. Isn't it graduation next weekend? Skipping town before something important like that . . . it's not exactly normal for you."

I pick at the fraying hem of my T-shirt. "How would you know what's normal for me?"

When I was thirteen, two important things happened: I realized I was falling for Alana, and I stopped speaking to my sister. *She'll say she knows what's best for you, but she won't.* That was Alana's familiar refrain. She was right. Jazmine had always been picky about the people I had in my life, and she never liked Alana.

After my sister graduated from Stanford, my dad gave our family lake house to her; despite not being biologically related, they'd always had a close relationship, and he wanted to help her succeed. He helped pay for her to get an online MBA when it became clear that architecture wasn't the career path she wanted, and with his guidance, Jazmine opened a shop in town.

My sister reached out to me plenty of times, but I never answered. The last time she came home was on Christmas morning three years ago, and I spent the whole time ignoring her in favor of texting Alana. We haven't seen each other since.

"If I don't know what's normal for you, why don't you tell me?" Jazmine asks in a tone more charitable and patient than I deserve.

I stare down at my disgusting sneakers coated in dirt, the cut along my leg that's finally stopped bleeding.

"You've got to know that—that Mom would be sad if she knew what's happened to us," Jazmine continues, and I know what it's costing her to say this out loud. The way her words quiver, bending but not breaking. "Maya, I'll always be here for you. You know that, right? I'm your big sister. If you need me . . ."

"That's not why I'm here. I just needed a place to crash, and I didn't have anywhere else to go."

Jazmine goes quiet again.

"Fine, Maya," she mutters. "Happy to be your last resort. Go up to your room. It's just how you left it."

. . .

The last bedroom at the end of the hall has always been mine.

I stand in the doorway unable to cross the threshold, twining a hair tie around my wrist. Jazmine's right: It's exactly how I left it. There's still a box of rock salt on the dresser. I hesitate. Glance over my shoulder. Walk to the box and shake a handful into my palm, rubbing the grains between my fingertips.

Old habits die hard. I scatter the salt in a thin line across the threshold.

The earliest ghost I can remember was my grandmother, visiting me when I was only three—too young to be frightened by her appearance in my bedroom, lit by the glow of my nightlight. It's possible there were others before her and I didn't notice. From that point on, my ghosts were everywhere. Outside the grocery store, lingering in Wilacre Park. They would ask me for help sometimes when they realized I could see them, because I stared just a little bit too long. If I looked close, these people were smoke. You could step through them, look through them. They barely existed.

But they did, of course. They existed to me.

For a while I tried to help them, talk with them, guide them, explain that they should move on. Every single time, they did. They just needed some extra encouragement, and I was happy to provide that.

But when Mom died and I realized she wasn't coming back, I decided I'd had enough. That's when I set my boundaries; it was on one of our trips to Lake Ember. The streets were lined with sycamore and oak trees bowing in the wind, a warm breeze so different from Los Angeles, and instead of yoga studios and vape shops, people browsed through witchy boutiques selling incense and gemstones. I spoke to a kind-faced woman behind a desk about the best crystals for psychic protection, and she sold me the same obsidian stone I've carried with me ever since. Jagged black volcanic glass. As long as I'm holding it, no ghost can get close to me.

Dropping my purse to the floor, I step into the bedroom. It's been years since I saw my last ghost. Honestly, I rarely let the events of my childhood haunt me. But it's impossible to walk through this tiny space—was it always this tiny?—and not remember the little girl who salted her doorways before falling asleep, furious that I couldn't see Mom, desperate to keep all other spirits at bay. I still carry the obsidian stone in my pocket, just in case.

I turn on the bedside table lamp, muscle memory leading

me to the switch tucked underneath a pink and white shade. Mom decorated this room for me when I was four and I helped, begging for unicorn wallpaper. Since then, Jazmine's stripped the walls and painted them a pale yellow, the only change she's made to the room. Can't say I blame her.

I pull my phone out of my pocket, although I don't know what I expect. An onslaught of text messages, worried missed calls? Dad's used to me disappearing, usually over to Alana's house. And, of course, there's nothing from Alana herself.

My lock screen photo is too bright in the dark room: me and Alana at Venice Beach in our ripped jean shorts and crop tops. The sight of her face, dark hair tangled in the wind, hits like a punch to the gut. This morning, she was my girlfriend. Tonight, she's my ex who hates me.

It's funny. By now, I can feel it when a friendship ends. Like dry rot, crumbling under a hiking boot, nothing but dust. But I loved Alana, loved her more than a crush, more than fleeting starlight streaking across a desolate sky. I loved her like she was the only thing. When love like that is stamped out, where does it go?

I shake my head to clear it, running a hand over my face. It was stupid of me to come up to Antelope Valley. Like Alana always says, I let my anxiety get the better of me. I can't start worrying, because that's what Alana wants: to prey on my anxiety and make me frantic. I know she's fine, because Alana's always fine—she's probably home right now talking shit about me to her mom. Tomorrow I'll drive down to LA and get back to my life. To school, to graduation. To figuring out a plan.

But what even *is* my life if I'm not Alana's girlfriend?

"Maya?"

My sister's voice is quiet. She's standing in the doorway, one hand resting against the frame. There's a soft sadness on her face, and I can tell she's still grappling with the fact that a stranger has somehow replaced her little sister.

I squeeze my eyes shut tight. A mistake, because flashes of the day flicker behind my closed lids. Sweat dripping down my back as I raced back down the trail at Antelope Valley, orange poppies blooming in every direction. White-hot anger propelling me down the freeway until I started to regret leaving Alana behind.

"I'm fine," I say, my voice small.

"Are you still seeing them?" Jazmine lowers her voice. "Your . . . you know . . ."

Ghosts, my brain fills in. I spin around to face my sister.

"I'm seventeen years old. You really think I still believe in that shit?" I narrow my eyes, and when I speak again, it's with Alana's voice. "Do *you* really believe in it? I thought you were supposed to be smart."

"Jeez, Maya. It was just a question."

"You've always thought I was crazy."

"Honey, I've never thought—"

"Yes, you did. I overheard Dad on the phone with you all the time." I hug my arms across my chest. "He was always trying to convince you that I would grow out of it. And look at that. I did. I'm fine."

"You're fine?" Jazmine's voice is a string pulled taut. "This is how fine looks? Listen, I can only imagine how hard it must be to manage your anxiety. I know a lot more than you realize, Maya—"

"Oh, well." I toss my hair. "Thank god we have a Mensa-level genius in our midst."

I turn to the window, staring toward the dark lake, but I can feel her eyes boring holes in my back.

"For the record," Jazmine says finally, and her voice is remarkably measured. "I've never thought you were crazy. Maybe I don't know what it's like to have anxiety, but I can understand feeling alone and sad. And scared. And motherless."

I sink down onto the window seat, pulling my knees up to my chest. The material is slightly worn after all these years, but it feels the same as ever.

"When I asked about the ghosts," Jazmine continues, "I wasn't trying to belittle you. I was only curious whether that had something to do with you leaving LA tonight. Whether something scared you. Your dad's worried about everything you've been going through . . . you know, your relationship with Alana."

"Oh, like Dad even pays attention to that."

"Of course he pays attention. You're his daughter. He's concerned about you. I feel like you assume we call each other to gossip about you, but we talk about you because we care," Jazmine says, her voice softening.

I don't dare turn to look at her.

"Maya, you can stay here as long as you need, okay? Come to work with me in the morning."

"I can't go to work with you. Tomorrow's Sunday. I have a graduation rehearsal in the afternoon."

"You can't take a mental health day? I'll call Coldwater for you."

I narrow my eyes. "AP tests are this week. Dad will freak if I'm not home studying."

"All right," she says gently. "We'll get you home tomorrow. You can at least grab a cup of tea before you head back to LA."

That's right—Jazmine's tea shop. The memory bubbles up from some secret location deep inside my mind. Probably one of the chatty emails she sent me over the years, the ones I skimmed and then deleted, feeling guilty.

"I'll wake you up at seven," she says. She thinks I don't notice, but when she turns toward the hallway, she pauses, noticing the salt lining my doorway. I know she's remembering all the nights I did this ritual as a little girl, back when we lived under the same roof. I take a slow breath, bracing for the accusations.

Instead, she steps over the salt line without a word. Leaving it unbroken. Keeping me safe. That's the part that makes me cry myself to sleep.

CHAPTER FIVE

WHEN WE STEP through the front doors of Blue Skies Tea Shop early the next morning, I have to catch my breath. It's like Jazmine's teenage bedroom duplicated. Golden string lights hang across the wide front window, worn Oriental rugs are strewn across the hardwood floor, and the entire space is packed with overstuffed armchairs. *Mom would've loved this,* I think automatically—she always helped us decorate our rooms, drove us to antiques shops to find cool pieces that no one else would have. But it hurts too much to think about Mom here.

"It's pretty," I mumble, pushing damp hair off my face.

Rain is sheeting down on the streets of Lake Ember, soaking both of us to the bone, which offers an easy explanation for why I'm shaking. I clench my fists, trying not to check my phone for the hundredth time. Alana still hasn't sent me a single text, and the uneasiness is melding with an oppressive guilt. I popped one of my prescribed anxiety pills on the drive over here and I'm still waiting for it to kick in.

Jazmine glances over, blissfully unaware of my discomfort. "Thanks! Hey, go sit down somewhere. I'll be right back."

And then she's off through the swinging saloon-style wooden door. I frown at the place she disappeared. Privately, I think it's kind of weird that Jazmine chose to open a tea shop; in high school, she could barely operate our Nespresso machine. Not to mention her stellar high school career, her Stanford education . . . only to end up *here*. Alana and I used to discuss this at length. Imagining making it to college graduation and then throwing your whole life away.

I pull a chair out from a table by the window, gazing blankly at the laundromat across the street. Would Alana *really* vanish without a trace just before graduation? I don't want to think so, but she's done all kinds of things in the past when I've disappointed her. In middle school, after I wouldn't let her copy my Pre-Algebra homework, she ignored me for a week and only spoke to Elise. Freshman year, we got into a huge fight because I wouldn't let her borrow my brand-new pink Nikes for soccer practice. I saw for the first time how Alana could turn on a dime, how she would laugh when I said the wrong answer in class, make me feel small.

But when she apologized—and she *always* apologized, bringing me cold brew coffee or scattering my favorite California poppies on my doorstep—she was nicer and more loving than ever. *I don't know why I acted like that. I was wrong. You deserve so much better, Maya, so much better than me.* I would tell her that I didn't deserve better. That with me, she would always have a thousand second chances.

My phone buzzes, jolting me back to life. I glance down: it's a text from my dad.

Hey kid, Jazmine told me you went up to visit. Next time let me know before you drive that far by yourself. Have fun!

I bite my lip, rereading his words. Unconcerned, almost careless. Maybe it's silly, but sometimes I long for a parent like Alana's mom, who tracks her phone's location and knows all her teachers' names. Mrs. Murray would sometimes swing by the Coldwater campus and pick up Alana for lunch just because she felt like it.

As if on command, a photo of Alana's mom hugging me fills up the screen. I swallow hard and lift the phone to my ear.

"Mrs. Murray?"

"Oh, honey, hi. I'm glad I tracked you down."

I hesitate, not sure what to say. Why is she calling? Anxiety roils in my stomach.

"Your dad mentioned you're up at Lake Ember. Did Alana go with you, by any chance?"

"No, I still haven't seen her. Or heard from her. Why?"

Mrs. Murray sighs. "Well, I'm trying to track her down as well. She isn't answering her phone, which has me really worried. You girls both have graduation rehearsal later today, right?" She doesn't wait for me to respond. "So I'm hoping she'll show up for that. But I called your father and he said you're at the lake. I was hoping you girls planned an impromptu trip and forgot to tell me."

"Oh. Um, no, she's not with me."

She barely seems to hear me. "It looks like the video doorbell picked her up walking down the driveway yesterday morning. When did you last see her, sweetie?"

My heart crashes against my rib cage. I try not to think of Antelope Valley, but it happens anyway. The wind rippling through the poppy fields, snow-capped mountains in the distance, the way Alana's ice-blue eyes narrowed like I was stupid, like I was a joke. The way I said *watch me* and walked away, leaving her there.

Stranding her.

Oh my god. I can't tell Mrs. Murray that.

"I-I'm sorry," I say carefully, picking at my cuticles. If I sound shaken enough, maybe she won't push the question. "If she's not at home right now, I don't know where she would be. Did you—did you check her location on your phone?"

"Yes, but it's just telling me *no location found.*" She sighs heavily. "I called the police first thing this morning, of course. They're looking into it. Don't worry, honey. I'll keep you posted."

My chest tightens, panic rising as we say goodbye. No location found? What the hell? So maybe the Mulholland Drive ping really was just a glitch, and I confronted Elise for nothing. The very thought makes me want to puke. Plus, now the police are involved?

The swinging doors to the tea shop's back room bursts open, making me jump and drop my phone. A dark-haired girl about my age explodes out of the kitchen, catching the doors with both hands, arms spread wide.

"*The Grey Woods Haunting,*" she says loudly, but cheerfully, like a normal person might remark upon the weather. "I remembered it!"

"Excuse me?"

"Oh." Her face falls as she takes me in, the doors swinging back and forth behind her. "Thought you were Emily."

"Sorry to disappoint," I say, not bothering to ask who the hell Emily is. My heart is still thundering in my ears. Mrs. Murray could be on the phone with the police right this minute. What will they do? How quickly will they be able to find Alana? And when they do, when she tells everyone what I did, they're all going to hate me.

"Rowan?" The door swings open again and my sister steps out, eyes sparkling and kind. She's holding a container of blueberry oolong tea in one hand. "You look like you need a task."

"Sorry, Jazz. I just got excited that I remembered the name of that show I was telling Emily about yesterday! You know, the one about the killer stalking innocent victims on a lake until they come back to haunt him?"

Jazmine thumps the container of tea down onto the counter, then pats Rowan on the head. She's wearing a pastel blue baseball cap. A delicate white cloud is sewn onto the front.

"I challenge you to watch something educational and lay off the creepy stuff. Hulu has some *great* documentaries lately that I think you'd really . . ."

My sister keeps talking, but I'm watching my phone. Any minute now, I'm sure that it'll light up with Mrs. Murray's face again, her voice cold and full of rage. *The police say you were with Alana at Antelope Valley. That you picked a fight and left her behind. Didn't even look back. Like a monster.*

"This is my little sister, Maya," Jazmine says. I jump at the sound of my name.

"Oh, right!" Rowan looks up with a lopsided grin, baseball cap sliding down into her eyes. Even across the room, I can tell that they're a piercing slate gray. "Maya Rosier. You seem like a Darjeeling girl. Am I right?"

I'm silent, just watching her.

"I'm never wrong about people's tea orders. That's why your sister hired me. I'm a tea prodigy."

"What a useful skill." I hear Alana in my own voice.

"Maya," my sister says. "Be nice. I'll come back to get you in two seconds."

Jazmine ducks back into the kitchen. Rowan smirks as she pours hot water into a ceramic teacup. Her black T-shirt is cuffed at the sleeves and her forearms are tanned and muscular, the kind of girl who probably spends a ton of time on the lake.

"You don't remember me, huh?" she asks. "It's okay. I'm not devastated or anything."

"I've never met you before. And I don't like Darjeeling."

Actually, I've never tried it—coffee is my thing, not tea. But I can't give her the satisfaction of enjoying whatever drink she concocted, thinking she knows me. I glance back down at my phone, passing it nervously from hand to hand.

"They call it the champagne of teas, you know?" Rowan hops over the counter and carries the tea to my small table by the window, setting it down with great fanfare. Her eyes flash, mischievous. The exact kind of energy I don't need in my life right now.

I pick up the teacup slowly and, without breaking eye contact with Rowan, pour its contents into a potted plant beside the table. Her eyes widen, the smile wiped off her face.

"I don't have time," I say quietly, "for your shit."

"You really don't remember me?"

"I really don't."

"It's okay. You always seemed a little self-centered. No offense." She leans back against the floral-papered wall, crossing her arms.

I look this girl in the eye, studying the way she smiles easily and the mismatched way her sleeves are rolled up. She's nothing like Alana. I hate her for it. I know it's irrational, but I do.

"Look," Rowan says, one sneaker scuffing the baseboard. She pulls a scrap of paper out of the back pocket of her jeans, scribbles on it with a ballpoint pen. "Here's my phone number. I'm happy to give you a Lake Ember grand tour. You seem like the type to lock yourself inside with the curtains drawn all day, and that's no way to spend a summer on a beautiful lake. Too Emily Dickinson."

"I'm not *staying* here. I'm going back to LA today." *I need to find my missing girlfriend.* Except she's not my girlfriend anymore. A wave of nausea rolls through my stomach and I push my now-empty teacup away, standing quickly. "Lake Ember is a place I used to go as a kid. Not anymore."

"You're literally here right now."

"Whatever," I snap, annoyance growing. "Anyway, I don't need a *tour*. Like, I grew up here."

She shakes her head. "Have you eaten oysters at Captain Harry's? Breakfast at Shoreline Diner? Have you windsurfed in the Summertime Sail-a-Thon or the—"

I hold up my hands in defeat. "Sorry, I'm not a loser."

My sister picks this exact moment to burst through the saloon doors.

"Maya," she says. "We need to go."

"Thank god." I breathe a sigh of relief, leaving Rowan behind me. "That girl is so . . ."

My voice fades as I take in Jazmine's expression. Her face is drained of all color. She grabs my forearm as we head through the door, bell jingling merrily overhead, and her fingers are ice-cold pressing against my skin.

"The police are on their way to my house," she hisses, tugging me along the sidewalk. "They're saying Alana Murray is missing. You want to tell me anything about this?"

. . .

The LAPD gave Jazmine an hour warning. This is just enough time to work my sister into an absolute frenzy. By the time we get back to her house, she's ricocheting around the living room with cleaning supplies like she was shot out of a pinball machine. It's clear that there's no way in hell I'm getting back to LA this afternoon.

"They're coming to talk to *you*, Maya. Do you know where Alana is? Is this why you fled Los Angeles?"

"Okay," I say, knotting my fingers together. "We shouldn't use the word *fled*, first of all. I came to visit you. I mean, you're my sister. There's no law against that."

Jazmine softens, resuming her dusting. Her expression reminds me of Mom, tugging at my heart in ways I can't explain.

"They'll probably ask me why I'm here and not on campus," I mumble as realization dawns on me. "I'm supposed to be at graduation rehearsal today."

She waves the feather duster at me. "I called Coldwater right after I hung up with Mrs. Murray. Told them you were sick."

"You lied?"

"Do you feel sick?" she asks dryly. Good point. My stomach is churning. "Right. So I didn't lie. Listen, no one will give you a hard time. Ms. Connors in the admin office still remembers me—tried to get me to commit to the alumni brunch in the fall, so I guess I have that to look forward to now."

"Do the cops think something bad happened to Alana?"

"Maya, I don't know."

"What if I'm a suspect?"

"You're not," she says firmly. "This isn't that kind of

situation. Alana's missing and they want to bring her home safe, and they know you're her girlfriend, so they want to talk to you. That's all this is."

Her girlfriend. I swallow hard. I want to believe my sister, but there's a tremble in her voice that makes me unsure she even believes herself.

When Detective Ramirez arrives in our living room, he greets Jazmine, even though she's a flurry of nerves. You'd think she were the one with an anxiety disorder.

"I don't know if this is a good idea—I'm not her legal guardian," Jazmine says, fidgeting with her hair, eyes darting to me and back to the detective. "She's a minor. Shouldn't her father be here?"

The detective smiles, his eyes crinkling at the corners. He can't be much older than my dad. "Not necessary in the state of California, Miss Reyes. Unless, of course, you want a parent here, Maya?"

"No," I say quickly. "No, I'm okay."

I shoot a quelling look in my sister's direction and she retreats into the kitchen. The detective gives another good-natured smile and sinks into the armchair.

"This won't take long, Maya. I know this is a stressful time for you, so I want to be clear that law enforcement is simply doing our due diligence and speaking to Alana Murray's closest friends. We want to bring her home safe."

"Right."

"Can you describe for me the nature of your relationship with Alana?"

"Our relationship? I don't know . . ." I chew on my lower lip. How am I supposed to distill almost eight years into a single sentence? "We love each other."

"And we're talking . . . romantic love?"

I exhale through my nose. Jesus Christ. So glad they could send Detective Heteronormativity. "Yes. I've been her girlfriend for three years."

But not anymore. Somehow, I don't think I should mention the breakup. The detective shifts in his seat, and my heart rate quickens.

"Can you tell me when you last saw Alana?"

This is it. Whatever I say now will seal my fate. If I'm honest, I say: the morning of May fourth, surrounded by wildflowers, my heart splintering and cracking open. I turned and walked away from her. I stranded her and haven't seen her since.

Instead, I say, "Friday, May third. It was the last day of classes for seniors."

"Thank you, Maya. And can you be more specific? What time did you last see her?"

I saw on some true crime documentary once that people can get through these types of conversations by sticking to their truth. Keeping their statements as simple as possible. Don't lie unless you absolutely have to.

"Our last class of the day was International Relations— that's one of the classes we have together. And then I didn't see her after school."

The detective hums, making a note on his yellow legal pad. I track the movement of his pen as it etches across the page, trying not to remember Alana sitting next to me in the classroom like she always did. Her green and blue plaid uniform kilt spread across her thighs, the way she pulled two bottles of Essie nail polish out of her pencil case and held them out to me. They clinked together in her palm. *Pick a color.*

"Alana was last seen by her mother early Friday morning. According to her mother, she was getting dressed for school. Melissa Murray then left for a work trip to Vancouver. However," the detective continues, "she's provided us with home security camera footage of Alana leaving the house the next day, just after eight thirty in the morning on May fourth."

"Oh," I say, trying to look politely interested instead of terrified.

"The camera never captured Alana returning home." He clears his throat and takes a long sip of coffee from the mug Jazmine filled for him. "Do you, by any chance, know where she might have been going?"

I hesitate for a second. If there's security footage of Alana leaving the house, does it show her climbing into my car? Is the detective waiting for me to tell him this? Long ago, Alana taught me that whenever faced with a question I don't want to deal with, it's best to answer with another question.

"Did you know there's a back way into Alana's house?"

His dark eyebrows raise. "What do you mean, a back way?"

"Well, there's a fence around the property, but there are a bunch of dogwood trees back by the pool. Sometimes, we . . ." I pause. "Are you going to tell Alana's mom everything I say?"

"Let's not worry about that."

"Um, sometimes we hop over the wooden fence and climb up the tree. Like, if I'm coming over late and we don't want her mom to hear the security camera chime, that's how I'd get in."

"And you think that Alana would've used this method to reenter her own home?"

"I'm just saying." I shrug, trying to ignore the squirming discomfort in my chest. "If she needed to sneak out of her house, she would've used the back way. She wouldn't have walked out the front door by the camera."

Detective Ramirez taps his pen against his notepad, studying my face.

"That's helpful, Maya," he says finally. "So you don't know where Alana was going on Saturday morning?"

I guess the video didn't show her getting into my car. Guilt and shame swirl in my stomach, threatening to devour me.

"I—I don't know."

He doesn't need to know because Alana is fine. Sleeping at the house of one of our classmates, probably, one who she can intimidate into secrecy, ensuring that I get all spun up with worry.

The detective makes a quiet humming noise. "Alana's mother was alerted by your teachers that Alana didn't show up to an AP Psychology study session this morning. She also told me that your school has a graduation rehearsal this afternoon, which it seems Alana will also miss. Is that unusual for her, to skip school obligations?"

"Um, I guess it's a little weird."

"And you're here, so I assume you're not planning to be at the rehearsal either," he notes. I think he's waiting for me to offer an explanation.

I swallow, trying to look like I could puke on him at any moment. It isn't difficult. "Yeah, getting over a stomach bug. My sister called the school this morning."

He nods absently, skimming his notepad. "Do you know where Alana is right now?"

"No." Finally, I can answer honestly. The words spill out of my mouth before I can stop them. "She won't answer my texts or calls. She doesn't have her location shared with me on her phone—but then, she never does. Her social media's gone dark. Wherever she is, she doesn't want to talk to me. I don't know why. But—but no, I don't know where she would've gone."

He hums again. I want to slap the coffee mug out of his hand and let it shatter.

"Thank you, Maya. This has been helpful, and I really appreciate your time and your honesty, okay? I promise we're going to do all we can to bring Alana home."

My honesty. I bite my lower lip, the finality of what I've done, the lie I've told, settling over me like a storm cloud thick with rain.

CHAPTER SIX

RELAX.

It's been hours since Detective Ramirez left, but I can't calm down. Evening has fallen, and even though Jazmine's tried to make me eat something a million times, I can't bring myself to. Going back to LA is out of the question today; the conversation with the detective has me frozen to the spot, and I'm scared to move in case that attracts more attention.

I pace back and forth in front of the twin bed, bare feet cold on the hardwood floor. *People go missing all the time. Alana's dramatic. She's trying to mess with you, and you're giving her the exact reaction she wants.*

I stretch my arms up high, folding my hands behind my head as I pace. Now that an actual police detective has shown up in my sister's living room to question me, it's getting harder to believe that Alana's playing a joke on me. Alana loves a good laugh at my expense, but there's no way she'd let a prank go far enough that the LAPD would get involved. What if this is something different—something real? They won't issue an

Amber Alert because she's eighteen. What if she's just ... gone, and no one can bring her back?

A hotel room. Some random classmate's basement. She could be anywhere. It fills me with dread—what will she say when she finally sees me again? But a new emotion also drifts to the surface.

Anger.

She shouldn't get to have this much control over my life, sending me spiraling with every move she makes. What if she's watching from afar, some bizarre test of my love for her? Like a sick attempt to get me to call off the breakup. I wouldn't put it past her. Well, if she's following me on social media to see my reaction, I need to show her that I'm fine on my own. Just like I told her on the trail yesterday. I can survive without her—no, not just that, I can *thrive* without her.

I pull my phone out of my pocket, uploading a lake photo that I took earlier that day to Instagram. I type out a quick caption next to a palm tree emoji: *getting away from it all.* There. If she sees that post, she'll know that I'm totally fine.

Which I am.

Breathe in, breathe out.

Completely fine.

Count three things that you see.

Empty water glass on my bedside table. Thin white curtains like gossamer, drifting in the breeze from the cracked-open window. Polaroid pictures emptied from my purse and strewn across the dresser in the corner. Alana, again and again and again: smiling with her head on my shoulder, laughing at a concert, balancing a joint between two fingers, kissing me on the cheek.

I climb onto the bed, barely registering how fast my breathing is ripping from my lungs—gasps that sting like knife cuts. Inside my mind, the panic is getting worse, building into something terrible and uncontrolled, and I toss my phone onto my bed, forgotten.

The pill case in my pocket is green plastic. I crack it open, let one tablet spill into my palm, swallow it down dry. If I can just hold on ten minutes, I won't tip over into full-blown panic. If I can fight it back for half an hour, I'll be numb enough to think about this without wanting to scream my throat raw.

I left her there. I *left* her there, in Antelope Valley without a way to get home, and if anything bad happened to her, it'll be my fault forever.

Squeezing my eyes shut, I reach into my other pocket and pull out my second fail-safe: a small, shiny black stone with jagged edges. Obsidian holds purification and protection properties, made for blocking out unwanted negative energy.

I stare at my reflection in the mirror over my dresser, barely recognizing the girl looking back at me. Her eyes are weighed down with black-and-blue watercolor bruises. I squeeze my fist around the obsidian stone, letting its edges dig into my palm, trying to hurt myself awake. The stone can only protect me as long as I'm carrying it.

Breathe in, breathe out. Toss the stone into my dresser drawer and slam it shut. Kick the salt line in my doorway, breaking it. There's only one person I want to talk to right now.

"Mom," I whisper, closing my eyes. If she loves me, she'll come. Maybe she's stayed away all this time to teach me some kind of lesson. But now, now that something terrible has happened, now that I need her more than ever, surely she'll be here.

She died when I was eight. There are really no guidebooks on what to do when this happens to you. Your mother gives birth to you and holds your hand through everything. She's not supposed to leave you, ever. One diagnosis, swift and sudden as a guillotine, and I was cut loose from everything I thought or believed.

But I thought things would be different—I mean, I could see ghosts. I saw them all the time, loitering outside shops on Ventura Boulevard, ducking in and out of shadows in the dark dining room of Dad's restaurant. They could speak to me, ask me questions, and when I answered them, they could hear me. Death meant something different for me. At Mom's funeral, I didn't even cry, because I knew she'd be waiting for me when I got home.

But she wasn't.

They lowered her into the ground, and that was it. She never came back up.

As a panicked eight-year-old, I tried everything I could. Dragged a Ouija board up to our attic and knelt over it, gripping the planchette and willing it to move. Stood in front of the mirror in my dark bathroom and chanted her name. I grew more and more desperate, setting up Dad's ancient camcorder to record all night in case she manifested while I was asleep. I put my tablet into incognito mode and googled *how to summon a ghost,* making a list in my homework notebook of different methods to try.

Nothing. Nothing.

That's when I started carrying the obsidian stone, sprinkling salt across my bedroom doorway. Taking every precaution to block them out. If Mom's ghost wasn't coming, I didn't want to see any at all.

"*Mom*," I say now, clenching my hands into fists to stop them from shaking.

The room is still and silent. Dust motes drift in the setting sunlight that prisms through the lace curtains, and the sight knifes through me, a searing confirmation that Mom isn't here. She will never be here. My mom, who once wallpapered this room and picked out the sunshine-yellow quilt, who kissed me on the forehead every night before turning out the light. I'd never considered that a parent's presence in your life could be ephemeral, that they could disappear down a bright white hospital hallway and never kiss your forehead again.

Where are you, I think but don't say. It's no use. She's never coming back.

Jazmine's voice rings up the stairwell, summoning me downstairs. I punch my pillow once, fury coursing through my veins, then head down to meet her.

My sister is in the kitchen, waiting with a hot pink mug filled with something that smells like chai. Bringing people hot beverages must be her love language.

"How are you doing?" Jazmine presses the mug into my hands. I accept it, staring down at the brown liquid. "I know that must have been weird, talking to the police."

"It was fine," I mutter.

She doesn't look like she believes this, but moves on, pulling her phone out of her back pocket.

"I wanted to show you this before you found it on your own," she says, sliding her phone across the kitchen table. Her browser is open to a tweet from the North Hollywood Community Police Station. The white letters swim together.

MISSING—Alana Marina Murray, 18 y/o white female, 5'6", brown hair, blue eyes.

Her senior photo, the one where she's wearing a white baby doll dress and laughing at the camera. Then there's a phone number to a tips hotline.

My eyes flutter closed. This can't be happening.

"Maya," my sister says, soft but urgent. "What do you know about this?"

"I didn't know anything until Mrs. Murray called me earlier today." I shove the phone back toward Jazmine; I can't look at that picture of Alana for one second longer. "She said Alana hadn't been answering her calls, so she was getting in touch with the cops. You know Melissa. She's overprotective, so everything has to be a big freaking deal. And I mean—yeah, Alana hasn't been answering my texts either, but she does stuff like this."

"She pretends to be missing?"

"Well, no. But the silent treatment part seems like the kind of thing she would do to scare me."

Jazmine stares at me. I can tell she's trying to figure out whether I'm kidding.

"Doesn't this feel so . . . dramatic?" I ask, clenching my hands around the mug of tea and trying to block out a shiver. "The MISSING poster . . . it just feels like a lot."

"Yeah, they're being really quick to classify this as a missing person's case," Jazmine says thoughtfully, looking back down at the phone. "Normally, they'd just say, like, *Oh, she's a runaway, give it a couple days.* But you know Melissa Murray. Influential, white, wealthy . . ."

Anxiety grips my lungs like a vise. Maybe if I could relax, I could talk to my sister like a normal girl would. She might understand if I started the story from the beginning. If I laid it bare, explained why I couldn't face her at thirteen. How I felt so imperfect, so unmoored, that I couldn't bear to look my own sister in the eye.

"Maya, I want you to know you can talk to me about whatever's going on, okay?" Jazmine leans across the kitchen table and I'm suddenly filled with fear that she'll touch me. I flinch away. "And if you know something about Alana . . ."

Our eyes meet. There's a long silence, a tacit understanding passing between us like smoke in the air.

"You watch a lot of those true crime shows," I say finally, and her eyebrows draw together in confusion. "It's true what they say, isn't it? When somebody goes missing, the first forty-eight hours . . ."

"Oh, hon." Her face crumbles. "Please don't think like that, okay? They'll find Alana. Those statistics are the worst things to focus on right now, trust me. They'll find her, and everything will go back to normal."

A shadow passes over the trees, casting the already-dim kitchen into murky shadow. This time, I can't block out my shiver. Stories like these, they live on television, in cautionary tales, in episodes of true crime podcasts. They don't happen to people I know, and they definitely don't happen to girls like Alana. Girls who hold fire in their palms and laugh at danger.

"Jazz, I broke up with her." My voice is barely more than a whisper. "I hadn't been happy for so long, and then she was making me so mad, saying all this stuff about how dependent I am. It wasn't true."

I turn away from my sister, not wanting to see the look

on her face, since she may or may not agree with this assessment.

"So I told her we needed to end it," I finish. "But she didn't take that well. We were up at Antelope Valley to see the superbloom, and I drove home without her."

"Okay," Jazmine says slowly. "And when was this?"

My mouth is dry. I clutch the mug tighter. "Um, yesterday. Saturday."

"Oh, Maya." She tilts her head back, closing her eyes. "Yesterday?"

"Yes."

"So when Alana left her house yesterday morning, was she ..."

"Getting into my car. Yeah. Mrs. Murray's camera must not have caught it."

"Okay," Jazmine says, letting her hands fall back down to the table. "Okay. Okay, this is fine. And now the police are involved because of Melissa Murray. Okay. Listen, I'm sure it'll be fine. Girls run away all the time, and they come home."

"You think?" I bite my lip.

"Yes, I think so." Jazmine takes a deep, cleansing breath. "If Alana really did run away, she'll be in major trouble when she comes back. It won't be long until the truth ..."

The kitchen light cuts off with a distinct click.

"... comes out," she finishes.

In slow unison, we lift our heads to the dead lightbulb hanging from a pull-string ceiling fan. There's just enough light from the darkening sky outside to make out Jazmine's silhouette across the table.

She stands up, pulls the string a couple times. It clicks but doesn't turn on.

"Power's out. Weird. Did you even hear any thunder?"

I walk to the window, the one that faces the lake, and press my palms against the glass. In the stillness I can hear a pattering of rain, and then, when I strain my ears, a low rumble. Trees along the shoreline sway in the wind, sending leaves scattering.

The thin hairs along my arms lift. I know this feeling, like a half-remembered childhood dream. The last time it happened, I was eight years old, but it's not something I could forget.

Something draining all the energy from the house. Absorbing it.

"One sec, Maya." My sister bangs around the kitchen, producing two flashlights from one of the drawers. She shakes one, batteries rattling. Its beam falls long across the linoleum floor. "I've got plenty of candles and there's a generator outside, but use this until I get back, okay?"

I nod, flinching in the light as it passes over my face. I just barely manage to conceal the rising hope that I'm sure is shining all over my face. The salt line that I kicked down in my doorway . . . removing the obsidian stone . . . I told Mom that I needed her, and she listened. After all these years, it's happening. She's *finally* coming back to me.

Jazmine pulls open the back door and the rain snarls and hisses, an unfamiliar sound that stops me in my tracks. We don't get storms like this in LA. Without hesitation, she walks right out into it. The second flashlight remains on the kitchen counter, for me, but I don't pick it up. Mingled fear and excitement course through my veins.

I sprint upstairs through the pressing darkness, banging my elbow into the railing on my way. Mom is coming to help. I don't know why she's stayed away for so long, but all that matters is she's coming back *now*, when I need her the most. My chest feels tight with emotion, a rare and sparkling relief and ecstasy mingled into an overwhelming blur. Tears clog my vision as I hit the landing, footsteps echoing the thunder outside.

Down the hallway, silver moonlight slices through the dark and makes knife-sharp shapes on the hardwood floor. I'm already planning what I'll say to Mom, the emotions that will burst out of me like fire, when I grab the doorknob to my room and my hand closes around something soft.

When I unfurl my palm, there are three orange petals from a California poppy.

Startled, I push the door open, blinking at the figure sitting on my bed.

"You ran so far."

Ice washes over me, and I swear my heart stops. I'm frozen, unbreathing.

"All that," Alana's ghost says, "just to get away from me."

INTERLUDE

FOUR YEARS EARLIER

IF THERE'S AN afterlife for particularly evil people, without a doubt it's a middle school dance.

Alana picked out my outfit for tonight. I sat on my bathroom counter while she drew swooping lines across my eyelids and fanned out my eyelashes with Lancôme mascara swiped from her mom's vanity. She had held up different dresses, neat on their hangers, against my body before settling on a dark green velvet one. I used to get ready for school dances with Livia, but we're not best friends anymore; now it's Alana. *I don't miss Livia,* I told myself.

"Perfect," Alana had said, stepping back to admire her handiwork through narrowed, scrutinizing eyes. "You look like a model."

I turned away to hide the pink flush creeping up my cheeks. No, I don't miss Livia at all.

Coldwater Canyon School for Girls doesn't do anything halfway. We arrive at 7:05 and the dance is already well underway: boys bussed in from nearby private schools surreptitiously passing joints in the parking lot, girls grouping together in the dark auditorium. Multicolored disco balls adorn the stage, casting chaotic rainbow light across the room.

I glance over at Alana, taking in her center-parted brown hair. She cut it shoulder-length at the end of the summer and it throws her stunning bone structure into sharp relief, cheekbones like cut glass. I know she'll never look at me like I want her to, never see me as anything more than the friend who follows her around like a puppy. But somehow—

"Let's not talk to *anybody* else tonight," she says, leaning in so close I can smell her perfume. It's something expensive and rare, also lifted from her mom's collection. She's wearing a simple blue bodycon dress, probably from Forever 21's sale rack, just to prove she doesn't need to shop on Rodeo Drive to look better than every girl in our class. It's a level of confidence I can't even comprehend—but then, I can't comprehend most things about Alana. "Won't that be funny?"

"To not talk to anybody else?" I wrinkle my nose. "That seems kind of cliquey."

"Therein lies the brilliance." Alana flicks me on the upper arm. She turns, hair bouncing, to survey the crowd. "Don't you think it's more fun if we're mysterious? If people are jealous of us? I mean, nobody else likes me more than you do anyway, right?"

I stammer, my brain playing this sentence on loop, parsing it for hidden meaning. *Like,* like we're best friends, or *like,* a very different kind? I can't ask for clarification or she'll think I'm a total loser. But how can I stand here looking at her and not be absolutely achingly, secretly, world-endingly in love with her?

It's the kind of moment I would discuss with our other

best friend, desperate for her help deciphering Alana's cryptic statements and hidden meanings. We do this often, attempt to decode the mystique that is Alana. I scan the room, and sure enough, Elise is on her way. She opted for a black satin dress that probably cost triple what Alana's did.

"Hey, Maya," Elise says, tossing her hair in the way we both picked up from Alana. "Where'd you get that dress?"

I shrug. "One of those boutiques on Tujunga Avenue. Alana helped me pick it out."

"You guys went shopping together?" Elise looks crestfallen. "When?"

"Does it matter?" Alana's ability to shoot people down with condescension has always been disarming. "Hey, we'll catch up with you later. Maya and I have some stuff to talk about."

Before Alana and I turn away, I catch Elise rolling her eyes.

Just like a movie, the song blends into the next, electric guitar notes blurred away by a high soprano. The world slows. Alana's grip on my arm is soft but sure, her eyes blazing sapphires.

"Like I told you," she whispers warm against my ear. "People are jealous of us."

Her hand finds mine, twisting our fingers together. She leads me out the opposite door of the auditorium, the one that leads to the courtyard, and the crowd parts for us. Glittering fairy lights are strung up in the trees, making everything feel like a dream.

"Why were you so mean to Elise?" I ask as soon as we're outside. Under the watchful gaze of sparkling stars and palm trees, the night is quiet. "She's our best friend."

"No, *we* are each other's best friends. We're better off just the two of us. We deserve each other, you know? Everyone else leaves in the end anyway."

I blink up at Alana, holding my breath as I realize she still hasn't let go of my hand. "What do you mean, everyone leaves?"

"Well, not everyone, I guess," she says, brushing a loose strand of hair out of my eyes. Our faces are so close that I can count the constellation of freckles strewn across her nose. "I mean, I'll never leave you."

In that moment I can see it—our lives unspooling symmetrically, tied together with red thread, never having to be without the other. And even though I don't know if I'll ever tell her, I know that I love her. I know it in the marrow of my bones, stitched together in my soul.

That was the first time she said those words to me, but they would become our mantra. A promise. A vow. *I will never leave you. I will never, ever leave you.*

CHAPTER SEVEN

I SQUEEZE MY eyes shut tight, then open them.

Alana rises from the bed, leaning against the frame. She's tall and perfect and whole, shimmering around the edges, and a cold shiver of horror washes over me as I process what I'm seeing. Dark brown hair falling past slim shoulders in waves. The outfit, exactly as I remember it from yesterday at the Antelope Valley poppy field: black leggings with a cropped white top, pristine sneakers.

Part of me wants to run to her, shove her: *Where have you been? Do you realize what you've done to people, how you've made them feel? How you've made* me *feel?* But I stay silent, staring, because no, she never realizes that. I stay silent, because she's dead.

I'm going to throw up.

Alana grins lazily. "So, what's new?"

I step back, clutching the doorframe so hard my knuckles turn white. There's a ringing in my ears, a horrible scratching feeling in my chest like my heart is trying to claw its way out.

This isn't real. There is no way this is real.

"You're not afraid of me, are you?" She walks toward me, a glittery glow radiating around her body like a halo. Blinking fast doesn't make the glow go away; I'm not hallucinating. "Because that would be quite the plot twist. You, the bravest little ghost hunter in town."

I dig my hand into my sweatpants pocket again, searching for my obsidian stone, before I remember that it's in the dresser. If it was in my pocket, it would've protected me. And I broke the salt line in the doorway, trying to let Mom in.

This is all my fault. All of it.

"I-I'm not . . ."

"I could kill you, you know." She leans gracefully against the dresser, examining her nails.

Fear lances through me. My mouth goes dry.

"My hands around your throat. Make it look like an accident. And we all know how sad that is, don't we? When a pretty teenage girl dies in an accident."

My chest tightens, every word I can think of evaporating. *She's just trying to scare me. She would never actually hurt me—she* can't *hurt me, because she's a ghost.* But even knowing this, the storm of grief inside me is growing by the second. Soon, it will be too deep for me to ever dream of traversing. Soon, I know the waves will pull me under, and I'll drown.

"Wh-what happened to you?" I whisper.

Alana laughs, high and musical, but it sounds far away. "Oh, like you care. Did you even notice I was gone?"

"Of course I did! I haven't thought about *anything* else. I thought you were playing a joke on me." I'm shocked at how clearly the words come out. "I thought you were going to just—just show up and call me dramatic for worrying."

Alana shrugs. "Well, you *are* dramatic, and you *do* worry too much. But that would've been a stupid joke. Where the hell would I even go? I'm always with you. Or . . . I was. You know, before the unceremonious breakup."

The word is what finally does it, breaking the dam inside me.

"I-I'm sorry," I say, and my voice rises and falls on a sob, my hands covering my mouth. "Alana, I'm so sorry."

"Yes, your favorite phrase." She narrows her blue eyes.

This is a trick of the light, a hoax. She's playing a joke on you, my brain screams.

"Alana, please. I'm so . . ."

"Sorry," she finishes in a whisper. Steps closer. I can almost smell the floral traces of her perfume, almost feel the warmth of her breath on my skin. "Maya, I know you're sorry. But a lot of good that does us now."

With that, she glides out of the room. Fades right through the door without opening it. I squeeze my eyes shut, willing myself to wake up from this nightmare. I'm tired, I'm anxious, I had to talk to the freaking police. When you're overly stressed, weird shit can happen. You can make yourself believe that you see things. Your brain can become your worst enemy, a dangerous adversary.

Because I remember how Alana looked when I last saw her, haloed by desert sunshine, a wildflower field sprawling into infinity behind her. I remember the piercing blue of her eyes, the warmth of her skin, the freckles sprinkled across her nose, the disbelieving arc of her eyebrows as she watched me turn away. She was angry, she was shocked, but she was alive. How does a girl go from that—alive, glowing in a field of flowers—to missing, to *dead*?

Breathe, I tell myself, trying to remember everything that years of therapy have taught me. *Name three things that you can see.* Shadowy tree branches scraping glass, the pinwheeling beam of Jazmine's flashlight against the sheeting rain. Alana in a lily white sundress drenched with blood, eye sockets hollow and black, a scream rattling its way out of her lungs—

"Alana," I say to the empty room. Everything familiar: Jazmine's books and candles lined up along the dresser, fluffy throw pillows covering my bed, moonlight pouring through the gauzy curtains. Everything wrong. *"Alana."*

She doesn't answer. She's gone, and I know in my heart that that's how she'll stay. That I wasn't dreaming or hallucinating or crazy. I know a haunting when I see one.

Soon, Alana's body will be frozen in a funeral home. I'll never again feel the sleep-warmth of her body next to me, the softness of her fingers lacing through mine, the earthy and flowery smell of her hair. Gone forever, under six feet of dirt.

She didn't even say goodbye.

My knees hit the floor. I bury my face in my hands and scream.

■ ■ ■

"This morning, the search continues for missing Los Angeles teen Alana Murray...."

"Search efforts organized by Alana's mother will be targeting areas of the San Fernando Valley near Alana's high school, Coldwater Canyon School for Girls...."

"At this time, police detectives have not stated whether they suspect foul play...."

Jazmine lets out a humorless laugh at this, springing forward to rest her elbows on her knees to stare at the television. Bright morning light spills through the living room windows, picking out lighter brown strands in her wavy hair.

"Whether they suspect foul play? Are you fucking kidding me?"

My sister's swearing is the thing that drags me up from underwater. I'm on the opposite end of the couch in the lake house's tiny living room, knees pulled to my chest, hugging a pillow. I can't remember her ever cursing in front of me before.

She half turns to face me. "Sorry, Maya. I just think the media coverage is getting a little out of hand here, you know? Alana must be . . ."

Her phone buzzes on the coffee table, interrupting her train of thought.

"Oh no," she mutters, seeing the name on the screen, then lifts it to her ear. Her eyes dart over to me; the distance between us is palpable. My sister and I don't really know how to talk to each other on good days, let alone amid disaster. "Hi, Will—yes, of course I heard. . . . Melissa Murray called yesterday. . . ."

My dad's on the phone. I tuck my hands between my knees, sinking lower into the couch like I can shrink myself down to invisible.

"Yes, she's sitting next to me . . . I don't know if that's a good idea. She's . . . she's not feeling her best today. Talking to that cop was hard for her, and I think the news might be sinking in . . ."

Jazmine's voice fades away and I'm floating, driftwood

cast astray by the current. Nothing touches me. Maybe it's the shock, or maybe it's the tablet of anxiety medication I popped upstairs, the double dosage my doctor said is okay for *emergencies*.

There's a phone in my hand, suddenly. Dimly, I remember that it's Monday and I'm supposed to be taking my AP Chem exam today. Maybe Dad's angry that I'm missing it. Not like it matters—it wouldn't have made a difference to Yale. Coldwater was doing a kindness in letting me sit for the exams. My results would be sent nowhere.

When I press Jazmine's phone to my ear, my dad is saying a lot of things without saying anything at all. Little phrases jump out at me:

Can't imagine how you must feel, kid.

Try not to watch the news, if you can help it.

If there's anything I can do.

I sit there still as a portrait, one hand holding the phone to my ear. Taste of acid in my mouth, light going out behind my eyes. I pity my father, the way that even drenched in years of his own grief, he's still unsure how to talk to me about darkness.

"Maya, did you hear me, kiddo?"

Shake my head to clear it. My thoughts scatter and fall like snow. "What?"

"Your friends are planning a candlelight vigil at school tonight," Dad says, and I get the sense this isn't the first time he's patiently explained this. "To show support for the search party and for Mrs. Murray. I think it might be a good idea for you to go, but it's up to you, kid. If you want to go, I'll come get you. What d'you say?"

My brain is catching on those two words: *your friends.* I

barely know what a candlelight vigil is, but I don't have the energy to ask the question, let alone explain to him that I no longer have any friends.

"Okay," I say instead, wishing for Mom. And not just her ghost, not a flickering spectral being, but my living, breathing mom, who could help take on all this pain so I wouldn't have to feel it all by myself.

CHAPTER EIGHT

NORTH HOLLYWOOD, LOS ANGELES (KABC)—A
candlelight vigil is planned for tonight at 8:00 p.m.
for 18-year-old Alana Murray, the young local woman
who has been missing since May 4.

The vigil will be held on the athletic fields at
Coldwater Canyon School for Girls, the private
college preparatory school Murray is due to graduate
from on Saturday.

Murray's disappearance has shaken the community,
says a neighbor who did not wish to be identified.

"She's a real sweet kid," the neighbor told reporters this
morning. "Never causes any problems around here. For
her poor mother's sake, I hope she'll be home soon."

The candlelight vigil is being organized by two of
Alana's classmates and senior class copresidents
Madison Kim and Elise Carter-Holloway.

"It feels like the least we can do," said Carter-Holloway, who will also graduate from Coldwater Canyon School on Saturday. "We just want Alana home safe. Plus, we want to show support to her mom."

Alana Murray's parents are offering a reward of $100,000 for information that leads to their daughter's safe return.

■ ■ ■

When the sun drifts lower toward the horizon, it takes my courage with it. I'm curled on the living room couch, staring at the TV and biting my nails down to the cuticle. Jazmine put on a Disney movie just like she used to when I was a kid and she'd get stuck babysitting me. Back then, she'd rip a page out of her sketchbook and teach me how to draw a character, kneeling beside me at our coffee table.

Now, she's in the kitchen banging around. Something spicy and aromatic fills the air, but instead of making me hungry, my stomach turns. When was the last time I had something to eat? I can't even remember. I've been stuck here since morning, since Jazmine and Dad decided that I shouldn't drive back down to LA by myself. *Not safe*, Jazmine had muttered on the phone, and I wondered what she was envisioning: me yanking the wheel and spinning off the 5 or vanishing in the Los Padres National Forest. She thinks I'm crazy.

Now, an engine roars in the driveway and I jump. Over the sound of the creaking trees and the water lapping at the shoreline, I hear faint notes of Bon Jovi from a car radio. Dad's here to pick me up.

"Is that your dad?" Jazmine calls from the kitchen, voice brimming with false positivity. I can't bring myself to answer her. A key jingles in the lock, and then my father's on the threshold, looking grizzled and world-weary. He couldn't make it until now because of some chaos at his restaurant, and I'm sure he's got the staff working doubles to cover for him because of this.

Because of me.

The image flashes into my mind before I can stop it: last fall, me, lying on my bed sobbing. Dad picking me up with a strength and care that surprised me, my arms and legs dangling limply. The way I pressed my forehead against the passenger-side window in his car as he sped along dark streets—I needed to feel something cold, something solid, something steady. The whooshing cool air in the hospital hallway when he checked me in, reciting my full name and birth date.

He's stuck here, checking me into this inpatient facility, I thought with a sorrow that cloaked me like a blanket. Stifled my ability to breathe. *He never asked for a mentally ill daughter. His life is upended because of me. This is all because of me.*

"That's what you're gonna wear?" he asks me now, in greeting.

I glance down. Black T-shirt, black jeans, sneakers. Everything but the sneakers was borrowed from Jazmine; none of it fits me right.

"What's wrong with this?"

"It's a little macabre." Dad gives me a weak attempt at a smile, but I just stare at him. "Kiddo, everything's gonna be fine. We'll come back up to get your car in a couple days, okay?"

"You'd better leave if you want to make it to the vigil,"

Jazmine says, sticking her head out from the kitchen. "Maya, it was . . . nice of you to visit."

"Yeah." I'm only half paying attention, tugging my purse over one shoulder. "Yeah, it was great."

• • ■

The interior of Dad's car smells like peppermint and sage, just like it has my entire life. I pull my feet up onto the seat and wrap my arms around my legs.

"You really shouldn't do that," he says casually. It's been quiet except for the music thudding through the speakers. "I heard a story on the news about some girl who sat like that and when the driver slammed on the brakes, her kneecaps went straight through her eyeballs."

I smirk despite myself. "Oh, you just made that up. Like the time you said I shouldn't wear headphones during a thunderstorm because lightning could strike the car and fry my brain."

"And what happened?" Dad taps the side of his head. "They started making wireless headphones."

I roll my eyes, watching the lights of Los Angeles twinkle through the falling dark. He's trying to make me laugh, but it won't work. There's only space in my mind for one thought: *Alana's dead, and it's all my fault.*

Up ahead there's nothing but a river of red taillights as we inch along the freeway. Traffic on the 101 is nothing new to me, but it's jarring to reenter after the calm of Lake Ember. I stare into the lights, letting them burn my eyes until my vision goes fuzzy.

"Maya, I hope you aren't losing too much sleep over this,"

81

Dad says. His voice is low, and I wonder if he's been rehearsing a speech in his head this entire time. We're only a couple miles from school. "The cops are taking this case seriously. Alana's not one to run away from home, and they know that. And with Melissa Murray putting pressure on them? They're gonna take this city apart to find her."

"Why didn't Jazmine want to drive me to the vigil?" I ask, mainly to divert this train of thought. "It's kind of rude she made you drive all the way up to the lake and back."

"Kid, she didn't *make* me do anything. I offered."

I watch him out of the corner of my eye.

"Jazmine's having a hard time with this whole thing. She doesn't . . ." He pauses, drumming his fingers on the steering wheel. "She doesn't really know how to talk to you about Alana, I guess."

"You mean she hates Alana."

"Now, why would you say that?"

"She always wanted Alana out of my life."

"Nah, she didn't." The exit sign looms up ahead and he hits the turn signal. "It's been years since your sister even *saw* Alana. And, well, there's no denying that Alana was sort of a . . . tricky kid back then. Spirited. Kinda noisy. Jazmine never knew what to do with kids like that, especially since you were quieter and calmer, and I think she watched you two together and thought, jeez, is Maya really happy around this girl? And as you got older—I mean, you're always miserable because of Alana."

"That's not true," I say softly, knotting my fingers together. "I was—I'm happy with her."

My dad has been mild-mannered this entire conversation, but as he eases off the exit and onto the main drag that'll take us to school, something seems to flare up inside him. He snorts. "That's how happy looked on you, huh?"

And I know he's remembering it. My bed at Ocean Vista Recovery Center—nobody ever said the "recovery center" part out loud—with its crisp white sheets. The way I sat on top of the bed in sweatpants and a giant hoodie, feeling like an imposter for even being there.

"I was doing fine," I say now.

He senses the hardness in my voice and pulls back. "I just think that Alana doesn't make things very easy for you."

I lick my chapped lips as we turn into the Coldwater Canyon School parking lot, which is already packed. My dad is doing his best, but it's hard to commend him for that when all I want is Mom. Even though she never met Alana, she would know what to say. She would know I loved Alana, and that love was real. She would wrap me in her arms and unpack it for me, everything I need to know, everything I need to do.

Outside the car window, a nausea-inducing number of people have already congregated on the soccer field. Way more than just my class. It looks like the entire student body. All around us, girls I half recognize are spilling out of cars with their parents, siblings, friends, everyone speaking in hushed voices.

She's dead, you idiots! I want to scream. *She's dead, and she's never coming back.*

Coldwater's campus was modeled after the elite East Coast boarding schools, a brick-and-stone monstrosity that looks bizarre surrounded by palm trees and sagebrush. But somehow, at night, it's not so weird. Someone is handing out white tapered candles near the entrance to the athletic field, and the effect is stunning. There must be fifty people already on the field, clutching their candles, standing in silence. Like a sea of stars. If I could make myself forget the purpose of this whole thing, it would be beautiful.

"You don't have to come with me," I tell Dad. "Really. I'm sure you don't want to be here."

"I care about Alana too, kid. And Melissa. Don't worry, I'll go off and give her my best wishes so I'm not cramping your style. You meet up with your friends."

After he pats me on the shoulder and heads off across the parking lot, I take a deep calming breath, trying to ignore the plunging sadness at the realization that Dad is clueless enough to think I still have friends here. I keep my head down, hair falling across my face, and accept a candle from the girl handing them out at the edge of the field. The school grounds are eerily dark, palm trees bending in the unnatural wind that carries across the open space. I've never been to a school function that was this quiet. But, of course, the quiet only lasts so long.

I hear the first whisper as I enter the crowd. *Maya.* It's like a curse word, something you mutter when you're scared and surprised. *Maya. Maya Rosier.*

Even in the dark, I can make out faces in flickering candlelight, people glancing at me in a way that makes it clear they're trying not to be obvious.

I heard she was with Alana the day she disappeared—
Well, of course she was, they're always together.
If she does know something, she's not talking.

I try to imagine how Alana would want me to act; toss my hair back, stand tall, unbreakable. But then I catch sight of three girls standing in a circle by a towering oak tree, not even bothering to lower their voices, and my resolve crumbles. One of the girls is Madison Kim, the copresident of our senior class.

"—stayed home, I heard," one girl is saying, a junior in a Coldwater Soccer sweatshirt. "Addie Castillo said she saw her before the AP Enviro exam this morning and she looked like she'd been crying."

"Crying? Elise?" Madison asks skeptically.

"I was surprised too." The younger girl lowers her voice. "No one's *really* worried that Alana's missing, right? She obviously just ran away."

I step backward involuntarily, colliding with the girl behind me. We realize who the other is at the same moment, our eyes locking.

"Isabelle," I blurt out. Elise's little sister. "What are you doing here?"

"Oh, just hanging out," she says airily, then rolls her eyes dramatically. "What do you think I'm doing here, Maya?"

"S-sorry. I was just surprised." Heart in my throat, I take another step back. I can remember Isabelle begging me and Elise to take her trick-or-treating, the way she skipped along the sidewalk and grabbed my hand when she saw a scary lawn decoration. Now, she's two inches taller than me.

"So I'm guessing you didn't find Alana the other day? You know, when you were looking for her at my house?"

I bite back the frantic rush of anxiety that's making my legs shake. "No. Obviously."

"People are talking," Isabelle says, eyes widening. "Look, Maya, I don't hate you or anything. Even after the way you treated my sister. But you better watch your back, okay? You know everybody at school thinks that you're keeping her location secret from the cops?"

"Why would I do that?"

"There are a million theories. Maybe Alana's blackmailing

85

you, maybe it's all an elaborate senior prank." She ticks them off on her fingers, nails painted her favorite shade of pale pink—Essie Ballet Slippers, I remember with a pang. The Carter-Holloway sisters always had the best nail polish collection; I used to help Isabelle paint her nails when she was little. Her voice is completely innocent when she adds, "Maybe you're trying to get the reward money to buy your way into one of those colleges that rejected you."

I reel backward.

"What are you—how do you—"

No one is supposed to know this—no one but Alana and my father. Could Alana have possibly told her? No, why the hell would Alana talk to the little sister of our former best friend? Plus, Alana did a lot of questionable things, but she'd never tell my secrets.

"I'm not trying to be mean. I just think that if people are talking about you, you should know why," Isabelle whispers. It raises the hairs on the back of my neck. "There are no secrets at Coldwater. Hell, the teachers probably even gossip about us."

I grip my candle so tightly that my knuckles turn white.

She gives me a sad, searching look, then turns away, curly brown ponytail swinging. I stare blankly, confused, and watch her go, then I run for it.

The trees swallow me up, a barrier between the field and the parking lot, and I push through to the other side, stumbling out onto asphalt. I bend forward, struggling to catch my breath, one hand still clutching the stupid candle.

Isabelle was lying—she *has* to be lying. But what was it, then? A lucky guess? She's right about my shitty grades, which started plummeting at the start of senior year along with my mental health. No number of extra therapy sessions per week could boost my AP Chemistry grade, could stop my Honors English teacher from handing back my essays face down, disappointment etched in every line of his face. No amount of medication could stop the panic attacks that sent me running to the school bathroom during AP Calculus tests. It was the fights with Alana that made everything worse—the peaks and valleys of my depression, the sudden lightning storms of anxiety that overtook my brain.

But Alana was also the only thing that made it all better. In the bathroom between classes, I would splash cold water on my face and reread our texts, searching for reassurance in her words: *You're doing fine, Maya. I'll help you study this weekend. I will never leave you.*

I imagine her alive and gazing at me with dreamy blue eyes, telling me that our fight was all just a big misunderstanding. That she isn't angry at me for breaking up with her. That she doesn't hate me for leaving her at Antelope Valley to face whatever happened.

No. She doesn't care about you, screams the nagging voice in the back of my mind, and it sounds a lot like Livia, my childhood best friend who warned me off Alana time and time again. It sounds like Jazmine, her voice ragged with frustration. *She doesn't love you. She was going to keep on treating you terribly, talking down to you, hurting you more and more every day. That's not what someone does when they love you.*

"She's dead," I whisper to myself. "None of that matters anymore."

I straighten up, wiping away forehead sweat with the back of my hand. It's then that I see it: a flickering white light, like a moth but bigger. It dances along the ground like the beam of a flashlight.

There's something mesmerizing about the light, like a lantern carried by an invisible hand. Against my better judgment, I push my hair out of my face and follow the light as it bobs in front of me. A will-o'-the-wisp leading me into the deep darkness. Transfixed, I cross the parking lot, following the light as it guides me toward the towering academic buildings of Coldwater's Upper School.

My heart rate speeds up, the familiar anxious hum cranking up to a roar in my ears. Probably a side effect of the surprise conversation with Isabelle. Plus, I don't like to be alone, especially not in the dark. Even here on this campus where I would know my way around blindfolded, I still feel uneasy ducking behind palm trees, wandering around the Science building at night while it's completely deserted. Every nerve ending in my body is electrified.

Up ahead is the courtyard. I duck past a willow tree, swallowing down my discomfort, which feels like a visceral presence pushing against me. Alana and I used to sneak out here during all the school dances, but we spent plenty of daylight hours here too. There's the bench where we did homework, the garden where I helped her run lines for the school musical. During the past year when Elise wouldn't even look at me, the courtyard felt like the only place I could get peace.

"I remember it too," a voice says behind me, and I almost drop my candle.

Alana is standing under the nearest palm tree. She glows on her own, a warm golden aura—I don't remember any of my ghosts glowing so brightly, but I'm not surprised. Of course Alana would have to outshine everyone, even in the afterlife.

"I said, I remember it too." Alana's voice is calm and sure.

"All the time we spent out here. That's what you were thinking about, right?"

Fear bleeds into a low-simmering anger. It's been growing over the past day. A pale blue pilot light just begging to ignite.

"I wasn't thinking about anything," I respond, but she's already shaking her head.

"You must feel awful, Maya. So guilty over what you did."

"I didn't do anything." The words burst out of me shaky and crackling, so I try again, force the syllables out with everything in me. I tighten my grip around the candle. "I didn't do *anything*, Alana. I didn't mean to leave you at Antelope Valley. You know that."

"Of course you meant to leave me." She wrinkles her nose, pulls her voice into a higher octave in the world's worst impression of me. "*You know what, Alana? I'm going home.* And then you flounced off with your car keys. That's the definition of leaving me."

I swallow back the bile rising in my throat. "Stop it."

"Stop hiding from your own mind," she says, sweet and singsong. "The truth is there, and if you sit with it long enough, you'll realize. You're smart. If you hadn't treated me like shit, broken up with me, and then left me on the trail—"

"Shut up."

"—I would still be alive right now."

I step closer to her, squeezing the candle even tighter. The flame flickers.

"I said shut up!"

"Maya, if you could relax for one freaking second, we could have a real conversation. Just trust me, okay?"

"*Trust me, Maya*," I repeat. It explodes out of me, mocking, twisting her words and turning them bitter. "*I know what's best for you, Maya. Fall in love with me and I'll rip your entire life apart, Maya.*"

"Oh, come on. I didn't *make* you fall in love with me."

"Fuck you." My eyes are burning and I blink hard, determined not to cry, not even now. "This is why I broke up with you—don't you get it? The way you talk to me . . ."

"Oh, quit being so sensitive. I'm dead. I can talk to you however I want."

"Alana—"

"Let's go back to why exactly you broke up with me, maybe. Because that part wasn't clear."

My voice breaks, almost a whisper. "What does it matter now?"

"I think I deserve to know."

"I just . . ." In this dark courtyard, overcome with misery, I honestly can't even remember the headspace I was in two days ago. "I think I needed to move on—"

"Move on?" Alana flickers like the flame of the candle I'm holding, halfway between here and somewhere else. Her hair is tangled around her shoulders. "You're trying to move on? They haven't even found my body. My parents don't even know what happened to me. But go off, I guess."

I picture Melissa Murray's face etched with worry lines. The way she always tells me she loves me in the throwaway manner to which I've become accustomed. Like it'll always be true. When she finds out, she'll despise me.

"They do deserve to know," I whisper, the words scraping my throat on the way out. "Tell me what happened to you, and I can explain it to them. . . ."

"You're afraid someone will find out what you did," Alana says. "That you left me."

My eyes dart up to meet hers.

"I can read it on your face, how scared you are." I swear I catch a glimpse of softness on her face as she says it. "Nobody knows you like I do."

I hesitate. The night is warm and still, the sky a deep, dark sapphire clogged with light pollution from the sprawling city just over the hill. No wind, not even a breeze. But somehow, the flame of the candle in my hands bends and wavers in the air. I wonder if she can tell that just looking at her causes me physical pain.

"Tell me what happened to you," I whisper, stepping closer. We're only a foot away from each other now. "Please, I have to know. Was it an accident, or—"

Alana's eyes are wide, searching my face.

"It's not a big deal," she says finally, coolly, and holds up a hand when I stammer in protest. "I slipped ... I fell ... I think I hit my head on the way down."

If it weren't for the unnatural cold and the eerie glow emanating from her, we could've been discussing restaurant choices for a Saturday night dinner. The color drains from my face.

"But where were you?" I ask. My voice sounds very far away. "Antelope Valley?"

"They'll find my body soon—I'm not worried about that. What I *am* worried about is how I can reverse this."

It takes a couple seconds for my brain to unscramble her words. "*Reverse* this?"

"Yeah." Alana's lips quirk up at the corners. "You're going to bring me back to life."

Another pause, and it draws out, aching. A slow wind picks up through the trees, undercut here and there with a burst of music from the vigil. After everything we've been through together, after everything she put me through, I can't believe we've ended up here. Me, tucked away in darkness, whispering to her ghost.

"There's no way for you to be alive again, Alana," I say, but my voice is weak and shaky, and she sees right through me. "I'm sorry. I wish there was."

"Oh, really?" She shakes her head, hair cascading. "I'm going to cut you a deal."

There it is, I think but don't say, almost choking on the bitterness. That's Alana. Always transactional, no matter how much I love her, no matter how much I'm willing to give her on my own. I hate her so much for putting me in this position—but I hate myself even more, because I know I will agree to whatever the deal is. Bring her back to life, no matter the cost.

"You're going to help me possess someone," she says.

I stare at her, sure I've heard wrong. "I'm—what?"

"Listen to me." Her voice is haughty. "You'll help me come back to life by possessing someone, or I will make sure everyone finds out that you left me in Antelope Valley."

I'm frozen to the spot, shivering against the cold. The temperature is dropping more and more with every passing second.

"That's the stupidest deal I've ever heard," I mutter. "Possession isn't real, and no one is going to find out—"

"Of course they are," she interrupts. Her eyes are narrowed, her gaze sharp as a blade. "They're already suspicious, the girls from our class. They think you're hiding something about my disappearance. The cops will interview them. Each one of them. And what do you think they'll say about you?"

"The cops already talked to me," I say. "They don't suspect me of anything."

"Not yet." Alana says darkly.

"I . . ." My eyes dart around the dark courtyard. It's no use. There's no way out of this. "Look, can't we talk about this some other time? Come visit me back at Lake Ember. We'll figure out a way—"

"Maya, come on. I thought you were Los Angeles's premier child ghost hunter. You're telling me you've never helped a ghost possess someone before?"

"No!" It explodes out of me. "I would . . . you know, talk with them a little bit, encourage them to move on. That's all. I was never a *ghost hunter*. I never learned anything about . . . possession."

"Well, this will be your first big adventure, then."

"Alana, you shouldn't mess around with this stuff. Trying to possess someone isn't a game. You'd be taking over someone else's body . . . a living person. It would almost be like—"

"Dying?" Alana finishes, smiling humorlessly.

My voice is small. "Yes."

We stare at each other for a minute, wind whistling through the trees. I want to ask her a thousand things. What did she think of in the last minutes of her life, and was she scared, and did she think of me? I want to know the answers so badly, but at the same time, it feels like there's a dagger shoved into my windpipe. *My fault.* Everything is always my fault.

"Alana, look, I know you want to be alive. Obviously, I want that too. But this is dangerous."

"You know what else is dangerous? Being accused of murder."

I shake my head. "You wouldn't do that to me."

"Wouldn't I?" She crosses her arms haughtily. "Maya, I can make it so much worse for you. I can make you look like the prime suspect if I want to."

"That's impossible. You can't even touch anything around you."

She takes the smallest of steps toward me. For a wild moment, I think she's going to try to hug me. But she focuses on the candle in my hand instead. The flame illuminates her face in a wash of yellow, stark against the dark courtyard—and then there's wind. Wind so strong I know it can't be natural whips around the buildings, howling. It bends the palms, sending fronds falling to the ground. It rattles the windows of classrooms surrounding us.

It pulls the candle right out of my grip, sending it sailing into the dry grass and sagebrush at my feet.

The wind feeds it, starving—I leap backward just as an entire row of desert shrubbery bursts into violent orange flames.

"You owe me," Alana says quietly, a snarl that chills me to the bone. "After what you did to me? You *owe* me."

And she's gone. A shadow, a nightmare that fades upon waking.

I'm alone with the fire.

My breath is coming in short gasps as I stare at the rising flames, one hand already pulling my phone out of my back pocket. It crackles, it *roars*, licking higher and higher, dangerously close to the Science building behind a row of palms. Terror overtakes me as I watch the flames climb. Trying not to think about what will happen if it spreads to the Chemistry room, I dial with fumbling fingers.

"911, what is your emergency?"

"I'm at Coldwater Canyon School," I pant, retreating slowly, unable to tear my eyes away from the blaze. "Fire—there's a fire in the courtyard. Please hurry."

If the woman on the other end answers me, I don't hear it. I hang up and take off running, phone in hand, sneakers kicking up dust. Instead of making a right toward the crowd at the vigil, I head left, out to the parking lot. Smoke is choking the air. Everyone will know soon—I already hear voices rising, silence breaking. I'm almost to the parking lot when my foot catches the curb and I fall hard to the ground.

"Shit," I mutter, kneeling on the asphalt and brushing my hands together. They're scraped, blood trailing down my palm, but otherwise I'm fine. I let out a shaky breath and lift my head, desperate to slow my heart rate, to breathe clean air—

And then I see it.

Bracketing the parking lot is the gymnasium wall, dark imposing brick. Words are scribbling fast across the surface, white as bone, like someone's finger-painting with volcanic ash. Each letter is tall and elegant and sure.

The words pound into my brain, louder and louder, with a slow, dawning horror.

I
will
never
leave
you

CHAPTER NINE

Coldwater Canyon School for Girls

Official Facebook Page

Located on a sprawling 10-acre Studio City campus, CCSG is a private, independent, college preparatory day school for girls in kindergarten through 12th grade.

May 7, 2024

Current students, parents, and alumnae:

Last night, during a vigil for missing CCSG student Alana Murray, a fire broke out in the school courtyard. 911 dispatchers responded to a call from an unknown source and the fire department quickly arrived on the scene. Fortunately, they were able to extinguish the blaze before it caused substantial damage to school property.

The Upper School Science wing will be closed for the next week as light repairs are performed, and AP exams will be held for juniors and seniors according to the predetermined schedule. Classes will continue as usual for kindergarten through eleventh grade.

We are saddened to share that the heroic firefighters who saved our school from potential destruction believe that this fire was set deliberately. We realize that due to the vigil, a larger than average number of people were congregating on the campus, many of whom are not part of our school community. Anyone with information regarding this incident is encouraged to come forward.

As ever, we remain united in our support of the search for Alana Murray. Counselors are available on campus for any students who are struggling with this ongoing situation.

Juliana Castillo

> Devastated that someone would try to harm our school community. My sweet daughter would have been so upset to miss her AP Government test if the school had burned down. Thanks to the firefighters!! #ColdwaterStrong !

Mary Rivers

> Coldwater parent here—we pay how much money in tuition (not even counting donations) and none of that is going toward fire safety?! This is Southern California, has anyone heard of WILDFIRES?

Jack Stevenson

I live pretty close to this school and it's really going downhill. Kids going missing and now a fire. When I was a kid, school was a haven for students. Sad the times we're living in. Has anyone checked to see if some teenager started this fire by smoking marijuana?

Ana Fernandez

@Jack Stevenson, uh, not sure how you would start a fire by smoking weed. What I want to know is the identity of the girl I saw running across the Upper School parking lot while the vigil was going on. I arrived late with my daughter and we watched her sprint toward the gymnasium. Rest assured I will be giving a FULL account to the police.

Catherine Carter-Holloway

These news articles and comments are taking the focus away from Alana, which I feel is deeply inappropriate. She's still missing, and my two daughters are just devastated. Can we redirect our focus, please? Visit www.whereisalanamurray.com if you have any information and need to get in touch with authorities.

• • •

The nightmares are like ghosts. Only I can't talk to them. I can't hide from them.

I draw a deep breath and let them pull me under.

They take shadow shapes at night and crawl across the floor of my bedroom, long and slow and eerie. They reach for me with smoky tendrils and take hold. On the night of the vigil, sleeping in my Los Angeles bedroom, I wake up every hour. Moonlight puddles on the floor and I shine my phone's flashlight into every dark corner.

Nothing, nothing. Just my own fear, sharp and electric. Waiting.

I dream of Alana alive again, solid and whole, blue eyes bright and so in love with me. My mind constructs a different girl who cares so deeply her blood runs red with it, who cracks open her rib cage and lets her heart unspool like crimson ribbon. When I apologize for breaking up with her, she takes my hands and tells me it's okay and I'm safe and we're fine now.

But no—

If I agree to help Alana possess someone, her eyes wouldn't glitter blue. If I searched her face for honesty and love, I wouldn't find it, because I wouldn't even know her. Her soul would be trapped in the body of someone else. It would be its own terrible grief. No matter what I choose to do, she'll be dead to me.

You owe it to me, dream Alana says. *You* left *me. Left me to die. You killed me.*

Fix it.

I sit bolt upright in bed, heart hammering, sweat dripping down my back. The palm fronds scraping my bedroom window sound like nails scratching. Something is watching me out in the dark, angry, staring through empty eye sockets. With shaking hands, I grab my pill case from beside my bed and swallow a tablet down dry.

The wind whispers through the cracked-open window, and it still sounds like Alana's voice in my ear.

If you don't help me, you're next.

...

The safest place for me.

That's how Dad phrases it on Tuesday morning when I wake from a sleepless night, standing in the upstairs bathroom and swiping concealer under my eyes. Lake Ember. It's a refuge—no one will bother me.

"But I have AP tests," I protest, shoving the concealer wand back into the tube with a satisfying pop. Dad shoots me a withering look from the hall, and I hear what he doesn't say—that shit doesn't matter anymore. I'm not going to college. Alana is dead—or, as far as the world knows, *missing*. Dad's done caring about my last-ditch attempts to turn my academic future around.

"I should've taken you up to the lake months ago," he grumbles, stomping downstairs, pulled by the sound of the gurgling Nespresso like it's a homing beacon. "If I could go back in time, I'd do it. There wasn't any need to put you through all that."

I freeze by the mirror, staring into my own brown eyes, surprised.

"All what?"

Silence. Down in the kitchen, he rummages through mugs.

"I thought you had all these friends," he calls finally. I sigh, twirling a mascara wand between my fingers, then tromp down the stairs to join him by the coffee maker. "But I didn't see you go up to any of them last night when we got to the vigil. Remember, all the girls you had over to swim? Didn't you go to the movies with a bunch of kids?"

Maybe in, like, eighth grade. I try not to roll my eyes. "Dad, I don't want to talk about this right now."

"They start being mean to you? Bullying you?"

"Why don't you ask Dr. Duarte, since you guys are in cahoots anyway?"

Now that I've invoked the name of my therapist, who's had way more conferences with my father over the past year than he'd probably prefer, I figure I've gotten the last word. Surely, he'll realize he's being overprotective and decide I can stay in LA.

Instead, he brings this up again and again as I pour my coffee into a thermos, as we pile into the car, as we head back up to Lake Ember. I know better than to try and fight it. I stopped speaking up about what I want a long time ago. Better to let myself get pulled around like driftwood in a current, surprised by where I land.

■ ■ ■

"For the last time," I sigh, flopping onto my back on the living room carpet at the lake house, "the conversation you saw me having was not a big deal. This girl came up to me—Elise's little sister. And she told me to watch my back because people are talking about me."

Dad is pacing back and forth by the front window, sipping on his second cup of coffee, this one lovingly brewed by Jazmine.

"Hmm," he says. "You're talking about Elise Carter-Holloway? I remember her. You used to bring her down to the restaurant sometimes."

"Why was Elise's sister talking to you like that?" Jazmine asks. She's perched on the couch, drinking tea instead of coffee, but she's still on edge. I can't help but wonder if she's pissed that I'm here, intruding on her life. If I were in my late twenties, cool and established and at peace, I wouldn't want my little sister saddling me with her drama. "I remember the Carter-Holloways. Catherine Holloway used to teach me piano. They were so nice."

"Look, it's no big deal. Isabelle wasn't trying to be mean. She was just teasing me about my grades."

"Your grades?" Jazmine is clutching her mug, looking at my dad. "What is there to tease you about your grades?"

A long silence stretches out, lazy as the sunbeams that fall across the floor and warm the carpet. Whoops. I didn't mean to let that one slip out. It's been so easy to fit back into Jazmine's life. Sometimes I forget that until a couple days ago, we'd had zero contact.

"It's nothing. I got some bad grades," I say finally. I don't tell her that it started in the fall, after a huge fight with Alana, when I succumbed to the depression that threatened to suffocate me. I don't tell her about the classes I missed while I was in the hospital for a week, how it felt to lie awake under those cold, crisp sheets. "It wasn't that big of a deal."

Dad sighs heavily, taking a long sip of his coffee. Jazmine and I both turn to look at him.

Hot shame rushes to my face. "Dad, it *wasn't* a big deal."

"Oh, all those college rejections weren't a big deal?" His tone is playful, but just serious enough to sting. And then, as if this isn't bad enough, he starts to list them out. "Bennington, Vassar, Bard, UC Berkeley, UCLA, Yale."

"Maya, why didn't you tell me?" Jazmine's on the verge of tears. *Because we don't fucking speak to each other,* I think but can't bring myself to say. "And Will—no one thought to clue me in?"

Dad opens his mouth, then closes it, glancing at me. I crush my thumb into the rug, grinding the tan fibers into nothing.

"Listen, it's not your business," I snap. "It's not your life."

"But those must've been your top choice schools—your reach schools, right? When do you find out about your safeties? You must have heard by now."

Again, Dad and I exchange a look. Those *were* my safeties, and he knows it. The threat of tears looms, a burning behind my eyes.

"Maya is still figuring things out," Dad says finally, and I look away. I can't bear to see even a shadow of shame or disappointment on his face. "I'm sure she'll end up in the place she's meant to be this fall."

Jazmine barely lets him finish the sentence. "Is she still going to therapy?"

"Well, I can make sure she goes, but I can't control what she talks about." He takes another sip of coffee.

"In case anyone's forgotten, I'm still here." It comes out cold, but I don't care. It hurts to hear them talk about my own therapy like this, like it isn't a personal thing between me and Dr. Duarte—who I do like, actually, and who's taught me how to walk myself back from panic spirals. Listening to my family, you'd think I sit on that couch every week staring at the clock. "Dad wants me to talk to Dr. Duarte about Alana, but I won't, because there's nothing to tell. Everybody's so convinced that Alana ruined my life...."

Her eyebrows lift. "*Did* Alana have anything to do with this? With your grades and the college rejections?"

"No!"

"Yes," Dad says at the same time.

My lips part and I stare at my father.

"What do you think she did, Dad?" I spit out. I would never talk to him like this if we were alone, but having my sister in the room gives me a strange confidence. "You think she called Yale and asked them to reject me, and they listened? Alana didn't have the power to mess up my life like this. Only I did."

That statement hangs over us like a heavy fog, finally permeated by the chime of my dad's ringtone. He sets his coffee down, frowning at the phone number, then walks into the kitchen to answer it, leaving me and teary-eyed Jazmine alone.

I sit up, eyes going directly to the living room mantel. On the far left is that gold-framed photo of me and Mom that I tried to ignore when I first arrived. In it, Mom is wrapping my toddler self in her arms, both of us laughing in the Venice Beach sand. No matter how hard I stare at that little girl, the unguarded happiness on her face, I'll never be her again.

Dad reenters, clutching his phone in his hand. He's biting his lower lip just like I do when I'm nervous.

"Maya," Dad says, business as usual. "This is Detective Ramirez on the phone. It sounds like they just have a couple quick questions for you about a 911 call you placed last night?"

My blood turns to ice. "What? No. Dad, talk to them for me. Please."

Apparently unable to handle another surprise, Jazmine stalks off into the kitchen. Dad stays. He switches the phone over to the speaker setting, giving me an encouraging nod, and despite my earlier anger, I feel a sudden rush of love for my father.

"Now," Dad says, "as my daughter is a minor, I won't be handing over the phone without being present in the room with her. And before she says a word, I'd like to know why it's important whether she placed a 911 call last night."

"The fire department has some concerns about the blaze being set intentionally," says Detective Ramirez, voice fuzzy through the phone. His tone is cordial, almost warm. Just two men shooting the shit. Completely different from the way the cop spoke to me. "I'm not sure if you've heard anything about—"

Dad cuts in. "The school put out a statement. I saw it this morning. Detective, you can't honestly think that my daughter would have *set* the fire."

"Sir, your daughter was the first on the scene. Several eyewitnesses spotted her running from the courtyard. We want to do our due diligence here and see what she has to say."

"I didn't do it," I say quickly. My hands are starting to sweat. I wipe them on my jeans. "Why would I do something like that?"

"I think," Dad says loudly, "that what Maya cares about most—what we *all* care about most here—is making sure Alana Murray is found safe."

I raise my voice. "You have to know what happened to her by now, don't you?"

"Maya." Dad's voice is sharp, chastising, but I don't drop it.

"It's been days. Do you have any leads? Any suspects?"

"Miss Rosier," the detective says with measured calm. "I'm not at liberty to disclose that information. We're still working to bring Alana home, but, Mr. Rosier, the fact that Maya was the first to call about the fire raised suspicions."

For the first time, Dad sounds genuinely irritated. "Detective, thanks for your diligence, but it doesn't seem like there's any issue here. The fire situation and Alana's missing persons case are obviously two different situations."

"Mr. Rosier, I'll cut to the chase here. It's our understanding that this case is beginning to generate public interest."

Public interest? I twist my shaking hands together in my lap. I know people love true crime podcasts and TV shows about serial killers, but it's only just sinking in how fucked up it all is. Alana's missing—*dead*—and just because she's a pretty, rich white girl, people are *interested.*

If what he's saying is true, she'll be all over social media. All over local news. All over the country.

"Look, I never meant to cause a problem," I say, trying to quell the rising hysteria in my voice. "I saw the fire, I called 911 like my dad always told me to. When I'm really anxious, I'm, like, hyperaware of my surroundings. That's what my therapist tells me anyway."

"I understand, Miss Rosier." Now that I've mentioned a mental health professional, he seems reluctant to press any further. He exchanges a series of pleasantries with my dad before the call ends, and I realize for the first time that my entire body is trembling.

My father tosses his phone onto the couch, then runs his hands over his face.

"Dad," I say, barely louder than a whisper. Fear prickles down my spine, ripples goose bumps along my arms. The idea of hopping in my car and heading south down the freeway makes me want to vomit. "I do think I should stay here. Just for a little while, though, right?"

It's not really what I want—dancing awkwardly around Jazmine, trying to act like we're loving sisters as my world falls apart. But the alternative seems so much worse. Trying to take AP exams on campus during all this will be impossible, and the world hasn't even realized that Alana is dead yet.

When they find out . . .

I can't even think about it.

"Yeah, kid," Dad says, watching me carefully. "Just for a little while."

I can barely register what he's saying. All I can think is, *Alana was right.* Maybe she can't touch me, can't push me, can't hit me, but she can destroy me in her own way. Just a simple breeze sending a candle sailing out of my hand and police officers are calling.

If she can make me look guilty of this, what else can she do?

Her words float back to me: *I can make it so much worse for you. I can make you look like the prime suspect.* Alana wants to come back to life so badly—of course she does. If I refuse to help her, I know her rage will be terrible. She'll stop at nothing to ruin my life. She'll accuse me of a murder I didn't commit. Somehow, she'll make sure I get caught.

And despite everything, despite her blackmailing me, I can't deny there's still part of me that can't imagine life without Alana.

Involuntarily, my eyes track back over to that photo on the mantel of Mom and me. Both of us smiling, no idea of what was to come. Since she died, my mother has missed nine of my birthday parties. Hundreds of soccer games and school plays and art shows. She never helped me get ready for a school dance or took me bra shopping or listened to me cry about secret middle school crushes. Death took all of that from me, and now it's taking Alana from me too.

I grit my teeth, heading for the stairs and leaving Jazmine and Dad behind me, the last broken remnants of my family.

I'm not ready to let go.

INTERLUDE

MY FRIENDSHIP WITH Livia Gonzales was never supposed to end.

We met in kindergarten at Coldwater, and she was like my sister. After Mom died and when Dad was away opening a new branch of the restaurant in San Juan Capistrano, I would stay at her house, both of us camping out in her giant canopy bed, eating popcorn out of mixing bowls. On the day I met Alana, ten years old, I was wearing the gold half-heart necklace that Livia and I shared. We had a history that Alana couldn't touch.

For that reason, we were doomed. I just didn't realize it until it was too late.

Elise was Alana's shiny new friend in middle school, a transfer student she handpicked and dangled in front of me. They happened to meet over the summer before Elise officially started at Coldwater; they were both attending this NorCal summer camp where they studied redwoods and sat around campfires learning dumb songs. It would never have occurred to Dad to sign me up for something like that.

"Look at my pictures from waterskiing with Elise," she would brag, shoving her phone in my face. They were both freckled and deeply tanned from their summer of bonding and friendship, and I loathed them for it. "Elise and I were on the same team for Color Wars and we totally pushed this one boy in the lake."

"She's awful," Livia tells me one chilly April morning in eighth grade. We're swinging side by side on the school playground. The toes of Livia's flip-flops drag in the mulch, but she doesn't seem to notice. "Seriously, Maya. Do you even think it's *fun* to hang out with Alana?"

I swallow past the lump in my throat. My swing skews to the left, back and forth, chains creaking. I can't tell my best friend that I've memorized Alana's favorite Bath and Body Works fragrance—Champagne Toast, fruity and sweet and wrapped in pink packaging—and that I bought it just so I could spray it in my room. I can't tell her about the way I watched Alana's Snapchat story twenty-six times last night, pressing my thumb against the screen to pause and study the exact sapphire blue of her eyes. I can't.

"She can be fun sometimes," I say carefully.

"Oh, yeah," Livia scoffs. "Fun when she's making her mom call the school at the start of eighth grade to move you into her advisory group so we couldn't be together, right?"

"I don't know for *sure* that's what happened."

"Fun when she plans a pool party and makes you guys swear not to tell me?"

"Her mom wouldn't let her invite too many people." I

squirm my way through the lie, glancing down at the plaid of my uniform skirt. "We just didn't want to hurt your feelings."

"Plus, you know that she's always trying to make you jealous, right?"

I know Livia isn't saying this like it's a good thing, but my heart flutters anyway.

"What do you mean?"

"It's so obvious, Maya. She'll, like, buy Elise a drink at Starbucks and then look over at you to see how you react." Her brown eyes are wide, fixed on my face. "Can you seriously not see it?"

"I don't know why Alana would want me to be jealous."

"You never even come to my house anymore," Livia says, her full lower lip slipping into a pout. A sudden burst of annoyance rises in me like a wave, so powerful that I leap off the swing, landing neatly on my feet.

"Liv, quit being such a baby," I snap, turning to face her. My abandoned swing is still lilting back and forth. "Maybe if you were a little bit more mature, I *would* come over more."

Alana is across the playground chatting with a couple other girls, including Elise, a fact that's been percolating in my mind for the past ten minutes. I know she's been watching me too. When I stride across the lush grass, Livia already forgotten behind me, Alana propels herself into an elaborate cartwheel. The girls surrounding her laugh, Elise applauding like a total suck-up. By the time I reach Alana's side, she's upright, silky brown hair tossed back.

"Hey," she greets me, smirking, voice low enough so that only I can hear. "Saw you over there with Little Livy."

"She was being *so* annoying." The words can't spill out fast enough.

Alana grins, pretending to glance at her watch. "Tick, tick. The school year will be over soon. Remember what we talked about? Not bringing any friends into high school who don't bring you joy?"

It's easy to laugh on the sunny playground, our classmates watching us with admiration. It's easy to feel happy with Alana as my ally. It's all so easy.

...

I'm not proud of the way I do it.

Liv, I type, thumbs moving slowly across my phone's keyboard. *I'm really sorry, but I don't think we should hang out anymore. I feel like we're growing up into different people. It's just easier this way.*

Gray dots skip across the screen for five minutes before Livia's message comes through.

Yeah, easier for you.

I swallow hard, think of the future I could have with Alana. The way I lie in my dark bedroom imagining her lips pressing against mine in the school hallway. I love her, I know I do.

I can keep her by my side. If it comes at a cost, I will pay it.

Livia, please don't be like this.

Maybe after this blows over with Alana, we can talk about it some more.

Liv??

But that's it. Our decade of friendship ends as fast as the swoosh of a falling ax. Firm and final and forever. At the end of the year, Livia transfers to Berkley-Carlisle, a super-exclusive private high school in Santa Monica.

I see her sometimes in the years afterward. Restaurants in

NoHo, our old favorite boba place at CityWalk. Every single time, her head is held high. And I watch her life unfold on social media, scrolling through photos of her and her boyfriend. She gets the first chair violin spot in the school orchestra, plays on the soccer team, competes in Model United Nations. She goes to prom in a beautiful dress and gets into USC, her dream school. She looks like she feels just fine.

Alana tells me, *I told you so.*

Alana tells me, *You never needed her anyway.*

Alana tells me, *She was crazy.*

But a fault line cracks inside me, jagged, tearing. I think something between us breaks. No matter how hard I try, it never repairs.

Because now Alana isn't just the girl who lit the fire in my heart—she's the girl who took my best friend away from me.

CHAPTER TEN

HuffPost

A Los Angeles Teenager Is Missing.
Why Do We Care?

by Allie Kingston, Contributor
May 8, 2024

The disappearance of Los Angeles teenager Alana Murray on May 4 took her local community, the San Fernando Valley, by storm. Her family and friends searched parks, trails, and even the sprawling cement expanse of the LA River. They posted fliers on telephone poles and in windows of shops that Alana frequented. A candlelight vigil was held at her private all-girls high school.

But quickly, something else began to happen. The rest of the country started paying attention.

Even though Alana has only been confirmed missing for three days, the hashtag #WhereIsAlanaMurray brings up over 5,000 posts on Instagram and over 10,000 videos on TikTok. The posters, mainly hyper-fixated teenagers and true crime buffs, speculate over the location where Alana may have been last seen and analyze her social media posts with a depth and precision typically only found in the FBI's Behavioral Analysis Unit. Turn on the news, and you'll see overeager reporters standing in front of Alana's school or outside her favorite coffee shop.

So why all the attention?

Let's get the obvious out of the way: Eighteen-year-old Alana Murray is white, wealthy, and beautiful, with a shock of long dark hair and striking blue eyes. Her mother, Melissa Cartwright Murray, is showrunner of the hit teen drama *Little Secrets,* a position she's held for five years. Indeed, some are remarking that a missing daughter storyline could be ripped from an episode of Murray's show.

Alana attends the prestigious Coldwater Canyon School for Girls, a cutthroat independent college preparatory school that students can attend from kindergarten through twelfth grade. Girls at Coldwater load their course schedule with APs, take practice SATs in their preteen years, and are often the star-studded offspring of Hollywood big shots— the very definition of "nepo babies."

In a typical year, the National Missing and Unidentified Persons System states that more than 600,000 people go missing. Of these, over 40 percent are people of color. Many of these teenagers don't have a parent like Melissa Murray, who can immediately offer up reward money for a safe return or persuade the LAPD to launch an instant investigation. Quite frankly, girls like Alana Murray typically don't go missing—and when they do, the world watches. With popcorn.

To skim through Alana's social media is to enjoy a jaunt through a privileged Southern California teen girl's sun-kissed life. See her dip her toes in her backyard infinity pool, see her browse the boutiques strewn along the famed Rodeo Drive. Surely one reason Alana's case has captivated Gen Z observers is her relationship with her longtime girlfriend, Coldwater classmate Maya Rosier. Sweetly pretty and demure, Maya offers a pleasant contrast to her partner—the Ingrid Bergman to Alana's Elizabeth Taylor. Posts spanning years prove they were deeply in love, and, to quote many of this case's most obsessive followers, the relationship is "goals."

Con't. below

■ ■ ■

Voicemails from my dad always start the same way.

"Hey, Papaya, it's Dad!" Like I've gone blind and can't read my phone's call history. "Made it back to LA just fine. Jazmine will take good care of you, and in the meantime I'm sending you some of your clothes and stuff. Not to worry about everything that happened at the vigil. Text me. Proud of you, sweetheart."

I tug a T-shirt over my head, worn cotton sliding over my cold skin. The morning air seeps in through cracks in the floorboards, the window, and makes me shiver. *Proud of you, sweetheart.* As if I've done anything in the past year that could possibly make him proud.

Walking into the kitchen, I type out a quick reply to Dad, *All good here* with a thumbs-up emoji. The floor is freezing under my bare feet. I skim my fingers along the papered walls, white and yellow florals. It's a narrow two-story house, but everything about the design is updated, from the stainless-steel appliances in the kitchen to the super-shiny windows with plastic locks. Dad helped Jazmine renovate it when she moved in, but older details that I remember from my childhood visits still pop up here and there, like the exposed wood beams crossing the ceiling.

I jam a coffee pod into the Keurig and lean up against the counter while it brews, glancing down at my phone.

The coffee maker splutters to a stop. I pour the coffee into one of Jazmine's Stanford University mugs sitting on the counter. When I pick it up, I notice a scrap of paper tucked under it. My sister's handwriting is scrawled across in half cursive.

Maya—

Have to run into Blue Skies for the morning rush. Feel free to walk over for some tea if you want! Here's a spare house key. Call if you need me.

Love ya,
J

I sip my coffee, contemplating this. What the hell am I going to do here in Lake Ember? Jazmine and Dad and I never decided on the length of my stay; taking exams at Coldwater is out of the question, and it's not like I'm desperate to get back home to hang with my many friends. I could hide out at Blue Skies, try to distract myself from my disastrous life, drink some tea—but that dark-haired girl, Rowan, flashes into my mind. Her stupid blue baseball cap and annoying questions. Involuntarily, I slide my hand into the pocket of my jean shorts, searching for my obsidian stone, before I remember that it's still upstairs in the drawer. Then it hits me.

There *is* a place in Lake Ember I can go. One that would be much more helpful.

Google Maps refers to Major Arcana as a "metaphysical supply store," which I guess is accurate enough. As a kid visiting the lake, it was a home away from home. With Jazmine's supervision, I would make the five-minute walk into town and browse the tiny store with wide eyes, tracing my fingers over craggy bits of crystal, from stunning blue azurite to warm citrine. The woman who owned the shop, Valeria, took such good care of me that eventually Jazmine let me go shopping there alone. Valeria taught me how to burn incense—peppermint when doing my homework, lavender when I was stressed out—and went over my star chart in detail, worrying about the conflicts between my Venus in Gemini and my Cancer sun.

My entire childhood, the only people who knew I could see ghosts were Jazmine and Alana. I never directly told the woman at Major Arcana anything, but somehow, she knew. After Mom died and I was desperate to contact her, Valeria would answer my questions about ghosts patiently, with a knowing look in her eye. There were beanbag chairs at the back of the shop and I'd curl up there with books about famous hauntings and resurrections and summoning rituals; she let me stay there for hours.

If there's anyone in Lake Ember who might be able to help me now, it's Valeria. There's no way I can help Alana with her possession idea; I need some kind of counterplan, and I need it fast. If I'm going to thwart Alana's attempts at possession, I need to understand it first.

On my way out of Jazmine's house, I let the front door slam shut behind me. The yard is washed in sunlight, but I shiver anyway, arms wrapping around my chest. I can't shake the feeling that Alana's behind every tree, peeking out.

I turn onto Hacienda Avenue. This is a busier street, the one that leads right into the heart of town, cars whooshing past. Years ago, during childhood summers, I'd see ghosts wandering these streets as the sun set, leaning up against trees, skulking outside stores, waiting for someone to look their way. Today, there isn't a single one.

That's not the only difference. Things have clearly gotten trendier in Lake Ember. Thick swaths of trees have been carved away to accommodate the construction of cheerful bed-and-breakfasts, cozy wine bars, vegan cafés. When I cut across to Mira Monte Road, the main street that runs through town, I actually see a couple groups of tourists snapping photos. So weird.

Last time I was here, Major Arcana was tucked between a hole-in-the-wall coffee shop and a gas station that looked preserved in time from the 1960s, one pathetic palm tree clinging to life out front. Now, the storefront looms ahead, its gold and purple logo repainted in fresh, bright hues—and it's flanked by a chic Italian restaurant and a Starbucks. I suck in a deep breath, bracing myself to face Valeria again after all these years. At least after I've gotten the answers I need, I can grab a venti cold brew.

A gong sounds when I push open the door. Despite the changes on the street, the inside of Major Arcana looks the same as ever. A worn Ukrainian flag hangs along the far wall, faded blue and yellow. There's the same velvet carpet, the same tall glass cases filled with peacock feathers and bleached animal skulls. Scents of patchouli and rosemary cloud the air, so thick that I wave a hand in front of my face.

Part of me expected Valeria to be standing right there like she was expecting me. Instead, there's no one in the shop at all. Stupid to think otherwise—I can't imagine that this place is a major tourist attraction, and just because Valeria is a self-professed psychic doesn't mean she'll see me coming.

I bend over the counter at the front of the shop, an ancient cash register perched on its surface. Below the glass, there's a display of gold-encrusted tarot cards inlaid with gemstones, an assortment of moonstone and quartz necklaces spread out across a bed of black fabric. I'm leaning closer, examining a giant, iridescent pendant shaped like a beetle, when a door slams shut behind me and I almost jump out of my skin again.

"Hey! Can I help you find something?"

I whirl around, leaning up against the glass counter, one hand over my heart. "Oh my god, you scared the—"

We realize it at the same time.

"Maya?"

"*Rowan?*"

"What the hell are you doing here? Was Bath and Body Works closed?"

"What are *you* doing here?"

"I work here," Rowan from Blue Skies says matter-of-factly. Without her tea shop uniform, she looks vaguely spooky, dressed in all black from head to toe. Her dark hair is up in a ponytail, revealing an undercut.

"But you work with my sister."

The smirk fades from Rowan's face. "I realize I probably sound like I'm speaking a foreign language to you, princess, but people can have two jobs at once. Maybe you've heard the age-old phrase *making ends meet?*"

I roll my eyes. "Listen. I need to speak with Valeria Sokolov. Your boss, probably?"

"That's one word for her," Rowan snorts, glancing over her shoulder and raising her voice. "Oh, Mother?"

Mother? No fucking way. But sure enough, the back door swings open—beyond it I can see a small, cramped office space with a computer that looks like it's from the 90s—and Valeria steps out, carrying a stack of leatherbound books.

I turn back to Rowan, staring at her slate gray eyes, the stubborn set of her mouth. *That's* why she looks so familiar. Rowan Sokolov, Valeria's daughter, the one who was always running around town with a gaggle of lake kids. I used to hide from them in here, shuffling tarot cards and reading every book I could get my hands on. I still have tons of them that I bought with allowance money.

"What is it now, Row?" Valeria asks, sounding world-weary. She looks as glamorous and dramatic as I remember: thick black hair streaked with silver and twisted into a chic top knot, heavy winged eyeliner. Even despite the early summer heat, she's wearing an amethyst-colored turtleneck.

Rowan smirks. "Another LA girl looking for manifestation crystals."

"Wh—no!" I splutter. "No, that's not why I'm here."

"Rowan, honestly . . ." Valeria says, shaking her head. She sets the stack of books down on the counter behind me with a thump, then wipes her brow as she turns around. "I'm sorry about my daughter. She—"

Valeria's kind eyes widen as she takes me in.

"I'm sorry," she says again. "Have you been in here before?"

"I—yeah. When I was a kid." I lick my lips. "It's—I'm Maya Rosier?"

At the name, her expression bursts into sunlight. Before I know it, I'm engulfed in a hug.

"Little Maya! Oh, sweetheart, I'm so sorry I didn't recognize you. You're so grown up. How old were you last time you were in here? Eleven, twelve?"

"Thirteen," I mumble as she lets go of me. "I was kind of short for my age."

"Well, it's wonderful to see you, dear. I wondered about you when you stopped coming in."

"Rosier was always too cool to talk to the townies," Rowan says.

I shoot her a sidelong glance. "I never saw you in here."

"No, I had better things to do. Tried to talk to you once on the beach—I bet you don't even remember. You were so quiet back then."

"Oh, Miss Maya was a sweetheart. Very knowledgeable

little girl too." Valeria turns to me, fondness in her eyes. "You always asked great questions."

"I'm actually here with another question," I blurt out, before Rowan can derail me further. "If that's okay."

"Of course!" Valeria exclaims, clapping her hands together. Jeweled bangle bracelets on her wrist chime like little bells. "What do you need?"

"Um, basically, I need to learn more about . . ." I glance over at Rowan, who's just standing there, hands in her pockets. "Sorry. Do you need to be here?"

She fixes me with an offended glare. "I work here. Man, they really don't teach listening comprehension in private school."

"I just need some space. This is . . . something personal."

Her dark eyebrows shoot up. "Personal? Are you planning an exorcism or something?"

My hesitation lasts a beat too long.

"Maya," Valeria says gently. "Why don't you ask me for whatever you need help with, and Rowan will quietly get back to work? You two can catch up later."

Rowan makes a big show of huffing and looking annoyed, but she listens to her mom, stomping off to the back room in her combat boots. Neither of us mentions that catching up with each other is the last thing we want to do.

"I'm sorry I haven't been to visit in a while," I tell Valeria. "It wasn't my choice, really. You know my sister, right? Jazmine Reyes?"

"Of course." She smiles warmly. "And I knew your mother. Lillia."

I blink, surprised. "You—you knew my mom?"

"She came in here often during the summers. You might

not remember . . . you were so small. The two of us spoke about all kinds of things. I gave her a few readings, you know. And Lillia did love to talk about you."

My face flushes pink. Everything else suddenly seems unimportant. "She did?"

"Oh, like every mother does."

"Jazmine never really . . ?" I glance over my shoulder. Rowan is banging away at something in the back behind a closed door. It's safe to talk. "After our mom died, my sister never really understood me."

"Ah," Valeria says with a lamenting sigh, moving over to the glass cabinet at the front of the shop. She clicks open the back and begins to lightly dust the artifacts inside with a delicate feathery brush. "It can be hard with sisters, Maya. I'm sure Jazmine tries her best."

"Jazmine and I had different relationships with Mom, I think." I shrug, eyes moving slowly across the spread of gemstones inside the glass cabinet. "So we were never really close after Mom was gone."

Valeria smiles. "I have an older sister myself, so I think I know what you're getting at."

I bite my lip, leaning forward to rest my elbows on the glass cabinet as Valeria continues to dust. "Sometimes I wish there was a way I could talk to my mom now and ask if she's proud of me. Like, if I turned out okay. I wish there was a way she could come back, you know?"

Valeria pauses, feather duster in hand, back to me. Then she turns slowly.

"Forgive me for being so blunt," she says, "but surely you've seen your mother's ghost?"

"No. I never have. She never came back."

She rests her duster on the glass cabinet. "I'm sorry to hear that. I wonder if perhaps that's a kindness."

I stare at her, trying to figure out what she means, but she keeps talking.

"Sweetheart, I remember when you came into the shop just after your mother passed. You must've been—what, eight years old? Tiny little thing. Stronger than most children would've been. What you can do, Maya, is a gift and a curse. To be a mediator between our world and the next—it's not for the fainthearted."

What you can do. I swallow, wondering if I should correct her with the truth: that I don't do any of it anymore. That Alana's the first ghost I've seen in years. If she expects me to be some kind of ghost prodigy, I'm a letdown. But I can't bring myself to admit it.

"Honestly, I'm just wondering, um . . ."

Her eyebrows raise, waiting, but she doesn't rush me.

"Wondering about, um . . . how it would be possible for a ghost to possess someone. And come back to life that way."

Valeria's expression changes, a shroud of mist lifting off the tops of trees. Her dark eyebrows draw together. "You'd be okay with your mother's spirit possessing some innocent human vessel?"

"I'm just curious whether it's possible."

"There are plenty of things that fall within the realm of possibility, regardless of whether they should," Valeria says darkly, sinking into a velvet pouf behind the counter. "Plus, from what little I know about Lillia, I doubt she would ever agree to something like that. Possession is a violent act, Maya. It rips a soul from a living body and forces it into a sort of limbo. The dead should move on to whatever comes next, rather than remaining on earth to commit such an unspeakable act."

I worry at my bottom lip, staring at a collection of amethyst gems. "But if the ghost was really dead set on possessing someone—sorry about the pun—can a living person stand in their way?"

"It has happened before." Valeria's gaze burns me; I have no choice but to look up. "There are some very determined spirits who will stop at nothing to finish business they've left on earth. Your purpose, Maya, your very existence, hinges on making sure *this does not happen.*"

She hits the counter with one bejeweled hand, punctuating each word.

"You've been given a beautiful gift. I'm sure it doesn't always feel like that, but you have. Your responsibility to this world is to guard it from the deep, damaging psychic interference such a possession would cause."

Damaging psychic interference? My heart is pounding so loudly I'm sure that even Rowan in the back room can hear it.

"Okay," I mumble, slightly put off by the fire blazing across Valeria's face. "Sorry that I asked. I was only curious, I promise."

Valeria's expression softens. "You must learn to live with the memories. Live with the love Lillia gave you here on earth and carry that with you." My face must give me away because she smiles. "Believe me, I know it's a pale imitation of a mother's love. But it's something."

"Yeah." I nod. "I guess it's something."

Alana's face flashes into my mind—the quick and practiced way she'd tie her hair into a ponytail while we hiked at

Fryman Canyon, the way she always sang along loudly to that dumb Donna Lewis song on long car rides. Valeria's right that my mom would never want to possess someone to come back to life, but Alana is another story. And now that I know that possession is actually a real thing that ghosts can do, the fear is almost overwhelming.

The back door slams and Rowan wanders through, gray eyes sparkling.

"So, what's up, Rosier? You got a ghost in your house?"

I roll my eyes, turning back to Valeria. "It was really nice to see you—"

"When can I come over and see it?" Rowan interrupts.

"One week from never," I shoot back.

"But I can help! I've banished *plenty* of ghosts before."

"No you haven't, Rowan." Valeria lifts her feather duster to the stained-glass window. "You play at paranormal investigating, nothing more."

I watch the smile slide off Rowan's face. For the first time since we met, she doesn't have a snappy retort.

"It was wonderful to see you, Maya. Come back for anything else you might need," Valeria says, sliding a couple books into a paper bag. "Take these. I remember you always loved reading. Learn as much as you can. Keep yourself safe."

Back out on the sunny sidewalk, I keep my head down. I'm desperate to talk to somebody, but what am I going to do, call my dad and tell him that Alana's ghost manifests in my bedroom? Ask how dangerous he thinks it would be to bring her back to life? And Jazmine's out of the question.

I wind back down Mira Monte Road, lost in thought. Possession is a terrible act, Valeria made that much clear. The one thing Alana wants, *needs* from me, I can't give her.

But there's one thing I can do: help her move on. How many times did I do that as a kid? Talk with a ghost, find out what was keeping them tethered to earth. As soon as they figured it out, they'd vanish. I'm not sure what exactly is keeping Alana here—her love for me? Her sudden, traumatic death? Sheer willpower? But if I keep engaging with her, keep talking to her, maybe I can get her to move on peacefully.

It's my only option. I left Alana to die. If I can't give her a peaceful resolution, then my life might as well be over too.

INTERLUDE

TWO YEARS EARLIER

IT DOESN'T MATTER if Dr. Duarte's office is cute. I'm determined to hate her.

"Maya, welcome," she says warmly, like she can read my mind. Her office is a backyard cottage, roses and sea lavender crawling elegantly up the cream-painted walls, and when I trudged up the front walk, the floral smell clogged my nostrils.

Now I'm standing at the threshold, staring around; this place is definitely a converted shed. The walls are shiplap adorned with paintings of beachy scenes, and a vanilla sandalwood candle flickers from her narrow writing desk. A silver MacBook, closed, is perched atop it.

Dr. Duarte herself doesn't look old enough to be a doctor. Or a psychiatrist, I guess. Her black hair is impeccably curled into beachy waves, and she wears fun glasses: bright teal, round. Her clothing is simple: linen slacks and a plain T-shirt. I can tell that this entire experience is geared to make me feel comfortable; instead, I want to crawl out of my skin.

"Sixteen next month!" Dr. Duarte says brightly, gesturing toward her couch. It's bubblegum pink, adorned with throw pillows in the shapes of fruit. A lemon, an orange slice. "That's exciting. Any plans to get your license?"

"I hate driving on the freeway," I say, plopping down on the couch and hugging the lemon pillow.

"That's universal, I think." She smiles. This whole time, she hasn't risen from her desk chair. She doesn't continue speaking either—doesn't shuffle through notes, tap away at her keyboard.

She just looks at me.

"You probably know that you're my fourth therapist," I blurt out. Her dumb tactic worked, but I have to get this out in the open just in case she *doesn't* know. "I'm difficult to work with. My first therapist just said *mm-hmm* a lot and wrote in a notebook—she was probably doodling. The second one wanted me to be hopped up on meds instead of listening to anything I said. And the third one told my dad that we weren't a good fit."

"That's interesting," Dr. Duarte says thoughtfully, even though I'm suddenly certain she knew this already. "Did you feel like the third one wasn't a good fit?"

"She didn't listen to me," I mumble, picking at the frayed hem of my jean shorts.

"That must have been really frustrating. What was it that you wanted her to hear?" The therapist pulls open a desk drawer and produces a bag of Jolly Ranchers. Holds it out to me.

"I only like apple," I say, which isn't true—I just feel like being difficult because I don't want to be here. She tosses me a lime green candy and I catch it, crinkling the wrapper between my fingers. "Well, so, I would tell her about my girl-friend. We've been together for about a year, but this b—I mean, this woman—kept saying *Oh yes, friendships between teenage girls can be very intense.*"

Dr. Duarte wrinkles her nose. "Eww."

"Yeah, major eww. I told my dad, *You don't pay her $175 an hour for her to sit here being a homophobe,* and thankfully, he heard me on that." I twist the candy wrapper. "So I'm here."

"Well, I'm glad you are." Dr. Duarte pops a red Jolly Rancher in her mouth. "So, a year with your girlfriend? That's exciting. Is there anything about her that you'd like to share?"

"Um, not really. Her name's Alana. She's a Scorpio, and she has a husky—his name is Balto and he sings along to Taylor Swift songs, but only the re-recordings, so we say that he's an unproblematic fave. She has blue eyes. And she's so funny. We spend almost every day together. And she just makes me feel, like, special."

My new therapist smiles, and I have the sense that she's trying to suppress a laugh. "She sounds wonderful, Maya. How does she make you feel special?"

"Just little stuff—it's hard to explain. Like, I planned a beach trip one time for a bunch of girls in our class, but she convinced me that it would be more fun if just the two of us went. She was totally right, though. It wasn't her being con-trolling or anything. A lot of the things we do together are just the two of us."

Dr. Duarte's smile fades just slightly. "Do you like it that way? Or do you wish your friends could come along?"

"I mean, yeah. I don't think everything needs to be a pri-vate date all the time. But it's what Alana wants, so . . ." I trail off, shrugging.

"But what you want is important too, Maya. Right?" she asks.

"I guess, but I'm her girlfriend," I say, sucking on my Jolly Rancher. It's more sour than I expected. "I'm all she has. Listen, maybe this sounds bad, but our relationship is really good. I feel really lucky to have found her when I'm still a teenager."

"You know Alana better than I do, of course," Dr. Duarte says, giving me a polite nod. "But do you really think you're *all* she has? The person you just described to me—that sounds like a girl with a pretty full life. Surely she has a loving family, friends. . . ."

"But she cares about me the most," I interrupt. "That's what she tells me all the time. And I care about her the most too. More than my family. More than my friends. Well, and some of my friends I don't even *talk* to anymore because of Alana, so that's—"

Dr. Duarte holds up a hand, frowning. "Friends you don't talk to anymore?"

I pause, not sure I should have admitted this. Of course, it's my own fault, because I never know how to shut up. "Alana doesn't like it if I'm friends with people who are too clingy, or aren't cool enough, or whatever. She's super smart about that stuff. She realized I was making my half sister into a substitute for my dead mom, so I stopped talking to her too."

There's a long, shivering silence, during which I become certain I've said too much.

"Maya," Dr. Duarte says quietly. "I'm sorry to hear that."

"It's no big loss," I mumble, but even as the words leave my lips, images flicker inside my mind. Jazmine giving me a piggyback ride on the walk to kindergarten, braiding my hair by the pool during hot summers, yelling at a boy on our block who teased me for still having training wheels on my bike. On the day of Mom's funeral, my sister cried alone in her bathroom so I wouldn't have to see one more sad person that day.

"Does your sister reach out to you?" Dr. Duarte asks, her voice still soft, like I'll shatter.

"I don't want to talk about this."

"I understand." She pauses, watching me. "I do wonder if you've ever considered whether Alana does these things to gain power over you. That can't feel fun to you."

"Gain power over me?" I ask, wrinkling my nose. "That sounds kind of intense. Like you think she's abusive or something."

Dr. Duarte opens her mouth, pauses. Closes it. "When you say *abusive,* what does that bring to mind?"

"Like, a guy who beats his wife or something. Gets drunk and screams and yells."

She nods slowly. "Those would definitely be characterized as abusive, yes. But I want to make sure you're clear that there are versions of abuse that are different from what you might be thinking of: hitting, kicking, bruising, swearing. Sometimes in a relationship, one person will demean and criticize the other by manipulating their partner's emotions. That's emotional abuse."

"I—" My mouth opens, but the words get jammed somewhere on their way to my brain. "Look, I get what you're saying, but it's not like that with Alana."

"From what you've told me, it sounds like Alana likes to be in control of situations. I wonder if, in these situations, she tells you things you want to hear. Perhaps without regard that they might be hurtful things."

I stare at her. I've been to psychics before, of course, mostly as a kid in Lake Ember having my fortune told at Major Arcana. Valeria spreading tarot cards across a purple velvet tablecloth, teaching me about the lightning-struck Tower. The shivering change that only Death can bring. Her predictions and claims were eerie, but they were nothing compared to sitting in this stuffy therapist's office, listening to someone tell me how it feels to be loved by someone who takes pleasure in breaking you.

"I don't say this to scare you," Dr. Duarte continues softly.

"Alana is *not* abusive," I snap, even though what she just described feels so, *so* real, something I could hold in my hands and squeeze the life out of.

"No one form of abuse is better or worse than another." Dr. Duarte leans forward in her chair, studying me again. "But often, victims of emotional abuse think that what they suffered isn't important. If they don't have cuts or black eyes, for instance, they might not even realize that what they're enduring is abuse. Maya, again, I'm not trying to scare you. But I'm bringing this up because some things you're saying are kind of alarming to me."

"No," I say again, and I'm furious to realize that tears are streaming down my face. "You're wrong. You don't even *know* her. Why would you say that as soon as I walk in the room? Did my dad make you say this?"

"Maya, no—" Dr. Duarte is saying, rising from her chair, but I'm faster.

Bursting out the door, sprinting down the walkway. I don't stop until I'm on the sidewalk, breaths coming in short gasps. I shrink down to the ground, arms wrapping around my knees to make myself small.

I'll never go back, I tell myself. *Never ever. She doesn't know Alana.*

But there was something compelling in her words—the way she listened to me without judging. The way she took things I said and grew them into something bigger and more meaningful. Despite myself, I want to learn more. I want to know.

For the next two years, I don't miss a single weekly session.

CHAPTER ELEVEN

UP IN MY room that night, the sill is already damp with rain from the window I left open. Rain in Lake Ember is much more common than in Los Angeles, and Dad always hated it because no one here knows how to drive in it, so traffic slows to a crawl. Still, I can't help but notice that it's storming more than usual.

Anxiety has been humming in my chest all day and hasn't abated. I fish my little pill container out of my pocket, slip one tablet into my mouth, and swallow it down dry. I feel homesick for a place that doesn't exist anymore. Alana and I in the middle of the night, whispering secrets; Alana and I at school, my every move shaped by her guidance. Without her, I'm unmoored, almost drowning. How am I supposed to do this on my own?

Thunder crashes outside, sudden and deafening, and I almost jump out of my skin. A gust of evening wind roars through the open window. The air is petrichor-thick, drenched in the scent of pine. I stand by the window breathing heavy, running a hand through my hair, and when I look down, there it is: another handful of California poppy petals scattered across the hardwood floor, sunset orange.

I crouch, gathering them into my hands.

"Hey, Maya."

Slowly, I look up. Alana's perched on top of the dresser, kicking her ankles lightly against the drawers, making them rattle. That's new. She couldn't interact with her surroundings last time she was here, couldn't even touch the candle back at Coldwater during the vigil. She had to blow it out of my hand.

"Same shit, different day, huh?" Her voice is light, like we're chatting about the weather. "How was the vigil after we said goodbye? Think you looked sad enough?"

"I don't know. I didn't stay." I straighten up and let the petals float back down to the floor. To avoid looking at her, I ease the window shut. My palms are sweating and I try to wipe them on my shorts without her noticing. She doesn't need to know how much I love her, how much I miss her. "And what do you mean, sad enough?"

She waves a careless hand toward me. "You always manage to make yourself look guilty as hell. Panicking, calling 911. Leave it to you to make a scene."

"I wasn't . . ." I lick my lips, trying to slow my breath. "Were you watching me?"

"You can't always see me," she offers by way of an explanation. "Oh, don't look at me like that, Maya. I still can't manifest anywhere unless it's dark, but I've gotta say, when I can sneak around during daylight, I get to see all kinds of good stuff."

My heart slams against my rib cage—how much did she hear?

"For example, the cops came sniffing around, just like I told you they would. Do you believe me now? How powerful I can be? And your chat with that goth lesbian was entertaining."

"Who?"

Alana bursts out laughing. "Maya, this is why you never got the good parts in the school plays. God. The girl you were talking to today! What's her story?"

"I don't know what you're talking about—" I say, even as beads of sweat form along my hairline. These accusations, insinuations, aren't new. Alana's always jumping on me for this stuff: *Why did you comment a flame emoji on this girl's Instagram?* They're always unfounded, but she hates when my attention is directed at a girl who isn't her.

"I mean, it did come as somewhat of a surprise," Alana interrupts. "So soon after breaking up with me—so soon after my *tragic* death. And plus, she's really not your type."

"Alana, stop," I say with as much bravado as I can muster, but both of us hear the tremble in my voice. "It's not like that. She's just some random girl. Anyway, aren't you sick of picking fights with me all the time?"

"Hey, I liked that witchy place you went to." Alana wiggles her fingers dramatically at me. "Spooky."

I'm relieved that she's moved on from Rowan, but still, the thought of her watching me live my life makes me nauseous. Time to redirect her, make her believe that I'm going all in on her plan.

"We need to be prepared for your possession ritual," I say a little too quickly. "I've decided, I'm definitely going to help you with this, so you can stop playing games with me, okay?

That's why I went to Major Arcana. The same shop where I got my obsidian stone when I was a kid—remember?"

I yank open my dresser drawer and pull out the black stone, holding it up like an adult distracting a kid with something sparkly. Alana takes a step back. Of course: The stone's energy will block her out. I haven't been carrying it for this exact reason.

"Oh," she says, wrinkling her nose. "That thing. I don't know, Maya, it looks fake."

"It's not. It's volcanic glass, and it's super powerful. It contradicts negative energy, heightens your self-control, and wraps you in protection."

"And what exactly do you need protection from? Any scary ghosts try to hurt you, I'll kick their asses. You don't have to worry about that." She waves a dismissive hand. "For all we know, that stone will burst into flames the second we start the possession ritual. It's a *protective* stone, right? What we're doing isn't exactly protection."

"I guess, but ..."

"Maya," she says. "You don't need it."

My mouth goes dry at the thought of not holding on to my obsidian stone. Even if I'm not actively using it, it's comforting for me to have it around, just like my anxiety meds. But I have to prove that Alana and I are on the same side here. I move toward the bedside table, thinking of slipping it into a drawer, but Alana shakes her head.

"Try again," she singsongs, and on her command, my bedroom window lifts with an eerie creak.

I stare at the curtains rippling in the sudden breeze. "I'm not sure that's a good idea."

"Why? I just said you're safe with me around. Get rid of it, Maya."

There's a burning at the back of my eyes.

"You know how it works between you and me," she says quietly. "I tell you what's best for you, and you do it."

Before I can think twice, I toss my stone out the crack in the window. It vanishes into the darkness below. Immediately, I feel vulnerable, but I'm not going to show Alana that.

"There you go. Okay. Now that we've dispensed with the dramatics, do you want to tell me more about this girl at the psychic shop?"

I turn away, easing the window shut. "Alana, I don't know. I knew her mom when I was a kid. They sell books about any topic you could ever want—gemstones, incense, astrology. . . ."

"And your little girlfriend—"

"She's *not* my—"

"She works there?"

"Yeah. I guess she helps her mom."

"I wonder what she would say if she knew you were being blamed for arson." Alana's voice is thoughtful. She hops down off the dresser, a smile playing across her face. I know this expression well. It's the way she looks when she's set a perfect snare and someone is about to step right into it.

"No one's blaming me for arson," I snap. "The cops believed my dad."

"Oh yeah? Check your phone."

Without taking my eyes off Alana, I grab my phone from the bedside table where I left it charging. I open up a new tab, searching "Coldwater Canyon School fire."

LOCAL NEWS

Suspicions Grow Regarding Fire at Coldwater Canyon School for Girls

Posted: May 8, 2024

Still reeling from the sudden disappearance of eighteen-year-old high school senior Alana Murray, the community surrounding Studio City's Coldwater Canyon School for Girls is now reckoning with a suspicious fire that occurred during a candlelight vigil.

"It was a tribute to honor Alana and show support to her family," one of Murray's classmates, who requested to remain anonymous, said to KTLA. "The fact that somebody would be this disrespectful—if the fire *was* actually started on purpose—well, it's really messed up."

Police detectives have not yet determined whether the fire was set deliberately, but many of the vigil's attendees are growing increasingly suspicious. Our reporters obtained a 911 call placed from Coldwater Canyon School's campus on the night of the vigil. This call alerted first responders to the blaze. While the caller does not identify themselves, sources have claimed it is the voice of Murray's girlfriend, seventeen-year-old Maya Rosier.

Alana Murray's classmate and friend, Elise Carter-Holloway, uploaded a TikTok this morning in which she appeared to react to the 911 call.

"I think the question we should all be asking ourselves is, Why was Maya in the courtyard at all? Why wasn't she at the vigil?" Carter-Holloway asks her viewers in the video, which has quickly amassed 300,000 views and hundreds of comments.

Rosier's family could not be reached for comment.

"What the fuck?"

My hands are shaking. I drop the phone onto my bed like it's a live snake.

"Terrible, right?" Alana asks, blue eyes glittering in a way that makes me certain she doesn't think this situation is terrible in the slightest. "They've invoked your name on TikTok."

"Couldn't reach my family for comment? You're telling me they called my dad about this shit? This is so stupid! Why . . ." My heart is pounding, the entire room feeling blurry and far away. "Why are people talking about this on social media?"

"Everybody loves a mystery, Maya," she says, and right on cue, lightning flashes outside my window. "And everybody's a true crime junkie these days—you should know that. It's your own fault for calling 911 and creating this drama anyway."

"Sorry that I didn't want our school to burn down," I snap; sometimes it's easier to channel my anxiety into anger. "What, do you *want* to get me thrown in jail?"

Maybe I can get angry, but Alana can conjure a rage that burns, incinerates, destroys. She advances on me fast with a whoosh of cold air and I stumble backward, my spine slamming into the windowsill.

"I told you I could make you look guilty, and I think we've proved that I can, haven't we? In case you've forgotten, Maya, *you're* the one who left me on that trail. You're the reason I'm not home with my mom." A hissed breath, low and terrible. "You're the reason I'm dead."

Her words hang in the crackling silence, undercut by a low rumble of thunder.

"I know," I whisper. "You think I don't know that?"

"You're on everybody's radar now, Maya. Even the police have an eye on you." She smirks down at me. Rain patters outside the window. "Only I can save you. Or destroy you. Your pick."

I say nothing, my heart trapped in a vise grip of panic. All I can hear is *You're the reason I'm dead.*

"Alana, I already told you," I say, barely a whisper. "I promise I'll help you with this. But look, before we even start, you need to *really* know what you're signing up for. Like, do you understand what you'd be doing if you possess a living person?"

She rolls her eyes. "I wouldn't be hurting anybody."

"You literally would be," I say, chewing on a hangnail. "Possession is . . . well, from what I understand, it's really complicated. And I don't know how to do it permanently."

"I don't care," she shoots back, lunging toward me again. My bedroom lights are extinguished with a *whoosh.* I reel backward. "Maya, you have no idea what it's like, sitting here knowing I'm dead and not being able to do a thing about it. Especially when there *is* something I can do. A way out."

"I know, but . . ."

"Do you know I came looking for you, after you left?" Her voice softens, and suddenly we're twelve and she's crying to me about her parents' divorce. Pitiful, lost, worthy of being saved. "I was sure you wouldn't actually leave me. After a couple minutes, I followed you all the way back down the trail, down to the parking lot."

I press my lips together tight, blinking fast to keep myself from tearing up.

"But you were leaving. I couldn't fucking believe it. I watched you slam the car door shut. Drove right out of the parking lot without even looking back to see if I was there."

The room is swimming with thick air, making it hard to breathe. I try not to let on how desperate I am to ask this question: "So what—what happened to you next?"

"I didn't want to go back down to LA, not right away." Something glints in her eyes. "I wanted you to worry about me. I wanted you to feel bad."

Amid my panic, my stomach gives a triumphant lurch. I *knew* that was something she would do. I knew she would hide out somewhere to teach me a lesson.

"So, you found some place near Antelope Valley to hunker down and make me feel like shit until I realized you were missing?" I try to focus on her terrifying, glowing face. "Alana . . . didn't you think that was insane? Your mom doesn't even know where you are. She's worried about you."

"Obviously I was planning to be back before she got home from Vancouver," she snarls. "When you're *dead*, you can't exactly send a text."

"So where did you go? What happened?"

She just watches me through narrowed eyes.

"Okay," I say, my lower lip quivering, a desperate weight of dread settling into my stomach. *Don't cry, don't cry.* "Fine, you don't have to tell me. I already told you I'll help you. What do you want—to possess me, or . . ."

She laughs, high and cold. "Possess *you*? Definitely not."

"So who, then?"

"Your little girlfriend."

I stare at her, confused, and she rolls her eyes.

"Rowan," she says. The name sounds alien on her lips.

"Are—are you serious?"

"What?" she asks. "Do you have a problem with that?"

"No," I say, trying to force my voice to be steady. Fake it, keep up the act. That's all I have to do for now. "Of course I don't have a problem with it. Just stop calling some random person my girlfriend when I've only ever spoken to her twice. It's weird."

"As you wish," Alana says, curtsying, and I want to slap her for trapping me in the middle of something so terrible when she knows I would never, ever turn my back on her.

She's pacing now, eyes gleaming in the moonlight. Outside, the wind has finally stilled, but there's a weird howling being carried through the trees.

"Rowan doesn't like me," I tell Alana, sinking down onto the window seat and trying to wrap my head around this conversation. "She thinks I'm some spoiled Valley Girl, probably. And she's obnoxious."

Alana snorts. "Is it important that you like each other?"

"Possession feeds off connection," I recite from one of the books Valeria gave me. Since I got home from Major Arcana, I've read each of those books cover to cover. They're dense and confusing and I can't tell if any information in there is even *true*, but at least it's something. "You might be able to force your way into an unwilling person who you don't really know, but it would be difficult. The victim's defenses need to be down for this to work, so they have to trust you. You haven't met this girl, so trust me. Her guard is *all* the way up."

"Oh, come on," Alana says, brushing my concerns aside with a wave of her hand. "Making people like you is the easy part."

She holds out one hand, palm facing me, and I reach out. I can just barely feel her touch—condensation on the other side of the glass. Almost warm. Almost real.

"We'll start planning soon, okay?"

"Why not right now?"

"Because . . ." Alana lowers her voice. "I think you're about to have your hands full."

The howling, wailing, louder and louder now. Lightning illuminates my bedroom—

No, not lightning. Lights.

Flicker in, flicker out. They wash Alana's face in red, blue, red, blue. A police car rushing down our street. A siren, screaming through the night. I hear voices outside, panicked.

My lips part in horror. Alana just watches me, and watches me, and then she grins.

"Finally," she says. "Looks like they found me."

CHAPTER TWELVE

OBITUARIES
Los Angeles Daily News

Alana Marina Murray, 18

Alana M. Murray, 18, of North Hollywood, was discovered deceased on the evening of May 8, 2024. She was born in Denver, Colorado, and moved to Los Angeles with her mother at the age of ten. Alana was a senior at Coldwater Canyon School for Girls, where she played soccer and lacrosse, served on the Student Council, participated in school plays, and achieved stellar grades. She would have attended Smith College this fall.

When not at school, Alana loved to sing, take photos, hike, and read fantasy novels. She was an avid practitioner of yoga and a frequent volunteer at the San Fernando Valley Sunshine Animal Shelter.

Alana adored spending time with her many friends and will be deeply missed by all who knew her and her joyous, infectious spirit.

Alana is survived by her loving parents, Melissa Cartwright Murray of North Hollywood and Anton Murray of Denver, Colorado; grandparents Patrick and Dahlia Murray of Boulder, Colorado; and several aunts, uncles, and cousins who loved her dearly. She also leaves behind Balto, her beloved husky. She was preceded in death by her maternal grandparents, John and Ella Cartwright.

Details of Alana's Celebration of Life are forthcoming, but it will be held at Elysian Fields Memorial Park and Funeral Home. The family will receive friends following the service. In lieu of flowers, please consider making a contribution in Alana's memory to the San Fernando Valley Sunshine Animal Shelter in Burbank.

■ ■ ■

There are three words that I dread hearing from anyone in my family. On the back porch the morning after Alana's body was pulled from the waters of Lake Ember, Jazmine finally says them.

"Are you okay?"

There's a screen separating the porch from the rest of the house. I stand behind it, watching my sister. When we were younger, she never wore her hair down. It would be twisted into a half ponytail, a messy bun, even a French braid. Today, it's loose and skimming her collarbones. She's wearing a camisole the color of a seashell, playing with the strap as she watches me over her shoulder.

"Hurry up," she says, but not in a mean way. "Don't let bugs into the house."

There are two wooden rocking chairs on the porch. She's sitting in one of them, a can of LaCroix in one hand. I walk past her and sink down onto the porch steps instead.

"Detective Ramirez called me this morning," Jazmine says into the quiet air. I don't turn around. "I told him that the lake was special to Alana, just like it's special to you. I emailed him a whole bunch of photos of you guys here together, as kids. I don't know if he really cared enough to see the photos, but I felt like it was important to show him."

I tug my Coldwater baseball cap lower over my eyes. The turquoise sky is streaked with pale clouds, the sun a brilliant, blinding orb rising high over the water's surface.

"You already knew she was dead, didn't you?"

Hearing someone else say *dead* sends a chill down my spine, and I angle away from Jazmine so she can't see the look on my face. I'm numb, rooted to the spot, unable to speak. My reaction last night, when I ran downstairs to a house washed in police car lights, had told my sister everything. They had already pulled Alana from the water's edge at that point, tucked her into a body bag. I didn't see any of it. Jazmine hugged me, crying into my hair, but I didn't cry. I don't cry, even now.

Dave Lopez, one of Jazmine's neighbors, was the one who found her. He'd walked the mile over to the dock last night to cover up his pontoon boat as the storm was starting, worried about the newly replaced white leather seats getting damaged.

Her body was half submerged in the water, half on the little rocky beach that leads to the boat docks. That's all I heard about it, because Jazmine has refused to let me watch the news; she even took my phone away overnight, tucking it in the drawer of her bedside table, so I couldn't search for further details. As if I wanted to know them.

"I had a feeling," I say to my sister now.

"Yeah. I figured." There's something strange, constricted, about Jazmine's voice.

I look down, trying to avoid facing the lake, but it's impossible. The surface glints in the brilliant morning sun. Blinding me. Normally by this hour of the morning, the lake would be filled with boaters, swimmers leaping off docks into the pristine water with a joyous shout followed by a splash. Sound carries so easily over the water. Today, a hush has fallen over Lake Ember. No one wants to set foot in the lake that claimed Alana's life.

Jazmine's eyes are boring a hole into the back of my head.

"Maya, your graduation this weekend . . . you know you don't have to go."

I bite my lip against the onslaught of tears threatening to spill over. It's Thursday, just a couple days away from the graduation ceremony. The idea of walking into that room in a white dress, collecting a diploma onstage, feels impossible.

"It's really important to you, I know," Jazmine continues. *You know?* I think. *You don't know anything about me.* "But with everything else going on, I thought you might not want to face that whole auditorium of people."

Letting the silence settle, I stare at the splintering wood of the porch steps, sun-warmed beneath me. The sharp edge presses against the backs of my thighs.

"I don't care," I mumble finally. "About graduation. About any of it."

"Okay. I'll call your dad. Explain everything. And listen . . ." She hesitates, and I chance a glance over my shoulder. Her dark eyes are watching me carefully, like she's sizing me up. Like she might be a little afraid of me. "The way I reacted when you told me about your college rejections . . . I'm so sorry, Maya. That caught me off guard, so I said some things I didn't mean. People don't need college to be successful, you know? Despite what they tell you at Coldwater."

I snort. "You needed a college degree to open up Blue Skies."

"Yeah, but I didn't get my business degree until later, re-member? Listen, Maya, you can change your mind a hundred times. I want you to know that. You have years, decades, to decide where you see yourself."

Yeah, I do. But Alana doesn't.

Jazmine stands up, brushes a quick hand across the top of my head, and walks back into the house, letting the screen door slam. Her life has been disrupted, and it's all my fault. No wonder she barely wants to be around me.

She doesn't know what's coming, but I do. She has no idea how quickly I will lose her love. How quickly I will make it happen.

Where do I see myself? I close my eyes, lean back against the railing, and green and purple swirls across the sky. Some-where northern and freezing, icy water that creaks and groans, crooked and bare trees that line the horizon. A little log cabin with one of those wood-burning stoves. I'll cook myself break-fast, lunch, and dinner, and I won't have a table—I'll just sit on the floor, listen to the wind, feel light. Maybe I'll have a dog. A loyal one who only follows me.

In the deep dark, we'll walk outside—I'll get him a little coat so he won't be too cold, and I'll wear my puffy North Face and thick hiking boots, and we'll wade through the snow. Cold powder. The northern lights will scream through the silence and I'll hold my breath.

Alone wouldn't feel so bad like that. Just me and a dog and the sky.

. . .

Jazmine is in her bedroom on the phone with Dad, I assume discussing my request to skip out on graduation. As the afternoon sun pours through my window, I grab a tank top and a pair of frayed jean shorts out of the box of stuff Dad sent me, dressing quickly.

The room feels quiet without Alana's ghost skulking around. Although who knows, she could be watching anyway. The thought sends a chill creeping up my spine. It was bad enough realizing that Alana can manifest every night to haunt me if she wants to, but now I have to worry about her invisibly spying on everything I do during the day.

There's a creaking from the hallway, my sister speaking in a low voice. I wait until she's descended the staircase before tiptoeing out of my room and peeking down around the railing. Jazmine's in the kitchen, cradling her phone between her ear and shoulder.

". . . said there were signs of foul play," she's saying. "That's the rumor, anyway. And there was no reason for Alana to be up here, right? ... It can't be a coincidence that Maya decides to come up to Lake Ember for the first time in *years* and then they find Alana's body here days later. She must know something."

I swallow hard, tightening my hand against the railing. Is that why she seemed weird around me earlier? Does my own sister suspect me now?

"Yeah, I heard they're coming to town. The Carter-Holloway girl, right?" She lowers her voice and I strain to hear the words that come next. "Down by Reservoir Road. I saw the cars lining up...."

Holding my breath, I ease my way down the stairs, avoiding the creakiest step. Is she serious?

Is Elise in Lake Ember?

...

The cars are parked all along Chaparral Street, bumper to bumper. I'm grateful I decided to borrow Jazmine's creaky old bike, because it would've been a real task to navigate my car down here without sideswiping anyone. I navigate around the bend of the road that I'm pretty sure connects to Reservoir eventually.

Thunder rumbles low in the distance. Through the trees, I can just see the gray surface of the lake, dull on this cloudy day, and I avert my eyes fast. This weather reminds me of when I was a kid swimming in our pool as the clouds rolled in. Rain is rare in Los Angeles, so you just let it happen. The memories sting now. I remember Alana and me, twelve with skinny legs and matching braids, jumping off the deep end of my backyard pool. I would float underwater at the bottom of the pool and look up, watch the raindrops hit the water's surface. The world from upside down.

Was that how Alana felt when she died?

Stop it. I shake my head, trying to block out the intrusive thought, but it batters against my brain anyway. I don't know a lot about drowning, other than the fact that it's one of the worst ways to die (is there a good way?)—but I know Alana could swim. I remember her practicing her backstroke in my pool, showing off with backward dives. She honed her skills at that stupid summer camp where she met Elise, the two of them spending all summer making up synchronized routines. I can't picture her sinking beneath the murky water, pulled down by seaweed and suffocated in the depths. Trying to breathe, lungs filling with silt, wishing I was there to pull her out—

I clench my fists. *Pull yourself together.*

No sooner do I think this than I see an ominous white van looming up ahead, the KLSC logo emblazoned on the side. It jogs a memory from the news my dad used to watch at the lake house every summer: Santa Clarita County local news. My stomach turns over as I climb off my bike awkwardly, squinting down the winding street.

There's a buzzing in my pocket. I tug my phone out, frowning at the screen.

> **Jazmine Reyes** ✦˖💌
> hey maya, where are you?

> **Jazmine Reyes** ✦˖💌
> if you're out, make sure to stay away from reservoir road, okay?

just give me a call when you can??

Missed call from Jazmine Reyes ✨🌿
Missed call from Jazmine Reyes ✨🌿

My heart is banging against my rib cage. Only half aware of what I'm doing, I lean Jazmine's bike up against a tree and jog down the street.

For the first time since it all happened, images explode behind my eyes. What does a body look like when it's been submerged in water for days? I had imagined her porcelain-pale, laid out on a bed of sand by the boat dock, hands folded angelically on her chest. Stupid. People—corpses—don't stay perfect in the water. Her skin was probably blue from freezing, eyes wide and staring—

I press a hand against my chest, trying to breathe. Up ahead, a knot of people are squeezed together in a clearing, the lake just a gray glint in the background. A voice rings out loud and clear over the crowd.

". . . to all of you who have come to pay your respects today, thank you," a woman says. Her voice wavers so much I don't immediately recognize it, but then it clicks into place. Melissa Murray cuts a forlorn figure at the front of the crowd of mourners, round sunglasses obscuring her blue eyes. Instead of black, she's dressed in all white.

"It means more than I can say. Please—please join me in a moment of silence."

It falls, immediate. Deafening. Wind rustles leaves in the trees high above me. Water laps against the shore. People bow their heads and no one moves, no one breathes. I press my fingers tight against the bark of my tree, hidden.

They're all here. Parents of girls from my class, people from town. This is like the candlelight vigil, but so, so much worse.

Somebody taps me on the shoulder and it takes everything in me not to scream. I whirl around.

Rowan Sokolov is behind me, dressed in a black T-shirt with the sleeves rolled up. Her slate gray eyes are sparkling with interest.

"They're talking about the body they found in the lake," she whispers. "Did you hear about that? Pretty fucking freaky, huh? Nothing like this *ever* happens here."

"I know her," I say coldly.

Rowan freezes, color draining from her face. I step closer to the group of mourners—and my heart stutters and skips. Mrs. Murray is still standing at the podium, but she's moving aside to allow a tight knot of teenage girls to step up beside her. They cluster so closely together that it's hard for me to pick out who is who, but I would recognize Elise anywhere. She looks the same as ever, strong and steady, coral lipstick applied perfectly, dark curls pulled back with a headband.

"Alana Murray was my best friend," she says into the mic, staring straight ahead, and the lie hits me like a dagger to the chest. "She was kind and funny, athletic and smart. Everyone who met her loved her. Her death was a tragedy that will forever shape my life. I will never forget her, but it's important that we find out how she ended up here. I urge anyone with information about Alana's death to come forward."

I stare at Elise's face and feel the string holding me to my old life snap.

"Thank you, sweetie," Mrs. Murray says quietly, and my heart drops. "Detective Stephen Ramirez from the LAPD and Santa Clarita Sheriff Joanna McKinley will join me now—I'd like to thank them for all of their . . . their hard work over the past few days as we searched for Alana."

A woman who I don't know steps up to the microphone, auburn hair pulled back into a sleek ponytail. Her face is gaunt and solemn.

"First and foremost, I would like to extend my most sincere condolences to not only Melissa and Anton Murray, but to the entire Murray family, and all those who loved Alana deeply." Sheriff McKinley's voice is like a wire pulled tight. "I ask that you please respect their privacy as they grieve their beloved daughter. While you are likely aware that a body confirmed to be Alana Murray was located on the shores of Lake Ember early last night, the cause of her death has not been determined at this time."

She takes a deep breath, seeming to steel herself. "However, at this time we do believe that foul play was likely involved. We are treating this investigation as a potential homicide."

A gasp ripples through the assembled crowd, followed by snippets of chatter.

Sheriff McKinley raises her voice. "The boat launch, beaches, and lake will remain closed to the public until further notice."

This is how it always starts, with a ringing in my ears. A slow acceleration like a roller coaster climbing the track, then the sharp plummet where my body goes numb. Panic.

"Hey," Rowan says sharply. I can barely see her, but I feel her hovering over me—I'm kneeling in the grass somehow. "Hey, Rosier, are you okay?"

"I'm fine," I say, even as I taste saliva gathering in my mouth, a telltale sign that I'm seconds from vomiting all over the ground. *Homicide.* They think someone *killed* her? "Just go. Leave me alone."

"—remind you all that this is an active, ongoing investigation." Sheriff McKinley is speaking again. "Lake Ember locals, we ask you to please respect the boundaries of this investigation and to not interfere in any way."

The world is too far away. It's too close. It hits me again and again, a rush of colors and noise pressing up against me and suffocating me, too fast too fast. Ringing in my ears, hollowness inside me, a black hole spreading and spreading.

Name three things you can see.

My nails scratching hard along my arm, leaving white marks. The carpet of leaves and dirt and twigs, too much too much.

Name . . . okay, start over. Name three things you can see.

A shadowy figure approaching Alana at Antelope Valley, dragging her into a van while she screams, and driving her to the closest body of water—a dump site. The barrel of a gun raised in her direction. Thick hands wrapping around her throat and pressing tight, squeezing the air out of her lungs.

Rowan stoops down an inch or two until she can look me directly in the eye.

"Hey, it's okay! It's okay. Look at me, Rosier. I'm gonna get you out of here."

I force myself to focus on Rowan's face. Her dark eyebrows are knitted together in concern as she wraps an arm around my shoulder, steering me toward another well-worn path that turns into a paved road.

We did it. We left them behind. I survived.

I suck in a long, slow breath. Pulling myself together takes time. Sometimes it hurts, like glass shards taped back together, keeping their sharp edges. But I can always do it eventually.

"S-sorry." I gulp, trying to ignore the worried crease that appears between Rowan's eyebrows. I squeeze my hands up my forearms as we walk, trying to jolt myself out of my panic spiral. "My sister's bike. I left it somewhere."

"It's no big deal, I'll find it later."

I wipe a hand across my face, which is now coated with a thin sheen of sweat. "Nobody even thought to tell me about it."

"The press conference?" Rowan asks, and I notice for the first time that she's literally holding me up. One warm arm is tight around my shoulders, fingers digging into my skin, as we trudge along the road in the direction of Jazmine's house.

"Yeah," I say, shuddering. "How could they just stand there and . . . and say that? They think someone killed her. They should've told me first."

"I'm sorry. That—that really sucks." Rowan shoots a sidelong glance at me. "Were those your friends? Those girls at the podium?"

I want to say no, I've never seen them before in my life, I don't know them at all, because that's what it feels like. But it's not true. I remember Elise in the school bathroom, forehead pressed to mine, trying to get me to breathe in sync with her during my panic attacks. "My sister gets them too," she said. "They always end. It's not forever. Breathe slow." I loved her so much for that. After school, she bought me a peach green tea lemonade and told me that anxiety isn't anything to be ashamed of. It was honest and real and she understood. She was my friend and she *understood*.

"Yeah." My throat is dry and my voice comes out hoarse. "Something like that."

INTERLUDE

———

ONE YEAR EARLIER

IT'S THE LAST week of junior year, and I start that Monday the way I start every morning: hopping into the passenger seat of Elise Carter-Holloway's car.

"Got your favorite!" she sings out over the shriek of the radio, shaking a pink Stanley tumbler at me. The ice rattles. Elise is particular about certain luxuries: no need for a fancy car, hence the ancient Camry with no air-conditioning or Bluetooth capabilities, but she can only start her morning with cold brew from home. She always makes mine at six in the morning and bottles it. The Stanley has my name printed neatly across the front, embellished with Sharpie-markered flowers and smiley faces.

"Thanks." I grin, accepting the tumbler and taking a big sip from the straw. "So, is this the summer you're finally going to accept cold air into your life, or . . . ?"

"Maya, that would be giving in." Elise has a knack for smiling even when she sounds fake-exasperated. It's comforting, makes me feel like no matter what, she's never *really* annoyed with me. "I've made it a whole year with the Hadesmobile. Plus, this way we get beautiful springtime fresh air."

"Yeah, by cranking these window handle thingies like it's 1950."

"So, temp check on Miss Alana?" Elise asks, flipping her turn signal as we ease around the corner from my house. "Are we picking her up today?"

I hesitate. Over the past few years, Elise has become a professional at navigating my relationship with Alana—at least, in my opinion. Who knows if she actually feels that way. Regardless, she understands that things are different with us. That we need our time to ourselves for dates and anniversaries, that we have sleepovers she's not part of. It was definitely easier when we were a group of three equals, but I would never go back to that. Not when I finally have what I want: Alana and I, girlfriends for two years now.

But Elise can sense the changes in the air, like a weather barometer. She picks up on tension before I do sometimes—if my eyes are red-rimmed because Alana made me cry over something stupid, if Alana's in a bad mood because I told her I felt too anxious to go out for dinner. She does her best to defuse the tension, but I'm sure it weighs on her. If I were her, I would fucking hate being the best friend of a couple.

"I think Alana's mom was gonna drop her off today on the way to some meeting," I lie easily. Whether Elise believes me or not, I have no idea. But she winks, heart-shaped sunglasses sliding low on her nose, and just like that, we glide past Alana's street.

...

That afternoon after classes, I'm changing into a sports bra in the locker room when I sense someone hovering behind me. I turn and there's Madison Kim, short black hair just skimming the tips of her prominent collarbones. She's already changed into her clothes for soccer practice; watching me carefully, she itches her ankle with the tip of one Nike sneaker.

"Hey," I say, giving her a funny look. Madison's cool; we have Pre-Calc together.

"Hi, Maya." Her voice is soft, like she's talking to a puppy in a shelter. I pause, just standing there in my bra and shorts. "Listen, if you ever need anything in practice, you know you can ask me, right?"

"Wh—" The question is so bizarre, although seemingly kind, that I have no idea how to process it. "Um, that's really nice, Madison."

"You know, if you need some water or to take a breather." She's still using that voice. Does she think I suddenly suck at soccer or something? I'm not great, sure, but I'm solid at defense and always have been. "My mom takes Zoloft, so I know it can make people feel a little weird sometimes."

I stiffen, cold all over. My mouth goes dry.

"I don't—did somebody say . . ."

"Oh, the team was just talking about it earlier," Madison says, still completely innocent, like she's doing me some great kindness. "You know, ways to help you with your problems."

Panic rises in my chest, tightening my airways; without thinking about how it'll look, I raise a hand to press against my throat. On the other side of the lockers, there's a sudden rise and fall of laughter—my teammates giggling. One of the girls pokes her head around the corner, then disappears.

Listening to every word, I'm sure. Convinced that I'm some kind of monster.

Barely aware of my movements, I grab my uniform polo and tug it on.

"I didn't mean to upset you." Madison looks really alarmed now, watching me step into my sneakers; my legs are shaking. "I heard that you have panic attacks, right? The nurse holds on to your meds for you in case you totally freak out?"

Nausea churns my stomach, bile rising up my throat. Somehow, I make it out of the locker room, out of the athletic building, before puking up my entire lunch on the sidewalk of the senior parking lot, and that's where Alana finds me.

Her hand is steady and sure against my back.

"Oh my god, I'm gonna kill her," she snarls. "Elise must've told everyone."

"W-why would she do that?" I choke, still bent over, hair falling across my face. With a practiced hand, Alana pulls the strands away, holding them in a loose ponytail at the nape of my neck. "Why would she want to hurt me?"

"Some people just don't think." Alana's rage grounds me, keeps me safe. "Do you want me to take you home?"

"No." I straighten up and wipe my mouth with the back of my hand. "No, I think I want to be alone."

. . .

I catch an Uber home but remember too late that my phone location is shared with Elise. She must check it, because when I hop out of the car, backpack swinging over one shoulder, she's already standing in my driveway. The stupid Camry with peeling black paint is parked crooked along my street.

"Maya," she says instantly. "I heard what happened. I—"

"Of course you did," I spit. Behind me, there's a roar as my Uber guns it back down the street. "Elise, what the fuck? I thought you had my back! All the girls on the team magically know about my anxiety and think I'm some kind of—"

"Maya," Elise interrupts, reaching for me. Golden bracelets jingle around her wrist. "Listen to me, okay? I didn't tell them. I would never betray you."

"I don't believe that. Madison knew stuff that I only told *you*. About—about the school nurse."

"Why would you not believe me?" Her voice shakes, lower lip wobbling, the telltale sign of her brewing tears.

Alana taught me better, I want to scream, but I don't, because she won't get it. Alana taught me long ago that everyone I love will leave me, and they'll do it because I'm too difficult. And here it is, spoken into existence. Elise thinks I'm messed up, broken. No one wants to deal with a friend like that.

Mom died. Dad checked out. Jazmine doesn't visit. Livia hates me. Elise is the next name I'll add to my list.

She reaches for me, but I tug out of her grip, my backpack falling to the driveway. The zipper splits and my pencil case breaks open with a clatter.

"Don't touch me!" Dimly, I'm aware of how loud my voice is.

"If they know all of that and they're laughing at you, then they're shitty friends, Maya!" Elise shouts. A tear spills down her cheek. "I don't know what else to tell you! And I wasn't the *only* person you told this stuff to, don't you remember? Alana knows too. Clearly, you placed your trust in the wrong fucking person—"

163

"Yeah, I guess I did," I shoot back. "Get the hell out of my life, Elise. I *never* want to see you again, do you understand me?"

She stares at me, an anguished, searching look that I can't quite understand. It's a look that will revisit me in dreams for years, although I don't know that yet. All I know is that Elise Carter-Holloway was my friend, and now she's a stranger.

Worse than that. She's an enemy.

Alana says, *She was never good with secrets.*

Alana says, *She loves gossip more than she ever loved you.*

Alana says, *What did I tell you? People always leave. But I will never leave you.*

It's just the two of us now.

CHAPTER THIRTEEN

DARK WATER Podcast, Season 3, Episode 1—Transcript

KATIE FITZGERALD: Welcome back to another episode of *Dark Water,* where the air is always chilly, the sky is always stormy, and, of course, the waters are always treacherous and deep. Here on *Dark Water,* we investigate some of the most terrifying true crimes to ever occur on the seas, lakes, and rivers of our terrifying planet—so let's dive right in.

[DARK WATER theme song plays]

KATIE: Hey, friends! You're listening to *Dark Water,* hosted by me, Katie Fitzgerald, and my hype-person and ever-faithful sidekick, Ty Jackson. Today, we're kicking off season three by taking you to sunny Southern California. Lake Ember, a reservoir tucked away in the stunning Los Padres National Forest, is not necessarily known as a Los Angeles County hot spot. Relatively quiet, this lake welcomes families for fishing, boating, and kayaking. By all accounts, it's a beautiful place to bring the kids for a day in the sunshine.

It's the last place you'd ever expect to find a dead body.

TY: Aw, shit. I should've seen this coming.

KATIE: Now, this week, Ty, we're going to tread carefully as we discuss this case, as it's an active one. That's right—just yesterday, the body of high school senior Alana Murray was discovered at the east end of Lake Ember by a lake community resident. Alana had been reported missing by her mother three days prior. But before we talk about the specifics concerning Alana Murray's tragic death, and the mysterious circumstances that are still part of an ongoing LAPD investigation as we speak, I want to talk about her life.

Here's what we know about Alana Murray: She was popular, athletic, intelligent—headed off to Smith College in the fall, as a matter of fact. But intriguingly, she was also a young queer woman. Of course, as members of the LGBTQ+ community ourselves, Alana's story really reached out and grabbed us.

TY: Sure—I mean, you never know, right? What was her home life like? Could somebody at school have made her a target?

KATIE: Well, as this investigation is still in progress, we won't speculate much further, but it does makes me worry about the mental health of today's queer youth. Local sources have stated that Alana had a girlfriend, one of her high school classmates, although the girlfriend in question has yet to speak up about Alana's tragic death.

TY: Well, sure! She probably feels awful. That poor girl. Imagine finding the courage to love someone proudly and openly as a teenager, and then losing her before your eyes. I wouldn't wish that on my worst enemy.

KATIE: The Alana Murray case is compelling because so many of us can see ourselves in her, right? A young queer person just trying to find her place in the world, excited to go off to college, navigating complicated relationships.

TY: Totally relatable.

KATIE: Exactly. And that's why we're going to talk more about Alana herself: not just a victim who washed up on the shores of a California lake, but a beautiful and talented person who lit up the lives of everyone she knew.

So here's what we know: Alana Marina Murray was born on November 8, 2005, to Melissa and Anton Murray. At the time, the family was living in Denver, Colorado, and life was a bit of a struggle for them. Melissa was a middle-school English teacher, and Anton was a seasonal ski instructor. Things looked up after their divorce; Melissa inherited some money from a parent, and her screenwriting career took off. She moved with Alana to Los Angeles in 2016, and Alana was enrolled in the prestigious Coldwater Canyon School for Girls.

Here are the quick things to know about Alana Murray, according to her past social media posts: She was a Scorpio—I know you were going to ask, Ty! She was a skilled athlete, playing soccer and lacrosse, and she volunteered at a local animal shelter during her free time. Her favorite holiday was New Year's Eve, she saw Taylor Swift in concert five times, and more than anything, she loved her girlfriend, Maya Rosier.

And what do we know about Maya, you might ask? Well, the girlfriend Alana left behind is known as a stellar student—you have to be to go to that school—and she excels in math and science. Up until her senior year, she was active on campus, joining Student Council, the GSA, and Girls Who Code. But then . . .

TY: Then what?!

KATIE: Her social media goes mysteriously dark. Well . . . not dark, just weird. It just becomes a shrine to Alana.

TY: Jeez.

KATIE: And that's not even the most interesting part. Many of our loyal listeners have been tweeting about this ongoing case, wanting us to cover it, because of an interesting connection between Maya Rosier and the location where Alana's body was found.

Property records in the public domain tell us that Maya's father owns a house on Lake Ember—a house that was actually purchased in the 1970s by his father, a real estate developer. Dig deeper into Maya and Alana's social media and you'll find that both girls have a history with the lake. It seems like they spent quite a bit of time vacationing there together as preteens.

TY: Well, it's kind of weird, but it could be a coincidence, right? Lots of rich people from LA probably have vacation homes up there.

KATIE: That was my thought at first—totally a coincidence. But then our viewers pointed out that according to her Instagram, Maya Rosier was actually at her family's lake house when Alana's body was found.

■ ■ ■

At night, Alana's ghost returns, just like I knew she would.

Ever since Rowan brought me home in the afternoon, tear-streaked and still on the shaky edges of a panic attack, my sister has been fussing over me. She made me lie down in my room to recover, bringing me tea in her favorite Stanford mug and talking to Rowan in a hushed voice in the kitchen. Although Rowan has no idea how to speak in a hushed voice, so I could catch the gist of their conversation through phrases that rose up the stairwell.

You're saying her girlfriend was the dead girl . . .

friends are in Lake Ember . . .

difficult relationship . . .

wouldn't have bothered her if I'd known . . .

I rolled over, burying my face in my pillow, willing sleep to claim me. Unfortunately, it's not that easy. It's been hours, and I'm still wide awake, under the watchful eye of Alana. For once, she doesn't seem to want to talk.

Moonlight pools on the floor and I watch it through slitted eyes, the way she paces through the silver glow without casting a shadow. The pacing is unnerving—in life, she could sit still for hours on end, reading a book or getting lost in a new album on Spotify. After a while, she sits down against my closet door, knees pulled to her chest.

"Was my mom crying?" Alana asks finally. I'm hovering somewhere between sleep and waking, and at the sound of her voice, I roll over onto my side, blankets rustling.

"She was sad," I tell her. My voice is hoarse. "But I didn't see her cry."

"That's probably good. Mom would be embarrassed to cry on national TV."

I swallow hard. "How did you know it's national news? It looked local."

"Eavesdropping on your sister's TV. She was watching the coverage earlier."

"You're not going to tell me anything, are you?" I ask, brushing the sleep from my eyes. "Nothing about what happened to you?"

She sidesteps the question completely. "How long do you think you have until they find out you were the last person to see me alive?"

I sit up in bed, pushing my hair off my face. "Who?"

"The cops. Duh." She stands up, walking to the foot of my bed. I'm not yet used to the way she moves. Alana was graceful in life, but in death, there's a preternatural quality to the way she walks, gliding like a breath of air, like fog appearing on a windowpane.

I freeze, eyes widening. "What are you talking about? Is that even true?"

"That's what they'll think." She lets out a humorless laugh, and I watch her stare toward my bedroom window, take in the dark trees washed in silver moonlight, the water lapping gently at the shore. "If I were you—and thank god I'm not, for myriad reasons—I would be working really, really hard on getting my story straight right about now."

And then before I can blink, before I can breathe, before I can do anything at all, she's gone again. She's gone, and I'm still sitting here in the cold dark, trying to catch my breath.

She's lying, I tell myself. *Lying to scare you. Don't believe a word of it. She's gone, and you need to rest so you can figure out how to get through this.*

But I don't sleep. I watch the shadows fall, long and slow and sinister across the hardwood floor, for hours.

. . .

The next morning dawns bright and beautiful. Sunshine peeks through cracks in the clouds and speckles the driveway. I watch it from my bed, still in my pajamas, willing myself to leave the house.

I swing my legs over the side of my bed, the events of yesterday still rattling around in my mind. It's not easy for me to forget the way Rowan guided me out of the woods until I was back at the house. Not many people know how to talk me down from a panic attack like that, and even fewer people would've cared enough to try. My first day of art camp in middle school, I had a panic attack in my cabin and got sent home by counselors who rolled their eyes behind my back. The people who were supposed to help me failed me—but Rowan didn't fail me at all.

And now Alana wants me to lead her to her doom.

I owe Rowan a thank-you for what she did. The thought of willingly seeking her out makes me nauseous, but I push past it and head out the door anyway.

It's not a long walk to Blue Skies—ten minutes tops, trees lining the road, bowing in the breeze. Before I know it, the hand-painted wooden sign is dangling over my head, a melodic bell chiming as customers stroll in and out.

It's 9:30 in the morning. I imagine Rowan will be in the back, dealing with the morning rush, but when I walk in, she's deep in conversation with a table full of girls around our age.

". . . and so I told them, maybe I just like wearing them short! Long nails just get in the way."

The girls all shriek with laughter.

"You are *awful*!"

"Rowan, you did *not*!"

"I did, but then I said, 'You know, when I'm working on cars.' He had no idea what I was talking about."

"That's so funny," one girl exclaims.

I bite the inside of my cheek so hard I taste copper. Nothing indicates an amusing joke more than somebody loudly proclaiming how funny it is.

It looks like Rowan's about to launch into some other stupid story, but when she adjusts her pale blue baseball cap and looks up, she catches my eye. I cross my arms, watching her with my eyebrows raised.

"'Scuse me, guys," she says to the group, looking right into my eyes. "Apparently the Valley Girl princess I ordered just arrived."

As she walks over, the four girls at the table stare at me like they're trying to singe a hole right through me. I try to keep my attention focused on Rowan.

"Sorry," I say, not bothering to lower my voice. "I didn't mean to tear you away from your groupies."

She smirks, lopsided. "Jealous, Rosier?"

"Not even a little bit."

"How are you doing today?" Rowan asks, her smirk fading. It rattles me for a second.

"I . . . I'm fine."

"I'm just gonna be blunt—if I'm teasing you too much, please just tell me, and I'll stop giving you shit."

My mouth opens, then closes again. I was prepared for more banter, not empathy.

"No," I say finally. "It's okay. I just came to say, um . . . thanks. For yesterday. That was a really hard thing for me to witness, and I don't know what I would've done if you hadn't been there. So. Thank you."

173

Rowan's eyebrows raise. I can tell she's caught off guard, but she says, "It was no problem, Rosier."

I bite my lip. "Okay. Yeah. So . . . that's why I came here."

"Do you want to hang out?" she asks. "If I were you, I wouldn't want to just . . . sit at home by myself."

I look at Rowan's face, gray eyes wide and full of concern. Think of how Alana wants to possess her, destroy her. A spider capturing its prey in a gossamer web, so thin and perfect it might almost be invisible.

And just like that, I'm *crying*. Crying in the tea shop, in front of everyone. Crying, really crying, for the first time in months.

A warm hand presses against the center of my back, guiding me through the door and out onto the sidewalk.

"Sorry." My voice is choked by tears and snot, which makes me want to disintegrate.

"Don't be sorry for crying, Rosier."

I wipe my cold hands across my cheeks. My tears feel like fire.

"Again, if you want me to leave you alone, I promise I will," Rowan says. "Rest assured that you bug me just as much as I bug you. However! You seem like a girl who's in dire need of a distraction, so I'd be more than happy to provide one."

"No, I don't need a distraction." I can't make the hard edge come back into my voice, can't channel Alana when there are tears streaming down my face. This is a disaster. "I can't think about anything else—I need to know what happened to Alana. That probably sounds like a bad idea, but it's how I feel. I want to go there."

Rowan frowns, eyes scanning my face. "Okay. Go where?"

"Where she died." I wipe the tears away impatiently.

Rowan is watching me carefully, but it's different than the way Jazmine's been looking at me. Like I'm a specimen to be analyzed, or a delicate vial of poison that could shatter and spill at any moment. Maybe Rowan really does think I'm annoying, but when she smiles at me, it's encouraging, kind. She pulls off her baseball cap and shakes out her short black hair.

"Listen, my shift's over in half an hour. I can get Emily to cover for me." She glances over at the shop, then back at me. "You shouldn't go alone."

CHAPTER FOURTEEN

Thread: twitter.com/allisawyer97

Allison Sawyer

@allisawyer97

Been following the Alana Murray situation and it's just wild, seriously. I saw a photo of Alana Murray and her girlfriend, I guess her name is Maya? Well, I was hiking last weekend and saw two girls, and I KNOW it was the two of them.

12:08 PM–May 10, 2024-2.1M Views

> **Allison Sawyer @allisawyer97**
>
> Replying to @allisawyer97
>
> Okay, my replies are out of control, so: 1) it was definitely her hiking with Alana and 2) yes I have called the police and given them a statement. This was before Alana was declared missing, morning of May 4. Again, yes I'm certain it was these two girls.

Allison Sawyer @allisawyer97

Replying to @allisawyer97

A couple people are asking me about the dynamic between them. I went up and asked if they were okay because they were definitely in the middle of an argument. The girl with lighter hair (maya) looked like she was about to hit alana so I walked up to check on them. Maya didn't talk to me at all but alana did.

Allison Sawyer @allisawyer97

Replying to @allisawyer97

alana said that things were fine and that neither of them needed help. Most important thing I noticed is that alana seemed really quiet, almost shy, not like how people in the media are describing her. She told me they were talking about school and could barely meet my eyes

Allison Sawyer @allisawyer97

Replying to @allisawyer97

People are asking me if I think maya is guilty. I can't answer that, when I saw them they were at antelope valley and the lake where alana ended up being found is about 15-20 mins away. I don't even know if the two girls drove together. I can only tell you what I saw: them having a heated conversation and alana sounding nervous to talk to me

Allison Sawyer @allisawyer97

Replying to @allisawyer97

I've provided my statement to police and from here on out, it's in their hands. I'm closing my DMs because this is getting way too much attention.

···

Rowan's car is an abomination, a box on wheels. It started rattling before we'd even left Mira Monte Road, and as she cuts a sharp right and heads back toward the lake, I start to wonder if the wheels might fall off.

"What *is* this thing?" I ask as we drive along a road that winds through dense trees, the air thick with the scent of pine. "It looks like the car from Jurassic Park."

"An Isuzu Trooper," she says proudly. Like I'm just supposed to know what that means. We rattle past a rambling mansion flying a battered California flag, half-buried in trees. Creaking oaks, a brick shed with firewood stacked outside, a tiny cottage with a blooming flower and succulent garden out front.

"So you're *sure* you're okay going to the lake?" Rowan asks.

"I'll be fine. I look out at the lake every day and feel okay," I lie. The truth is that at night, the water breaking across rocks on the shoreline keeps me awake, staring at the ceiling. Wondering what it would be like to gasp for air and choke on briny lake water instead, sink like a stone into the murky depths.

"Take a look out the window," Rowan says, pointing like a cheerful tour guide. I can't help but wonder if she's just trying to distract me. "Lake Ember High! That's where I went."

The building is warm red brick, two stories, freshly mowed green grass stretching out front and dotted with benches and weathered picnic tables. It looks nice—small, manageable, the kind of place where nothing too terrible could possibly happen. Instantly, I'm jealous of her. I'm envious of her cool mom, her non-anxious brain, her town full of friends who would never turn their backs on her.

"It's a small school—like, three hundred of us. So we all

knew each other. Everybody went to Lake Ember Elementary, then to the middle school, then here. No other options, except for the ones that got shipped off to fancy boarding schools." She brushes her hair out of her eyes. "For the privileged, of course."

My cheeks flush. I haven't had a reason to tell her, but Coldwater Canyon School for Girls is about as far from this place as possible. Tucked along Mulholland Drive, it's a series of sprawling stone buildings blocked from the real world with an iron gate, classrooms where all the students sit around Harkness tables and share ideas without raising their hands. At graduation, we wear white dresses and carry single-stem roses and parade across the auditorium stage.

Or, I guess, *they* wear white dresses. Not me.

"Are you okay?" Rowan asks, noting my expression. The lake is closer now, glinting through the trees as she turns off Main Street. I flinch away from the sight. "You just graduated, right?"

My lip quivers. Great. I can't cry in front of Rowan *again*. "No, it's tomorrow. I'm not going back to LA for it. I'll still get my diploma and everything, but I felt like ... with everything going on ..."

I trail off.

Rowan glances over curiously. I run a hand over my face.

"I don't even remember my first day at Coldwater. Isn't that weird? I started there so long ago—I was five. My dad has pictures, so I know I wore this dumb dress with a big sunflower on it and walked across the stage for kindergarten orientation, but that's all. That school was my home since before I can remember, and now I won't even get to say goodbye." I slump lower in my seat. "At graduation, you walk across the same stage. It's supposed to be like you're completing a journey. Wear a white dress, carry a red rose. I spent my whole life thinking I would do that."

"That makes sense." Rowan taps her fingers on the steering wheel. "That would make me sad, too."

"I mean, it's not like anybody will miss me. They all think I'm a freak." I lick my lips, staring at the trees as they fly by. "I'm not going to college next year, and at a school like mine, where they're priming you for college by the time you can read, that's suicide. I messed up this year. By the end of the fall, my favorite teachers would barely look at me. They all taught Jazmine, who, as you know, is the light of everyone's fucking life, and none of them could figure out why I wasn't more like her."

Rowan cocks her head sympathetically.

"It wasn't always like this." My voice is strained. "For years, I *loved* school. I was really involved. Student council, the honor committee, all that crap. I tried theater, piano lessons, the soccer team. I wanted to try everything. But then . . ."

Rowan eases the car off Lake Street, heading down the short dirt road that leads to the boat launch. I take a deep breath. I don't want to talk about this, especially not here, but somehow I can't make myself stop.

"My mom died." Next to me, I feel Rowan tense. "She was sick. It happened when I was eight, but I didn't really let myself feel it until I was older. Everything I did was to make her proud—good grades, all the activities and awards. But then, things got . . . bad. I messed up."

"Rosier, I'm—"

"Yale was my first choice." I push past her interruption. Each word is handpicked, careful. It's not true, but the truth doesn't matter anymore. "My mom went there, so I applied early decision. But ... turns out places like that don't want you if your grades start sucking because you've had a total mental breakdown, which I did at the start of senior year. So."

"I'm sorry," Rowan says, gentler than I've ever heard her. She puts the car in park, but neither of us get out. "Are you—"

"Yes," I say, opening the passenger-side door. It creaks ominously. "I'm sure I want to do this."

The beach at the boat launch is different from the one I went to as a kid; that one was sandy and wide, perfect for spreading towels on the ground or doing cannonballs off the dock that jutted into the cool water. We were never allowed to play at this one. The sand is rough and sprinkled through with rocks. It's a thoroughfare used for getting to your boats, dragging plastic coolers, hopping into kayaks while wearing water shoes.

Today, all the boats are docked; going out onto the lake is still forbidden by the local police. Bright yellow caution tape wraps around the launch, blocking the entrance and rippling in the breeze. I try not to think about what they could be looking for here: blood spattered on wood, maybe, or chestnut strands of hair caught in cracks between the boards.

I bite my lip, studying the cool gray surface of the lake. They found Alana *here*?

"What happened to you?" It takes me a second to realize I spoke out loud. The wind picks up and I hug my arms around my chest, staring into the water's depths. What was the last thing Alana remembers seeing? Maybe the rainbow flutter of a windsurfer sail, maybe the chipped wood of a dock. The turquoise sky stretching out, cloudless—or the velvet expanse of night, sprinkled with silver stars.

"Your . . . I think the words you used were *mental break-down?*" Rowan says hesitantly, stepping up next to me. Her boots sink in the sand. "Do you want to talk about that?"

I look over at her, because it's easier than facing the lake. "The thing is, Alana's not a bad person or anything. But at the start of senior year, we were fighting a lot. I wasn't myself, and my panic attacks were getting worse. Dad was worried, and then I had this awful fight with Alana. It was the last straw for me, I think. I spent a little bit of time in the hospital."

Rowan's face is impassive. "Your friends . . . didn't they help you?"

"Nah. I didn't have anyone left. For years, my best friend had been this girl named Elise, but we . . . fell out of touch." I squint up at the clouds dotting the bright sky, making them into patterns. Move on fast, because as always, talking about Elise feels like suffocating. "I lost other friends too. We just grew apart, I guess. By senior year, Alana was the only person who I hung out with. And a lot of the time, it was . . ."

Awful. She was so mean, cruel and cunning like a dagger blade. She made me so scared.

I shake my head hard. I can't say that, it's not even true. Alana loves me, protects me. *I will never leave you*—it's a promise that no matter how many people walk away from me, whether it's Mom dying or friends leaving, Alana never will. Even in death, she isn't leaving me.

"High school is the fucking worst, dude," Rowan says.

"Do you . . . have a lot of friends around here?" I ask. "From high school?"

"I wouldn't say a lot." Rowan frowns thoughtfully. "I graduated last year. Me and all the lake kids, we grew up together like siblings. It was fun, but then they all moved on. And college ended up not being an option for me."

"I'm sorry," I say automatically. At Coldwater, as I'm well aware, this is a fate worse than death, eliciting hushed tones. But Rowan just shrugs.

"Hey, I'm not. I saved myself from tens of thousands in student loans. I started working at Mom's shop in my freshman year of high school, and then Jazmine hired me at Blue Skies, which was so nice of her. I love working there. We get all our regular customers. Your sister even lets me put my own coffee concoctions on the menu sometimes, even though Blue Skies is supposed to be strictly a tea shop."

"That's pretty cool."

"Very cool." She lowers her voice like she's about to reveal state secrets. "I'm the one who came up with the idea to put clouds on the mugs."

"Wow," I say dryly. "I had no idea that I was convening with one of the greatest minds of our time."

Quiet stretches on and on, and all I hear are trees rustling in the wind around us, faraway cars chugging up and down the street.

"Hey," Rowan says finally, and it's a new voice, one I haven't heard before. "Want a story?"

I shrug, picking at the hem of my denim shorts.

"Once upon a time—is this a bad way to start a story?" She pauses, waiting for me to smile. "Okay. Once upon a time, there was a princess. She had everything: a mother, the queen, who loved her more than life itself. A father, the king, who traveled far and wide to go on adventures and quests. And yet, she was never happy. Her mother always had one foot out the door. Her father stopped coming home. The princess would make friends, and then they would leave. She would fall in love, but it was all wrong, every single time."

Rowan stretches out her arms and squints up at the sky. *"Something must be wrong with me,* the princess told herself. What could she have done to deserve losing these things? Why would her father leave like that? Her mother let her grief take over. She couldn't follow her mother there. So what do you think she did?"

"I don't know."

"She built a new castle. One with sapphires and garnets and diamonds embedded in the walls, ornate fireplaces to keep warm all winter long. Even when the wind howled, or rainstorms whipped through her kingdom, or snow fell in heavy piles outside her front door, she was warm, and safe, and protected, and loved. But here's the most important thing that she remembered when building her castle—a lock on the door."

I look over, eyes narrowed. "Why is that important?"

What I really mean is, *Why did you need a lock?*

"Because no one could ever enter again unless she let them."

A chill prickles up my spine, raises the thin hairs on my arms.

She kneels down in the sand. After a beat, I join her, the grains digging into my bare knees. Side by side, we watch the water slosh against the shoreline. There's no wake, no boats to churn waves to roll toward us. Only the wind moving through the trees, breaking through the eerie quiet like breath.

"I know we can't answer your question of what happened to Alana," Rowan says quietly. "But I hope it helps to come here, you know? You don't need to be afraid."

She gets to her feet, extending a hand to pull me up. I hesitate for a second—what would Alana want me to do?—and then take it. Her palm is warm and there's something weird about the way our hands fit together, like an electric current running between us.

I drop her hand fast and wipe my palms on my shorts for good measure.

Of course I need to be afraid. Rowan just doesn't know it.

CHAPTER FIFTEEN

r/AlanaMurray

About Community: On May 5, 2024, Alana Marina Murray was reported missing by her mother. She was last seen leaving home on the morning of May 4. On May 8, her body was recovered in Lake Ember after reports of a dead body were made to the local authorities. As of today, the medical examiner has not provided a cause of death. This community's purpose is to foster healthy and helpful discussion of what might have happened to Alana, and to seek justice on her behalf. Any toxic comments or harassment will be deleted.

---

grav3undigger
okay so let's dive into the friend circle. everybody's heard that they're focusing on the friends right?? does anybody

live in the area or know people at that school? who were alana's friends?

trucrmthrowaway4578
Did some instagram creeping because it's what I do best. I got names y'all. These are all people who appear in her pics and comment regularly:

    Elise Carter-Holloway

    Maya Rosier

    Madison Kim

    Addie Castillo

    Tyson Becker

    Mackenzie Jameson

    Nathaniel Chen

AveragePasta
did anybody see that girl elise on the news the other night? clearly really distraught and was super close with alana

> **_RealZodiac420**
> dude fr?? that chick is always like seconds away from being like "live laugh love!" lmaooo i'm sorry, no disrespect, but she's fake as shit
>
> **foggymorningstar**
> That's so not funny. A girl is dead. Take your disrespect to tiktok
>
> **OG_nightsta1ker**
> Wait those girls from the school are sus as hell. They've held like a thousand memorials for this girl, who tf does that?

foggymorningstar

Everyone grieves differently.

xxNightmareQu33n

GUYS GUYS WAIT WTF!!! I JUST LOOKED AT MAYA
ROSIER'S INSTAGRAM AND SHE'S NOT EVEN IN LA. LOOK
AT THIS PIC SHE POSTED LAST WEEK

> **newsjunkie890**
>
> Whoa yeah . . . what is up with that caption? "Getting
> away from it all"??? What'd she do, go on vacation
> after her girlfriend died?! How close do you think she
> was with Alana Murray?
>
> **xxNightmareQu33n**
>
> super fucking close. they're in tons of pics together
> starting in like 2016. there's like, pictures of this girl
> with alana's MOM
>
> **korrasami4evr**
>
> Omg guys. I found maya rosier's spotify (here) and
> she was adding songs on her travel playlist THE DAY
> AFTER ALANA WENT MISSING . . . plus, look at that
> photo in the "getting away from it all" post. IS THAT
> THE SAME LAKE WHERE THEY FOUND ALANA?
>
> **tedcruzzodiac69**
>
> my cousin's friend knows somebody @ that school
> and she said they were lesbians
>
> **girlonfyre**
>
> WAIT THAT PICTURE IS LAKE EMBER! BITCH IM
> FUCKING LOOOOSING IT
>
> **twelvenightsatkarls**
>
> Holy shit. Maya Rosier just jumped to suspect #1 in
> my mind at least. Plus, look at her sister's Instagram.

Maya's SMILING in this selfie and her gf is dead? Seriously?

_champagne_problems

You guys are so obsessed with this case it's creepy.

This is about a real girl who died, not a game of Clue.

korrasami4evr

I was looking at tiktok and a bunch of girls are saying that maya came to elise's house a couple days before alana's body was found and she was looking for alana!! Someone got a pic of her there!

xxNightmareQu33n

OOOOOH SHIT THE PLOT THICKENS

■ ■ ■

When I walk through the front door after my outing with Rowan, Jazmine is bustling around the house, loudly regaling me with anecdotes from the crew at Blue Skies, flinging open the windows to the breezy, sunny afternoon. She's trying hard, I know, and I appreciate it. I chat with her in the kitchen, accept a glass of cold lemonade, and after about fifteen minutes I'm able to place the weird feeling settling into my stomach.

It's something close to happiness.

For the first time, I let myself wonder—what if I never went back to LA? If I faded into obscurity, surely there would be no one back home who would even miss me.

But no, it wouldn't matter. There's still Alana, and turning my back on her is impossible.

At Jazmine's urging, I take my sketchbook out to the back porch and unpack my charcoal pencils from my backpack.

I've been drawing my whole life, although I stopped this year when everything fell apart. When I was little, I would sketch every ghost who appeared to me. It was almost like a journal, a way of making sure each of them mattered, and with enough practice, I became pretty competent at portraits.

In high school, so much about me changed. The drawings changed too.

I pull my latest sketchbook out of my bag. At the end of every school year, I replace the book, so this one represents senior year. The drawings blur as I flip through them fast. Alana standing in front of her kitchen window and twisting her hair into a half bun. Alana in her school uniform, sitting on the stone steps in front of Coldwater, glaring.

I can't disappear in Lake Ember, no matter how much I might want to. I can't hide when Alana will hunt me down to the ends of the earth to get what she wants.

Sighing, I flip to a blank page at the back of the sketchbook, spinning my charcoal pencil between two fingers before letting it skim across the paper. It's muscle memory, coming back to me without a second thought, even though I haven't drawn in months. Alana's words from our last conversation, right before they pulled her body from the lake, are still ringing in my ears: *You know how it works between you and me.*

And I do. I still remember that ache of familiarity, but I don't know if that means I want to go back. There's nothing I could do differently, no better, more perfect words. Every fight we had in my living room, the Valley sparkling like diamonds scattered by a careless hand below us—it's all written in stone. The fights are finished. And so are those girls we used to be, glaring at each other from either end of the room, shouting hateful words to drown the other out. It's all changed forever, the room haunted by our ghosts. Maybe that's all hauntings really are anyway. Lingering love that caught fire and burned away.

Out across the lake, a hawk screeches an echoing call, jolting me back to life. I stare down at the page in disbelief. A charcoal-sketched Rowan stares up at me. Black hair in a short ponytail, jawline sharp, eyes narrow and contemplative.

I slam the sketchbook shut and walk back into the house.

●●●

"So how was it?"

Alana's ghost pops up behind me while I'm in front of the bathroom mirror brushing the tangles out of my hair. I clap a hand over my mouth to keep from screaming. I should've expected this; no salt line in the bathroom doorway. And, of course, still no obsidian stone.

"Jesus. Do you have to appear out of thin air like that?"

"It's part of my irresistible charm. So how'd it go with *Rowan*?" I hate how she says it, draws the name out long and slow and singsong, like the subject of one of our elementary school crushes. "What'd you guys do together?"

She hops up onto the bathroom counter, crossing her legs.

"It wasn't a big deal. We just went down to the lake."

Alana pouts. I recognize the look in her eyes. It used to mean fondness and affection, the kind I craved. I'm not sure what it means anymore.

"It's not fair. *I* want to do normal stuff again."

"Well, don't worry," I say carefully. Keep up the act. Don't let her suspect that I have no plans to help her possess Rowan. I grab my toothbrush from my toiletry bag, holding it under the running water, trying to remain casual. "Soon, you'll be able to."

There's a creak in the hallway—Jazmine spying on me, probably. Making eye contact with Alana, I hold a finger to my lips. We watch each other until my sister walks back down the stairs.

"As soon as we get her possessed, I'll go back to LA with you. Obviously," Alana continues. "And we can figure it out from there."

I twist the sink handle hard, shutting the water off. She's struck a nerve.

"And in this imaginary world," I say, "are we in a relationship, or am I just your henchman?"

"What do you mean by henchman?"

"Alana." I whirl on her, jaw set. My rage overpowers my fear of confronting her. "I broke up with you. Do you remember that conversation, or did you assume that your death just canceled it out?"

She tilts her head, a small smile creeping across her freckled face. "Oh, the drama queen has finally arrived! I was wondering when she would be here. I've missed her."

"Answer the question."

Her eyes are ocean blue, blank and still and calm as she looks at me. I'm not going to get an answer, which is so perfectly Alana it makes me want to send my fist through the wall.

"Does it really matter?" she asks finally, voice placid. "I thought it was pretty good, what we had. Remember the funnel cakes we would get at the Santa Monica Pier? That time we spied on the guy Elise liked at the skate park? Or how about the time you were crying last fall because you got a C on that big AP History test, so we walked to get cheese fries?"

"You can't just rattle off a list of memories and expect me to feel something."

"So feel this," she hisses, reaching for me. Her fingers are snowdrift-cold and soft, pressing into my jaw, tilting my chin so that I have no choice but to look her right in the eye. It hits me like a bullet: *She can touch me now.* "You knew, didn't you, even back in middle school? Every time Coldwater had a dance, you and I ditched our friends to hang out and gossip outside. Just you and me. And you knew we'd be together forever."

Panic squeezes around my heart, an iron fist.

Alana's voice is nothing but a whisper now, a low hum. "You knew they talked about us, didn't you, Maya? Because they were jealous, or because they thought two girls dating was weird, or because they thought we were doing it for attention. But I was never afraid of what they said about us."

"Neither was I."

"I really did think we were going to be like that forever," she laments, not letting go of my jaw. Her breath is cool wind on my face. "But I think we just wanted different things. I think we went down different paths, don't you agree?"

"That's the same bullshit you used to tell your mom."

Back at the beginning of senior year, Alana and I had one of our legendary fights. We didn't speak for two days. Dad had come to my room, wire-rimmed reading glasses on, tapping on my half-open door. *Melissa Murray says you and Alana are going down different paths,* he had reported. He'd sounded so amused, like this was cute. I'd already thrown up twice that night and was blinking at him through bloodshot eyes. Two days later, he'd check me into the psychiatric hospital for the short stint that would cause my downward academic spiral.

My heart stutters. Her words are all it takes for me to summon my courage.

"Hey, I have a question. Are you aware that Elise is acting like she's your best friend?"

Alana laughs, leaning back against the wall. "Maya, I have no idea why that girl does anything she does. You're probably imagining things."

"You were at Elise's house the weekend you died." I say it fast before I lose my nerve. "Was I imagining that?"

"Elise's house?" She frowns. "No, I wasn't there."

"Stop acting like I'm making this up! Just because you're dead—"

"Ouch. Do you even hear yourself?"

"—doesn't mean you can act like my feelings and thoughts aren't valid."

"Honestly, I don't even know where you're getting this." Alana turns to study her reflection in the bathroom mirror, fluffing her perfect hair. "Like I gave a shit about that clingy bitch. Always jealous of us. *Spend time with me, Alana! You never text me anymore!* You made the right choice when you ditched her last year."

I stare at her, anger simmering. A *choice*? A choice to ditch my friend? Is that how she sees it? There was never any choice.

"She was here at the lake," I say, clenching my fists. It's hard to tell, but Alana's face seems to go pale. "Elise was here when the police did a press conference. Talking about how you guys were best friends."

"And you believe her?" Alana snorts. "She's lying so she can get five minutes of fame. Listen, Elise treated you like shit. Friend groups of three are doomed from the start, and she was my friend first, before she got to know you. The stuff she would say behind your back . . . well, you're better off not knowing. Remember how she gossiped to the girls on the soccer team about you?"

I bite my lip, watching Alana's expression for some trace of a lie. Honestly, I don't want to believe her, but I'll never be able to forget the way Elise turned on me so quickly, sharing my personal business with the whole school.

"All of this is irrelevant, because you don't need any of your old friends anyway," Alana adds.

"I don't?"

"No. When you bring me back to life, it'll just be you and me again, like it always was. Everything will be perfect." She turns from the mirror. I can feel a cold, whispering wind emanating from her. It's painfully easy to imagine us falling back together, like none of this ever happened. I wouldn't have to traverse new relationships, just stay safe in Alana's protection forever. But it's impossible, because I won't do that to Rowan. I won't let Alana win.

"And speaking of which, what's the update on the plan?"

"Oh . . . yeah." I clench my fists, forcing myself to concentrate. I twist my face into an expression that hopefully resembles determination. "I just need to study a little more before we can attempt anything, okay? Read up on this stuff."

Alana blinks, surprised. "Why do you need to *study*?"

"I've never helped a ghost possess anyone before," I snap. "Somehow I don't think it's the kind of thing you should attempt without doing your homework first."

A door slams downstairs. Both of us freeze.

"Maya, get down here, please!" Jazmine calls from the steps. I jump, dropping my toothbrush onto the sink. My heart skips at her tone. It's urgent, measured calm; Mom used to call us like that all the time just before a big lecture. When I glance over my shoulder, Alana has vanished. Slowly, I ease the bathroom door open and head downstairs. Night has fallen, dinner dishes already cleared away. Who could possibly be visiting now?

Downstairs, Jazmine is sitting at the kitchen table with Detective Ramirez, who looks exhausted. Black-framed glasses slide down the bridge of his nose and he's clutching a Styrofoam coffee cup.

"Maya, you remember the detective," Jazmine says. If I weren't so scared, it would be easy to laugh at her stick-straight posture. Her hands are resting on the table, squeezed tight to keep them from shaking. "He's back with a few questions."

"Again?" It's all I can think to ask.

"Sorry, Maya. I wanted to be sure I'm solid on the facts. I'm grateful for your cooperation today. Now . . ." Detective Ramirez taps a ballpoint pen against the yellow legal pad that's cracked open on the kitchen table. I stare down at the stupid yellow paper. It's already covered in scribbles. "Can you take a seat?"

My hands press into the back of the kitchen chair. "You guys think Alana's death was . . . that there was foul play involved, right? I heard them say that yesterday, down by the lake."

His brow furrows. "You were at the press conference?"

"Are you here because you know what happened to her?" Breathless anticipation has taken hold of me. I can feel Jazmine's eyes boring into me, but I don't turn toward her.

"I'm not here to talk about Alana Murray's manner of death today, Miss Rosier," he says, watching me carefully.

"But—"

"Let's start at the beginning, when you first met Alana," Detective Ramirez says. "When was that?"

I slump into the kitchen chair, resigned. He's clearly focused on whatever line of questioning this is, and I'm not going to get any answers. "Um, on the first day of fifth grade. She and her mom had just moved from Denver, and Alana got into Coldwater on a partial scholarship."

"Coldwater Canyon School for Girls," he reads from the open folder next to his notebook. "Good school, huh? Ivy League feeder. Small. And were you friends right away?"

I breathe in, remembering Alana's face on the first day. Freckles and round blue eyes. Her nails were painted with turquoise polish, and during lunch, we sat on the stone front steps drinking lemonade out of plastic bottles. Back then, before Alana and her mom had money, she seemed smaller and angrier.

"We became friends pretty quickly," I tell Detective Ramirez. "She wasn't happy to be in LA—she didn't like that her new house was small. There's always been something about Alana . . . her face, I guess. You just want to help her."

And you're supposed to be helping by finding out what happened to her, Detective. But you won't even talk to me about it.

"And at what point did your relationship with Alana become romantic?"

I swallow hard. "We got together in freshman year."

"And was your relationship well received by your friends?"

"Which friends?"

Ramirez shrugs. "Any of 'em."

"Well, I don't think anyone really cared. There was *some*

gossip, but it was just random girls and their internalized homophobia. They didn't even know us."

"Okay," he says slowly, like this is meaningless to him. "And at the time of Alana's disappearance last weekend, were you two in a fight?"

I pause, licking my lips. "Why would you ask that?"

"A credible witness places you at . . ." He skims his notes, frowning. "The Antelope Valley California Poppy Reserve on the morning of Saturday, May fourth."

Blood drains from my face.

"Which would contradict the information you provided in our previous interview. You see, Maya, that's why I'm here to speak with you again." The detective looks up at me, steepling his fingers thoughtfully. "Why did you lie?"

I pause, wishing my brain would work faster. Lie after lie unspools in my mind, but they're no good—every single one will unravel under scrutiny. *Fight*, I can imagine Alana saying. For all I know, she's watching me right now. *Don't let him get to you like this.*

"I'm sorry, who is this witness?" I ask, forcing the quiver out of my voice.

"Well, I'm not at liberty to share a name, but we spoke to an eyewitness who was on that trail on May fourth. She's stating that she saw two young brunette girls on the hiking trail that day in the middle of an argument."

"And she thinks that girl was me?" The confusion in my voice sounds so fake to my own ears, but Jazmine is looking back and forth between us, tense. She better not say anything. I know I can fake it well enough to get through this. At least, I hope I can. "Did she take photos of the girls?"

"Ah . . ." Detective Ramirez hesitates, glancing at his folder like it's going to print out a helpful Polaroid. "No. No photos. Just an eyewitness account. When provided with a photo of you, the witness was confident that you were the second girl she saw."

"She saw a photo of a white girl with brown hair and brown eyes and thinks it was me," I say, forcing out a humorless laugh. "Sorry, Detective, but that's . . . that's pretty silly, isn't it? We have a million classmates who fit that same description."

"So you're saying that you *weren't* at Antelope Valley that day."

Lie. It doesn't fucking matter. It's not like you *killed Alana.*

"No. I've been to the superbloom before, but the girl arguing with Alana wasn't me." I'm shocked at how easily this falls out of my mouth. "Honestly, Alana and I didn't really even fight, ever. She would just . . . say mean things when she got upset with me, which isn't the same as a fight."

Detective Ramirez takes a long look at me. Sips his coffee.

"You and Alana were pretty close, it sounds like. Did you share things like email passwords? Lock screen codes?"

"No," I say honestly. "Not really. Alana didn't want me rooting around in her stuff."

"So you don't know the password to her iMac."

"No," I repeat, but as I say it, a picture floats into my mind: myself in Alana's messy bedroom before I realized she was missing, trying to log on to her computer. Oh my god.

"Because we have a record of someone logging on to Alana's computer on May fourth—a timestamp when it would've been impossible for her to do so."

"Probably her mom," I say easily. "Was Mrs. Murray home by that point?"

Ramirez pauses, shuffling papers. Gotcha.

"And could you tell me why you chose to travel to Lake Ember on the evening of May fourth, Maya? Even though you'd realized your girlfriend was not responding to your texts or calls, and per your conversation with her mother, her whereabouts were unaccounted for?"

I widen my eyes, glancing at Jazmine. Whether she's trying to or not, she puts on a perfect act, meeting my gaze with enormous, teary eyes.

"I missed my sister," I say.

Of all the lies I've told tonight, this is the one that makes me feel the worst. Jazmine rises from her chair, walks to the sink to pour herself a glass of water. I want to rest my head on the table and cry.

"One last question for you tonight, Maya," Detective Ramirez says. "Did Alana ever provoke you? Hurt you?"

I blink, startled by this question. He probably means did she ever hit you, scratch you, make you bleed. But my lungs constrict and I remember the coldness settling in Alana's eyes during so many fights, like I was nothing but dust. I remember her laugh, glass-sharp.

"No," I answer, my voice a dull blade. "No, never."

"Well, Miss Rosier," he says, setting the coffee cup down slowly. "Then I guess we're done for tonight."

INTERLUDE

——

EIGHT MONTHS EARLIER

I'M NOT AFRAID of death.

I've seen it my whole life—not just the extinguishing of the flame, but the cold stillness that follows, the whisper-breath filling the quiet that only I can hear. No, I'm not even afraid of hauntings.

It's endings that I hate.

The morning of September first feels like an ending, and I wake up anxious. Sunlight pours in through my open curtains. I was hoping to sleep late—it's a Sunday and tomorrow's Labor Day, so school is the furthest thing from my mind. But nope, something has awakened me before nine. A tapping on my window.

I rub my eyes, trying to make sense of what I'm seeing. Alana, brown hair long over her shoulders, has scaled the tree in our yard. She's grinning at me through the glass pane.

"What the hell are you doing?" I unlatch the window and push it open, laughing despite myself. "You could break your neck sitting out there. Watching me sleep like you're Edward Cullen."

"It was early," she says through her laugh, kicking her feet aimlessly at the windowsill. She's wearing a pair of athletic shorts and an oversized T-shirt. I grab her suntanned calves and try to angle her feet through the window. "I didn't want to bug your dad."

"You wouldn't be bugging him. He would want you to use the door like a normal person."

I yank hard and Alana tumbles through the window, taking out my desk lamp with one sneaker. We both hit my bedroom carpet hard. Our laughs sound identical; at least, until I see her trademark lavender backpack swinging over her shoulder. It's the one she only uses for school stuff. My laugh dies out.

"Are you seriously working on college apps on a holiday weekend?"

"Early decision waits for no one, Maya." She wrinkles her nose. Like she needs to remind me. The November deadline for early decision applications feels closer every day. "Speaking of which, why were you *still* asleep? Don't you have, like, a million things to do?"

"It's Sunday."

"Yeah, and?" She hops up onto my dresser, banging her heels against the drawers. "You wanna review my essay? This time I wrote a pretty good sob story about my dad. I figure if I hit 'em with the double whammy of lesbian teenager with divorced parents, maybe I could make some headway with Smith."

I roll my eyes, but then her words sink in. "Wait. Smith College? Like, the one in Massachusetts?"

She nods, tossing her hair. Heels kicking, *bam bam bam.*

"Weren't—weren't we both doing UC Berkeley early decision?" Suddenly, I'm doubting everything, even though *of course* that was the plan. We'd talked about it for years, bought matching sweatshirts last year during our campus visit.

"Oh." Alana waves me off with one hand. She has a fresh manicure, pale pink, which must mean she's going to blow off our scheduled nail salon date tomorrow. "Yeah, but Mrs. Connelly was talking about Smith in College Counseling the other day and it just sounded so nice. Did you know about all the traditions they have? You live in houses—like, real houses, not gross dorms—and it's supposed to be one of the most haunted campuses in the United States. Plus, you know who went there?"

"Sylvia Plath," I say. "Every depressed teenage girl knows that."

"I thought you'd be more excited for me." Finally, Alana stops slamming her feet against my dresser. She pouts, resting her elbows on her knees.

I turn so I won't have to see her miserable face, and root through my closet for a pair of jeans. "No, I think it's cool that you're applying, but it just goes against our plan. So I guess that's confusing."

"UC Berkeley is a really good school, but I dunno, Maya ... do you really want to stay in California for the next four years? I want to see the world." She spreads her arms out dramatically.

Massachusetts is the world? I think skeptically but have the sense to keep it to myself.

"I remember Elise said she wanted to apply to Smith." I sigh, flopping backward onto my unmade bed.

"You're still fixating on Elise, huh? Every time I say anything these days, it's like, *Elise also thinks that. Elise also does that.*"

"I don't say it every time," I say, even though insecurity creeps in. Maybe she's right.

"Maya, I don't understand why it matters what Elise wants." Alana laughs, high and cold. "Who cares?"

"I care. We're not friends anymore. It reminds me of the whole thing with . . . with Livia." I squeeze my eyes shut tight because even though it was years ago, thinking of Livia still hurts.

"Someday," Alana says, "we'll be married and live in some beautiful place, and you won't ever think about the crazy bitches we knew in high school. It'll just be you and me. The way it's supposed to be."

"How is that going to happen if we go to college on different coasts?"

"You used to always talk about going to Yale like your mom did," Alana says easily. "Apply early decision there instead."

"But I don't know if I want—"

"Maya!" she interrupts, exasperated, flinging herself off the dresser. "I came over because I thought you'd be excited about my news. Smith could be *so* great for me, you know? But you don't ever seem happy about stuff I tell you anymore. I don't know what your deal is. We're finally seniors! Don't you want to support me?"

I bite my lip, staring over at my desk, where a pile of homework has already accumulated. AP US History is a blur of names and dates and the textbook weighs as much as a boulder. I thought I was pretty good at French, but I already have a paper due on Tuesday and it seems like every one of the language's grammatical rules flew out of my brain over the summer. And that's not even mentioning my other APs, Calculus and Chem. The anxiety is like a lead block crushing my chest.

How am I ever going to survive this year? All the older girls at Coldwater always said that this was the year to fuck around and get drunk at parties, but all I've done so far is panic.

"Do you ever think we're just, like . . . headed down different paths?"

It's Alana who asks this. I stare at her, well aware that I haven't brushed my hair or my teeth and probably got about four hours of sleep last night.

"Well, up until five minutes ago, I thought we were headed down the same path."

"You have this inability," Alana says, starting to pace my floor, "to accept any good news I ever tell you. If it doesn't pertain to your life, it doesn't matter to you. That's selfish, Maya. Can't you see how selfish that is, to only care about changes in my life in proportion to how they affect *you*?"

She says *you* like I'm nothing, a dying star in an endless night sky, pathetic ancient light that still shines down as best as it can. I'm not selfish—at least, I don't *think* I am—but I don't know how to refute this, and panic unfolds frantically in my chest.

"I *do* care about other people." My voice shakes. "I care about you. I was just surprised because UC Berkeley was our plan for so long."

Alana waves a hand, disregarding this. "It was never a *plan*, Maya. Never set in stone."

I think of the post on her Instagram last year, the two of us posing side by side on campus in our matching crewnecks, grinning at the camera. Her caption was *future UCB roomies!* It got over 100 likes. This *was* the plan, I remind myself, like I do whenever I'm uncertain about Alana. I've scrolled back through her Instagram and her TikTok a hundred times over the past few weeks, trying to prove to myself that there's documentation of her love for me.

"Fine." I sink back onto my bed, shoving my trembling hands underneath my thighs. "Alana, that's fine if you don't want to do this with me anymore, but just go, okay? I just want to be alone."

I can't fathom having to sit here while she fills out the Smith application, telling me about the classroom where Gloria Steinem once sneezed or whatever. She's right—I can go to Yale. I can *definitely* go to Yale. Mom was a legacy, and I know I can write a good essay. School is hard right now, but if I can *just* focus and get these Alana-induced anxiety spirals to stop, I know I'll be able to keep my GPA high. I can survive this.

"Okay, Maya," she sneers, stepping closer, and I hate myself for concentrating on the smell of her rosewater shampoo. Her bright blue eyes flicker over to the pile of unfinished homework on my desk. "I'll go home. Looks like you've got plenty to work on."

You promise you won't leave me, right? I want to ask her, but I can't make myself do it.

After she leaves, her words echo in my mind: *Do you ever just think we're headed down different paths?* I've never once thought that. I thought our paths were intertwined permanently, a Gordian knot that neither of us would ever attempt to unravel. Now, I don't know what to think.

Dad finds me retching on the bathroom floor half an hour later—I haven't eaten in at least a day, so there's nothing in my stomach but bile. My heartbeat is hysterical in my ears, a pounding drumline. When he looks down at me, all I can do is cry.

That's the beginning of the end.

And I hate endings.

CHAPTER SIXTEEN

JAZMINE IS HAVING a game night.

"Are you *sure* you don't want to hang out with us, Maya?" she asks for the millionth time, bustling around the kitchen assembling a charcuterie board. A couple wine bottles are lined up neatly on the counter, six glasses placed behind them. She's wearing a faded apron over a flowing sundress. "Because, like I said, you're totally welcome. You don't need to hide in your room. My friends would love to meet you."

There's a tiny part of me—the part that made me cling to her legs when I was five years old and screech if she left the house—that wants to agree. Her friends seem nice. She has a whole group of them and they're all involved in the lake community, planning Catan and Mario Party nights, windsurfing and kayaking in the summer.

There's so much about my sister that I don't know. Maybe in another life where things were normal, we could actually talk about stuff. But no. She's stuck with a haunted little sister who lies to police officers instead.

"Thanks for inviting me," I mumble. I'm clinging to the stairwell with one hand, delaying my ascent as long as possible. "But I'm really tired. I'm probably just gonna read and go to bed early."

"Oh, I'm sure you are, after the day you had." Jazmine makes a sympathetic face. Again, I expect her to call me out for lying to Detective Ramirez about Antelope Valley, about my reason for coming to Lake Ember. But she doesn't. I think she feels too sorry for me. "I drove down Reservoir Road earlier and it looks like the press has all cleared out. They were lingering awhile, searching for some intrigue or clues, but they're gone now."

I chew my lip for a minute, stuck between acting like I don't care and begging for the answer I desperately need. The latter wins.

"You promise?"

She nods. "I promise. But anyway, how's Rowan doing? I'm so happy you guys are talking. She's seriously the nicest girl."

"Jazmine, we're not *talking*." I pull back, leaning against the wall. Outside the kitchen window, the silver moon is gleaming, trees bending in a gentle evening breeze. Alana could be back at any moment, and the last thing I need is for her to overhear my sister waxing poetic about some girl she thinks I'm dating.

"Okay," Jazmine says wryly, shaking a package of crackers so they fall onto a large plate. "Well, whatever you're doing with her, keep it up. She's had a rough go of it too. I'm sure you guys have a lot in common. Oh, and on her way out this afternoon, she told me that she's having a party tonight—maybe you could stop by, meet some people."

"If I'm too tired for your party, I'm definitely too tired for hers."

She laughs. "You got me there. Oh, that reminds me . . ."

Jazmine sets down the charcuterie platter, rooting around in the mail tray that sits by the back door. Then she turns back to me, holding . . .

"Is that a *rose?*"

"Somebody dropped it off," my sister says, placing tremendous emphasis on *somebody*. I reach out, completely confused, accepting a single long-stemmed red rose attached with string to a cream-colored envelope. "I'll let you open it."

Holding the rose between two fingers, I carefully tear open the envelope as I walk up the stairs to my bedroom. Inside is a stiff piece of paper. I don't recognize the handwriting, but immediately, I know what this is supposed to be.

Coldwater Canyon School for Girls, it says in impressive, arching calligraphy that swoops across the top of the small card. And below it:

This certifies that

Maya Elisabeth Rosier
has satisfactorily completed the course of study in being the most feisty, loquacious, and all-around kickass girl this uptight educational institution has ever seen. And seeing as we're located in LA, that's really saying something. She is hereby awarded this
High School Diploma
and is therefore entitled to one fantastic cup of coffee brewed by her favorite tea shop worker, who knows she prefers cold brew to tea.

I flip the card over, laughing as fresh tears well up in my eyes.

hey Rosier—I know it sucks that you won't get to walk at your graduation tomorrow but LOOK, YOU STILL GRADUATED! OMG I KNEW YOU COULD DO IT! ever since i first met you five days ago, I believed in you! I'm serious about the coffee, come by soon and I'll make you some. You're the baddest and strongest bitch in this whole town. See ya soon, Rowan

I settle onto the window seat, knees pulled to my chest, reading it again and again. It's not long before I have it memorized. The sky is deepening to a dark sapphire, nighttime crickets rustling and chirping in the trees. Bullfrogs along the lake's edge croak into the night. When I was a kid, I thought there was no place in the world more peaceful than this.

"Nice night."

I jump, dropping the card and the rose. *Shit.* I really need to start protecting myself again. Earlier, I dug through Jazmine's hydrangeas and violets, trying to find my obsidian stone, but it seems like it's gone forever.

"Do you always have to make such a dramatic entrance?" I ask, trying to steady myself. "Like, could you knock before manifesting?"

"Wow, what a welcome."

I hop up off the window seat, slamming the card and rose in my underwear drawer before she can remark on them. Alana is sitting at the foot of my bed, hair long and center-parted, still wearing that cropped white top and black leggings. Smiling at me with closed lips. It's a nice smile. A not-mad smile. For now, at least.

"Hey, Maya, you know what I was thinking about?" She

smirks. I lean up against the dresser. "Your sixteenth birthday at the macaroni and cheese place. Remember? It was like, a gastropub or something, and I found it on Instagram because tons of famous people go there. There was that candle in the middle of the table and we both made wishes and blew it out. What did you wish for?"

"I don't remember."

But I do—Los Angeles sunset hazy pinks and oranges, the rumble of traffic, a breeze that blew the palm tree above us back and forth. Alana's hair in two long braids, mascara thickening her lashes and falling in loose flecks under her eyes; I could tell because I looked at her so close, I paid so much fucking attention.

"No, but seriously," Alana says, and she snaps her fingers, disappearing, then reappearing right beside me. I whip around, stumbling back against the opposite wall. "I know what you wished for. I always knew what you were wishing for. Because I was wishing for the same thing. And look where it got us."

I shoot her a simmering glare. "Shut up."

"You never even seem excited to see me. You complain that I'm scaring you, that I'm being difficult." Her voice is cold. "You're letting me go."

"I'm not," I lie quickly.

"That was a nice rose you were holding, by the way."

It's like being plunged into a bucket of ice. Of course she wouldn't miss that.

"That was a graduation gift," I say quickly. "From my dad."

"Mr. Rosier sent you a long-stemmed red rose. Okay." Alana smirks. She tucks her hair behind her ears. "You can't fool me. I *know* you. I know you better than anybody. I've given up everything for you. But you won't give up a single thing for me."

"That's not fair," I snap. "You haven't held up *your* end of the deal. You said that if I agreed to help you with this possession thing, you'd make sure I was safe from blame. Well, I don't know what you see or hear when you're off wherever you are, but people are blaming me left and right. Girls from our school are on TikTok gaining thousands of followers talking about me, Elise and all those other Coldwater girls are traipsing around Lake Ember holding cheesy memorials claiming they're your best friends, and you don't even want to know what they're saying on Reddit. . . ."

"You go on Reddit?" Alana wrinkles her nose. "Eww."

"That's not the point," I say, exasperated. "The point is that you promised me I wouldn't look guilty, and now everybody thinks I am."

"Maya, you're the one lying to the police. Don't you think that's the bigger issue here?"

I pause, caught. Pray she can't tell my hands are shaking.

"Just relax." She rolls her eyes, enormous and blue even in the dim light. "From here on out, you need to do as I say and quit making things more difficult for yourself. You can't lie *again,* so I'll make sure no one can prove you were with me at Antelope Valley that day. They've found my body, and now it won't be long before they find out the truth."

What's the truth? I want to ask, but the words stick in my throat and won't come out. I lean forward, eyes fixed on her.

"Nobody caused my death. I slipped, I fell, I drowned," she says softly. She sounds so much younger, like when we were kids whispering secrets. I fell for it as a little girl at sleepovers, but I won't fall for it now.

"If that's the truth, then why are the cops saying it was a homicide?"

Alana sighs. "Maya, come on. I was a completely healthy teenage girl. When someone young drops dead, it's either an undiagnosed illness, suicide, an accident, or homicide. Illnesses? Nope. Suicide? I'm not like you. So that leaves accident or homicide. They picked homicide. How am I supposed to know why? I wasn't in the room when they made the decision."

I stare at her, unable to find words.

"Anyway. Like I said, you need to do as I say. And clearly, you're no help with possession." Alana looks up at the ceiling, thinking. "Maybe I'm overcomplicating things. Maybe this is one of those things where you learn by doing."

My heart skitters, finally jarring me back to life. Rowan's face flashes into my mind. "No! No, don't do that to her. I'll—"

"Oh," Alana breathes, cocking her head to the side. Her tone freezes the breath in my lungs. "Oh. *Don't do that to her.* I think I know what's going on here."

"What are you talking about?"

"This girl. Rowan. She's not just someone, is she, Maya?"

"Don't be stupid," I say, trying to keep my voice level. I need to steer Alana away from this line of questioning, and I need to do it fast. Her anger will come on sudden as a freak thunderstorm and just as terrible.

"Tell me what happened between the two of you."

"Alana, you're being insane. Why are you accusing me of dumb shit when we should be talking about something more serious? Like, have you even thought about the repercussions of possessing someone?"

Her eyes glint. "Define repercussions."

"Uh, for example, what happens to Rowan's soul when you jump into her body?"

She lets out a slow breath, punctuated by a shrug.

"You don't know?" I ask in disbelief. "You haven't even thought about it?"

"No, Maya, when I'm wandering around the spiritual realm, I'm not worrying about your little girlfriend's soul."

"She's not my—"

"If we don't do this, I'll be gone. Forever." Alana's voice is cold steel, but I know her well enough to hear the fear wavering under the surface. "Where I'll go . . . it's dark. Lonely. Away from you. Look, do you want me to show you what it's like for me? Would that be easier for your tiny brain to comprehend?"

I open my mouth, but she's quicker, stronger. Her arm shoots out and grabs me. Her fingers lock around my wrist, strong as iron, with a pain that sends me slamming to the hardwood floor on my knees. The world spins around me.

"It's so fun to catch you off guard," Alana says, but her voice sounds far away. Fuzzy.

There's a cracking sound, like ice out in the middle of the lake just before the drop. Some otherworldly force slams me flat on my back, knocking the air clean out of my lungs. Alana's grip tightens impossibly around both my wrists until I can't breathe, convinced my bones are splintering, and just when the pain becomes too much to bear, it vanishes.

The floor under my spine, hard and cold.

My breath comes in short gasps and the world around me goes black.

And then my eyes burst open, and I'm someone new.

Snow-coated city streets and I'm so small, purple mittens sliding off my delicate hands, twirling on the icy sidewalk. Swinging open a wooden front door, kicking off my boots in a dark hallway. A small house with squishy carpet under my feet. Screaming from another room.

I run up a narrow staircase, palms pressed over my ears. My room is the first one on the right and I dive in, kicking the door closed with my socked foot, sobs racking my body. Dad's voice downstairs—

no, not my dad, Alana's dad—

you stupid bitch, do you even realize that rent is going up next year? No? No, of course you don't, all you do is piss away our money and focus on your stupid writing, Alana deserves better than a self-centered bitch of a mother,

and I'm screaming *stop* through the crack below the door but no one hears—

I blink and I'm nowhere, lost in the dark. Everything blurs past me: city smog and mango tajin candy on my tongue, neon buzzing and mountains staggering so high above me.

I pinwheel through the darkness, bursting into a new scene: It's Alana's first house in LA, the one out in Van Nuys by the 99 Cent Store. The one where Mrs. Murray and Alana lived just before Mrs. Murray got her first fancy TV job and her inheritance money.

Shaking in the cold air rattling from the window unit air conditioner; my soccer uniform is baggy, shorts hanging to my knees, and my arms are thin and pale as I wrap them around my torso. Melissa's sitting at the rickety kitchen table with envelopes and scratch paper spread out across the surface, a calculator in one hand and a pen in the other. Tortoiseshell glasses push back her frizzy, dishwater blond hair.

Alana, if you can't keep your grades up, there's no reason to keep you at that school—

NO! It tears out of me.

Twenty thousand dollars a year after your scholarship. I know that doesn't mean anything to you, but do you know what I could do for this family if we could keep that money? I could take you to Disneyland. We could keep the power on and groceries from Gelson's in the fridge all the time. You could go shopping at the Westfield Mall with Maya and Elise and actually buy the clothes that they buy, do you get what I'm saying? And we could afford a house.

I don't want to leave Coldwater. It comes out alien and wrong, twisted by sobs. *I don't want to leave Maya. Please, Mom . . .*

When you're paying taxes, when you have a job and are helping with rent, we'll talk about what you want, she snarls. I thought I knew Melissa Murray so well, but I've never heard her like this. Never seen her face blotchy from crying and eyes puffy from exhaustion. She looks at me, at Alana, like I'm a bug she wants to squash.

"Melissa," I choke out, determined to reach through time and make her hear me. But she doesn't, and the world spins into black again. I fall into another place, another time.

I'm an eleven-year-old Alana standing outside my best friend's house—*my* house—all the windows dark except for one: a golden nightlight shines from upstairs. I take a shuddering breath, gathering courage; the night air is pressing against me like a blanket. With a quick glance at the empty driveway, I sprint up the front walk—

The alarm beeps loud and sharp against my skull, but I punch the passcode into the keypad on the wall—fingernails painted turquoise, quick and practiced like I've entered this a million times—

Up the stairs, I start crying, and by the time I shove open Maya's—my—bedroom door, my body is shaking.

I watch myself sit up in bed, brown hair tousled, grabbing a pink flashlight and swinging its beam frantically across the room—

Maya, it's me, I choke out through sobs. *It's Alana. I'm sorry—*

Why are you sorry? Pause. *Why are you crying?*

I'm never gonna see my dad again, and that's all it takes for me to collapse to the carpet in a ball. Rustling of blankets, footsteps rush toward me—

Are they getting a divorce for real?

Yeah, it sounds like it—and Mom says he won't pay for Coldwater because he doesn't want me at some school for spoiled Hollywood girls.

I lift my tear-streaked face and see my own face staring down, brown eyes huge in the dark, filling with tears of sympathy. My face is a perfect echo of Alana's. Warm arms wrap around me, hold me tight.

You'll be fine, my voice says softly, a hand gripping the back of my head. *There are merit scholarships and stuff you could get—*

My grades aren't good enough for that—

The arms squeeze tighter. *Okay. My mom left me some money when she died. I could—*

No. I shake my head hard. *No way. That's your money.*

But I want to help—

Maya, Alana's voice shakes. *Just be my best friend, okay? Please don't leave.*

The images unspool fast—

I'm pushing open the front door of the North Hollywood house, a sleek, enormous mansion all in white, and I gasp, twirling around to take it all in—

Scoring the winning goal on the soccer field, pumping my fist in the air—

Running through the backyard with Balto, tossing a ball for him to catch, watching it arc through the air—

Holding tight to Elise's hand while we skip down a dock at summer camp, a cold gray lake glinting ahead, both of us giggling—

The memory stalls and skips and throws me forward hard, like a car slamming on its brakes. I know exactly where I am.

The poppy fields at Antelope Valley.

Gold and beautiful and sprawling, a strange planet, beautiful as home. I turn my head to the right, ponytail swinging over my shoulder, and there's—

me, Maya, almond-shaped brown eyes staring right back at me

fear carved on my face like porcelain

I didn't know it ever showed like that

I thought I hid it better

and my lips move, and I hear Alana say,

You're breaking up with me? Really.

I watch myself blink, stung—hear my own voice: *You know we would both be happier that way.* I want to say sorry, but how do you say sorry when you're just trying to give yourself your best chance?

Don't tell me how I feel.

I know you better than anyone.

Oh, you'd love to think that's true.

And even though I can't read Alana's mind, I can feel it—the ache when you press against a barely healed bruise, the scream that builds inside your lungs. We're both thinking it. The promise we always made to each other: *I will never leave you.*

I stand there and I watch myself leave her.

My muscles strain with the effort of trying to keep myself there, stuck in that moment, surrounded by California poppies and fresh mountain air and visceral, stinging heartbreak. If I stay, maybe I'll find out what happened. But it's no use. I'm ripped out, gasping, aching—

My eyes wrench open and I sit up, breathing hard. I'm back at the lake house. The hardwood floor of my bedroom and the familiar walls. There's never been a more beautiful sight. But something doesn't feel right.

Panting, I grab the bedpost and haul myself to a standing position. Alana's ghost is gone, and in her absence, the mirror over the dresser is watching me.

My nails dig into the dresser wood and I stare at the girl looking back at me.

She's me. She's got my tangled brown hair, my chapped lips and round face, but she also has the daring glint of Alana's eyes. Alana's fury, and something else. It's terrible, a chasm I can't let myself fall into. But it pulls me down anyway. There's a roiling storm in my heart that does not belong to me.

Hate, I think, recoiling with shock.

Hate. I hate myself.

My eyes lock onto the girl's reflection, the girl who's

somewhere between Alana and myself. Stare so hard I might crack glass. There's something else there, tucked within the hate.

Scared. I'm so scared.

The second I realize this, every light in the room is extinguished and I'm bending in half against cold wind, wrapping my arms around my body tight. I open my mouth to scream for help but nothing comes out. Not even a whisper.

I suck in a deep breath and take off running through the dark, but on both sides, there's nothing but walls of smudged, cracked glass. Like a long, dirty window from an abandoned hallway. Tripping over my feet, I slow to a stop, walking closer—past the grime and spiderwebbing cracks, there are human-shaped shadows ducking and whirling, trying to escape my gaze.

"Hey," I say, hoarse, a voice that's somewhere between Alana's and my own. "Hello? Who's out there?"

One of the shadows steps up close to the window. Squinting so hard my eyes start to water, I walk up to it, faint recognition tugging at the edges of my consciousness. It's a woman, dark and blurry around the edges. My hand lifts, and hers does too. Our palms meet on either side of the glass wall.

"Mom?" I whisper.

I would know her anywhere: brown hair like mine, small and solemn-faced. But when I press my palms against the glass and stare hungrily at the person on the other side, I can't see the details of her face. That's okay. I know it's her. The sight unlocks something within me, and I choke on my own sob.

"You need to banish her," Mom says, but her voice sounds weird. Not right.

"*Banish* her? How am I supposed to do that?" I ask desperately. "I've never banished a ghost before. All my other ghosts wanted to leave, but Alana will do anything to stay."

"You'll have to work hard, but you'll be able to do it. I promise. You're strong enough."

"I'm not strong," I whisper, lower lip trembling. "I'm not brave."

"You *are*. Banish her and you'll finally be able to live your own life."

My lips part. I want to say that she's wrong, that my life with Alana has been beautiful and there's not a second I would change. But then I think about sketching on the back porch of the lake house until the sun slips over the glittering horizon. Curling up on the window seat with a book, all of Lake Ember unexplored and waiting, sprawling before me. A whole world that I can make my own.

I slam my fist against the glass wall one last time, a shout of rage bursting from me. It shatters, glass shards falling like snow and coating the ground. In a sudden light before plunging me into nothingness, I see the figure who I thought was Mom for just a second, completely clear.

It wasn't Mom. It was me.

With a crack like lightning, I wake up curled on the floor, shivering. Pins and needles scrape every nerve ending, my body on fire. My face is slick with warm tears and my legs are shaking. Alana's ghost is leaning against the windowsill, watching me with trepidation.

I stare up at her, throat dry. "What the *fuck*, Alana?"

Alana grins down at me. "I guess that's all I have to do. Well, shit."

But I barely hear her. My entire body is drenched in cold sweat. "You can't just jump into my body without asking. That was—"

"I just wanted to know that I could," Alana interrupts, waving me off. "I wanted to prove that I can do this without you. And look at that, it looks like I can!"

"What's that place?" I ask, sitting up slowly. My head is pounding. "That dark hallway with the glass walls."

Alana presses her lips together tight. "I don't know what you're talking about."

"Is that where you go when you're . . . when you're not here?"

She doesn't even seem to hear me. "God. I just can't believe how easy that was."

"Alana, of course it was easy for us. We've always been practically the same person anyway! If you possess Rowan . . ." My voice slows as I process this new, dawning horror. "If you possess her, I don't think it's safe. I don't think it's temporary. She'll still be there inside your mind, inside the same body . . . *trapped.* She'll be in that dark hallway, won't she? Half dead, but not alive. Forever."

She shrugs. "There's no other way."

"Uh, there is, actually. There's the way where you don't suppress somebody's soul and hop into their body like it's a freaking subway car."

"You're acting like I'm a monster," Alana says, hurt flashing across her face. For a second, she looks like that crying little girl on my bedroom floor, folding into my embrace. "Look, I didn't mean for your life to get so messed up. You're the one who broke up with me."

They were right.

It's all I can think, a roaring in my ears growing louder, louder. Dad. Livia. Jazmine.

They all said Alana was hurting me. And they were right.

I stand up slowly, one hand tightening around my side. Pain lances through my body, down my arms, tingling my fingers. I flex them and wiggle them around. After that experience, my entire body feels wrong. As I walk toward Alana at the window, I catch my reflection in the mirror and am overwhelmingly relieved to see my usual pale, scared self looking back at me.

Our fingers overlap on the windowsill. She's like fog, like smoke on the wind, but I can almost feel the heat coming from her body.

"You'll help me, Maya," Alana says quietly. "I know you will. You've lost so much already. You can't lose me too."

"Yeah," I say. "Yeah, I've lost a lot. But you know what else?"

"What, Maya?" she asks, voice flat.

I lean in close enough to count every freckle on her face. "With every loss, I got stronger. Just think how strong I'll be after losing you."

I watch the shock register on her face. We stand there, an impossible staredown.

"Maya, you can't be this stupid," she whispers. "We have a deal. You help me do this, and you're safe—"

My arm shoots out, grabbing a fistful of white cotton shirt and pulling her close to me, teeth bared. Until this moment, I wasn't even sure if I could touch her.

But I can. I *can*. The realization sends a bolt of triumph reverberating through my body.

If I can do this, what else am I capable of?

"Alana, I'm done," I spit out, gripping so hard my knuckles

turn white. Her eyes are round and huge, twin moons. "This is evil. If you want to possess somebody, you're going to have to do it on your own."

The smile vanishes from her face. "You tried to get rid of me once before, Maya. Didn't work out so well for you, huh?"

I let go of her hard, shoving backward, and I'm pleased to see her stumble into the windowsill. I've never had a ghost stick around this long, but I assume that the longer they stay, the more they can interact with their surroundings. This is getting dire—I can't let Alana stay here much longer.

I thought maybe she would go peacefully, given time, but now, realizing that she's comfortable enough to possess me, I'm not so sure. Banishing her will be the only way forward. I know it now.

"Are you telling me that you still want to haunt me even when you've learned to possess someone on your own?" I try to make my voice as scornful as possible, determined to cut her with my words the same way she does to me. Try to keep myself sounding strong. "You don't have better things to do but stick around and hurt me?"

"Maya, of course not," Alana says, serene. "I love you."

My eyes squeeze shut tight and I clench my fists, sucking in a long breath. Lightness in my head, floating, a bitter taste in my mouth. I have to go find Valeria, and I have to do it now.

I turn, and I walk out of my bedroom, and I don't look back.

INTERLUDE

———

SEVEN MONTHS EARLIER

"**WRITE A LETTER,**" they tell me.

"You don't have to send it. Just get everything down on paper."

They leave me with paper. They leave me with a pen—this surprises me. Shouldn't they be scared that I'll jam it into my eyeball or something?

The thought makes me laugh, which makes me worry that I'm more fucked-up than I realize, and I shove the paper and pen into my nightstand and don't look at it until night has fallen and moonlight is pooling silver across the hideous linoleum of this godforsaken hospital room.

I don't want to be at Ocean Vista Recovery Center. *A peaceful seaside oasis to heal,* it says on the brochure. I want to light the thing on fire. They took my phone. Alana thinks I'm at my grandmother's house. The idea of her unread texts piling up makes me nauseous.

To distract myself, I grab the paper. If I can just quiet my mind . . .

Dear Alana,
I write.
Things I love about us: Our inside jokes. Playing with your dog. Swimming in your pool. Shopping for each other's Christmas presents at the same time. Making mac and cheese at midnight.
"You don't have to send it."
Feeling important when you listen to what I'm saying. Glowing because you think I'm pretty. The way the world watches us hand in hand and they don't think anything mean or judgmental, they just think, Wow, those girls have got their shit together.
"You don't have to send it."
Knowing they hate us, all the girls at Coldwater. Knowing that no one on earth is more important to you than me.
"You don't have to send it."
I tear the letter into strips, then shred them over a trash can in the bathroom. Back in my temporary room, I climb onto the crisp, sterile sheets and start over, balancing a notebook on my lap.

Dear Alana,

In my dreams, you're a wildfire.
Beautiful from a distance, but you destroy
everything you touch. I've seen it myself, burning
my eyes, the way you rip wings off beautiful things
and watch them die. The friendships you obliterate
because—I don't know—you're bored that day.
I know it's only a matter of time before you destroy
me too.
That's why I'm here. They sent me here because I
seemed depressed, I "wouldn't eat." Like I was refusing

or something. It wasn't that. I couldn't eat. Every
single thing made me nauseous and that's because of
you. Because I'm scared all the time.

Scared of what you'll say, or what you won't say.
Scared of your reaction if I don't pick up the phone fast
enough. Scared of your laugh when it's mean and cold
and directed at me in front of people, supposed to make
me feel small. Scared I'll like a book or movie that
you think is stupid. Scared I'll say something that'll
embarrass you. Scared that one day you'll wake up
bored and fall in love with the first girl who looks at
you for longer than a millisecond.

I love you, and that will be enough. Forever.
You love me, and that will be enough. For now.

CHAPTER SEVENTEEN

I BIKE AROUND the lake to Lilting Brook Road, hell-bent on finding Valeria, mind racing. She'll know how to banish Alana, how to send her on. It's not until the house comes into view that I remember that Rowan is having her stupid party tonight.

I guess I have Alana's possession to thank for scrambling my brain. I still don't feel well—my palms are clammy, slicking the bike handlebars with cold sweat, and my body feels light. It's like anxiety but worse somehow. Sick in a way I can't describe.

My eyes narrow as I force myself to concentrate on my surroundings. Rowan's house is smaller than I expected. A green A-frame, tire swing down by the shoreline. The backyard is larger than Jazmine's, grassy and leading down to a rickety dock that juts out into the water. Moonlight washes across her yard and sparkles on the lake. As usual, I look away.

Music blares inside the house so loudly that I can hear it before I even turn down her driveway. I hop off Jazmine's bike and lean it up against an oak tree with a knotted trunk, distinctive enough that I won't forget it. Nausea swirls in my stomach. Probably it's another post-possession side effect, but I'm sure it also has something to do with the voices carrying from the dock, from the open windows of the house. I pat the pocket of my shorts, making sure my anxiety pill case is still there.

Will Valeria actually be here? It's seeming less likely by the second.

A white stone path winds to a front door with chipped paint. I pause there for half a second, thinking about knocking, but it seems dumb—the door isn't even closed, just resting against the frame. And it smells good, I can tell that already. Having been to my share of gross house parties in LA, the nice smell is what gives me the courage to walk in.

I'm prepared to be ignored, because who could even hear a door creak open with all this noise? But the first person I see bounding toward me is Rowan. I don't notice anything else.

"You came!" she yells, wrapping me in a hug that I don't reciprocate. "I tried to really hype the party up to Jazmine at work today! Told her I thought you'd flake out on me."

"You're not wearing black." I don't know why I say it. Again, my brain is scrambled.

Rowan laughs, throwing her head back. She's holding a bottle of water in one hand, which surprises me—a quick scan of the tiny living room shows that everybody's either cracking open beer cans or sitting on the carpet drinking from bottles of wine. A fat orange cat winds through people's legs, meowing loudly.

"It's not a uniform or anything," she says, pulling back. Her baggy green T-shirt is tucked into another pair of ripped jeans.

I try not to notice the collar falling low, below her collarbone. "Why? Are you disappointed? Should I change into my Blue Skies hat to fulfill your fantasies?"

"No. Sorry. I was actually, um, looking for your mom."

Rowan stares at me, completely caught off guard, then lets out a cackle of laughter even louder than the previous one.

"Mom has an apartment over the store," she says finally, wiping tears of laughter from the corners of her eyes. "She comes back to the house sometimes, but honestly, it's mostly me, especially since tourist season's ramping up. So, did you and my mom have fun plans?"

"Shut up." I wrap my arms across my chest defensively. I really can't afford distractions, not when Alana's made me so angry. "So she's in town tonight?"

"No, she's in Ojai," Rowan says, and my stomach drops. "Visiting my aunt. Pretty sure she said she'll be back early tomorrow morning."

I swear under my breath, looking off into the crowd in the living room. I need to talk to her about banishing Alana *now*. What if she comes after Rowan next?

"Rosier, what's going on?" Rowan's smile fades as she takes in my expression.

"It's nothing. I just . . . needed your mom's help."

"Is it *that* urgent? You can't stay for the party?"

No, I start to say, but freeze, watching Rowan's friends laughing in the living room. Two girls are sharing a beer, passing it back and forth cheerfully, and they remind me of myself and Alana so strongly that all of a sudden I can't breathe. The song that's playing ends, and in the heartbeat moment before the next one starts, I see one of the girls lean forward to her friend and her words float through the air toward me.

". . . why you would say that, but I think drowning is the only option. You know somebody actually drowned in Lake Ember in, like, the eighties? It happens."

"Especially if she was drunk," the friend agrees, twisting her blond hair into a ponytail. "Have they said how old she is?"

She turned eighteen in November, I think, but the other girl just shrugs. "Dunno. I don't really think it's murder, though. The town is being so dramatic, getting all freaked out like Ted Bundy is stalking the streets. People drown all the time."

The bassline of the next song kicks in, obscuring the rest of their conversation. My eyes dart back to Rowan, but she's answering a text, appearing to have missed the whole thing.

Everyone is trying to figure out what happened to Alana. I'm the one who should have the best guess—I know her better than anyone. But I *don't.* I can't understand how she could've wound up in Lake Ember, and obviously, she's not talking to me about it.

"What do you have to drink?" I ask.

Rowan blinks and looks up from her phone, momentarily surprised by my quick subject change. "What do you want? I've got beer, White Claw . . ."

"You drink White Claw?" I snort before I can stop myself.

Rowan's eyes narrow. "No, smartass, but I have guests who do. Also, no need to diss the Claw."

"I was just surprised. It tastes like spiked Capri Sun."

She snorts, whacking me on the shoulder. It actually hurts a little, which I don't think she intended, so I don't say anything, just accept the bottle of Blue Moon she passes me. "Is this good enough for your sophisticated palate, Ms. Hepburn?"

I glance down at the bottle. "Was Audrey Hepburn an alcohol snob?"

"I have no idea. You just look like her a little bit." She reaches for the fridge, one of those vintage ones in canary yellow. "That beer's not for you, by the way."

My thumb is already worrying at the label, peeling it back. "It's not?"

"Nah. Not for my Royal Highness." Rowan slams a cabinet door shut, then whirls around. She's clutching a cut glass champagne flute in one hand, a dark green bottle in the other.

"Oh my god," I say, covering my laugh with one hand. "What is that?"

"Only the best. I worked as a bartender's assistant last winter at all these fancy holiday parties and *maybe* I swiped some of their cool shit. Rich people never miss it." I open my mouth to respond, but she doesn't stop talking. "I had this hidden in the back of the fridge behind the pickles so all these greedy assholes couldn't swipe it. Trade me?"

I hand her the frosty-cold bottle, and she presses the glass into my hand.

"How are you doing now?" Rowan asks, gray eyes suddenly serious. "Did it help at all to go down to the lake?"

"Oh," I say, surprised. "Yeah, honestly, it kind of did. It still freaks me out a little to be this close, but . . ."

"Understandable." She hops up on the kitchen counter, kicking her heels against the chipped wooden cabinet. I hesitate for a minute, then hoist myself up beside her. "I mean, she was your girlfriend."

I study the champagne glass, passing it from one hand to the other. *We were broken up,* I think but don't add. It doesn't feel right to say somehow, like it cheapens our relationship.

Immediately, I shake my head, disgusted by my own thought. *Cheapens our relationship?* Yeah, the beautiful, meaningful, healthy relationship between me and the girl who just possessed me. What is *wrong* with me?

"Okay." Rowan regards me seriously for another moment, then jumps down from the counter. "You look like a girl who needs to drink champagne on the dock."

Outside, the dock has cleared out, people trudging back along a well-worn grass path for the front door. Rowan calls out to some of them, waves to others.

"How do you know all these people?"

She shrugs. "High school. Work. Everybody either works at Blue Skies or comes in for chai. Lake towns are one of those creepy places where all the kids know each other growing up."

I think of LA, the sprawling heat of the city, anonymous faces. The summers I spent here in what I'm growing to realize was isolation from the locals, reading Jane Austen on the back porch and practicing flips off the boat dock with Alana.

"I don't think it's so creepy."

Rowan stops when we reach the dock, shifting her weight so the champagne bottle rests against her hip. One fist closes tight around the cork and she twists the bottle. I realize a second too late what's about to happen, reaching out a hand to stop her—

It pops anticlimactically, hissing, a trail of silvery smoke bursting out. Her smile is unmistakably proud.

"Hold out that glass," she says. I do, and I watch her as she pours. She passes me the glass and I take it by the stem.

"You really didn't have to put this in a fancy glass. It's a nice one, I can tell."

"Yeah. Waterford."

"You're kidding me."

"I don't kid about luxury Irish crystal," she says seriously, but when I sneak a look out of the corner of my eye I can see her smirking. Then she points straight ahead, out across the lake.

"See that house out there?"

"Yeah." I squint, barely making out a dark shape. Some of the first-floor lights are on, spilling out across the water. "I see it."

"That's your house. Well, Jazmine's house."

"Oh, seriously?"

Rowan tosses her short hair; even in the dark, I can tell, because there's a particular scent of shampoo that clings to it. "Yep. It's easier to see in the daytime, obviously. It's a pretty view. Jazmine takes great care of her garden. Sometimes I sit out here at night and look over."

"Oh yeah?" I turn toward her, smirking. "Should I change the porch lightbulb to a green one so you can pine for me more effectively?"

She raises her eyebrows. "Oh, she's clever, huh?"

My front teeth press into my lower lip, leave a mark. I shouldn't say things like that. Alana would be impressed with a solid literary reference, but she'd hate everything else about this conversation.

Out past the dock, I watch stars flicker across the twilight blue sky, trees with wind-creaky branches. Normally, the lake would be packed with boats humming along, kicking up a wake. But everything is eerily silent, the water and beaches deserted. Tainted by the fresh horror of a girl's body floating to the surface.

Before I realize what I'm doing, I've drained my entire champagne flute.

"You sure you're okay, Rosier?" Rowan asks.

"I'm sorry. It's just getting to be a lot. All these girls who haven't even been my friends in years saying all kinds of shit to the media . . ." My voice cracks, but for once, I don't hide it. "I'm scared that they're going to paint it like I'm guilty."

"Look, even if they do keep talking to the media, and even if they do say questionable shit, the truth *always* comes out. I'm gonna tell you something I don't usually tell people."

"You don't have to."

"No, I want to. So, my grandmother died when I was young. I understand the grieving process and how it changes and contorts over time—you might not even realize it yet, but it's like fighting demons every single day. But you're *strong*, Rosier—I know I haven't known you for very long, but you *are*, and I wish you knew."

Guilt lances through me. *I do know,* I want to say, but the words tangle up inside me and won't come out. Wordlessly, I take the bottle from Rowan; she holds on to it for a second, hesitating, before relinquishing it to me. When I lift it to my lips, she doesn't comment on it.

"And here's a secret," she says quietly. "Nobody broke you. Okay? In your worst moments when you feel small, like you've been torn into pieces, I want you to remember that, okay? Maybe sometime in your life, someone tried to break you, but they couldn't, Maya."

I lift my head, wiping stray tears off my cheeks before she can see, trying to calm my racing heart. I knock back another gulp of champagne.

She's never called me Maya before.

The thought explodes like fireworks inside me, crackling

and popping in all the brightest colors. But before she can say anything else, she's interrupted by a chirp. We both look down, startled, to see a large, orange cat winding around my legs.

"Wilde!" Rowan exclaims gleefully. "The life of the party! What are you doing all the way down here, bud?"

"Wilde, like Oscar?"

"Olivia," she corrects. I can't tell if she's joking.

"Is she supposed to be doing this?" I'm afraid to move.

Rowan laughs, bending down and scuffing her knuckles against Wilde's little chin. "Yeah, it means she likes you. Wilde is a good judge of character. She loves the lake, too. Guards it."

"Hey, Rowan . . ."

"What's up?"

"I'm sorry that I've been kind of weird around you. You were nice to me today, and I just . . ." I pause, imagining how the next couple sentences could go. *You see, the ghost of my ex-girlfriend has been wandering around Jazmine's house, plotting to possess you and snuff out your soul. Oh, and by the way, she thinks I'm going to help her do it.*

Rowan sips her drink. "It's fine."

"No, it's really not. I just wanted you to know that I have a hard time talking to people sometimes. Alana taught me how to act around other people. How to get what I want. Sometimes I act like her, and I don't mean it."

"I get it."

"Plus, I, um, have an anxiety disorder, basically. Things weren't always this hard for me. I used to be normal."

Rowan tucks a stray piece of hair behind my ear. She leans close to me, close enough that in the moonlight and the flickering glow from the citronella torches, I can see faint freckles scattered across her cheeks. "Well, I think you're normal. Honestly."

My eyes meet hers. I think a lot of things, things like *this is stupid* and *this is a horrible decision* and *this is not even a decision at all.*

And then, before I have time to figure out what the hell she's doing, she leans forward and splashes me with water.

I flinch, recoiling, laughter bursting from me. "What the fuck? That's so cold!"

She's already getting to her feet, laughing to herself. Her back is turned so I can barely make out the words when she says them.

She says, "You look happy tonight."

■ ■ ■

The rest of the night passes in a blur. After a while, I'm not thinking about how Alana possessed me, how I need to banish her to save both of us. I'm not thinking about anything at all.

Rowan's little house is warm and bright, and after finishing the bottle of champagne I'm relaxed enough to move into tequila shots with a bunch of girls in the kitchen. They chase each one with a sip of cider from a sweaty can, so I follow their lead. There's a lull in conversation and Rowan turns around. I'm tipsy enough to stumble into her, but she catches me with strong hands and holds me upright.

"Did you like the champagne?" she asks, leaning in so her lips brush my ear. I assume this was accidental.

"Yeah, it was fine."

"Fine?" She pulls back, laughing. "Should be better than fine."

"What do you mean?"

"It was a Dom Perignon '02."

I gasp, smacking both palms against her shoulders. "*That's* what you gave me to drink? Oh my god, and I drank it all!"

"Maya, it's fine." Everything's blurry but she looks like a movie star when she laughs, head thrown back. "What'd I tell you? Only the best for Her Royal Highness."

"Actually, you said *my* Royal Highness," I correct before I can stop myself. She opens her mouth, but I interrupt, pink flush creeping across my cheeks that's only half because of the alcohol. "Look, you should've just given me cheap beer like everyb—why do you even *have* Dom Perignon in your house?"

"Remember, I told you I swiped it?" She laughs. "Listen, I hope you're having a good time."

We both turn to watch as people filter in and out of the kitchen. Some of the remaining partygoers are laughing over an elaborate drinking game in the tiny living room. It all seems so nice, so calm. So normal.

"I want to feel normal," I tell Rowan, who's leaning up against the counter. Everything looks blurry and gold-washed. I blink slowly, eyelashes feathering against my cheeks. "Do you ever just wish that? That you could be normal?"

"Never once," Rowan answers smoothly.

"Well, yeah, of course," I grumble. "You're cool. Look at this—all these friends you have. It's bullshit."

"Excuse me?"

I stare down at my shoes, but I can hear a note of amusement in Rowan's voice.

"You probably don't even have to try and people like you.

I try *so hard*." My voice trembles, surprising me. "All the time. All I do is try. And what the fuck do I get for it? People keep leaving, people keep dying."

"Rosier—"

But I'm not listening to her anymore. I'm not thinking about how the house is full of people, how it's late, how Alana's ghost possessed me just a couple hours ago, how the police could very likely be preparing to accuse me of murder. All I'm thinking about is Rowan, who's nice to me. Who brought me a long-stemmed rose and looks across the moonlight-flecked lake toward my house.

The last thing I'm aware of is the cool gray of her eyes, the faint dusting of freckles across her cheeks that I can only see when I lean close. The warmth when I press my lips to hers, tasting sparkling champagne. Her fingers tightening around my upper arms—

and pushing me away.

My heart sinks, my vision sharpens.

"Maya," Rowan says, eyes wide, face sheet white. "Listen . . ."

"Oh god." The words spill out and I yank out of her grasp. "I'm sorry. I'm so sorry."

"No, no—" Rowan reaches for me, but I've already crossed the kitchen, turning away so that my hair falls across my face. "It's okay, I didn't mean to hurt your feelings. You're just—"

"Fucked-up. I know," I spit out, and somehow I'm rushing through the living room, out into the windy dark. Trees creak around me as I cross the driveway in search of Jazmine's bike. I swear under my breath, spinning back and forth. I thought I left it in an obvious place.

"Maya!" The house's front door slams shut. *Damn it.* Rowan's sprinting up the driveway in my direction. "Listen to me, please—I'm not mad. I didn't mean to . . . You're just going through so much right now, okay? You drank a lot. I didn't want you to do something you'd regret."

The silver metal of the bike catches the moonlight and relief floods through me. I dart toward it, hopping on before Rowan can catch up to me. And then I pedal off, the world dark and frantic and enveloping me with tendrils of electric fear.

Rowan's words follow me on the wind, but they can't catch me.

CHAPTER EIGHTEEN

I DON'T KNOW how I make it home, drunk and teary-eyed and weaving along the dirt road that wraps around the lake, but somehow, I do.

The first floor of Jazmine's house is dark except for a glowing kitchen nightlight. I stumble up the back porch, fumble with the lock—judging from the upstairs lights and the creaking floorboards, I'm assuming Jazmine is awake and chatting on the phone. Her guests probably went home hours ago. I don't think she'll be upset that I went to Rowan's, but still, I don't want to talk about it with her. I ease my way around the screen door, and something crunches under my shoe.

I freeze, lifting my foot, reaching down. A sharp pain lances across the palm of my hand.

"Shit." I fumble in the dark for the switch. Warm yellow light floods the room.

I gasp, my back slamming against the door.

Every cabinet is open, one still swinging on its hinges. Wineglasses, mason jars, champagne flutes, every type of glass imaginable has been thrown onto the linoleum, shattering into pieces. Some are crushed so finely that it looks like a snowstorm blew through. A shard is embedded in the bottom of my shoe. Leaning against the fridge, I carefully pull it out, wincing at the ribbon of blood trickling from my palm. Droplets sprinkle the floor like rain.

Alana's revenge—I should've expected this.

I close my eyes. Breathe in, breathe out. Make a plan.

Okay. I hoist myself up onto the counter, crawling awkwardly over the sink—it's then that I realize I'm definitely still not sober yet, the kitchen sink wheeling wildly beneath me—and hop down as soon as I've reached a clear spot on the floor. The broom is exactly where I remember, in the pantry, and I have almost everything swept up by the time I hear my sister creaking her way down the upstairs hallway.

"Maya?" Jazmine calls, bare feet thumping down the staircase. "Is that you?"

"Shit, shit, shit," I mumble, turning wildly from left to right, broom in hand. At my feet, there's a dustpan filled with glass shards. My hand is still bleeding.

"Maya?"

My back is to the doorway as I rinse my cut at the sink, pressing a damp paper towel against my palm and raising it high to stop the bleeding. I bite my lip against the stinging pain as Jazmine rounds the corner, then turn around to face her.

My sister's wearing her pajamas, flannel pants with an oversized Stanford tee. In one hand, she's clutching her phone.

"Jesus!" she exclaims, taking in the sight. "Oh my gosh—Maya, what happened? Are you bleeding?"

"No," I say automatically as blood trickles down my arm.

"You are! Come here." She whips a package of Band-Aids out from under the sink at the speed of light, cracking it open and shaking one out into her hand. "And there's glass all over the floor? What happened?"

"I, um, dropped some stuff."

She pauses midway through unwrapping a Band-Aid like she's going to question this, then shakes her head. "It's okay. I'll help you clean it up."

"No, don't worry about it—sorry, you were on the phone and I interrupted you."

"It's okay. I was talking to your dad." She pauses, eyeing me with such a weird look that fear clenches in my stomach.

"Wait, is Dad okay? Did something happen?"

"Oh, no, your dad's fine. It's about . . . Alana."

My breathing stutters and stalls. "What now?"

"Apparently Melissa Murray's ex-husband is in town, and they've decided to hold the funeral service tomorrow. It'll be a memorial service in the morning, and then a . . . a burial in the afternoon. Your dad just wanted to make sure we knew. He mentioned he's been texting you a bit too, but I told him you've had a lot on your plate."

Jazmine takes my hand gently, unfurling my fist and delicately placing a bandage over the cut on my palm. The gesture is so careful, so reminiscent of Mom, that I almost cry.

"Oh," I say quietly. Now I know what people mean when they talk about sobering up quickly. It feels unbelievable that I could've just been kissing Rowan—oh my *god*, I kissed *Rowan*—an hour ago.

"Would you like to go to the memorial?" Jazmine asks,

giving my hand a light squeeze before letting it go. I wish Mom was here to comfort me, but honestly, my sister is the next best thing. "Whatever you choose is okay."

"It's graduation tomorrow." I hear this like someone else is saying it, a ghostly vestige of my old self.

Her eyes soften. "Graduation was postponed. In light of the circumstances."

"But how can they be burying her already?" I hold my bandaged hand close to my chest. "Don't they . . . don't they have to . . ."

But I can't think of anything, any reason her burial should be postponed. It sinks over me slowly like fog: Alana's dead. Alana Murray, my best friend, my girlfriend, the person I loved more than anyone else, is *dead* and she's never coming back. Not even through possession. After I banish her, that'll be it.

And now I'll have to stand by her grave, acting like everything's normal.

"I know this is a lot," Jazmine says, watching me carefully. "You can let me know in the morning what you decide. If you want to go, I'll drive down with you, and your dad will be there too. Head up to bed, okay? I'll clean this stuff up."

"No, I can do it. I'm almost finished anyway." I grab the broom with my bandaged hand. "It's my mess."

My sister shrugs, turning away, but I catch her glancing back at me before she leaves the kitchen. She's worrying about me. If she had any idea what I was really up against, she would never sleep again.

Her footsteps creak up the staircase. I stand with the broom clutched in one hand, squeezing tight, trying to count the seconds as I breathe, in and out, in and out. Jazmine's bedroom door closes, silence falls.

And the screen door crashes open behind me.

Barely catching a scream before it bursts out of my lungs, I whirl around, letting the broom clatter to the floor. The door bounces off a kitchen cabinet, warm night air pouring in. A rumble of thunder carries on the wind. Impossible—it's been a perfect, clear night. But no, of course, there's one explanation.

I take cautious steps toward the doorway, squinting to see anything in the blackness beyond. There's a breeze, but nowhere near strong enough to blow a closed door wide open. As soon as I reach the back porch, I see it: a trail of poppy petals, dark as bloodstains, sprinkled across the floorboards.

"Maya."

It sounds like wind through the trees high above, goose bumps rippling on my forearms making the hairs stand on end. I don't see Alana, but I hear her.

"I can't say I'm surprised." Her voice is clearer now. Behind me. I spin around, heart in my throat—she's standing with her back to the doorway, blocking my entrance, trapping me out in the hot dark. Golden light from the kitchen outlines her like a halo.

"What are you talking about?"

"You should know better than to throw yourself at people. What, you really thought she was going to kiss you back? You thought she was going to fall in love with you?" She laughs, and I hate her, I hate her, I hate her.

"I didn't think—"

"Too. Much. Work," Alana says, overenunciating each word. "Even if she thinks you're cute now, how cute will it be when she has to hold your hand every time you have a panic attack and remind you to breathe?"

"Fuck you."

Alana smirks, long hair falling over her shoulders as she leans close.

"We deserve each other, you and me," she whispers. "Always have. Always will."

I push away, facing out toward the lake. Jazmine left a citronella candle on the railing. Needing to do something with my hands, I grab the matchbook and strike one against the box, the sound violent and jarring in the still night air. Dip the match against the wick and watch it explode into light.

"And when Rowan gets tired of you," Alana says behind me, "because she will, because everyone always has, because they'll *always* get tired of you, Maya—you'll miss me. More than you can even imagine."

I stare at the candle flame. It casts long shadows that spill along the backyard as it slopes down to the lake that claimed Alana's life, water gently lapping against rocks.

"By the time you realize how much you need me, it'll be too late." Her palm presses against my shoulder. It's ice-cold and light as breath, but I feel it. When she speaks again, there's a waver in her voice, and this is the only thing that could get me to turn around.

"I'll be six feet underground. Gone. I'll be a carved marble headstone that you come to visit once a year. If ever." Alana's lower lip quivers. I blink, sure I'm imagining the genuine sadness on her face. "Hopefully you'll bring me some nice flowers, at least."

"I will," I tell her.

"You will what?"

"Bring you flowers."

We both fall silent. Long after she disappears, I stand rooted to the spot, bare feet freezing, until the candle burns itself out and the night wraps me in darkness.

■ ■ ■

According to Google, Major Arcana opens at nine in the morning. At 8:57 I'm already there, leaning Jazmine's bike up against the brick exterior wall with a Starbucks cold brew clutched in one hand.

"Maya!" Valeria sees me through the glass storefront window, hurrying to unlock the door. A variety of bells jingle out a welcome; it sounds like Santa's sleigh just rolled into town. "My goodness. What brings you here so early?"

"Hi—I'm sorry to bother you," I stammer as she hurries me inside to a welcome burst of air-conditioning. "I wouldn't have come over this early if it wasn't urgent."

Valeria frowns, holding a hair tie between her teeth so she can collect her black hair into a high ponytail. She's wearing thick-rimmed glasses and looks exhausted, probably from her early morning arrival back in town. I don't give myself time to feel guilty about bothering her.

"An emergency?" she asks.

"Somewhat."

She snaps the hair tie around her ponytail in a swift motion. "This doesn't have anything to do with the questions you were asking me about possession last week, I hope."

"Oh, um, no." I sip my coffee nervously, watching her bustle around behind the counter. "I wanted to ask you about banishing ghosts."

"Banishing them? Haven't you ever done that before? I assumed . . ."

"No, I haven't," I say honestly. "Not really. I've never had anybody refuse to leave before."

"And this one is refusing."

I hesitate, but she continues anyway.

"You know the typical protective steps, I assume?" Valeria sounds like my Latin teacher grilling us on declensions.

"Well, kind of." I lick my lips nervously. "I salt the doorways. Ever since I was a kid, I've been doing that."

"If you find you need a banishment ritual, something more powerful . . ." She reaches for the stack of books lined up on the wall behind her, selecting a few and sliding them toward me. "These have always worked well enough for me. You'll want to burn a fire—here, I'll write this down for you."

I watch, mesmerized, as she rips a piece of paper off a stenographer's pad from behind the counter.

"Burn a fire," she continues, "and within it, you'll make a sacrifice. If you can get ahold of an item that belonged to the deceased, that makes for a perfect sacrifice. Finally, you'll want to use a sacred phrase as a type of invocation—this is common in many rituals. Even if you're not religious, try to find something that resonates with you personally."

"Okay," I say somewhat skeptically, taking the paper from Valeria. "That's everything?"

"Most importantly, should a spirit become violent—should it attempt to possess you or someone else—you'll need to be strong. This will intimidate the spirit and force it out."

My mouth goes dry. "But how—how do I make myself strong?"

"Find out *why* the spirit wants to remain here on earth so

badly," Valeria says, concentrating hard on my face. "Do this with authority. Do not be afraid. When you've reminded the spirit that you're the one in charge, and you're the one with the power to decide when it can move on—that's very humbling. Never forget, Maya, that *you* are the one with the inner strength. With the mental fortitude."

I swallow past a lump in my throat. Wishing I believed her.

CHAPTER NINETEEN

Cause of death determined in Alana Murray disappearance case

By Jack Abramowitz, Lacey Lopez

Updated 9:08 AM PT, Saturday, May 11, 2024

(CNN) A break in the Alana Murray investigation came early Saturday morning, when Los Angeles County Coroner Don Werner attributed the teenager's tragic death to blunt force trauma. As of press time, exact details regarding Alana Murray's death have not been released to the public.

The death of Murray, an 18-year-old whose remains were pulled from the waters of Santa Clarita County's Lake Ember on May 8, has rocked the community. Coldwater Canyon School for Girls, the

Studio City private school Murray attended, held a moment of silence at a Friday evening memorial. The school's graduation ceremony, originally scheduled for today, has been postponed by a week. During this ceremony, Murray would have received her high school diploma. Instead, the diploma will be presented to her mother, who will also accept a posthumous Coldwater Citizenship Award on her daughter's behalf.

Several close friends of Murray's spoke briefly during Friday's memorial.

"Alana was beautiful and brave, and she loved everyone around her," graduating senior Madison Kim read. "She was a vibrant spirit and a true friend. As the police have stated, the circumstances surrounding her death are suspicious. It breaks my heart to think that someone Alana knew and loved might have information regarding her death. Again, if anyone knows why Alana was in Lake Ember that day, please come forward."

But perhaps the most emotional tribute came from classmate Elise Carter-Holloway, a longtime friend of Murray's.

"It's tremendously moving to ruminate on the impact Alana made on us all," she spoke through tears. "We are truly all better for knowing her."

Speculation regarding Alana Murray's disappearance and subsequent death has run rampant on social media. A popular subject of discussion in recent days is Maya Rosier, a Coldwater Canyon School senior who was absent from the memorial and, records show, has a family home on Lake Ember. Many users believe she was Murray's girlfriend, while school officials have refused to comment on Murray's personal life.

...

The only funeral I've ever been to before was Mom's, and I was so young that the entire thing is a blur of lilies, uncomfortable clothing, and adults I didn't remember giving me hugs I didn't ask for. When I walk in through the doors of the funeral home in Burbank later that morning, Jazmine by my side, I feel like I've stumbled onto an alien planet.

A giant poster-sized version of Alana's senior picture greets me in the lobby, which is trying really hard to look like someone's welcoming living room. The furniture is pristine, the carpet bursting with a dark green and deep violet floral print, and the white-painted walls are sprinkled here and there with generic paintings of things like sailboats and pastoral countryside. There are no windows. It's like a room that exists outside of time.

"Are you okay?" Jazmine whispers in my ear.

I swallow hard and nod. If it wasn't completely lame, I would ask her to hold my hand. It's hard to make out people's identities as I scan the room, since everyone's dressed in black, but it's obvious that there are more young people here than at your average funeral. People are congregating by two immense double doors that lead to the chapel, where the carpet turns to a lush red velvet and pews line both sides. There are fewer people in there, and with one quick glance, I realize why. That's the receiving line.

Dad meets us as we approach the chapel. His button-down shirt is wrinkled like he just pulled it out of the dryer. First, he hugs Jazmine, then turns to me, eyes full of concern and protectiveness. It reminds me of when I was little and he always had the softest spot for me, the first to volunteer to come get me from a sleepover when I was homesick. During the past year, I've detached from him; when he pulls me into a hug, somehow, I can feel how this detachment has hurt him, and it makes my body heavy with regret.

At the front of the chapel, Melissa Murray is standing by the closed casket, a tall man at her side—it takes me a second to recognize him as Alana's shitty dad, who I haven't seen in years. He's wearing a suit and looking morose. Both of them are engaged in a somber conversation with Alana's AP English Lit teacher.

I look up at Jazmine. *Do I have to go in there?* I ask silently.

She blinks back down at me, eyes full of pity. I can tell she's not going to force me, but I also know I don't really have a choice.

After sucking in a deep breath, I motion for my sister to follow me, and we join the receiving line. I try to ignore the giant framed senior portrait propped up along the wall, Alana's long hair perfectly curled while she smirks into the camera. Calligraphy is superimposed across the bottom in glittering gold.

ALANA MARINA MURRAY
November 8, 2005—May 4, 2024

I stare at her face so that I don't have to think about what's waiting for me at the front of the room. A polished wood casket latched shut—

Blunt force trauma, my brain screams, and I press a hand to my mouth, suddenly afraid I might throw up—

Concentrate on the sprawl of flowers adorning the casket: lush white lilies, lavender roses, baby pink carnations. The smell makes me want to gag.

All I see behind my eyes is broken glass sprinkled across the lake house kitchen floor like bits of ice, blood spilling down my palm. All I hear is the anger that crackled in Alana's voice when she told me that I was the only one who could save her.

I swallow, twisting my hair into a ponytail just to have something to do with my hands. Standing in this air-conditioned room, all of these problems feel like a fairy tale. Alana's ghost has become a regular fixture in my life, so how is it possible that her body is in that box at the front of the room? It's impossible, surreal. The receiving line is still moving, and despite taking my anxiety meds this morning, I can feel a rising swell of abject panic in my chest.

Suddenly, Melissa and Anton Murray are right in front of me. I'm not sure how that happened so quickly.

"Oh, honey," Melissa says—but she's talking to Jazmine, not me. Her perfume is intense, settling over me like a cloud. Sunglasses hang around her neck on a pearl chain. Why won't she look at me? "Thank you so much for coming. It means the world."

I open my mouth to speak up, to make her see me, but I can't.

Alana's dad hugs me, tears in his eyes, even though I

have no clue if he remembers who I am. Then I break away, Jazmine murmuring condolences to Alana's parents behind me. Melissa still hasn't said a word to me.

She's dead, a voice says flatly inside my head. *She's dead because you left her alone on the trail, and now she's never coming back. All these people are here today, mourning her, because of what you did. Mrs. Murray hates you now because of what you did.*

I almost trip over my feet in my hurry to back away from her parents. Anxiety skitters up and down my bare arms, and I hug myself around my chest to keep from shivering.

Jazmine catches me, an arm slung around my shoulders.

"Maya," she says quietly, smoothing my hair with her free hand. She guides me back toward the lobby, talking softly along the way. "It's okay. That was a lot, you know? You probably don't remember Mom's—well, anyway, nobody expects anybody to be calm and collected at a funeral. You're doing great. Would you like to leave?"

"I—" My teeth are chattering. No matter how hard I try, I can't force the words out.

I blink and Dad is next to me, a warm, reassuring hand on my back. He's got a strained look on his face. I wonder if it's discomfort from being at some kind of social gathering that's not hosted by his restaurant, or just the general funeral atmosphere.

"Look at this," Dad says in a clear attempt to distract me. I try to focus on what he's pointing out. Thanks to my therapist, my father knows all the old tricks: name three things you can see, two things you can touch.

Different-sized posterboards have been propped up on easels around the lobby. People dressed in black wander around, smiling sadly as they examine the photos that have been glued

255

to each board. It only takes a minute to realize that they're set up in chronological order, starting with a photo of Melissa lying in a hospital bed and holding a newborn Alana.

"Who put these together?" I ask, stepping closer to the first poster. There's a Polaroid of a toddler Alana in a snowsuit, standing outside what must have been her childhood home in Denver. I'm imagining Mrs. Murray sitting in her dark kitchen, gluing photos to posterboard; the mental image fills me with a hollowness I can't comprehend.

"Some of the girls from your class, I think. That's what Melissa said." Dad rests a hand on my shoulder.

I freeze, staring at the next posterboard. Horror settles into my stomach, making my arms and legs feel heavy. Slowly, I drag myself forward to examine the posters more closely—but no, it's true. There are ten posterboards documenting Alana's eighteen years, each one featuring photos from pivotal moments of her life.

And I'm not in any of them.

It's like a nightmare where your feet are frozen to the ground, unable to run, unable to scream. Whoever made this rewrote Alana's life. They erased me from everything: The play that Alana, Elise, and I starred in back in sixth grade. Alana grinning and posing in a feather boa at my thirteenth birthday party. Alana hugging Elise at our eighth grade graduation. Alana, Elise, Madison, and a bunch of other girls on the first day of freshman year.

I step up to the board from this past year. There's no way they'll be able to erase me from this one. We were together almost every minute that I can remember, sheltered and hidden away from the rest of the world, just the way Alana wanted it.

I barely spoke to anyone else, even my own family, because I only belonged to Alana.

"Dad," I ask quietly. "Who did you say made these?"

"Oh, I don't remember what Melissa said—I think the Carter-Holloway kid was one of them."

I move closer, squinting at the posterboards. More people are congregating in the area, a blur of bodies and a hum of soft, respectful voices. There's my AP English teacher, there's the soccer coach from when we were in middle school. I blink hard, trying to focus on the photos, when a woman I don't know appears at my elbow.

"Oh, her poor girlfriend," she says quietly, and I jump, turning. She's addressing a man in a black polo; both of them are unfamiliar, and instead of staring down at me like I expect, they're focused on the posters. "This must be so hard for her."

I follow the line of their gaze. Amid the photos of Alana on the soccer team and hugging her mom by the Christmas tree, there are pictures of Alana with Elise. Way too many. They're squeezed in a booth at Katsuya, laughing over plates of sushi, weirdly close. Elise's arms draped around Alana's shoulders while they pose in formal dresses, Alana's midnight black and Elise's pristine white. I saw that dress hanging in Alana's closet and she told me her mom bought it for her to wear to a family party, but I can tell the photo was taken at this year's winter dance, which I skipped since I was having a bad anxiety day. I'd spent the entire night sobbing in my room and texted Alana, begging her to come over. She'd told me she was sick and would call me in the morning.

The last photo is a selfie, Elise holding out her phone to capture Alana's head resting on her shoulder. Alana is smiling at the camera, but Elise is looking at Alana. Immediately, I can pinpoint the day the photo was taken. Alana and I had a big fight in February over nothing, me crying about how she would forget about me when she went to college, her looking at me in disgust and telling me she couldn't handle my tears. That I was too much. I was too difficult. I screamed at her to just *go*, then, and I can still see her behind my closed eyelids: pale pink T-shirt, jean shorts, hair loose and long. She had cut bangs herself that weekend, Valentine's Day weekend, both of us laughing in my bathroom. They came out crooked. She only had them for a day before heading to the stylist to get them fixed.

This picture could only have been taken that same day. She must have left my house and headed straight for Elise's.

How long had this been going on? Did they go to the winter dance *together*? Spend Valentine's Day together? A wave of nausea rolls over me—I can't remember a single holiday we spent together in the past year, a date we went on in public. I don't want to believe it, but I think it might be true. She's been with Elise, and I've been the ghost.

White-hot anger explodes behind my eyelids like fireworks. I don't even realize how fast I'm walking until I hear Jazmine and Dad calling my name across the lobby. My hands hit the back doors of the funeral home; they slam open, banging into the wall on both sides, and I storm out into the blinding sunlight at exactly the perfect time.

Elise is closing the door of her parents' glossy black SUV when I reach her. It takes her a minute to realize who she's looking at: her eyes are wide, lined with mascara, and all I can think about is tearing her apart with my bare hands.

"You fucking *liar*," I spit out.

Dimly, I'm aware of my dad yelling my name across the parking lot, of Elise's parents climbing out of the car in a flurry of movement. I don't care. I don't care about any of it.

Before Elise can speak, my fist collides with her face, sending her spinning to the asphalt. She goes down hard, and I stand above her, gasping for air. And the world explodes.

"Maya!" my dad roars from somewhere behind me.

"Whoa!" Elise's dad shouts. "What the hell?"

I launch myself at Elise again, but someone catches me around the waist, straining to hold me back.

"No, let me go," I choke out. "She—she . . ."

"Stop it, Maya," a voice hisses in my ear, and through my rage and panic, I can pick out the voice of Elise's little sister, Isabelle. I twist in her arms. She's surprisingly strong, her grip like a vise. "Seriously. Calm down."

I sink an elbow into her stomach, satisfied when she stumbles backward, releasing me. But not for long—Dad grabs me, and there's no breaking away. He wrestles me toward his car.

Jazmine is frantic, scurrying forward. "Mr. Carter, Mrs. Holloway, I'm so sorry—please excuse my sister, it's a hard day for everyone, you know? This is—Elise, I'm so sorry, can I get you some ice, or . . . ?"

Elise looks up from the ground, spitting dark hair out of her mouth. Her mother is fussing over her, trying to pull her to her feet, but Elise swats her away. Our eyes lock, and an electric current of understanding passes between us. She says something, low as a rumble of thunder. In the chaos, I can't make it out, but I think it's *I loved her more.*

Her hand presses against her face, where I can already see an angry red welt forming. When she scrambles up, I see that her knees are scraped and bloody. Good.

"Looks like you were right about her, sweetheart," their father says gruffly as Jazmine yanks open the backseat of our Audi and Dad shoves me in, like I'm being loaded into a cop car. "Violent fucking kid."

...

No one knows Alana Murray like I do.

The world can think what they want, but I'm the one who watched her sleep when we were twelve years old and she had spent the entire night crying at my house because her father forgot her birthday. In the moonlight, I counted her freckles, watched her dark eyelashes fall in shadow across her cheeks. I didn't have the words for what I felt back then, but I do now.

By the time Jazmine and I arrive at the burial plot that afternoon, I've carved myself out of stone. I stand still and expressionless as Melissa Murray sobs behind her sunglasses. I don't flinch when people stare at me, when they whisper my name, call me crazy, a monster. I definitely don't cry, not even when everyone lays red roses on top of her casket.

Because when their backs are turned, I feel a sudden, urgent gust of cold wind ripple through the grove. My skirt flutters against my thighs and I look down, startled; for a second, it almost felt like somebody brushed my hand. But no—lying in the perfectly manicured grass is a small handful of California poppy petals.

I scoop them up silently. Hold them in my closed fist until the line moves and it's my turn to press my hand against her coffin lid. And I let the petals fall like rain.

CHAPTER TWENTY

DAD LEAVES IT up to Jazmine to discipline me, which is how I know I'm in deep shit. His temper strikes like lightning, rendering him speechless, and I know from experience it will take some time for the anger to burn away. He's back to work, back to his life, and I'm trapped here in Jazmine's car barreling up the 101. We're almost in Lake Ember before she'll speak to me.

"Maya, I'm trying to go easy on you here, because you're obviously going through a lot," she says, fiddling with her Jeep's air-conditioning. "But do you want to tell me why you thought your behavior was at all appropriate?"

"No," I say quietly. "I know it wasn't appropriate."

I bite my thumbnail, waiting for Jazmine to say more, but she's quiet until we pull into her driveway. My car is still there, looking pathetic and deserted; Jazmine parks next to it. She cuts the ignition and we both sit there, silence descending on us like a dense fog.

"When your dad called about the funeral," my sister says, hands still resting on the steering wheel, "he thought you should go, but I thought it would be too traumatic for you. But then he said, *We shouldn't deprive Maya of her chance to mourn and say goodbye.* We're the adults, so when all is said and done, I guess this was our mistake."

She doesn't look at me, just stares straight out at the sprawling yard and the lake beyond, glistening in the sunlight. Silent and empty still.

I swallow, looking down at my phone in my lap so I don't have to face her.

"Your dad can't constantly supervise you in LA the way you apparently need," Jazmine is saying. "So you'll stay here. And I'm finding you a new therapist in the area."

"Fine."

My sister turns to me then. Out of the corner of my eye, I can see the curiosity on her face, finally overpowering her anger.

"Why did you hit her? Elise, I mean. What did she do to you?"

I yank open the passenger door and jump out onto the driveway.

■ ■

Up in my room, I pack my incense bundle and light it with a match, holding it in every corner of my bedroom to clear it of all negative energy. Breathe in cedar, frankincense.

Then, I drag a plastic laundry basket from the bathroom into my room and fill it up with everything I need to get rid of: a Coldwater Canyon T-shirt from the end of the school year that everyone autographed in Sharpie. A pack of birthday cards from Alana that I tied with a scrunchie and stowed in my suitcase, lipstick kisses and *I love you* scrawled on the envelopes. Polaroids that lit up her eyes in electric blue, that sent my smile sparkling.

My dresser drawers rattle and slam, slipping out of my shaking hands. I throw my clothes onto the floor in a pile. There's a couple of Alana's T-shirts that I wore to sleep, jean cutoffs I made with Elise, a tank top I wore when we all went to a street fair. All the clothes my dad sent when I came up to stay here.

Burn it all.

I stomp down the staircase with everything clutched in my arms, through the kitchen, where I grab a book of matches from the pantry. Slam the back door, let it bang on its hinges. If Jazmine hears me, she doesn't try to stop me.

Elise and Alana. Elise and Alana. I make it out the back door before I have to stop, dropping the basket, bending over, hands on my knees, and gagging into the bushes. I haven't eaten since breakfast, and I choke on stomach acid and bile.

All those times Elise would breathe with me through my anxiety, all the things I told her about my fears about the future. She would hold my hand and tell me everything was going to be okay. And other people must have known—there are no secrets at Coldwater. The thought of the other girls in our class covering for the two of them while they snuck around behind my back acting like soulmates, staring lovingly into each other's eyes, is impossible. It's unthinkable.

But I know it happened. Those photos on the posters—they weren't fake.

And as much as I hate it, I can hear it. Alana whispering

to Elise in the dead of night, the quiet hours where you can be honest and unheard. I can imagine what she probably said. *Maya and I fight all the time. She'll be fine with us being together.*

I can't believe I didn't realize this was happening. I'm an *idiot*. Is Alana really that diabolical that she could kiss me, sleep in the same bed as me, and . . . be with someone else? It crashes down around me, panic spiking through my veins— the devastating realization that maybe I never really knew her at all.

But why wouldn't Alana just break up with me? If she wanted to be with somebody else, why not just cut me loose? In the weeks leading up to Antelope Valley, I had agonized over whether I should end our relationship. Whether I could handle the pain, whether Alana would fight me on the decision, whether I had the strength to stand up to her and tell her I was done. At the end of the day, I was strong enough to end our relationship. Alana wasn't.

What else did she lie about?

The thought creeps in, intrusive and aching, and it makes me sink down into the grass by the firepit, head in my hands. There are so many possibilities, so many question marks. If Alana could keep this secret, what else was she hiding?

Her ghost isn't here, but still I can see her eyes so clearly, narrowed, full lips twisting into a smirk. Something is dragging through my chest, roaring, metal scraping metal and setting off sparks.

I don't want any part of Alana anymore. I don't want to see her, talk to her, wear her clothes, hold on to her memories. I want to let it all burn.

Strike a match, watch the world waver from the other side

of the flames, the coals turning bone white. Something hot rages in my chest, like my heart is catching fire too.

"That was a really shitty thing to put me through," I choke out, just in case Alana's still here, invisible and listening. I don't just mean the past week, the hauntings. I mean all of it. "And I won't let you control me anymore."

A *sacred phrase*, I think. If only I could think of something, maybe this could be the fire that banishes her forever. But my mind is blank.

Outside, all I hear is flames crackling, water lapping against the dock. Name three things you can see: Trees curving in the evening wind. The lake house behind me, still and calm. Every piece of clothing I own lighting up as I throw it into the fire.

I think part of me is waiting for Alana to show up, to defy logic and manifest in the slowly fading sunlight, but she doesn't.

Maybe I finally caught her by surprise.

Maybe she has no power over me after all.

Maybe she's in the trees, invisible and dark and stunned into silence.

Maybe she was never real.

■ ■ ■

I sit by the fire as the sun slips over the horizon, watching the flames lick the sky.

Jazmine finally comes down to the firepit when everything has burnt away to ash, carrying a sandwich on a paper plate, and we eat side by side. She pretends not to notice the tears streaming down my cheeks.

"Do you want to come inside?" she asks.

I shake my head, still unable to speak, so she leaves me alone and heads back into the house. I don't move until night has fallen and a sudden sound shakes me back to life.

Footsteps on gravel, keys jingling. Fear clenches in my stomach. Is it Dad, coming to drag me back to LA? But when I whirl around, Rowan is jogging toward me.

My cheeks flush with red-hot shame. Great. The last person I want to see.

"Are you okay?" she asks, barely sounding winded despite the absolute sprint she just did down from the driveway. "I got home from work and Jazmine texted me—said to check in with you because . . ." She trails off, taking in the scene. "Were you having a bonfire or something?"

Behind my eyelids, the flames still flicker. Every item of clothing I packed for Lake Ember, every single thing here that reminds me of Alana, incinerated, a powdery dust pile in the firepit. I wonder who on earth will possibly understand why I did that.

"I was just sending smoke signals in your direction," I say, a pathetic attempt at humor.

Rowan laughs nervously. "But you're okay?"

"Yeah, basically." I bite my lip, wondering how much I can bring myself to say. "I, um . . . I went to Alana's funeral today."

"Oh my god." She claps a hand over her mouth. "Okay, uh, Jazmine could've led with that. How was it? I mean—forget I said that. That's a horrible question."

I wave her off. "Nah, it's fine. It sucked, and I found out she had been cheating on me with one of my old friends, so I punched the girl in the face."

"You . . . ?" Rowan gapes at me. "I think I need to sit down."

266

I pat the log next to me. She sinks down, closer to me than usual, her bare arm brushing against mine. I turn to her. Setting sunlight plays across the sharp angles of her face.

"That fucking sucks," she says finally, turning to look at me. "Alana was cheating on you? For how long?"

I shrug heavily.

"Don't know. I don't know if I want to know. The girl, Elise . . ." My voice snags on her name. It feels like poison coming up, scorching my throat. "We used to be friends. Good friends. I stopped hanging out with her a while ago. Alana said I was a bad friend to all these girls, but now, I don't know. . . ."

"Shit." Rowan exhales through her nose. I study her in periphery; dark circles pool like watercolors under her eyes.

"Are *you* okay?" I ask, frowning. "You look really tired."

"It's nothing. I haven't been sleeping well." Is it my imagination, or does she look kind of . . . scared? I don't think I've ever seen fear on Rowan's face before. "You know my mom's been out of town the past couple days, and the house has been quiet as usual. Or . . . really *not* quiet."

I raise my eyebrows. "What does that mean?"

"Nothing." She forces a laugh, but I know someone trying to seem brave when I see them. "Just some weird noises late at night. The other night, I came downstairs and my front door was cracked open. But I *know* I locked it. Just weird shit like that."

Electricity jolts to my heart, buzzing like neon.

"Weird shit," I repeat, looking at her carefully. "For sure. Hey, you must have some stuff in your house from your mom's shop, right? I didn't notice last time I was there."

"From Major Arcana? Oh my god, yeah. Pretty sure every surface is coated in incense."

"Good," I say, and my shoulders slump in relief. At least there's *something* keeping Alana out.

We're quiet for a beat, and I imagine reaching out, grabbing Rowan's hand. But I can't. She's made it clear she doesn't want anything to do with me, at least not in that way. And now, Rowan is in danger because of me. I'm *sure* the noises she's talking about are coming from Alana . . . but somehow, Alana hasn't succeeded in possessing her yet. Maybe she's just not strong enough. But she will be soon, if I don't find the strength to banish her ghost.

Rowan will never be safe.

It settles over me, another terrible realization I wish I could ignore. It's not enough to just be polite, cordial, normal to Rowan. If I spend time with her and Alana assumes that it's because I care about her, I'm signing her death sentence. But maybe if I create some distance, Alana will target someone else. Maybe she'll just target me. That would probably be safest for everyone, anyway.

"What are you thinking about?" Rowan's gray eyes are narrow. I have the bizarre sense that she's trying to read my mind. "You look worried."

"Yeah," I say bitterly, resting my chin in my hands. "Of course I'm worried. Alana was—Alana is dangerous."

I hug my knees to my chest, blinking down at the charred remains of the fire.

"Well," Rowan says slowly, the way you talk to somebody who's feverish and hallucinating. "Even if she was dangerous, she can't hurt you anymore. So—try not to worry about it. Actually, I know that's shitty advice since you have anxiety. You can forget I said that. I just mean . . ."

"She can still hurt me."

There's a long silence, during which I can tell Rowan is trying to work out what I mean.

"Yeah, I'm sure the memory of her is—"

"Rowan." I tilt my head back to the jet black sky, exasperated.

She's quiet, and I can practically hear the wheels turning in her head. The things I said to her mom at Major Arcana. Talking about Alana in the present tense.

"I can still see her," I whisper. "I can still talk to her. And she can see and talk to me."

"Okay. Okay." Rowan takes a deep breath. "You can see her, um . . . her ghost. Is that what you're telling me?"

"Unfortunately."

"Rosier, what the hell are you going to do? Does your sister know about this?"

"She knows about the ghosts in general, but after my mom died, I stopped seeing them." I pause. "She doesn't know I've been seeing Alana's ghost."

"But you said you had an obsidian stone for protection. Can you use that to keep Alana away?"

I sigh heavily, stretching my legs out in the grass. "Alana made me chuck it out the window a while ago, and now it's gone. I looked in the garden. It's nowhere. And I can't get another one—your mom didn't have any at Major Arcana, I checked."

"Well, maybe there's another option." She unclasps a golden chain around her neck, fumbling under the collar of her shirt. I watch as she takes off a necklace and extends it to me. A black stone ringed with ornate gold filigree, lying flat in her palm.

My lips part in surprise. "Rowan, what—"

"This was my mother's. Well, my grandmother's first, I think. A family heirloom. But anyway, it's obsidian." Rowan's cheeks flush as she takes in my expression. "You know my mother's obsessed with you. I don't think they would mind if you used it for a while. Especially if it'll give you any protection at all."

I stare at her, lips parting in surprise. Rowan has *had* an obsidian stone this entire time?

"No," I say quickly. "No, thank you."

"Oh . . . okay." The pink flush on Rowan's cheeks darkens. "No problem."

"Sorry, I don't mean *no* in a mean way—I just think you should keep it."

My brain is whirring frantically. Alana must not have been able to possess Rowan yet because of the obsidian stone. As long as she keeps wearing it, Alana *won't* be able to possess her at all. It'll block her out. I'm so relieved that I laugh out loud, breathing and unlike myself.

Rowan hesitates for a moment, probably wondering what the hell is wrong with me, but then nods, fastening it around her own neck again.

"Whatever you say, Rosier."

"Thanks for never thinking I'm weird," I blurt out.

"What do you mean?"

"My ex would've made fun of me for that. For wanting you to wear the necklace with no explanation. But you just believed me. Nobody's ever done that before."

Rowan looks shocked. "That's surprising."

"No, I'm serious." I stare down at the grass. Something uncomfortable is squirming deep inside my chest. Sadness rolls over me like a thundercloud, sudden and sure. "I don't think I've been a very good friend."

"Rosier, yes you have. Don't talk about yourself like that."

A laugh slips out, humorless. "If you only knew."

"If I only knew what?" Rowan's face is so open, encouraging, that somehow it actually makes me mad. The thundercloud darkens, promising rain. Suddenly, there's a weird, animalistic desire inside my heart to hurt her—to take her trust and shatter it. The craving is so strong and intense that it scares me.

"Alana wants to come back to life," I blurt out.

Rowan freezes.

"What are you talking about?"

"She has this big plan," I mumble, the cloud of sadness threatening to suffocate me. "She was going to possess somebody, and I was going to help her do it, except I didn't know how. . . ."

"Well, yeah," Rowan says, like this is obvious. "Possession isn't a real thing."

"Of course it is."

"No, Rosier, that's something from horror movies. Stories that kids tell at sleepovers. It doesn't *really* happen—my mother never . . ."

"Well, maybe your mother just doesn't trust you with this kind of information," I snap. I don't mean it to come out so harsh, but there it is nonetheless. Blood pounds in my ears. *Nice job*, Alana cackles somewhere in the back of my mind. *But I know you can be meaner. Do it.* "Look, you have *no* clue what I've been going through. There's a million true crime junkies wading through TikTok and Reddit, saying all kinds of stuff about me and my friends and Alana and her family—"

"Your friends?" Rowan repeats, eyebrows lifting. "Those girls aren't your—"

"No, don't act like you know anything about my life!" I stand up fast, blood rushing to my head. "Don't act like you know what kind of pressures I'm under—the horrible stuff I've had to do...."

"What horrible stuff?" Rowan asks, and it's the tone that gets me. Gentle, like I'm seconds from shattering. Understanding. Soft.

She thinks you're crazy, the voice hisses in my ear. *She doesn't want you. She rejected you. Tell her the truth. Hurt her.*

"Alana wanted to possess you," I tell Rowan. "And she wanted me to help her do it."

Our eyes meet. Rowan's face has gone very white.

"No, that's not . . . I mean, *me?*"

I nod once.

"You weren't going to actually do it, were you?"

I steel myself. "I thought about it."

"Come on. That can't be true."

I slide away from her, wrapping my arms around my chest. I regret it already, but when I scramble for the right words, Alana's voice is still ringing in my ears. Why can't I block her out?

Good. But you can do better.

"Of course it's true," I snap at Rowan. "Why else do you think I talked to you in the first place?"

The hurt on Rowan's face is instantaneous, and regret floods through me like rain—I want to reach for her, I want to cry, apologize, tell her I didn't mean it. But this is who Alana has made me. Someone who scratches and claws, who fights back. Who never breaks. I don't know how to get my old self back.

Without a word, Rowan stands up and walks away from the firepit. She trudges through the grass, back up toward the driveway.

It knocks the air from my lungs, and I stare after her. My mind flashes to Alana on the trail, surrounded by wildflowers, watching me go.

That's when I hear it.

Along the shoreline, through the trees, something is coming. I feel it like breath on the back of my neck, like a chill inside my lungs. The air thickens as if it were clogged with smoke.

"Rowan?" I ask into the night, scrambling awkwardly to my feet, even though I know she's not there. Her footsteps crunch against gravel. Any minute now, she'll be gone and I'll be here in the suffocating dark, trapped with whatever is advancing on me.

And I have a pretty good idea of what it is.

"Rowan," I call, louder now. I trip over my own feet in my hurry to get up to the driveway. Tears of fright bloom in my eyes, clouding my vision. I'm certain that it's Alana, and I'm also certain that there's absolutely no way I will ever be able to outrun her.

A hand closes around my wrist, and I scream.

"Shush! It's fine. It's me," Rowan hisses in my ear. She's at my side, both of us frozen at the edge of the driveway, the house to our left.

"Do you feel that?"

"Yeah." There it is again: an unsettling trace of fear glinting across her face.

"Maya," she whispers, and the use of my first name silences me instantly. "I think you should get inside the house."

Slowly, slowly, I track her gaze into the copse of trees twenty feet to the right. They lead to the lake's shore, densely packed and smelling of pine. I know we're both hearing the same thing.

A slow, methodical snapping of twigs.

The crunching of footsteps.

Someone coming closer, closer.

"When I say go, we run into the house and hide," Rowan hisses, and I bite down on my lip so hard I taste blood, nodding. I'm staring straight ahead, concentrating on a faint shimmer of golden light just past the tree line.

"*Go.*"

We slip on the wet grass, sprinting toward Jazmine's back porch. All I can think of is warning my sister, but when I catch sight of the driveway, my Toyota is the only car there.

"Where's Jazmine?" I pant, trying to catch my breath. Maybe it's my imagination, but I swear that I can hear a stirring behind us like wind picking up through the trees. I swear it's breathing down my neck, nipping at my heels.

The back door slams behind us. Rowan points wordlessly at a notepad on the kitchen counter, and we approach it together. My sister's handwriting scrawls across the page.

M—Went to Ralph's to get some ginger ale and snacks for you. Try to rest if you can. It'll be okay. Love, J

Rowan and I exchange a glance. My throat constricts, but I'm too panicked to let myself feel any other emotion.

"I don't think we should hide," I choke out. "I think we need to go."

Rowan gives me a perfunctory nod. "Get your stuff. I'll help you."

Together, we race up the stairs. We crash down the hallway, into my room—

But I don't have anything anymore. All that matters is my backpack, shoved into a corner beside the dresser and filled with my meds, laptop, basic toiletries. I swing it over one shoulder, grab my car keys from the bedside table.

"Where are we going?" Rowan asks, eyes wide.

"I don't know." My heart is thundering in my ears. Somewhere below me, there's a creak, eerily similar to the sound the screen door makes when you ease it open. "But I don't think we're safe in this house. Come on, I'll drive."

As we pound back down the stairs, the house's lights switch off—

One, the hallway.

Two, the kitchen.

Three, the living room.

Rowan's hand clenches around my wrist as we leap off the front porch, back out into the chilly night. I hold my car keys tight in my fist, like they'll really do anything to save me.

Four, the porch light extinguishes just as our feet hit the driveway.

Gasps are ripping out of my throat as Rowan shoves me into the driver's seat. In a lightning flash, she's darting around to the passenger side. Key in the ignition, my breath still coming in hysterical gulps. The car splutters and stops. Rowan pounds a fist against the glove compartment.

"Come on! You're a Toyota, you're better than this."

"Oh my god," I hiss, trying the starter again. Nothing.

Rowan slams a hand on the power lock, and I'm breathing too hard to note that car locks probably don't work against ghosts.

My hands are shaking as I jam the key into the ignition again. Nothing.

Wind howls outside the window, trees bending so hard that leaves scatter across the main road. A shadow has obscured the moon, making everything that much darker. I crank the key hard for the fourth time and my car finally, mercifully starts. We fly out of the driveway like a bullet from a gun.

■ ■ ■

For five minutes, the silence is glass; finally, I get the courage to break it.

"Listen, maybe we should just go down to LA." My voice almost sounds normal. "It's only an hour drive this time of night."

"Don't you think that'll be the first place Alana will look for you?"

"Rowan, she's a ghost. I don't think there's anywhere I could go that she wouldn't find me." We're both quiet for a minute, letting that horrible realization sink in.

"LA sounds fine," Rowan says finally, remarkably composed.

I squint into the night, watching desert landscape and craggy bluffs whizzing by. I've made this drive with Alana so many times, shuttled back and forth with my dad on summertime trips to Lake Ember. We let the quiet fall like a blanket, an hour of stillness, no words exchanged.

When LA is finally glittering up ahead, Rowan glances over at me, one elbow resting on the window. "You okay?"

"Yeah. You just might need to distract me," I mumble, gripping the wheel tight.

"Okay," Rowan says, missing nothing. "Um . . . let's see. What's a good distraction? Do you want a joke?"

I shrug.

"All right. Knock knock."

"Rowan." I let out a shaky laugh. "A knock-knock joke? Seriously?"

"Well, you didn't give me a clear answer regarding joke delivery!"

"Okay, fine. Who's there?"

"Who."

I roll my eyes heavenward. "Who who?"

"There's an owl in here!"

"Never tell me a joke again," I say, raising my voice to be heard over her peals of laughter. "That was horrific."

"How can I entertain you, then, princess?"

I think for a minute, still trying to suppress my laughter. "Tell me something about yourself."

"Suddenly it's like I'm back at summer camp."

"It's not an icebreaker. The ice has already been broken. I'm just curious."

Rowan sighs wearily, but she's smiling, and that's how I learn that she loves camping and classic literature, how she memorized passages from *Pride and Prejudice* for fun when she was in middle school. I learn that she was a theater kid, but she was actually good, and starred in Lake Ember High School's extremely low-budget production of *Wicked* during her senior year.

"I can't see ghosts at all," she tells me as we rattle along the freeway, "but I always wished I did. My mother was convinced she could. She's . . . eccentric, as you know."

"I always thought Valeria was so sweet, but she seemed kinda short with you at Major Arcana the other day."

Rowan smirks, not taking her eyes off the road. "It's a long sob story. She wasn't the most present mother, and my dad stopped speaking to us when he got remarried. Like I told you, Mom stays in the apartment above Major Arcana most of the time. She traveled a lot when I was young, did psychic readings. Sometimes it was like she could read everyone's mind except mine. It makes me feel really trapped sometimes, honestly."

"That makes sense, yeah."

"Oh," she hurries, "and of course you've had it way worse, with your mom—"

"No, no, it's fine." I wave her off. "I understand. If someone really loves you, they won't trap you. They'll let you be free."

Rowan's lips part in surprise and she turns just slightly to look at me, our eyes locking.

"I wouldn't believe her," says a casual, drawling voice from the backseat.

I scream, whirling around in my seat.

The last thing I remember, after the screech of tires and the crunch of metal, after the stench of burnt rubber and the high-pitched whine of panic in my ears, are Alana's cool blue eyes blazing straight into mine.

CHAPTER TWENTY-ONE

"**I SWEAR,**" I say for what feels like the millionth time in the last half hour. "I saw her. She was sitting right there in the backseat."

"Yeah, I saw her too."

When my car spun off the road and into a parking area, I was able to crank the steering wheel fast enough that we missed any buildings, which is a miracle in the crowded Valley. Unfortunately, I couldn't steer around the tree on the corner. We're standing on the side of the road, which is mercifully quiet this late at night, both of us staring as the hulking piece of metal is loaded onto a tow truck.

"Look, at least we're alive." Rowan pats my shoulder.

"My car," I say mournfully, staring after my Toyota. The EMTs have come and gone, given us both a clean bill of health, but my whole body still feels numb and shaky from shock, and I can tell the misery over my car will linger. "My dad is going to kill me for this. I saved up allowance money for months."

Rowan smirks, turning to look at me. "*Allowance* money? For *months*?"

"What?"

"Nothing. Spoken like a true Valley Girl princess."

"Look, now that we're actually in the Valley, you've got to stop calling me that. It's so embarrassing." I tug my phone out of my back pocket. "And I'm not a princess."

"What are you doing?"

"Calling an Uber to take us to my dad's house."

Rowan grins, cocking her head to the side. I can tell teasing me is making her feel better—honestly, it's having the same effect on me—so I don't tell her to shut up. "Why wouldn't you just call your dad?"

"Uh, because he's at his restaurant?"

Even with my eyes on my phone, focused on ordering the Uber, I can tell that Rowan's hiding a smile behind her hand.

"Ugh," I mutter. "What?"

"Nothing. You're right, you're not a princess."

The car will be here in four minutes. I sigh, letting my arms fall to my sides, and take in the familiar surroundings: a Gelson's parking lot, the distant roar of cars down the freeway, palm trees swaying in the late-night breeze. All of these should be comforting sights of home, but I can't shake the adrenaline pounding through my veins.

Rowan is watching me carefully. "You don't think Alana's still after us?"

The tow truck revs into gear, pulling out onto Laurel Canyon with my Toyota along for the ride.

"Honestly?" I tell her. "She's probably so pissed off by now that she'll never stop."

There's a long pause while we both digest this information. Then I suck in a deep breath, turn to look up at her. Rowan's eyes are dark and serious in the moonlight.

"Hey, um . . ." I let my shoulder bang into hers. "I'm really sorry about what I said back at the lake. How mean I was to you. That—that wasn't me. Or at least, that's not the person I'm trying to be. If that makes sense."

Rowan's expression shifts into pensiveness. She doesn't say anything, but the silence is comforting, wrapping around me like a blanket in the uncharacteristically chilly night.

"It's like I told you. I act like Alana and I don't mean to." My voice wavers with tears. "I'm really trying to figure out why."

Without a word, Rowan reaches out and grabs my hand. She doesn't let go.

...

My house is quiet, all the lights switched off except for the nightlight Dad always keeps plugged in by the kitchen counter. I move through the hallway turning all of them on.

"Damn," Rowan says, trailing behind me. "RIP your dad's electric bill."

"I *hate* dark houses."

"Oh?" I can tell she's just barely holding back a laugh. "A ghost hunter who's afraid of the dark. That's a new one."

"Look, I know you're scared too. Quit trying to deflect with humor." I shoot a scathing look in her direction. "And also, I'm not a *ghost hunter.*"

I push open my bedroom door, and my stomach flips over for reasons that have nothing to do with Alana-induced panic. Last time I was here, the morning after the vigil, I had no idea I'd be returning with Rowan. I would've, you know, put away my stuffed animals. Not left a pink bra lying on the floor. The usual.

Everything has changed since then. It's bizarre to stare around at the lavender-painted walls and realize that this space, at least, has stayed the same.

"So this is the famous Maya Rosier's room!" Rowan stretches out her arms, twirling around, and flops backward onto my bed. I kick the bra under my closet door before she can see. "Exactly as posh as I assumed it would be."

"Don't say posh. That's so weird."

I lean up against the doorframe self-consciously, trying to see my bedroom through her eyes. I've had floral bedding for as long as I can remember, and surely it looks like something a princess would pick out. There are Polaroids of me and Alana taped to the wall above my desk, which is littered with textbooks and gum wrappers. Nail polish bottles and three-wick candles are scattered messily across the top of my dresser. Opening my closet, I push past a collection of suitcases and a box of childhood stuffed animals, producing a box of Morton's salt and a plastic baggie filled with incense bundles.

"So what's the game plan?" Rowan asks, watching me trudge toward the doorway with the salt. "Making margaritas?"

"Very funny," I say wearily. "It's called salting the entryways. Surely you know about that from your mom. Pass me that lighter, will you?"

She tosses me a purple lighter from my bedside table. I catch it, light the incense bundle, watch the embers glow. As I carry it from one corner of the room to the next, my phone starts buzzing in my back pocket.

"Someone's calling you?" Rowan asks, sitting up on my bed. "It's, like, almost midnight."

"Five minutes in the Valley and you're already, like, talking like me." I shove the incense bundle into an empty coffee mug on my desk and pull out my phone. "Oh, it's fine. It's only Jazmine."

I hit Answer, but before I can say a word, my sister is berating me.

"Do you ever think about other people, Maya?" she asks, somewhere between exasperated and hysterical. I flinch instinctively. "You couldn't give me a call or leave a note? You just had to head off with Rowan on some road trip?"

"How did you know I'm with Rowan?"

"She texted me an hour ago to let me know you were okay. At least one of you is responsible."

I meet Rowan's eyes across the room. She waggles her fingers at me.

"Look, Jazz, everything's fine." I run a hand over my face. My heart is sinking, remembering Jazmine's note about running out to pick up snacks and ginger ale for me. Surely, any day now she'll realize how much better her life was before her fuckup of a little sister resurfaced. "We're at my house, Dad's house, and honestly, we're just super tired and want to go to sleep, so . . . I mean, I'm tired and want to go to sleep. I don't know what Rowan wants."

Rowan's watching me, slouched at the edge of my bed, eyebrows raised. This is the worst thing that's ever happened.

"It's okay," Jazmine's saying on the phone. "I'm glad you're safe, and honestly, you saved me a drive, so tell Rowan thanks for me."

"What do you mean?"

"Your dad called me while I was at the store—he got a call from Detective Ramirez. They want you to come into the station tomorrow, so your father wanted me to bring you down. I guess Sheriff McKinley is in town partnering on the investigation."

My jaw drops. "Again? No, that's insane—why? Why do I have to talk to them *again*? They determined Alana's cause of death."

Blunt force trauma, I repeat inside my head. *Not drowning. Suspicious.*

Of course they're still looking into this. Of course nobody can let it go.

"Sweetie, I don't know. He didn't tell me."

"Do they—do they think that *I* did it, or something?"

"Maya, I'm sure they don't." There's a scuffling noise on the other end. "I'm texting you something, okay? I didn't want you to see it, but I think . . . I think it's only fair that you're prepared, because I'm sure the police will bring it up."

I sigh, covering my face with my hand. I can't say what I'm thinking: Alana is keeping her word. Somehow, she's behind this. She's going to make sure I'm blamed for her murder. Soon I'll be in so deep that there will be no way out.

"There," Jazmine says. "Look at the Instagram post I just sent."

I put my phone on speaker so I can look at the screen. The message from Jazmine appears, and at first it looks innocuous, just a video. But then I peer closer, tapping through, and the bottom drops out of my stomach.

There I am in my black A-line dress, briskly approaching the Carter-Holloways' SUV. You can't see my face, but I recognize my brown hair pushed back by a velvet headband. There's Elise, expression open and fearful—I don't remember her looking that afraid—and the camera shakes and skitters as its owner hurries across the lot to get us both in frame. My voice, too quiet for a phone microphone to capture. Dad jogs into frame, and he's closer so you can hear it: "*Maya!*"

My fist, cracking against her face. Elise, falling to the asphalt like a rag doll. I stand above her, staring down, just staring, as the video keeps rolling. Elise's famous father approaching, Isabelle darting around him to grab me before I can get to Elise again. The camera zooms in on Elise, head bowed, one hand raising to gently cup her jaw.

That's where it ends.

Openmouthed, I stare at my phone. Keep staring for so long that Rowan gets twitchy, repeating my name over and over.

"Who posted this?" I say out loud, finally. My voice sounds weird and shaky. "Why . . . why would somebody do this? These people don't even know me. Why does anyone care?"

It's a stupid question. I realize this the second it leaves my mouth. This is circulating everywhere, of course—Instagram is the least of my problems. People will analyze it across social media. Journalists will go wild in their articles, calling me a problem child, or worse. The Carter-Holloways are well known, beloved, and I'm no one but the mentally ill exgirlfriend of a dead girl.

Rowan hops off the bed and pads across the floor to me. When she peeks over my shoulder at the phone screen, which has started replaying the viral video, I hear her gasp.

"Maya, when you do something like that in public . . ." Jazmine's voice is strained. "You realize how this looks. And the police will ask you about it, no doubt."

Rowan is uncharacteristically silent, watching me.

"Don't read the comments," Jazmine adds, so I tap the screen and read the comments.

These LA kids are absolutely sick

This girl needs mental help, what the fuck

The cops were called, right?? #JusticeForElise

What a psycho. If she can punch some random girl in a parking lot, what else is she capable of?

"Oh my god," I choke out. "The cops are definitely going to think I . . ."

"Rosier, they'd have to prove it," Rowan says reasonably.

"Listen, do you want me to come down there? I can get one of the girls to open up Blue Skies. . . ," Jazmine offers.

"No. I'm . . . I'll be okay. Thanks for telling me."

"Okay. Call me tomorrow."

I end the call and stare at Rowan, taking a deep breath.

"It sure is exciting to be you," she deadpans.

"I can't believe this," I say, biting my lip so I don't cry. Maybe if I keep as calm as possible, this will start to feel normal. "What do you think the police are going to say about the video?"

"I don't know," Rowan says, wrinkling her nose at her phone. She tosses it away; it lands on my bed. "But don't Google yourself for, like, three to five business weeks."

My breath hitches. "Oh my god. Is it everywhere?"

"Not everywhere." She looks at me with pity. "But I wouldn't get upset—"

Rowan tries to stop me from grabbing her phone, but I'm faster. I catch a glimpse of a few screaming headlines marching across her internet browser before she rips it out of my hands.

VIOLENT ALTERCATION OUTSIDE VALLEY TEEN ALANA MURRAY'S FUNERAL SHOCKS ONLOOKERS

COFFINSIDE BRAWL! WITNESSES SPOT
ALANA MURRAY'S GIRLFRIEND ASSAULTING
SCHOOLMATES

I sink down onto my bed, not even resisting as Rowan wrestles her phone out of my grasp.

"The future of journalism is bleak," she says dryly. "Don't look at it, okay, Rosier? It's been a shitty day, huh?" She pauses. "To put it lightly. Want to get some sleep?"

"Yeah." I yank open a dresser drawer, pulling out some sweatpants and an oversized T-shirt, which I chuck across the room at Rowan. "Here. You should at least be comfortable if you're hiding out from my ex's vengeful ghost."

"My, how considerate."

I grab my own pajamas and dart into my bedroom's attached bathroom, certain that Rowan is the kind of person who can unabashedly take her clothes off in front of anyone. Sure enough, I catch a glimpse of her standing there in a black sports bra before I make it to the next room.

"I can crash on the floor," Rowan calls. "This carpet looks super comfortable. Or the living room, but you might wanna text your dad ahead of time so he doesn't think some random lesbian broke into his house."

"Honestly, I think he'd just be glad I'm making friends." I pull on an old tank top that seems like a good compromise between *deliberately sloppy* and *trying too hard*. Who knew this would be so much work? "Also, um, you don't have to sleep on the floor. That's so sad. You can just, um, sleep in my bed. There aren't really any other comfortable options, so . . . take what you can get."

My cheeks are flaming red. There's no way I can walk out of this bathroom now.

"Okay, Rosier," Rowan says, and I can hear the laugh in her voice. "You really mean to tell me that in a house this big, there's only one bed?"

I push the bathroom door open carefully. The sight of her sitting on my bed and wearing my clothes almost makes me want to cry; it's too intimate.

"Listen, I know I apologized earlier, but I just want you to know . . . I didn't mean that horrible stuff I said back at the lake. I was never going to help Alana possess you. Maybe I considered it for a fraction of a second, but that was it, I swear."

Rowan looks uncharacteristically serious. "People do all kinds of stuff when they're trying to survive, Rosier. It's okay. I forgive you."

I let out a breath so heavy that my shoulders slump. Looking back, I can't quite remember the last time I apologized to someone and received such a thoughtful, honest acceptance. With Rowan, I don't think I need to be afraid.

For the first time, I don't think of orbiting around Alana like she's my second sun, letting her bleed me dry, the two of us alone in the blazing desert heat. Instead, I think of Rowan. Of her gray eyes like ice, the way her raspy voice goes quiet when she reassures me.

She falls silent, but I sit up for a long moment, staring out my bedroom window at the city lights glittering like jewels strewn by a careless hand. And I don't think about the news articles and the Reddit posts blaming me for Alana's death, the people who are waiting to see me fall. I don't think about the police station, and I don't even think about Alana's cold blue eyes glaring at me from the backseat of my car.

CHAPTER TWENTY-TWO

ALANA'S MOM IS losing it.

"I'm telling you, she knows more than she's saying!"

My fingers curl around the plastic arms of my chair in the police station waiting room, knuckles turning white. Melissa is in one of the adjacent rooms speaking to the police, but her voice is loud and clear, as though she's screaming in my ear. I've never heard her like this before.

"She assaulted a girl at my daughter's funeral, for god's sake! She's violent! You're not listening to me—"

It's been almost a full day since Rowan and I showed up in Los Angeles, but every minute has been incredibly painful. There are so many things I can't tell my family without sounding crazy; it's not like I can explain that Alana's ghost drove us out of Lake Ember, so I told Dad that Rowan, my new friend and Jazmine's employee, offered to accompany me to LA so I didn't have to make the drive alone.

Feeling bad about trapping Rowan in Los Angeles, I'd suggested that she get out of the house and do something fun this afternoon while I waste away in this police station. She asked for hiking recommendations, so I called her an Uber and sent her off to Fryman Canyon, one of my favorite trails. Sitting here and staring at my hands under the harsh fluorescent lights, I wish more than anything I could be with her, sunshine on my face and the Valley sprawling before me.

"Maya runs away to Lake Ember." Melissa again, loud and sharp. I jump at the sound of my own name. "Doesn't come home. And then four days later, *my daughter's body* turns up in Lake Ember! You think that's a coincidence?"

Next to me, Dad takes off his glasses and rubs the bridge of his nose. I watch him guiltily, listening to the lights buzzing. Once again, I've ripped him away from some activity he'd rather be doing with his Sunday—testing new recipes, prepping for an event at the restaurant—and embedded him in the tangled web that is my life.

"I buried my daughter yesterday!" There's a slam, like a chair dropping to the floor, a fist hitting a table. "That girl sitting in your lobby is saying that she knows nothing, but we *all* know that's a lie."

Melissa Murray was there the day I got my first period. I don't know why this memory pops into my head as I'm sitting in a dismal police station waiting room in North Hollywood, counting speckles on the tile floor, but it does. I was twelve and it happened in the middle of the night, and I was so embarrassed that tears welled in my eyes when I woke her up. But she folded the bedsheets with incredible precision, whisking them off to the laundry room like it was no big deal. Alana didn't even know. Melissa sat on the tile floor of the master bathroom with me, showing me a variety of pads and tampons and explaining the pros and cons of both. She made us waffles for breakfast. Mine had extra whipped cream.

And now, to Melissa Murray, I am *that girl.*

"Kiddo," Dad says quietly, gruff. "If you know something..."

"Dad, just let me deal with it."

The door across the waiting room swings open and a woman with a blond ponytail and wide green eyes sticks her head out, a badge gleaming on her navy jacket.

"Miss Rosier, my name is Detective Adler, and I'll be speaking with you today. Please come on back with me. Shouldn't take long. We appreciate your time."

Startled, I glance up. "I'm not talking to Detective Ramirez?"

"No," she says simply, without a smile.

I clench my hands into fists, nails digging into my palms, and follow her. They switched up the person interviewing me—why? Because they know I lied to Ramirez? Because they think I'll be more comfortable talking to a woman? My thoughts are skittering out of control; it was a mistake not to take my anxiety meds this morning. I need to be knocked out, sedated.

The room is impersonal, gray, and fluorescent. There must be cameras hidden somewhere. I remember grainy black-and-white film footage from crime shows, the kind Elise and I devoured while Alana said they were stupid—she meant they scared her. Cops sat in rooms just like this one and asked girls questions to break them. Confused them, made them talk in circles, deprived them of water and contact with family until they confessed to imaginary crimes.

Stop. Fucking stop it. That won't happen to me.

Detective Adler clears her throat and sinks into a metal

chair across from me, steepling her fingers and studying me. I study her right back.

"Maya, I know this is a difficult time," she starts. I knot my hands together in my lap. "I'm also aware that you've already spoken to my colleague, Detective Ramirez. My hope is that we can keep this as quick as possible—"

"I want to help you," I say slowly. "But I already talked to Detective Ramirez several times, and I just don't know . . ."

Detective Adler's eyes flicker over me, and I shiver involuntarily. It's like being x-rayed, knowing that someone is seeing parts of you that you don't even understand. That you might not even know are there.

"Maya, you're here today—and *I* am here today—because there were inconsistencies in your earlier statements," she says. "My job is to correct these inconsistencies. We're all seeking the truth here, right? To give Alana's poor mother some peace?"

Anxiety ripples through me, like a pebble thrown into water.

"Miss Murray's death was ruled a homicide. In these cases, we need to do our due diligence. I'm sure you understand." She doesn't wait for me to answer. "Now, before we get started, do you need anything? Water, coffee?"

"Um, actually, is there a restroom around here?"

The detective's eyes are still narrowed, but she pushes back her chair and gets to her feet. "I'll walk you there, but don't take long, okay?"

I nod wordlessly. Follow her down labyrinthine hallways until we reach the restroom.

"I'll wait right here," she says, and the steely note of warning kicks my heart into overdrive. Somehow, I've become the type of person who can't even be trusted to walk into a bathroom alone.

I stumble through the door, locking it behind me with shaking hands before I collapse against the sink. A dam breaks inside me and hot, real tears spill over, streaming down my cheeks, dripping off my chin. When I take a breath, it comes out like a death rattle. The tap water is ice but I don't wait for it to turn warm, splashing it onto my face with both hands and letting it soak my pink T-shirt. Close my eyes, pretend like I can wash it all away.

Slowly, I ease my eyes open, preparing myself to not recognize my reflection. But when I lift my head, I see exactly what I expect. A pale and shivering and scared girl under fluorescent lights.

And behind me—

"Hey, Maya."

I jump, gripping the edges of the sink, staring at the mirror. Alana is behind me, glaring. Perfect hair, undisturbed by the air-conditioning that rattles through the vent. There's no smile on her face, no light in her glowing blue eyes. She looks like a nightmare come to life.

"It's been a minute," she says, voice as sharp as a razor's edge. "How's life?"

"Get out."

"Nah, I don't think I will. Don't misunderstand me," Alana drawls, walking around me to lean casually up against the bathroom counter. "I don't have any desire to spend time with traitors. But I just couldn't resist seeing the look on your face. Little Miss Yale hopeful Maya Rosier being questioned in a police station? I wish I had a camera."

"How can you even be here? It's daytime."

"Every day that you don't banish me, I get stronger," she says in a singsong, snapping her fingers.

The bathroom lights switch off, plunging us into darkness.

Trying to act like this doesn't rattle me, I yank a handful of brown paper towels from the dispenser and pat my face dry.

"I'm not afraid of you," I lie.

She laughs. "Oh, of course you are. But you don't need to be afraid, Maya. I have no interest in sticking around for somebody as disloyal as you."

"Oh, so I'm the disloyal one?"

The lights flicker back on. Alana is so close I can see the way her eyelashes cling together like the points of snowflakes. I flinch, fear clutching at my heart despite my best attempts to steel myself.

"I knew you were going to have a whole freakout about Elise when you found out. Listen, it wasn't a big deal."

"Did you love her?" I can't resist asking.

"Love," she repeats, laughing. Diverts away. "Elise was there for me when you weren't. Like, I know you had a shitty time with your depression this year, okay? But you weren't exactly around, and was I just supposed to stop living my life while you pulled yourself together?"

"So you didn't love *me*, is what I'm getting."

"Someday maybe you'll learn that love isn't black and white," Alana says, grin fading. "It isn't all or nothing. Too bad I won't be around to see when you finally figure that out."

"What the hell are you talking about?"

"I'm telling you that this is my goodbye."

"You don't mean that." *Like you would ever leave me alone,* I think.

"Really, there's no need for you to be so dramatic when there's such a simple solution." She leans up against the paper towel dispenser, examining her nails. "If you're still down to help me possess your soft butch dream girl, I'll make sure you get out of this one safely."

Staring into the mirror, I watch a muscle in my jaw twitch. She has no idea how, regardless of outcome, this situation will follow me for the rest of my life. The way this grief will etch itself into my soul, a haunting all its own. How I'll never remember how to trust again, because the person I trusted most in the world let me down. How I'll love girls in the future but always glance over my shoulder, always salt the doorways, for fear that they, too, will betray me.

"I think it's too late for that," I whisper. "Even if you wanted to."

Fear and adrenaline thrum in my eardrums, blocking out the whoosh of the air-conditioning, the drip of water from the faucet. If Detective Adler hears me talking to myself in here, forget it. I'm done.

Alana laughs, and for a second I can almost pretend that things are normal.

"You know, you could just tell me." I turn around so my lower back presses against the wet sink. "Didn't you hear how upset your mom was? Tell me what happened to you. Tell me who—who killed you, and quit changing the subject whenever I ask."

"Oh, didn't you hear?" Alana says sweetly, pink lips pursing into a smile. "It was that girl, Maya Rosier. She found out her girlfriend was cheating on her and snapped. Lured her to their favorite childhood vacation spot and knocked her out—you know she's capable of that, didn't you see what she did to that poor girl in the parking lot at the funeral? Then she watched Alana drown and didn't even flinch."

"Alana, shut up."

"Her lawyers entered an insanity plea—after all, she was always *so* disturbed."

There's a spark of something deep inside me, some fire that ignited after her death. It's not a tactic I learned from Alana . . . it's something I came up with all on my own. Slowly, achingly, I'm teaching myself to be strong.

I arrange my face into the most neutral expression possible.

"Well, I'm out of here." I turn back to the sink, stick my hands under the automatic faucet. Lather with cheap pink hand soap, rinse. "Bye, Alana."

There's a note of disbelief in her voice. "That's the goodbye I get, huh?"

"Yes. Bye."

I dry my hands with brown paper from the dispenser, ball it up, toss it toward the trash can. It sails in a wide arc before landing softly, a slam dunk.

"Of all the times for you to not cry," she says disparagingly.

I'm not even trying to listen. I'm done. I walk out to meet the detective in the hallway.

. . .

"You realize you're waiving your right to a lawyer," Detective Adler says as soon as we're back in the interrogation room. "Your father doesn't think this is the wisest choice."

"That's great for him," I say in my politest voice, even

though my heart is slamming against my rib cage. "But I don't want or need a lawyer, because I didn't do anything wrong."

She frowns, studying me, and rests her elbows on the metal table that separates us. I think she's a little younger than I originally figured, maybe even in her late twenties. She's wearing charcoal eyeliner and a mascara that clumps her lashes together. "State your full name for the record, please."

"Maya Elisabeth Rosier."

She purses her lips, flipping open a manila folder that looks similar to the one Detective Ramirez had back in Lake Ember. "Describe the events of May fourth to me, please."

I chew my bottom lip, trying to ignore the roiling nausea. "Well, I, um, woke up. I had breakfast."

"And what did you have?"

I try to remember what Dad has in the kitchen that doesn't require actual cooking. Most of the time, I skip breakfast on school days or grab a granola bar from the vending machine when I get there. "Cereal. I don't remember what kind."

"Okay. And then?"

"I spent the day studying."

"What subject?"

"Pretty sure I was looking over my AP French notes."

"Advanced Placement French," Detective Adler repeats. "You're sure?"

My mouth is uncomfortably dry. No words come out, so I nod once.

"Interesting," the detective says, tapping her open folder, "because your teacher, Madame Poirier, told us that you were not eligible to take the AP exam. You were getting credit for the course, but due to your poor grade in the class, she met with you and the two of you decided you wouldn't take the test."

I freeze, hands knotted together in my lap. How did I forget that?

"Maya, your lies about what you did on the morning of May fourth are particularly troubling. Not to mention the fact that you lied to Detective Ramirez multiple times." She trails a manicured nail down a sheet of paper in her folder. "I'm not sure if you're aware that several eyewitnesses have described two girls who bear a resemblance to yourself and Alana arguing on the trail at Antelope Valley."

"Oh," I say, then can't think of anything to add.

"Later that day, you made sure you were seen by your classmates actively searching for Alana and appearing concerned. Then you headed north to your sister's house, where you knew she would protect you, and posted a photo on Instagram with the caption *getting away from it all.* At Alana's funeral, you were seen physically assaulting Elise Carter-Holloway in the parking lot, the girl with whom Alana was cheating."

My hand brushes my cheek, and I'm shocked to find that my skin is warm. Tears have been streaming down my face, splashing in my lap.

"N-no," I choke out, but there's no use. "The lake—it was meaningful to both of us. I have no idea how Alana got there from Antelope Valley, but I can imagine why she would want to go there. She loved Lake Ember just as much as I did."

"And the trail up at Antelope Valley?" Detective Adler asks. She reaches into her folder, produces a printed photograph. For a second, I have no idea why she's showing me this; it's a photo of a smiling college-age couple, making peace signs at the camera. They look happier than I can ever remember being. But then—

"In the background," the detective prompts. "Look familiar?"

It's blurry, but undeniable: the edge of the trail bending in the upper left corner, two girls walking side by side. We're far enough away that I can image we're happy too, but close enough that our identities are clear. The dark brown of Alana's hair, my favorite green backpack slung over my shoulder.

Detective Adler and I meet each other's eyes.

"Just tell me," she says, voice softer than I expect, and that's all it takes to break me.

"Yeah." A lone tear traces down my cheek, and I brush it back impatiently. "That's us."

The corners of Detective Adler's mouth quirk up, just slightly. A quiet triumph.

"I-I left her there," I whisper, leaning forward into the table. My ribs ache with the pain of holding back emotion. "We argued at Antelope Valley, and I broke up with her. She was making me so mad, and I just wanted to get away, so I left, but I didn't think that anything bad would happen to her...."

"How did you think Alana would get home?"

I bury my face in my hands. "I don't know. I just—I didn't think about it. She could've taken an Uber—we did that all the time."

"And your relationship with Alana ..."

My heart kicks up, a rapid drumbeat in my ears. Here it comes again: *Was it romantic? Did you love her? Did you think you were going to marry her? How cute.*

"Would you characterize it as abusive?"

"Wh—" I lift my head. All the air is knocked out of my

lungs, as though she had reached across the table and sucker punched me. "What are you talking about?"

"You were Alana's girlfriend for three years. Is that correct?"

"Yeah. Yes."

"Can you give me a couple adjectives to describe how you felt during that time?"

"Happy. Content." I shift in my chair. This is reminding me uncomfortably of a therapy session: Dr. Duarte watching me carefully, bright pink glasses sliding down the bridge of her nose. "Anxious, but then, I'm always kind of anxious. On edge."

"Tell me a little bit more about why you felt on edge, as you said, while you were with Alana."

I pick at my nail beds. "It's not a big deal. It was like . . . if you said the wrong thing to Alana—or not even the wrong thing, but just something she didn't like or approve of—it could be scary. She could turn on you so fast, and it was like a faucet. She could shut it off quickly too. You never knew what you were going to get."

My voice grows small, unsure. Bile rises in my throat. If I have to throw up, I'm not sure I could make it to a trash can.

"I watched her do it to other people," I say quietly. "Friends of ours. I was afraid it would happen to me."

"Afraid?" she repeats, and there's no sympathy in her eyes. Just a coldness that reminds me so, so much of Alana.

"Afraid that she would leave me."

"And she did leave you eventually. Because she was cheating on you, I understand."

I wince. There's the sharpness in my rib cage, the dagger jammed between my lungs, scratching and scraping and driving deeper each time I remember it.

"Who told you that?"

Detective Adler is quiet, watching me. But I catch her eyes flickering to the hallway. Somebody else here to be interviewed, maybe. Are they on my side, or trying to hurt me?

"Actually," I say slowly, fully aware that these are the words that will change everything. "I *didn't* know that Alana was cheating on me. I found that out at the funeral. Before Alana died, Elise and I weren't in contact, and I thought Alana had stopped hanging out with her too."

Detective Adler pauses, watching me. My heart is beating so loudly that I'm sure she can hear it. I try to think of a way to tell her that I loved Alana in the worst way you can love another person. Fear laced with compassion, empathy intertwined with disdain. She loved me like I was a butterfly she was trying to pin to a board, snapping its wings and twining them through with pins so that she could look at something beautiful once in a while.

But there are no easy ways to talk about this. I think back to Dr. Duarte, explaining the meaning of *emotional abuse* to me again and again, patient and sure. The way I fought her on it every time—*Alana's not like that.* I steel my jaw, tilt it with defiance.

"I'm sorry," I say, voice hoarse. "But I guess I just don't realize how this is relevant to the investigation. Do you think that she—she abused me, so I killed her to make it stop?"

"Maya, I'd like to read you something, and you can let me know if it sounds familiar. Sound good?"

I just stare at her, trying to slow the rhythm of my breathing. Tears are still leaking from the corners of my eyes. To calm myself, I tilt the chair backward, its front legs lifting from the floor.

She pulls a thin sheet of notebook paper from her folder

and clears her throat like she's about to give a presentation in class.

"Dear Alana. In my dreams, you're a wildfire."

My chair legs slam back down to the floor.

"Beautiful from a distance," Detective Adler continues, "but you destroy everything you touch. I've seen it myself, burning my eyes, the way you rip wings off beautiful things and watch them die."

The temperature in the room drops, freezing me from the inside out. My heart is stuttering inside my chest.

"How—how do you have this?"

"I know it's only a matter of time," she reads, not meeting my eyes, "before you destroy me too."

It's so strange to hear my words in her voice. I open my mouth, trying to get it out fast enough: this isn't *anything*, I just wrote it while I was in the hospital, and how do they even have access to it anyway? It didn't stay with the doctors or anything. I scribbled it in my own notebook, one that my dad chose when he packed up my things for me. It was my favorite shade of purple, dotted with glittery stars and planets on the cover. The sheet has been torn neatly from its binding. Someone did this.

I rack my brain—what the fuck did I do with that notebook when I got home from the hospital? After I got the generally clean bill of health, everything was so scattered as I met with the useless college counselor at Coldwater and cried in her office and tried to put my life back together. It was hard, and obviously Alana was pissed that I had fallen off the face of the earth for a week; I ended up telling her where I'd been, and her response was more interested than sympathetic. She wanted to know everything: Did I really wear grippy socks, like you always hear? Which belongings did they take away from me, and which were I allowed to keep? What did the therapists want to talk about?

She knew. It dawns on me slow and horrifying, like a rolling blackout, as I sit on the uncomfortable metal chair listening to Detective Adler reading my stupid letter. Alana knew about the notebook I used during my inpatient stay, because I showed it to her. After arriving home, I'd never opened that notebook again; Alana could've easily swiped it, even torn out pages. It would've been easy as anything, easy as a window left open and a light spring breeze, to make sure the cops found this when they searched her bedroom.

"I love you, and that will be enough. Forever," the detective finishes. "You love me, and that will be enough. For now."

I bite down on my lip, hard.

"*For now*," she repeats. "Her love would only be enough *for now*. Could you expand upon that?"

Blood pounds in my ears. "It was—I didn't *really* mean any of that. It was a creative writing exercise."

"Why did you think Alana would destroy you?"

I press my lips together, forcing myself to breathe slowly through my nose.

"Maya, I will ask you one more time," Detective Adler says, leaning back in her chair, eyes narrowed. "Would you characterize this relationship as abusive? Abusive enough, perhaps, to make you snap?"

Before I can answer, there's a rapping at the door. I jump, glancing over my shoulder.

The door swings open and a man strides in, LAPD badge

shining on his chest. Detective Adler immediately jolts at the sight of him, and I slump lower in my chair. I hoped I'd never have to see this guy again.

"Detective Ramirez, I'm in the middle of—"

"We're done here." The detective turns to me, jutting his chin out. "Miss Rosier, you can go meet your father in the waiting room."

It's presented as an option, but I recognize it for the command it is. Slowly, I unfold myself from the chair.

"I can—I can go?" I sniff, wiping my cheeks impatiently with the back of my hand.

"Ramirez, we have ample evidence here that Maya Rosier was present when Alana Murray died," Detective Adler protests, shuffling through the remaining papers on the table. I catch a glimpse of a printed photo from Alana's camera roll, her tanned arm slung over my shoulder while she winks at the camera. Photos of my family's lake house. Childhood photos of the two of us there, together.

"I'm aware," he answers, "but we've received new information. Detective, I'm bringing you into my office to go over the particulars. Miss Rosier, did you hear me tell you that you're free to go?"

"I don't understand." I stand up slowly, arms wrapped around my torso. Suddenly I realize I'm freezing in my thin T-shirt and shorts. "Why did you even make me come here if you were just going to let me go?"

"Did you hear me just say *new information*?" Ramirez barks, and suddenly I understand why Detective Adler looked freaked out as soon as he walked into the room. "Miss Rosier, I advise you to go back to your father."

I'm frozen. My legs are numb.

"*Now*," he snarls.

I'm halfway down the cold, institutional hallway when I see it: another small interrogation room like the one I was just in, a long table, one wall lined with a cracked mirror. There's a person inside this room, another girl just like me—she catches my attention through the square window in the metal door. My eyes have to refocus a couple times before I realize what I'm looking at.

Who I'm looking at.

Elise Carter-Holloway is sitting at the table, curls pushed off her face with a headband. There's a bruise blooming on her jaw where I hit her, a deep violet. She's sitting there calmly, dark lashes fanning across her cheeks, staring down at her folded hands. When I step closer and draw in a breath, she must sense me somehow, because her head snaps up.

We meet each other's eyes. Hers are round and completely surprised, and the surprise seems to shake something loose inside her. In one swift motion, she leaps from her chair and runs to the window. Anguish is etched in every shadow on her face.

Her palm slaps against the window and I jump back, startled. She's saying something again and again, *yelling* it, but the room must be soundproofed. I can barely hear her, but her eyes are welling with tears.

Confused, I study her face, trying desperately to read her lips.

I'm sorry.

I'm sorry.

Slowly, my hand rises to press against the cool glass of the window, mirroring her.

"You're sorry?" I ask. There's no way she can hear me. She doesn't even seem to realize I've spoken at all.

Maya, I'm so sorry.

Unconsciously, my other hand closes around the doorknob—I don't know if the cops locked her in there or not. Maybe all it would take is a simple movement of my wrist and I could step through that door, get all the answers I want. Look her right in the eye and demand that she tell me.

I hesitate for a long moment, fluorescent lights buzzing like a warning. I think I'm waiting to see what I'll do. But before I have the chance, Elise changes.

A shiver rolls over her entire body, like a cloud rolling slowly in front of the sun. She takes a step backward from the door, green eyes hardening. Her face goes slack and serious and devoid of emotion, even as a single mascara tear tracks its way down her cheek.

I watch her, unnerved. Wait for the screaming refrain of *I'm sorry* to start up again. But it's like she doesn't even remember what just happened. Her fingerprints still streak the glass, but she doesn't remember.

Her eyes won't leave my face. Slowly, slowly, her pink lips twitch into a cruel smirk.

I can try to act like I don't recognize what's happening all I want, but that won't make it true. The face looking at me is Elise's, but it isn't. Up above her head, the light bulb flickers.

I swallow hard, tearing my eyes away, and turn back to the cold hallway.

This time, I run.

...

"Maya! Maya Rosier!"

As soon as Dad and I step out of the police station, the world becomes a blur. Lights reflect the scorching late afternoon sun and aim it back at me, making me jolt backward and smack into my dad. His arm loops around my shoulder, pulling me close and guiding me through the mess of onlookers and reporters. I've seen this kind of scene before—I'm from LA, after all—but I've never been caught in the middle of it. It feels like the eye wall of a hurricane, and I'm being pelted with horrible questions on all sides.

My phone buzzes in my pocket. With shaking hands, I pull it out, trying to ignore the maelstrom of noise surrounding me.

> **Rowan Lake Ember** 👽😈💙
> hey are you okay??

> **Rowan Lake Ember** 👽😈💙
> stop talking to the cops maya read this

She's included a link to one of those dumb true crime blogs. The thumbnail shows a picture of Melissa Murray outside this same police station, probably on her way in earlier today. Her hair is perfectly blown out, sunglasses obscuring half of her face. SHOCKING BREAK IN THE ALANA MURRAY MURDER INVESTIGATION, the words scream below the picture.

"Maya!" one of the reporters shouts. I jump, looking up from my phone. "What do you have to say about the accusations?"

I frown, searching for the voice ringing above all the others. Accusations?

"What do you think about the bombshell revelation that Elise Carter-Holloway has confessed to police?"

I turn in the direction of that last voice, searching for the right reporter. The flashes and clicks increase to a cacophony.

"What?" I ask. Clear my throat. "Confessed? Who said that?"

"Honey." Dad's annoyed, pressing a hand between my shoulder blades. "Come on. We need to get to the car. Don't listen to these clowns."

"No, who said that?" My voice is stronger, louder now. "Elise confessed to something?"

"That she killed Alana!" One of the reporters finishes my sentence, a woman with a high ponytail who looks way too enthused to be delivering this news. A man next to her balances a giant, heavy camera on one shoulder, sweating under its weight. For the first time, I notice that she's clutching a KTLA-emblazoned microphone. "Did you have any idea that Elise was the last person to see Alana before she died, let alone the fact that she was responsible for Alana's tragic death?"

"What the fuck are you talking about?"

"Maya, enough!" Dad's voice booms from somewhere behind me. His hand finds my shoulder. "Come on. We're leaving."

"Elise was—she loved Alana," I continue, dimly aware that fuzzy microphones are being shoved in my face. "She didn't kill her. Why would she?"

"That's what we're all waiting to find out!" the reporter exclaims, like we're on a game show or something. There's a ringing in my ears, blood draining from my face.

"Maya," Dad says one more time, voice sharpening with concern, and that's the last thing I hear before I'm shoved into the passenger seat of our car.

CHAPTER TWENTY-THREE

SHOCKING BREAK IN THE ALANA MURRAY MURDER INVESTIGATION

Sunday, May 12, 2024

Yet another twist in the ongoing Alana Murray case came early this morning when 18-year-old Elise Carter-Holloway, daughter of prominent director Benjamin Carter and Grammy-winning film composer Catherine Holloway, turned herself in to authorities at the North Hollywood Police Station.

Insiders spoke to True Crime Central regarding Carter-Holloway's jaw-dropping confession. Alana Murray's missing cell phone has been confounding authorities, with the consensus that it was likely lost to the waters of the lake in which her body was found. However, along with her confession, Carter-Holloway was able to produce an iPhone that was confirmed to be Alana's.

Questioning is still ongoing at this time. If the phone hasn't been wiped, authorities will likely be doing a thorough investigation of its contents as this roller-coaster ride of an investigation continues. Stay tuned as we bring you up-to-the-minute updates.

Obsessed with everything true crime? You won't want to miss a minute of our nail-biting, pulse-pounding newsletter. Subscribe to True Crime Central today for updates on all the latest intriguing cases and ongoing trials as they unfold in the headlines. Stay safe out there!

■ ■ ■

Houses and palm trees blur past; we're tearing down Colfax Avenue, our house—and safety—just a couple minutes away. Dad's eyes are focused firmly on the road. Neither of us speaks. *I read it,* I text back to Rowan. *are you still hiking at fryman?*

> **Rowan Lake Ember** 👽💚
> yeah I'm still here, want to come meet me?

The tightness in my chest loosens. I'm about to respond when another text comes through.

> **Rowan Lake Ember** 👽💚
> maya wait

Three gray dots in a speech bubble appear at the corner of the screen, indicating that Rowan's typing.

Then they stop.

Start again.

Stop.

"Dad, do you mind if I go meet Rowan?" I ask, anxiously glancing down at my phone. What's she trying to tell me? "I won't be long, I promise."

"Maya, we're almost home. Plus, with everything going on right now, there's no way in hell you should be behind the wheel."

I sigh loudly. "C'mon, Rowan's up at the trail. It's not a long drive."

"Fryman Canyon?" he asks, easing to a stop at a red light. "I guess that's not far. I'll just drop you off and you guys can Uber back. But you need to text me when you're on your way home, okay? No more of this running wild without communicating."

"Ten four," I tell him, and he smiles despite himself.

It's only a five-minute drive to Fryman Canyon, but it feels like longer as I close my eyes and let the events of the past few hours wash over me. *Why* would Elise ever confess to something like this? Elise Carter-Holloway might be a lot of things, apparently, but she's not a murderer. In eighth grade, she cried when she accidentally drowned a spider in my pool. When we watched *The Ring* at Alana's house, she screamed so many times that we sent her off to bake cookies with Mrs. Murray. She was always helpful, kind. *Sweet*, even.

Well, until she hooked up with Alana behind my back and then confessed to murdering her.

I sigh, slumping lower in the passenger seat. Absolutely none of this makes sense.

By the time Dad drops me off at the trailhead, the sunset is starting to wash the sky in shades of orange and pink. Thankfully, it's almost deserted.

I haven't hiked since Antelope Valley and my muscles ache almost immediately. Rowan's last text said she'd meet me right at the trailhead, but knowing her she probably got distracted looking at flowers or something. As I trudge through the dirt, my mind is focused on Elise, the wild look in her eyes and the way she snapped so quickly into calm.

It was Alana possessing her. I know it was. I won't be able to breathe until I find Rowan and see that she's okay.

But, my brain insists as I pause to stretch out my calf muscles, heart stuttering, *if Alana could possess Elise once, she could do it again and again. What if she forced a false confession out of Elise?*

"Shut up," I mumble as I start walking again. There's no use getting myself freaked out about this, especially alone on a hiking trail where anxiety could easily spiral out of control. If Alana died of blunt force trauma and I wasn't the one who caused it, then *somebody* must have done it. The story about Elise makes sense—logically, if not emotionally.

I swallow and my throat feels painfully dry. How could Elise go from being Alana's friend to secret girlfriend to murderer?

If she found out you were still Alana's girlfriend, that nagging voice in my brain whispers.

The trail snakes higher and higher but it's familiar, so I barely have to think about where I'm going, when I need to turn. All I can think of is the sparse hope of freedom dangling before me, close enough that I can taste it. If Elise confessed to murdering Alana, I'm *free.* Nobody can blame me anymore. I can leave LA if I need to, I can start all over, and I can just be Maya Rosier, not Maya, Alana's girlfriend.

And then, just as I'm rounding the bend that looks out over the sprawling Valley below—

A single California poppy petal rests on the ground, just a few feet in front of me.

Coincidence. It's not like it's a rare flower or anything, I tell myself. But I slow down, and sure enough, every ten feet or so, there's another one.

A bright, golden-orange trail, leading me off the beaten path and onto an entirely new one.

I take a deep, shaky breath. Then, against my better judgment, I follow it.

The petals lead me up a hill that juts out awkwardly, choked with coastal sage scrub and chaparral, and I'm sweating by the time I reach the top. The trees are dense and lush. For a minute, I can almost pretend that I'm back at Lake Ember.

And then, squinting against the setting sun, I see her waving down at me.

"Maya!"

In the cloud-choked sunlight, Rowan's skin is bright porcelain, the knees of her jeans smeared with mud and dirt. Ribbon-thin cuts wend their way up her bare arms. My dark green backpack hangs between her shoulder blades; back home, I'd offered it to her in case she wanted to carry water bottles on her hike.

"What's wrong? What happened to you?" I try to spit it all out at once as I run to her. "Rowan, you'll never believe what happened at the police station. This is insane. Everybody's gone completely batshit."

"It's gonna be okay." Her eyes soften as she steps closer to me, grabbing my forearms gently. "Tell me what happened."

"Oh my god," I say, my voice wobbling with teary relief. "This police detective interrogated me about whether I felt like Alana was emotionally abusive, and then *another* cop comes in to tell me I can go, so I ran out of there, and it was *Elise*—"

Rowan frowns. I can't read her expression.

"You know, like in that article you sent me, about how she confessed—she had Alana's phone with her that whole time! That day I went to her house looking for Alana because her location said she was there . . . Elise must've had Alana's phone the *whole time*."

Rowan is staring, gray eyes wide. "That's so weird, Maya. Are you sure you're okay?"

"Yeah, I think I'm—wait." I frown. "How come you're calling me Maya all of a sudden?"

She opens her mouth, then closes it. "I . . . well, that's your name."

"I know, but . . ?"

"I know your name," she laughs. "No one knows you like I do."

Horror rolls over me in an icy wave.

"Rowan," I take one step backward, slow. "What did you just say?"

"I *said*," Rowan hisses, and her lips stretch into a smile that raises the thin hairs on the back of my neck. "No one knows you like I do."

My hands are shaking. I turn them over, see mud-streaked palms from collecting poppy petals on the winding path. Patterns like an inkblot test. When I suck in a breath of surprise, I taste brine and metal and packed earth. A slow fear grips my heart and squeezes tight.

"No," I say slowly, bringing my hands to my chest in terror. My finger brushes against something hard and solid underneath the fabric of my T-shirt. Confused, I dip one hand beneath the collar and pull out Rowan's protective obsidian necklace. It burns in my palm.

She must have put it around my neck last night while I was asleep. Thinking she was protecting me. Leaving herself vulnerable.

"What's wrong?" Her expression falters for a second, a flicker of confusion. She doesn't recognize the necklace. That's all the confirmation I need.

My fist collides with Rowan's jaw, sending her pinwheeling to the ground.

She lands in the dirt face down, and it's like a switch has been flipped. The gray sky opens up with a roar and the rain starts, falling in angry sheets that have me soaked to the bone in seconds. I reel backward, yanking my backpack off Rowan's shoulder. My own breathing is loud in my ears, ragged and hoarse over the knife pain that rakes up my windpipe. Thunder, a crashing heartbeat. The crack of heat lightning as it touches down nearby.

"*Alana,*" I scream, and I hate how my voice pitches up at the end, like a scared little girl. "What the *fuck* did you do to her?"

Rowan staggers to her feet, blood dripping from a cut on her forehead where she hit the ground, but she's laughing, wiping it away with a swipe of her palm.

"I knew you were going to figure it out too quickly. That's your fatal flaw, Maya. You're always thinking too hard."

"How the hell did you do that?" I ask, clinging desperately to one backpack strap. "You were possessing Elise an hour ago."

"Maya, you made me strong enough to do anything." She crosses her arms, cocky, but it looks all wrong on Rowan's face. "Your big mistake was keeping me around as long as you did, you know? You were too soft. Let me hang out, chat with you like old times. If you had just figured out a way to banish me on that very first night—if you were *smart* enough, and *strong* enough—well, that would've been a totally different story. With every day you kept me here, I got more powerful. You were a great practice target, obviously. But—"

She freezes, something shifting in her expression for the briefest second, but shakes it off.

"Fuck you," I snarl. "You're horrible."

"You can't hurt me, babe," she says, and it kills me to hear her call me this in Rowan's voice. "If you hurt me, you have to look at *Rowan's* face when you do it, and I *know* you can't bear to do that. You probably love her so much more than you ever loved me."

"Oh, shut up." I glare at her, rage shaking my limbs. "How many times do I have to tell you that I broke up with you? I knew that this had to end."

"Don't be ridiculous. You didn't know jack shit."

"Yes, I did. You know," I say, raising my voice over the rain, circling her slowly. "Your death made me into a different girl than the one you remember, but you'll never accept that. I'm so much more than you ever could have imagined, Alana. I got so much better, so much stronger. And I did all of that without you."

"Did you?" The words snarl, twist, mock. And then, sudden as a lightning strike, her entire facial expression changes: her eyes widen, her smile disappears.

Rowan reaches for me. Her hands grip my shoulders, fingers digging in.

"Do it!" she begs, shaking me, and I gasp. "Maya, you have to banish her. Do it soon. In the backpack I—"

Then she shakes her head, strands of damp hair whipping across her face, and Alana's smirk is back. She lets go of me fast. Every trace of Rowan is gone.

"Sorry," she says, just barely holding back a laugh. "Still getting the hang of things."

I point one shaking finger at Alana. "Leave her alone. Just face me yourself, you fucking coward. I'll give you whatever you want."

"Oh, Maya." She laughs, and it's so close to Rowan's actual laugh, carefree and happy, that I almost burst into tears. "You don't have anything I want."

"Oh yeah?" I narrow my eyes, watching her.

She pauses for a moment, confused, and that's all I need.

I grasp the obsidian necklace. "This is Rowan's," I tell her, letting the black stone rest in my palm. "She gave it to me because she cares about me and wants me to be safe. Safe from *you*. She took it off knowing that it would make it possible for you to possess her, and she did it anyway, because she didn't want you to hurt me."

There's a flicker of something in Alana's eyes. Jealousy. Hatred.

"She's not like you. She doesn't treat me like dirt," I continue in a low voice, brushing wet hair out of my eyes. "She's kind to me, and she cares so much."

"Stop it," Alana says, and I think I hear her voice, the higher-pitched whine I'm so familiar with, bleeding through. I know how she'll spiral at the possibility of me learning to love someone else, how she wants to be the only girl I love in the entire world. I need her to be weakened, uncertain.

"You already know that I kissed her." I smile humorlessly.

"But then, you have no right to get mad about that, seeing as you were fucking somebody else while we were in a relationship, apparently."

"I wasn't!" Alana screams, and that's really her now. When she lunges toward me in rage, her eyes have changed to crystal blue.

I duck away at the last minute, stumbling in the wet dirt that's rapidly turning into a river of mud. "Oh, you weren't? Well, I know you didn't love her, because you're treating her like shit right now. Making her give the cops a confession? She's eighteen, Alana. They'll try her as a fucking adult. Didn't you think about that?"

She shrugs.

"You're pathetic," I shoot back, and her smile falters. Clearly not the reaction she expected. "It's pathetic that the only way you can get what you want is by manipulating other people. Have you ever thought about just trying to be a nice person? A caring girlfriend? A good friend? You treated both me and Elise so badly, I bet she didn't even . . ."

I trail off, horrified awareness dawning. *I'm sorry. I'm sorry, Maya.*

"What did Elise think, about you and me? Did she think we were broken up?"

Alana hesitates, then rolls her eyes. "No. I told her that things were bad between us—which they *were*, if you need the reminder. I told her that you weren't in the right place to be in a relationship. Do you disagree?"

I exhale, tightening my grip around one backpack strap. "Whether I disagree or not doesn't matter. We were still together. You could've at least cut me loose."

"And make you spiral again?" Alana looks away, and I have

a feeling she doesn't want to look at me when she admits this. "I was scared to hurt you."

"Well, that worked out great," I say, voice dripping with sarcasm. "Clearly, you've avoided hurting me."

To do this, to banish her, I need to be strong, like Valeria said. I don't need to hurt her back, come up with the most cutting insult or cruelest words. Alana taught me how to cut people with words like knives, thinking that would help make me strong. But I don't need to be like Alana. She just needs to realize that I'm a whole, complete person without her.

"Alana, I don't want you to think I won't miss you," I say carefully. "Because of course I will, and I wish this hadn't happened to you, and I need to mourn the fact that it did. But I'll build a whole new life for myself and you won't be there. I'll go to college and make my own friends, and *I'll* be the one who decides if they're good, trustworthy people. I'll spend time with my family, and *I'll* determine if I'm using them as a crutch because I miss having a mother. Do you understand? I will rebuild my whole life, and you won't be a part of it."

I watch as Alana's pupils shrink to tiny black pinpricks. She stumbles backward, trying to get away from me, and I see it about to happen: her eyes changing, blue to gray to blue to gray, the air around her crackling with an unnatural energy.

When she hits the ground, it's Rowan who gets back up.

The shimmering ghost of Alana stares up at me from the dirt, long brown hair matted and tangled, blue eyes glittering up at me with hatred. She watches Rowan run to me, breath coming in gasps; I grab her and pull her to my side.

"You're *wrong*," Alana's ghost screams, scrambling to her feet.

She throws herself at me, Rowan yells my name, and that's the last thing I hear before I hit the ground. My head cracks against a tree root jutting out of the earth, and everything goes dark.

. . .

I wake to rain on my face.

The first thing I see is fog, unusual for Los Angeles. It swirls around me, chilling my already-freezing skin. Something soft pillows under my body. My limbs stretch out, spreading in different directions like I'm waking up from a thousand-year sleep.

I blink and try to focus on something. Anything other than swirling silver-gray. Peace flows through me, transformative and complete.

"Mom?" I whisper.

The coughing starts out of nowhere, but once I really get going, I can't stop. I choke on water, spit into the dirt. It's not Mom, but there's a mental clarity like fog lifting off trees, and I can't stop my thoughts from racing. This time, I'm not spiraling—it feels like taking a deep breath as each new realization hits me.

The way I discarded Livia, made her feel unimportant and useless, because Alana thought she was holding me back—that was a lie, that was controlling. There was nothing wrong with Livia. Alana just didn't want the competition.

Alana's story about Elise laughing to the whole soccer team about my anxiety—when I think about it, the whole story starts to crumble. Elise tried to tell me. That fight we had in my front yard—she drove over to tell me it was all Alana, tears glittering in her green eyes, and I called her a liar. I pushed her away because I didn't trust her, because Alana had taught me to trust no one. Since she was always helping me through mental health struggles, I figured she had betrayed me, so I shut her out.

And that's why Alana didn't want me talking to my sister. She knew that Jazmine didn't think Alana was healthy for me and was afraid she was going to get inside my head, pull us apart. So she told me that *I* was weak for making my sister a substitute for my mother. I stopped going to Lake Ember, stopped talking to Jazmine, because I didn't want to be weak.

I believed that I was the monster, spiraling out of control and causing pain to everyone around me. But I had it all wrong.

And just like that, I can hear everything.

Rain falls in sheets on the trail, hissing as it hits the trees above me. I squint through the fog; twenty feet away, Rowan is tied to the trunk of a towering oak, arms and legs bound by fraying rope; she looks murderous. At first, I think it's fear holding me in place, but no, no—I'm tied to a tree of my own, arms straining against a coiled rope. It digs into my skin, wrenching and scraping and dragging along my upper arms.

"Well, hello again," Alana says dryly. My head snaps up. The second we make eye contact, the rain slows to a pattering against the earth. "You can scream all you want, but nobody's listening. Well, except for darling Rowan over there, who's been nothing but a pain in my ass."

"Right back atcha," Rowan snaps. "Glad we could share this lovely moment together."

Silence holds me still against the tree. The anxiety descends again, that fear, ironclad and terrible. Rowan is in danger—she will always be in danger as long as Alana is around.

"Maya, I asked you for a simple favor." Alana places her hands on her hips, coming to a halt just in front of me. Her white shirt is still pristine, her hair long and wavy and perfectly dry. "A simple ritual that would let me live again. And you couldn't even do that for me, could you? No . . . instead you had to fall for this girl. You had to wreck everything."

I push against my restraints. "You can't just make commands and expect everyone to fall in line, Alana."

"You were always there for me, Maya. What changed?" She pouts. "What, you just met this girl and suddenly decided you didn't love me anymore?"

"No, I broke up with you, and then you died, which is a tragedy, but it wasn't my fault," I snap. "Are you ever going to tell me what happened, or just keep claiming that you don't remember?"

It's a bluff—for all I know, she really *doesn't* remember how she died, which is pretty common for ghosts who died violent deaths. But Alana hesitates.

"I couldn't tell you the full truth of what happened before," she says slowly.

"Why?"

"Because after you left me at Antelope Valley, I called Elise."

My entire body stiffens at the mention of her name.

"I hiked back down the trail, then I called her and asked her to pick me up." Her blue eyes light with excitement, and somehow I know that she's been desperate to tell me this story. To see my reaction. "I knew she was already in the area visiting her aunt, so it didn't take her long to get there. At first, I told her I was just hiking alone to take photos of the superbloom. It was still such a pretty day, and neither of us wanted to drive all the way back down to LA yet. So I told her there was a cool lake town nearby where we could hang out. I didn't mention that it was a place I used to go with you."

Alana shrugs. I'm pleased to see that she's having trouble meeting my eyes. "But she worked it out on her own."

"Well, yeah. She probably remembered us talking about Lake Ember, right?"

Alana nods. "We had walked down to the boat docks, and I saw your sister's kayak. I pointed it out to Elise—I was like, Jazmine Reyes won't mind if we borrow it. And from there, it spiraled. She got the truth out of me that you and I had been together the whole time, and not just together, but that . . ."

She trails off, eyes flickering over my face. There's a trace of fear I haven't seen in a while, and it reminds me of the little girl who used to cry on the bedroom floor about her parents, who ran to hug me the day she came home from summer camp. The girl I loved, still preserved in there somewhere, like a bug in amber.

"That I loved you," I offer, and she nods.

"Elise said I needed to end it with you, so I told her we already ended things, and that it was *you* who broke up with me. That just made her angry. She wanted *me* to be the one to end our relationship. And she was completely pissed off that I'd brought her to the lake where your family has a house."

"So, what? She drowned you?" Disbelief colors my voice, and Alana shakes her head.

"It was stupid. I should've just gotten in your sister's dumb kayak—it was such a pretty day up there, Maya. You would've really liked it. The lake's surface looked like glass, and the sky was so blue. But Elise and I had to have this stupid fight."

"How did you get in the water?"

"She pushed me," Alana says. "I don't think she meant for anything bad to happen. She said something about how I was hurting you and I needed to come clean—and shoved me as she was talking, but the dock was wet. Somebody had probably gotten out of their windsurfer not long before. It was slippery. I don't know . . ." Alana stares off into the distance, looking troubled. "It gets fuzzy after that. She pushed me, and I slipped. The water was so cold, and I hit my head on the dock on the way down."

My lips part. "She didn't even help you?"

Alana shrugs. "I have no clue. The last thing I remember is trying to take a breath and . . ."

Her voice trails off, fading into the low rumble of thunder that rolls across the valley. The rain has stopped, but heavy black clouds linger above our heads.

"And then it was dark," she finishes. Her eyes dart around like she's anticipating being watched. Like she's afraid of being overheard. "Maya, I hate it there."

The fear in her voice cuts like a knife, sharp in its familiarity. I remember when we were twelve and she called me homesick from summer camp after breaking into the office.

"I can't rescue you from death," I whisper. "You know I wish I could."

Alana's eyes burn like blue fire. "This is your chance to fix everything, Maya. I can possess *her* again, and we can be together, and everything can be like it was. It was never real with Elise. Not like with you and me."

During Alana's explanation of her death, I'd watched Rowan slowly, steadily work on the ropes binding her to the tree. Dark hair falls into her eyes, purple bruises are blooming around her wrists. Her throat. She looks so different from the girl I've come to know, electric and golden.

Into my mind pops a picture of the dark hallway where

I was trapped when Alana possessed me, the glass wall that I pressed my palms up against and screamed for Mom before realizing it was me. All those years that I pushed back tragedy and fought to live—that was me.

If I did that once, I can do it again.

"Don't send me back to that place." Alana's voice is a terrified whisper by my ear.

Rowan catches my eye, and even as soaking wet and dirt-covered as she is, she gives me a wink. Her gaze flickers to my backpack, then back to my face, chin jutting out—and I understand. As usual, Rowan is nothing if not prepared.

"Hey," Rowan says, loud enough for Alana to whirl around. With her back turned, I reach over my shoulder, straining against the rope that holds me back, and fumble with the zipper. There are cuts on my palms from when I fell; I wince at the pain, trying to shove it to the back of my mind. I manage to pull the zipper open a few inches, and when I reach through, my fingers brush cold metal. A sharp edge. Muscles wrenching uncomfortably, I tug out a pocketknife and flip it open. With Rowan still taunting Alana, I quickly saw the serrated edge against the rope.

"What do you want?" Alana snarls at Rowan.

"Just wanted to say thanks," Rowan says coolly, wrapping one end of the rope around her hand. "I always really wanted to have a thrilling paranormal experience like that. Now I can cross being possessed off my bucket list."

The first layer of rope falls to the ground with a soft thud, and it's just enough for me to wriggle myself free, yanking my backpack around my body and pulling the top pocket open fully. If Rowan knew what she was doing, she'll have packed the bag with everything we need—and sure enough, there are enough supplies to banish a whole army of ghosts. *If* I can figure out how to do it correctly. There's a matchbook, a loose T-shirt wrapped around a couple bundles of incense, even a shaker of salt that she must have swiped from the kitchen.

Alana is still effectively distracted. "You're kidding yourself if you think Maya could ever love someone like you," she laughs, cold bravado all too familiar.

I shake the matchbook out into my palm, crouching in the dirt. Somehow, it's dried out, much faster than natural. My hands are shaking so badly it takes a couple tries for me to get the match lit. But then it scrapes and catches, igniting my bundle of incense instantly. The heat is sharp and shocking and I reel back, surprised that something so powerful could've come from me. With a deep breath, I drop it into the chaparral brush nearest to me.

That's it—the first step that Valeria taught me, *burn a fire.* I lick my lips, grabbing the T-shirt from the backpack—it's one of Alana's, a soccer team T-shirt with her last name emblazoned on the back. The second I throw the cotton shirt into the blaze, it's engulfed, twisting and blackening, becoming unrecognizable.

"Maya," Alana says, sounding almost bored. Not even surprised that I managed to free myself. Through the flames and the haze of pain settling over me, she wavers, a dream of water in the desert. "This is dramatic, even for you. Can't we just have a nice conversation?"

What did Valeria say to do next? My eyes flicker shut. *A sacred phrase.*

"She's trying to get rid of you," Rowan snarls from behind me, her voice like the sharpest edge of a blade. "If you haven't realized."

Alana laughs, harsh over the crackling blaze. I'm not stupid—I'm from Southern California, and I know what it means to light a fire on a trail like this. The danger is obvious, and my time is extremely limited. All it will take is somebody in the houses below to smell smoke and this will all be over.

"I realize you probably think you know her, like, *so* well, but Maya would never do that," Alana says to Rowan. Her voice sounds weirdly far away. "We have a history that you know nothing about."

A history.

And just like that, it crystallizes. The sacred phrase—it's so simple, I can't believe it never occurred to me before.

I close my eyes, suck in a breath from the depths of my lungs, and climb uneasily to my feet.

"Alana," I call to get her attention. Her head snaps in my direction, eager and obedient now that she thinks I'll do her bidding. She steps closer, unafraid of the fire.

Maybe she's always had power over me, but I never realized—I have power over her too.

I say it again, just to get her to look at me one last time. "Alana."

Her eyebrows are raised, expression open. Trusting.

"I will never leave you," I say.

She flinches, surprised. "What?"

"I will never leave you."

"Maya . . ." Alana's eyes dart over to Rowan, who looks just as confused, then back to me. "What are you . . . ?"

Until I ran away to Lake Ember, I thought it was good that I'd trained myself to never cry, that I'd forced myself to become unbreakable. But standing here and looking at Alana, looking back on the mess my life became because she tried to change me, now I know—it's okay, even if you're the most breakable thing. It's okay to cry, to hide, to run when you need to.

That's what makes you strong.

I don't know if Alana notices that she's flickering out, but I do. It's different this time. I stare at her through the flames, count the constellation of freckles on her cheeks, because I know this will be the end. I stare at her even though I know she's only smoke.

"I will never leave you," I say, and when I brush a hand against my cheek, there are tears dampening my face. Off in the distance, a siren wails.

"Maya!" Alana's voice is electric with fear now—she steps close to the fire, as close as she dares. Her eyes are huge and pleading, but I don't break concentration, don't say anything other than the sacred oath she made me swear years ago. "Maya, don't do this . . . Maya, please—"

All of Los Angeles glitters in the sunset behind her, a tapestry of light, and I try to concentrate on that as I watch her fade into nothing, even as she sobs and screams my name. Our entire world, laid out like a sparkling blanket. Every lie Alana ever told me, but every promise she ever made me too.

I'll leave it behind. I know what it will do to me to walk away—but I've done harder things before. To save myself, I can do anything.

"I will never leave you," I say finally, my voice cracking around the words.

And she's gone. The fire overtakes her, kicking up higher on the dry grass, scorching the earth. She doesn't have time to say a word.

I stare into the fire. It flickers and turns white-hot, unforgiving, starting anew.

CHAPTER TWENTY-FOUR

THREE DAYS AFTER I banished Alana, Jazmine drives down from Lake Ember. She brings what she calls a "serotonin pizza"—pepperoni with extra black olives and mushrooms—and we eat it in the backyard, watching the sun lower over the tree line. Rowan, who's insisted on staying in the guest room for emotional support, makes me laugh out loud, and Jazmine tells embarrassing stories about me as a little kid, and everything falls together easy and sure.

Before Jazmine arrived, Rowan and I discussed Elise at length. Alana possessed her to force a confession, letting me go free . . . and that's the part where I hit a brick wall. Was the confession real, or another one of Alana's lies? Did Alana let me go because she still cared about me? Because when it came down to it, she couldn't bear to see me accused of murder? In the end, it's clear that she had the power to choose between the two of us, and she chose me.

Right now Elise is being held in a correctional facility in San Bernadino County awaiting her bail hearing. From what

I've heard in the news and through rumors flying around, Alana's story and Elise's statement to the police match up, so I need to let it go. It's not my job to figure out her fate.

"Do you think Elise will actually have to go to prison?" I ask Rowan by the pool, downing the last of my soda.

Rowan shrugs, uncharacteristically serious. "She confessed to second-degree manslaughter. That's a felony in California, so she could get up to four years in prison, yeah. Not enough to derail her life forever. Maybe she'll get a shot to start again when she gets out."

I frown, ripping up the label from my soda bottle. Late at night when I can't sleep, I still see Elise's face in my mind, distraught and screaming behind the window at the police station. *I'm sorry, Maya.*

I can only imagine what Alana must have been telling her about me. That I was crazy, probably. That she didn't love me. That I didn't matter. That we were only spending so much time together, still, because she felt bad for me. I can't even fathom if Alana's affection for Elise was real. All she ever craved was attention and praise, and she was getting that from both of us. That isn't love.

Sitting out by my backyard pool, I pick at the hem of the black T-shirt I've borrowed from Rowan. Soon I'll drive to the mall and start rebuilding a wardrobe of clothing that didn't get torched in the trauma bonfire. I'll reach out to people, try to make friends again; I've already unblocked Livia on Instagram, even mustering the courage to send her a message.

It's hard to imagine what things will be like now. Me wandering around my dad's giant house. He's already made it clear that if I want to keep living here, I'll have to take classes somewhere—whatever community college will take me in the fall, I guess. I'll have to get a job. All of that is fine. There are worse fates. But what will I do in the quiet moments?

Those are the moments when the ghosts come calling. Not the real ones—after Alana, those are gone for good. But the ones that creep behind my eyes during nightmares, that freeze me to the spot when my anxiety spikes.

That night when I'm getting ready for bed, Jazmine walks in, short hair twisted into a topknot. She's spending the night in her old room, even though Dad's been gradually turning it into a kitchen supply storage unit over the past few years.

"How's your room, aka the Williams Sonoma Outlet?" I ask, scrubbing a pink washcloth across my face as she appears in the doorway behind me.

"Oh, fine. I'm using a Le Creuset box as a bedside table."

I snort, rinsing off my facewash. "Glamorous."

"I just have to ask you one thing, Maya," my sister says. She slips into the bathroom and sits at the edge of the tub, slumping forward so that her elbows rest on her knees. A month ago, that statement would've filled me with anxiety; tonight, I just grab my bottle of lotion and squeeze it, letting it ribbon into my hand. Nothing can phase me anymore.

"Was that all because of Alana?"

I frown, studying my reflection in the mirror as I apply lotion to my face. "What part?"

"Why you suddenly didn't want anything to do with me when you were younger. Why you stopped visiting me."

"Oh." I freeze, hands falling to my sides. This has been such an integral part of my story that it never occurred to me

Jazmine wouldn't know about it. "Well . . . yeah. I think you were a threat, in her mind. Somebody I could confide in who wasn't her."

"Your sister?" Jazmine's voice is hard, shocked. "What, she doesn't have a sister, so nobody else is allowed to?"

"Probably something like that. Don't ask me how her mind worked." I lean against the sink, turning to face Jazmine. "But regardless of why she wanted it, I should never have listened to her. It was stupid. Alana had a way of making these rules and edicts sound so reasonable, you know? Like, it made perfect sense why I had to do what she said. I'm sorry, though. That was never fair to you."

"It wasn't." Jazmine lifts her head, her eyes full of sadness. "You know what I'd tell my friends? When I was eighteen, I lost my mom. When I was twenty-three, I lost my sister."

I watch her, my lower lip quivering.

"I'm sorry," I say again, and my voice breaks. I'm afraid that's not enough to undo the years of hurt I inflicted. I remember what I thought up in Lake Ember, what feels like a million years ago—that it was only a matter of time before she'd stop loving me, because I would make it happen.

She stands up, reaching for me, and I walk into her arms, tears streaking my face. "But now I can tell them that when I was twenty-seven, my sister came back to me," she says, one hand soft on the back of my head. "And I can't think of anything better than that."

• • •

Before I go to sleep, I wander downstairs in my pajamas and find Rowan still sitting out back by the pool. The lights make the water glow turquoise, casting a wavy glow across the small backyard. Rowan is still fully dressed in jeans and a black tank top, staring up at the sky.

"You really can't see stars here," she says. "Rosier, I don't know how you do it."

"You're being dramatic. The smog is nowhere near as bad as it used to be." I plop down on the lounge chair closest to hers. Looking over at her, a sense of safety settles over me, and before I'm even aware of it, a smile creeps onto my face.

It's weird, but I can't remember the last time I really smiled. It shocks me so much that I actually reach up and glide my fingers along my lips, tracing a pattern I thought I'd long forgotten. Everyone—my parents, my therapist, Alana—always talked about how I'd need to work to find a path back to happiness. But somewhere up north in a forgotten town tucked beside a moonlight-glistening lake, I think maybe happiness found a path back to me.

"So, hypothetical question." I turn to Rowan, an optimistic glow humming through my veins. "If I came up to Lake Ember at the end of the summer, would you give me a fall-themed orientation tour?"

Rowan brushes her hair out of her eyes. Even though it's been days since our confrontation with Alana, I can still see faint scratches on her pale arms, trace the bruises along her throat. When Alana possessed her, Rowan didn't take it lying down.

"Oh, sure. There's an apple orchard. I didn't show you that last time," she says. "I really don't think it would be fair for you to miss the apples."

Off in the distance, the city is coming to life. Cars rushing along the freeway, wind bending the palm trees, whispering.

"I'll be there," I answer. "You know, for the apples."

Maybe Rowan and I will never be like it was with Alana—whispering sleepover secrets, basking in the California sun. But we can be other things. Black coffee and lake water and ghost stories and champagne and witty comebacks. A safe place to land.

Rowan heads up to the guest room after saying goodnight, but I sit in my backyard, watching the taillights on the freeway like sparkling stars. For the first time in months, a weight lifts from my chest as I realize it's all over: the pain I've felt over ruining my school career, the anxiety Alana caused me. Of course, I know there will be hard days ahead, but at least now I'm confident that I can face them.

I close my eyes, listening to the rustling of wind, the far-off traffic. It sounds like home. And I try to imagine that if Mom could come back, if I could conjure her ghost to sit beside me, she would be proud of everything I've done.

My mom's eyes weren't brown like mine; they were gray-blue, like the ocean on a still day. When she tucked me in at night, she always sat on the same corner of my bed, and sometimes when I concentrate I can still feel her weight pressing into the mattress. I remember how when she walked past me in the living room, she would skim the top of my head with her hand; I remember how the rings on her fingers caught on stray tendrils of my hair; I remember how it annoyed me.

Everyone thinks I'll forget, but I remember everything. Everything small, everything aching. The memories are ghosts I keep alive.

. . .

Of course, I would be lying if I said I never think about Alana.

Rowan doesn't let me dwell on anything, but sometimes, she asks me questions about Alana and what things were like. Over the next few months, we talk on the phone about the hard things, but she also asks me about the times when it was good.

And each time, I tell her that we were extraordinary. We were unbreakable, until we broke. We were two girls who loved each other until it became easier to hurt each other. I lay them down on a bed of lilies and soft dirt, those girls we used to be. I bury them so that I can rise again.

I drive up to Lake Ember every now and then, and when I do, I leave the windows down. The air is dry and windy, whipping my hair back, and my heart lightens at the feeling. I let myself feel it all. I understand so much more.

When someone loves you, they don't hurt you on purpose.

If you think you need them like flames need oxygen, gasping, drowning, I want to tell you that you are wrong. You survive on your own. Nobody else props you up and nobody else can take credit for your triumphs. You are the phoenix. Fire is always fire. It destroys, it obliterates. But you can always rise again.

EPILOGUE

ONE YEAR LATER

ALANA MURRAY HAS been dead for twelve months and four days.

I try not to count, but I can't help it. Sometimes I don't think about her at all; sometimes I lie awake watching moonlight skim across the ceiling and I hold my breath, expecting her ghost to shimmer at the foot of the bed, eyes glittering with rage. Sometimes I wake up panicking from a nightmare that feels like being plunged into icy water.

The sun is setting low over the horizon, washing the world in gold, as I trek through the grass toward Alana's grave. Mrs. Murray chose one of the most beautiful spots in the whole cemetery to bury her daughter. Trees line the burial ground, looming tall and casting long, dramatic shadows. On the drive over, I'd stopped at a flower shop and bought a bouquet. Cold water drips off the flower stems, speckling my T-shirt like rain.

At her grave, stone and silent and still, I stand there.

The one thing people always fail to consider is just how complicated, how messy, how terrible girls can be. How our hearts can tangle into knots. A girl can scratch and claw, then trace bloody clouds with her fingernails. She can drown in spun-sugar kisses but claw out eyes like a carrion crow.

But one thing Alana knew—and so do I—is that girls are stronger than anything.

Stronger than the way the world tries to shatter us. Stronger, even, than death.

Kneeling, I place the bouquet against the cold headstone. I take a breath and wait to see if I'll cry, but I don't. I begin the long path back up to my car.

I leave her there.

ACKNOWLEDGMENTS

I've always believed that a good ghost story can move you. Some send shivers down your spine and lurk in nightmares. But in my opinion, there are all different types of ghosts. Some are feelings. Some are memories. Some wrap you in their arms, as persistent and consuming as grief, and demand to be dealt with. When I tentatively began drafting Maya and Alana's story in the early days of COVID-19 lockdown, my goal was to examine the way trauma can cling to us like a haunting. The characters took me on a journey I could have never imagined, and the story I excavated on those long, quiet nights became a beacon, leading me to new places, new friends, new goals. This story helped me achieve a dream I've carried since before I was old enough to speak, and I met so many incredible people along that journey. I hope you'll indulge me as I try to thank them all.

A million thanks to Chloe Seager, my rockstar agent and the kindest and most surefire advocate. Thank you for believing in this story and for being there every step of the way. Endless thanks also to Georgia McVeigh and the rest of the incredible Madeleine Milburn Literary Agency team.

This book wouldn't be nearly as heartbreaking without Hannah Hill, my incredible editor, who always pushed me to make things sadder and approved lines of dialogue I was nervous about. Hannah, thank you so much for your innate understanding of Maya and Alana, your thoughtful edits, and your patience as I wrangled with the timeline. You are a true superstar! Thanks also to the entire Delacorte Press and Random House Children's Books team, including Beverly Horowitz, Wendy Loggia, Tamar Schwartz, Colleen Fellingham, Lili Feinberg, Alison Kolani, Shannon Pender, Natali Cavanaugh, Stephanie Villar, Erica Stone, Katie Halata, and Natalie Capogrossi. I can't possibly express what a joy and an honor it is to publish this book with my dream imprint. I am also eternally grateful to Carolina Rodriguez Fuenmayor, Sarah Nichole Kaufman, Ray Shappell, Ken Crossland, and Liz Dresner for creating the most stunning cover and beautifully designed book; it's everything I hoped for.

Thanks to Clem Flanagan, Leonie Lock, Hannah Walker, and the team at Ink Road and Black & White Publishing for all your hard work to bring Maya's story across the pond. I couldn't be more grateful!

To Rachel Moore, the best and sparkliest friend a girl could have, for laughing and crying with me always. Thank you for reading so many versions of this book, even though Alana possessed you every time—now that's friendship! Endless thanks to my mentor and friend Rory Power, who believed in me (and Indie!) years ago and is still always up for a two-hour phone call. Thanks to the early readers of this book: Allison Saft, Alex Brown, Justine Pucella Winans, Kalla Harris, Kat Korpi, and Olivia Liu. Your enthusiasm kept me going through the toughest moments.

To my Pitch Wars mentors, Meredith Tate and Jamie Howard—you saw through to the heart of this book so early on, and I will be forever grateful! Thank you for all your guidance and siren emojis.

Skyla Arndt changed my life by sliding into my Twitter DMs and I've never been more thankful; thank you for all your sage publishing wisdom. Mackenzie Reed, my Aquarius soul sister and most trusted marketing advisor, I can always count on you for the sweetest words of encouragement or the driest wit known to man. Kat Korpi, thank you for your unflinching enthusiasm and for always encouraging me to girlboss my way through revisions. Crystal Seitz, my publishing twin, I am so glad we've gone on this journey together! Thank you to Joie, Lindsay, and Valerie—Copycats forever! To my entire Hex Quills family, where would I be without you? Thanks to Abby, Alex, Brit, Cassie, Darcy, Helena, Holly, Juliet, Kahlan, Kalla, Lindsey, Livy, Maria, Marina, Morgan, Olivia, Phoebe, Sam, Shay, and Wajudah for your steadfast friendship and serotonin.

To Kate, Liz, Katie, and Brittany, who have none of the bad qualities of the high school friends in this book and all of the good ones. Thanks also to Alexia and Ary, for your second chances and for reading this one early.

Thanks to my teachers at Lancaster Country Day School, especially Dr. Rudy Sharpe, and my Penn State professors Dr. Christian Weisser and Dr. Holly Ryan. To my fellow Writing Center tutors, what a privilege it was to be surrounded by so many talented writers during our chaotic college years. I wouldn't want to build an owl-shaped parade float during a thunderstorm with anyone else.

Thanks to Jude for your thoughtful insight and for answering my request for Reddit usernames with a proficiency that scared me a little. Thanks also to Phoebe for the astrology insight, Gary for his TV show naming assistance, and Alexa Donne for sharing her wealth of college application knowledge.

Thanks to my friends in LA, with love and endless gratitude—you know who you are. Special thank you to Elisabeth for teaching me how to weather every storm.

To my cat sons, Renegade and Roanoke: neither of you can read (I don't think?), but thanks for always making me smile and jumping on my keyboard. In loving memory of Ava, who sat beside me as I wrote the very first draft of this book late into the night, and always knew when I needed a dog to hug.

Thank you to Aunt Barbara and Uncle Bob for a lifetime of love, support, and lake house summers. The Lake Ember community was inspired in part by Bantam Lake, Lake Horace, and Hickory Hills Lake, all pivotal touchpoints in my family's history.

With tremendous thanks and love to Uncle Jerry and all the other aunts, uncles, and cousins who supported me over the years. And of course, thank you to my second family, Lisa, Julius, and Eric, for welcoming me into your hilarious chaos with open arms.

Eden, our life together is more beautiful, more powerful, than anything I could ever write. Thank you for loving Maya even in her most difficult moments, and thank you for loving me in mine.

To Dad, who always answers the phone, always hears my stories, and never once let me stop writing. Whether knowingly or not, you lit every light that has ever carried me out of darkness.

To Mom: "Yes, those are my words." I know you were with me through every page of this story.

Finally, to you, if you have ever felt silenced, alone, or afraid to name the trauma you've experienced. If you want to set fire to a past that haunts you, this book is me handing you the match. Let it burn.

ABOUT THE AUTHOR

Kara A. Kennedy has been telling ghost stories—and sometimes living them—since childhood. She holds a BA in Professional Writing from Penn State University, where she worked as a writing tutor and cultivated a love of coffee. She lives in a historic and possibly haunted home in Pennsylvania with her partner and their two cats. *I Will Never Leave You* is her debut novel.

karakennedywrites.com